According to one of the great writers of science fiction and fantasy, you are about to read an extraordinary novel...

"The <u>Interior Life</u> is not still another generic fantasy—it is a breath of fresh air, bearing originality, exciting narrative, vividly realized characters and settings, evocative writing—everything we have been waiting for all too long. This goes for the mundane part of the story too; there also are people one can care about."

—Poul Anderson

THE INTERIOR LIFE

KATHERINE BLAKE

THE INTERIOR LIFE

PS/2 is a trademark of IBM Corp.
UNIX is a trademark of Bell Laboratories.
LOGO is a trademark of Logo Computer Systems, Inc.
The Society for Creative Anachronism is real, but the Barony of Strange Sea is fictional.

A Baen Books Original

Baen Publishing Enterprises
260 Fifth Avenue
New York, N.Y. 10001

ISBN: 0-671-72010-4

Cover art by Tom Kidd

First printing, August 1990

Distributed by
SIMON & SCHUSTER
1230 Avenue of the Americas
New York, N.Y. 10020

Printed in the United States of America

HENRICO DILECTISSIMO FIDELI

CHAPTER 1

A Door Opens

A host of sparrows were hopping through the bright-berried pyracantha outside the kitchen window. Sue, with her forearms deep in greasy water, watched them with a look of envy. They might not know where their next meal was coming from, but at least after it arrived they never had to wash the dishes.

She stacked the last clean pan in the drainer and let the dirty water out of the sinks. The drain baskets were full of the usual fragments: cereal flakes, squashed berries, a scrap of egg white, coffee grounds. An hour ago it had all been edible food (if you were willing to stretch a point in favor of the coffee grounds). Now, without a finger having been laid on it, it was garbage and food for worms and fruit flies. She picked up the baskets by their metal nipples and dumped them into the garbage pail. (*I should make a compost pile*, she thought vaguely, *let it rot and dig it into the garden*. But she thought of compost every morning, and forgot it as soon as her hands were dried.) She brought the baskets back to the sinks and washed out the last few coffee grounds.

What she called "the garden" was made up of two scruffy lawns with meager trimmings. The back lawn had a covering of child-trampled crabgrass and one young apple tree whose best effort so far had been three undersized green lumps, and a sugar maple older than the house, for whose robust health Sue could not take the credit. The

3

front lawn was in slightly better shape; since it could be seen from the street, it got watered at intervals and mowed on weekends. It had an edging of standard-issue real-estate shrubs and a handful of dispirited flowers. Compost might have done them good, but they weren't likely to get it.

She wiped the tile, ran an inch of water into the sinks, and dribbled in some bleach to take out the latest generation of fruit stains. Then she took a step backward to inspect her handiwork. The dishes sparkled, the pots and pans gleamed, the purple stains were fading out before her eyes. But the rest of the kitchen was a disaster area— not dirty, exactly, because it had been cleaned not so long ago, but cluttered and chaotic. The garbage was at the overflowing point, trembling at the lip of the can; one more dead grapefruit rind or a stiff breeze would send it over. A cloud of moths rose from the bag of flour she'd forgotten to seal up again. Her six-year-old had lived up to his name by pencilling "MARK MARK MARK" along the wall under the paper towels. Comic books on the floor, fingermarks on the woodwork, and on the stove the sticky residue of the hot chocolate nine-year-old Kathy had made last night while her parents' backs were turned. It had all been neat and tidy forty-eight hours ago, and that was depressing. The clean sink was a single lily in an acre of pigweed—and twelve hours from now it would match the rest of the kitchen, and that was even more depressing.

And I thought once the kids were in school all day I could get this place cleaned up. She dampened a scrubber-backed sponge and attacked the stove. *The trouble with housework,* she mused, *is that it's so damn recurrent. I clean it up, they mess it up, and repeat from asterisk. I might as well be a Victorian chambermaid.* She set down the sponge over an encrusted stain and imagined herself in a long heavy black skirt (instead of grungy blue jeans), tight boots on her feet, a starched cap on her head. . . . *Running up and down the back stairs with my coal-scuttle and my ash-bucket sixteen hours a day. Ow, the young gentlemen, such a disorder as they do leave, to be sure.* Their muddy boots in the entryways, their muddy tennies on the stairs and their muddy clothes in heaps on the closet floor; midnight suppers in his Lordship's billiards room, half-emptied pop cans and peanut butter sandwiches stuffed down behind the sofa cushions didn't look much like champagne bottles and roast pheasant bones, but a girl's imagination had to do what it could with what it had . . . and the carpets to sweep with damp sawdust, and every foot of it rubbed up with the hand! There was something to be said for no-wax plastic after all. *And whenever I thought I'd got a breather, somebody would call "Sarah!" or "Jane!" and set me to work again.*

"Only I'd get paid for it," she muttered aloud. *And the upper crust were properly trained by their nannies and wouldn't leave their underwear in little piles on the floor where they stepped out of 'em. And they'd never set a toe in the kitchen in their lives.*

It just goes to show. The chocolate scurf on the front burner had softened, and she leaned hard on the sponge and scrubbed away. *There was that story about the guy who was sure he'd come from Somewhere Else, fallen through a time warp or something, and he didn't really belong here. He belonged in a world full of magic and derring-do, heroes and wizards and unicorns and virgins, he belonged in a castle instead of a high-rise apartment. Sure enough, one day a wizard showed up, hauled him back through the time hole and put him back into his Rightful Place in Life, in a castle. Mucking out the stables. And wherever I went, I'd find myself scrubbing the sink and picking up after other people.*

When I was little, she remembered, *I used to make up games like that—I'd be Cinderella, or Gretel in the witch's cottage, or the slave girl in the sultan's palace, cruelly forced to make my bed or wash the dishes. I suppose I got it from reading Mrs. Piggle-Wiggle.*

I ought to try it again—only all the people I used to be were such wimps, standing around feeling sorry for themselves. Kid fantasies. Then I got into high school and nothing was important but boys and clothes and dating and getting married. And now I'm grown up and I have a husband and a house and three kids, and what do I do in the real world? She dropped the sponge into the bleach solution. *I pick up garbage and I feel sorry for myself— and what do I do in my imagination? Repeat from asterisk.*

She looked out the window again. The sparrows had

taken fright at a dog, cat, or toddler and flown away. *The lucky stiffs.* Above the pyracantha something glinted in the sky, a 747, maybe, or a sea gull, the sun bright on its wings, high above the sparkling sea. She stood at a white-washed wall, chest-high, that ran along the top of the cliff north and south from the sea-keep. She could feel the gritti-ness of the mortar under her fingers, and the pressure against her breasts as she leaned far over the wall to see the shore below. A strip of clean sand ran along the cliff's foot, smooth and white. The shallow sea crept in on it with little wavelets, breakers only the height of your hand, that crumbled against the shore and whispered out again. And somewhere in the face of the cliff, almost under her feet and impossible to see no matter how she craned her neck, was the sea-gate, the door to the hidden passage from the keep above. Lord Andri and his companions must have left the keep by that way, but it didn't seem likely that she would get inside by the same door. There was no opening that she could see in the wall between here and the village, a matter of two miles. Or could she make it over the wall from here? It was a drop of at least twenty feet, and the cliff was smooth. Was there any rope in their saddlebags? She thought not, but it didn't matter. If she was going to have to climb into the sea-keep, she could find better places to do it.

"Marianella!"

"Coming, m'Lady."

Sue blinked. Her eyes hurt, as if she had been staring, unblinking and unseeing, for several minutes. She had been aware of the sinks, the solid floor she stood on, the pyracantha outside the window, but they had been entirely *unimportant* compared to the sights and sounds inside her head. And more than sights and sounds: she had felt the rough wall under her hands, smelled the salt/clam/seaweed smell of the sea. *Wow. Where have I been all these years?*

In the real world, she answered herself. *Welcome back.*

"Marianella?" Well, it beat "Sarah" or "Jane"—or even "Susan." So far, so good, but who *was* Marianella, and who was the lady she served—and why were they trying to get into a locked and empty castle, instead of riding down to the village to see if it had a decent inn? Or even a Howard Johnson's. Maybe she could find out.

It was just before noon, and the sun blazed on the white-washed walls of the sea-keep and westward on the sea beyond. From here she could see the walls of the Great Hall beyond the curtain wall and its slate roof, and the tall tower behind it that had been the original keep. All of it, apparently, quite empty.

Her boots crunched weathered shells as she made her way back to the front gate. The two horses stood there, her own brown Rowan and her Ladyship's black Pathfinder, gazing about them and touching noses. There was no grass here for them to eat, only the crushed shells from the mounds of ancient feasts.

The Lady Amalia stood before the gate, tall and fair in her black cloak. The salt wind had blown back her hood and drawn a strand of her golden hair across her face. "There's still no answer," she said.

"I don't believe there's a soul in the place," Marianella answered. "I've been all the way round from wall to wall, and there's only the one gate and it bolted from the inside. I can't get down to the sea-gate."

"They left by sea?"

"Seemingly." She took Rowan's bridle and led her to the edge of the moat—a mere dry ditch, about five feet wide and half-filled with shells. Even in the old days it had only been intended to stop a cavalry charge, not a team of sappers or one persistent visitor. She made Rowan stand at the edge and untied her sash.

"What are you doing?"

Marianella shrugged out of her full-skirted riding gown and laid it over a bush, and pulled her boots off. In her short linen shift she led the horse down the sloping side of the moat. "Breaking in." She climbed into the saddle, pulled up her feet, and cautiously stood up. Rowan, happily, was no fine lady's horse, but a placid beast with feet like soup plates and a back like a fishing dory. She stood fast, and Marianella's elbows now reached the top of the wall. She grabbed hold, slung one leg over the wall, and rolled over the top. The earth dug out of the moat had been piled inside the wall to make a walkway only four feet below the top. She padded along this walkway in her bare feet till she reached the top of the gate. There was a heavy wooden bar there, coated with bird-droppings, a lever to release the chain that held the bridge.

"Lady," she called, "is Rowan clear of the bridge? And are you?"

"Let me lead her away."

When she could see both Rowan and the Lady Amalia well out of the way, Marianella leaned with all her weight on the bar, and pushed it slowly down. The chain unwound, and the bridge descended and fell across the moat with a little puff of dust. Marianella scrambled down the gateside ladder to the bridge and went to retrieve her clothes. Her skirts back in place, and a certain degree of respectability with them, she led the horses by their trailing reins across the bridge and into the courtyard within the walls.

In a corner of the courtyard stood a well, with a trough next to it, and she led the horses there. She drew buckets of water and filled the trough, and let the beasts drink. Three sea gulls perched on the windlass took flight and flapped noisily away. There was no other motion. The courtyard was littered with trash, blown into corners by the wind: sand, straw, feathers, a scrap of linen cloth—but no food scraps, no horse droppings; the sea gulls had had the time to carry away everything they could eat.

Lady Amalia stood in the courtyard, a white lily wrapped in black silk, her tall body looking smaller, beginning to slump. Her face was pale; her strength, which had never faltered on the long ride from Tevrin, was ebbing now. Marianella left the horses to stand and ran across the pavement to the Lady; she grabbed and caught her just as she fell to her knees. "Bear up, m'Lady, just a moment now and I'll get you inside."

With the Lady leaning on her arm, stumbling on the flagstones, she led her to the great door of the keep. Marianella reached out to tug it open, but it stood fast: locked, like everything else. Well, her Ladyship had the second key.

"There's something terribly wrong," the lady said. "I can smell it."

Marianella sniffed. "All I smell is the sea."

Lady Amalia shook her head and backed up till she could lean against the wall. "I have to find it out. Here." She brought the key out of the deep-bottomed sleeve of her robe.

"Open the door." Marianella turned the key, and tugged, and the great door swung silently open.

Here was a smell, all right, but the prosaic stink of mold and garbage. She opened the door wide and wedged it open with a chunk of stone. Inside the door was a hall a few yards long, with another door at the end. The ceiling was pierced with holes, so that boiling water or the like could be poured down on unwelcome guests. But here also a bench had been placed for the comfort of lawful visitors and messengers, and she set the Lady down on it.

"You sit here where the air can blow in, and I'll set things to rights in there." The second door opened with the same key, and it led into the Great Hall.

It was dark inside, with no light but what leaked from the doorway and the old smoke-hole in the roof, and the first thing she did was to open all the shutters. The windows were small, mere arrow-slits, but every one had been tightly shuttered and closed with an iron bolt. This far west, no Darklander attack was likely; perhaps the shutters had been closed against a storm.

The Hall was a fine one, well-proportioned for its size, but its last occupants had left it in a fine mess. The trestle tables had been pushed askew, the benches stacked like cordwood, every flat surface littered with empty dishes, bones, fruit rinds.

This is where I came in, Sue thought. *Now I get to clean it all up.*

"Right," Marianella said aloud, hearing Rowan whinny in the courtyard. The stable door stood half-open. She pushed it wide: disorder, silence, and not even the smell of horses: the sea gulls and the sea air had cleaned everything away. *Half this place is rotting*, she thought, *and the other half's had its bones picked clean. Heavens, what an unchancy thought.*

In a loft overhead she found hay; last year's and not much of it, but still sweet enough. She filled the mangers, took saddles and saddlebags from the horses' backs, and gave them a quick rub with a wisp of hay. Proper grooming would have to wait a bit, till she'd found some human food. The saddlebags were practically empty. She slung them onto her back and trudged back to the hall. The Lady sat silent in the doorway, not opening her eyes.

Marianella found the kitchen in the usual lean-to at the far end of the hall. It had a window looking over the sea, and sticking her head out to get her bearings, she saw the finger-thin strip of beach below—the tide was high—and overhead a half-dozen sea gulls circling hopefully. "This is your lucky day, my good birds," she said. "We have a forty-one-course dinner, just for you. Selected cold orts from the sideboard."

She made trip after trip between the Hall and the kitchen. Sometimes she changed her path and brought in another bucket of water from the well, for scrubbing. Every kind of perished leftover went out the window; what the sea gulls wouldn't touch the crabs would no doubt find a use for.

Crabs? (Boiled, maybe, or stuffed with an herb sauce?) No, she had no time to go netting, not even to look for a net. There was some decent wine in the place, and a barrel of beer, and part of another barrel of flour that the weevils hadn't got to yet. She'd set some bread rising. There were worse meals than new bread and old wine, but she'd hoped for better for her Ladyship. Everything potted, dried, or salted had been eaten. She scowled, and threw out a green-furred bacon rind to the sea gulls. They all flew down to peck at it through the breakers, and with their screaming hushed Marianella heard another sound, a plaintive cooing somewhere overhead. She grinned suddenly, and followed her ears to the foot of a ladder that led to the kitchen roof.

Half an hour later a fire was burning steadily in the big kitchen fireplace. On its smallest spit a pigeon was roasting, in its chimney corner bread was rising, and the water in the big copper boiler was just starting to bubble. And the Hall, having fed the crabs and the sea gulls so lavishly, was looking and smelling much better.

And still there was no clue as to what had become of her Ladyship's brother, Lord Andri, nor of his companions the Lords Guiard and Zalmar. Andri had sent word at the beginning of summer to ask his sister to join him here. Months had gone by while she had made up her mind to come, and then made the journey. And in that time their Lordships had made up their minds to go, and had gone.

But before that they had done something to drive all their servants away (probably to the village; she would have to

look into that)—and after that they had let themselves out of
the sea-keep without unlocking door or window. . . .

Nonsense, they had gone out by the sea-gate and taken
ship, that was all. She hadn't yet found the secret door that
led to the passage, which must run underground to lead to
the beach. But it must be there somewhere. Three grown men
didn't suddenly sprout feathers and fly, or vanish in a puff of
smoke like a Darklander! . . .

"Hello," said a quiet voice behind her, and Marianella
clutched convulsively at the pigeon she was plucking, so that
she would surely have killed it if she hadn't done already.

"How—did—you—get—in—here?" she demanded of the
man who stood in the doorway, a man pleasant-looking
enough, twenty-five years old perhaps, not very tall and not
very dark, with a short curly beard and a pair of pale blue
eyes. He wore a homespun shirt and trews, and a leather
jerkin and boots, and a sea gull's white feather tucked behind
his ear.

"Over the bridge; you left it down," he said. "And in at the
door; you left it open. The lady at the door was asleep, so I
didn't take it upon myself to waken her." He smiled, a very
agreeable smile framed by the little curly beard. "Dear lady,
I've startled you half out of your wits, haven't I? Please
forgive me. I'm Kieran, and my father keeps the Blue Swan
down in the village, and my uncle Rolf used to be seneschal
here. Are you some of poor Lord Andri's people?"

"My Lady Amalia is Lord Andri's sister," she said. "We were
coming out here for the summer so that her Ladyship could
rest—she has the Sight and grows very weary in Tevrin." She
realized she was still holding the pigeon, and dropped it onto
the table. "Why do you say 'poor' Lord Andri? What's happened to him?"

The innkeeper's son shrugged. "Nothing that I know of,"
he said. "Perhaps he only went away. I came up to see if the
Swan was to expect guests, but it seems you intend to stay
here?" A raised eyebrow went with the question, and a glance
toward the chaotic Hall.

"I believe we do, but I suppose I ought to ask." She strode
through the Hall, Kieran trailing after, to where Lady Amalia
still sat by the door. "Lady, are we staying here?"

The Lady opened her eyes. "Yes. We have to find out what

happened." She turned her head to look at them. "You, now, you are—"

"Kieran. I am your Ladyship's servant," he said, bowing formally and correctly like a courtier. (Well, he had eyes, and could have used them while their Lordships were there.)

"I accept your service, Kieran," the Lady said. "Marianella will tell you what's needed." She closed her eyes again.

Kieran's eyes were round and wide. Marianella chuckled, and took his arm and led him away toward the bridge.

"I think you've just been appointed seneschal," she said. "That's the trouble with people with the Sight; they sum up in a few choice words a conversation you haven't had yet. I don't know about your uncle—"

"He's down at the Swan—in drink, whenever Father will let him have any; and he's not much use even when he's sober. I shall be very proud to be Lady Amalia's seneschal." He plucked the sea gull's feather from behind his ear, looked at it, and tossed it away as if unbecoming the dignity of his new office. "What's needed, then?"

"Provisions," Marianella said. "And bring the servants back. Hay for the horses, we haven't much here, and some grain. Soap," she went on, wrinkling her nose. "Scrubbing-brushes. Did I mention you're to bring the servants back? I assume they're village people."

"Oh, yes. I'll fetch them, if they'll come. I don't want to use force—let's see what persuasion can do." They were silent for a moment. "Well," he said, "and the sooner I'm gone the sooner I'll be back." He bent and took her hand, and kissed it as if she had been a great lady. "Till then," he said, and walked across the bridge and out of sight. Marianella went back to the kitchen.

Wow, Sue thought. *Where in the world did I get him?* She gripped the bottom of the laundry-room wastebasket and upended it into the garbage can. A cloud of lint rose into the air. *He's gorgeous. Where'd he come from?* She could still feel his soft lips against her hand. *I hope he comes back.*

She went back into the house and looked around. The kitchen was clean, the living room was clean, the laundry room was showing signs of having been nudged, and her feet hurt. Also it was two o'clock and she hadn't had lunch.

All right, fair's fair; I've been the scullery maid, now I'll be the lady. There were no pigeons in her kitchen, but she found a couple of pieces of fried chicken in the freezer and put them into the microwave. What else? Bread? Marianella would turn up her nose at the spongy stuff they got from the supermarket. Beer? She didn't like beer much. You could carry even a fantasy too far. Wine? They hadn't any—no, wait. Uncle Herman's Christmas present. She found the bottle, carefully laid on its side, at the back of a bottom cupboard behind Aunt Grace's linen table napkins. She took it out and stared at the label. The name, which was in French or German or something, didn't mean a thing to her. A pity; it was the sort of thing Lady Amalia would know. She rummaged in a drawer for the cork-screw, then stopped. Should she, really? All her favorite soap operas each had an example of the housewife as afternoon alcoholic . . . surely you couldn't turn into a total lush on one glassful. She twisted in the corkscrew, jimmied the cork out, and sniffed at the top of the bottle. That was a surprise: it smelled like wine, all right, but also like apples, and something spicy—vanilla, maybe. Not bad. The microwave chimed. She found the one good wineglass (wedding present) that the kids hadn't smashed during the past eight years, and filled it, and took it along with the microwaved chicken to the TV tray in the living room.

She pulled up one of the children's small chairs to rest her feet on. (They must still be Marianella's feet—they *hurt.*)

"My Lady," Marianella said, "will you come into the Hall? I've cleaned it and aired it, and I've got a bit of lunch for you." Amalia rose, and put aside her tangled thoughts, and went inside. Marianella had set a cup of wine for her, and a young roasted pigeon, and a chunk of the new bread. The air of the sea overlaid the smell of danger, and the shadows had drawn back a little, but only a little. She drew a curtain over her mind, as over a window to the east, and turned her back on it.

Sue completely forgot to watch any of her usual soaps. When she was tired of wondering where Andri and his friends had gotten to, she picked up a magazine she'd bought at the supermarket. She flipped through an article on how to avoid cancer by eating more vegetables, and another with a checklist on whether your marriage had hidden strengths, and concentrated on a several-page spread about women who cut their grocery bills in half by clipping out coupons and sending in proofs-of-purchase.

Very interesting, said the Lady Amalia's voice, or something very like it in her mind. *Are these supposed to be real women, or legal fictions? I don't recognize many of these names, but you have a great variety of wares on that list, and most of the households in your land are too small to use them all. You, for example, have yourself and your husband and only three children, all housebroken. So those diapers are not going to save you any money, however cheap they are. Nor the little crocks of baby food. Nor the stuff for gluing one's false teeth to the gums.*

If you had a bigger household, it would be different, Marianella put in. *Our household in Tevrin numbers several hundred: her Ladyship's family, men-at-arms, servants, and their families, with all the generations represented. We could find a use for everything from the baby food to the gum glue. But you couldn't, not unless you got together with several other families ... oh, I see, some people do but that's not your way. Yes, and someone would have to be steward and keep track of the expenditures, and that could be a burden.*

This, now, Lady Amalia continued, indicating an ad for a box of flavored rice mix. *Why not just mix the rice and the spices together when you're ready to cook them?*

It saves time, Marianella pointed out. *Remember she has no servants; it's every housewife for herself, and many of them work outside the home all day. Susan doesn't, but her children come home from school at three, just in time to be underfoot while she's cooking. Yes, I can see the virtue in having the stuff already mixed, but why not buy the rice and the spices and mix them yourself?*

Sue flipped through the magazine one more time, and tore out a recipe. Then she took her dishes to the kitchen sink and dropped the magazine in the wastebasket.

When the children came home, they found her cleaning the ashes, burnt foil wrappers, and scrap paper out of the fireplace. They stood in a row and stared. "Wow," said Mike after a few moments. "There's a *floor* here. What happened?"

No decent mother, it says in all the child-rearing books,

has favorites among her children. Nevertheless, if Sue had had to be marooned on a desert island with one of her kids, she would have picked Mike, the comedian.

Marianella looked the villagers up and down. A middle-aged woman, two aging men, and a youth with the first bristles of a beard just beginning to show through the pimples. They stood close together, glancing to either side, afraid—not of her, nor of the possible wrath of Lord Andri or his sister— afraid of something in the house.

(And these were the brave ones—the ones who had yielded to Kieran's persuasion. She would have to follow his lead and handle them gently.)

"Thanks a lot, Mike. Any of you have homework?"

"Spelling words," Kathy said, and let out an exaggerated sigh. Sue's fourth-grader was a traditionalist and a conformist. Doing her homework was no great chore for her— all three of the kids were reasonably bright—but she felt bound by the example of friends to complain about it. But she was already dutifully rummaging in her backpack for the spelling notebook.

"Fine. Go do them at the kitchen table."

The woman, Tama, had worked in the kitchen, and Marianella sent her there at once to see to it the second batch of bread didn't burn. "And slice up a pound or two of those onions Kieran sent. Where is he, anyway?"

"Please, ma'am," the boy, Jacko, whispered. "Master Kieran's in the stable, with Rigo the ostler, putting the fodder away."

"Do they need you to help?"

"No, ma'am. They sent me in here."

"Then take a bucket and fill me the kitchen cistern and the boiler. Then you can start scrubbing the tables."

"Mike, what about you?"

Mike had been standing on tiptoe for the past thirty seconds, waiting to be discovered in the act of *almost* dropping a cockleburr down his brother's neck. "Gaaah!" he shrieked, did an elaborate double take and fell to the floor. Mark, born unflappable, paid no attention.

"Homework, you two?" Sue repeated patiently.

"No homework," Mike said, and got up. "I did mine in class and the baby didn't get any."

"Then you get to clean up your room."

"I just remembered," Mike said. "I have to write a life of George Washington and design a Mars lander."

"I mean it," Sue said. "Toys in the toybox, trash in the trashcan, and bedding on the beds." Mark's ongoing project these days was turning the boys' room into a tent city of blankets and sheets draped over furniture and broomsticks. "You too, Mark. Blankets on the bed, sheets downstairs in the hamper, and all your other dirty clothes too. I'll tell you what. If you can get everything cleared up inside half an hour, I'll sweep your floor and then you can build tents till dinnertime."

"Okay!" Mark grabbed his brother's hand and led him up the stairs, protesting for form's sake but unable for once to think of a quip.

Of the men, Arvid was a little ratfaced man of middle age, and Brion an old grandfather (or at least great-uncle) with a bent back and a white beard. She set him to pushing a broom round the Great Hall, where he could keep warm, for it was now late afternoon and a chilling wind was blowing in from the sea.

Of the lot of them, Arvid was the most physically fit, but also the most frightened. He kept glancing at the doorways and the shadows that clustered in the Hall's high beams; it was clear that for twopence he'd run away, Kieran's persuasion or not. "Arvid, there are still a few hours of daylight left. You go up the road with a scythe and cut a load of herbs for the floor. We rode through a stand of sage up by those pine trees."

"C-O-A-S-T, coast," Kathy said as Sue came into the kitchen. "What's for dinner?"

"Ummmm," Sue said. "Hamburgers and whatever else I think up." Hamburger was in the fridge, green beans in the freezer. And rice in the cupboard. *That'll do,* Marianella commented. *Remember, when you're cooking any kind of grain, one and two makes three: one measure of grain and two of water makes three of cooked stuff. Only five people—use that big coffee mug for a measure. Now, what's to go in it. You could just plop a lot of butter on it, but let's see.* She looked over the spices. Cinnamon, cloves, *we'd like that fine in the Great Hall, but I don't think your people would eat it. What's this stuff? Curry? Yes, but only a little bit. You don't want to burn the children's tongues.*

"Or freak out my husband."

"What?" Kathy asked, looking up from her spelling.

"Nothing, dear, just muttering into my beard." She spoke lightly, but her blood ran cold and her face felt scarlet. Bad enough to be caught talking to yourself, let alone talking to . . . to . . . well, talking to yourself.

"You don't have a beard, Mom," said literal-minded Kathy, and went back to her spelling.

Maybe I should let the kids in on it, we could all pretend together, and get the place cleaned up once and for all—no, no, it wasn't a place for children. There was something wrong going on around there; what had frightened the villagers, and driven away the noblemen a few weeks later? *I'll have to find out. It's my fantasy, isn't it?*

She turned the rice, which had begun to boil, down to a simmer and covered it. "I'm going to go ream out the boys' room. Let me know when your homework's done."

By five-thirty the children's rooms, the bathtub, even the back porch was looking halfway civilized, and the pile of throwaways had filled the garbage can and three carton boxes stacked beside it. She'd have to make a dump run tomorrow, which meant putting gas in the car first. Two loads of laundry down and one to go, and all these dish-towels to put away. Meanwhile. . . .

The three tower rooms, each one stacked atop the next, had evidently been used as bedrooms by their Lordships. At the time the Great Hall had been built alongside the tower keep, some considerate mason had installed three fireplaces, one over the other and sharing a single flue that ran up the corner where round tower met rectangular Hall. The top room had four glazed windows, and an oaken wardrobe, and a fine bedstead heaped with featherbeds. That would be for the Lady. The second room had a plainer bedstead, and an oaken table. The third bed, though finely carven, sagged so with age that Marianella had it hauled away. Now the bottom room, level with the Great Hall, was bare except for two chairs, a lamp hanging from a wall bracket, and a faded carpet on the floor, so threadbare that its pattern could only be guessed at. She lit fires on the hearths and spread the featherbeds out to air. The sheets were thoroughly in need of changing, but there was plenty of clean linen, sweet with

lavender between the folds, in a cupboard. Just like a lot of
noblemen, never to think of changing the sheets. (If her
Ladyship had been here alone, which Heaven forbid, she'd
have managed to clean up after herself if no more.) It was of a
piece with everything else they'd done here—driven the servants away (how? she'd have to find out, once they got over
their fright) and then pigged it here till they couldn't stand it
any longer and left. (To go where? Kieran didn't seem to
know.)

She climbed the stairs once more, to look out the windows.
To the west the sea stretched flat and calm under the setting
sun. One thin flat cloud lay along the horizon, colored a
deepening rose. The fresh air was like wine, but very cold; she
closed the west window and latched it securely. From the east
window she caught a glimpse of Kieran's curly head, vanishing
into the stables as she watched. Above the shelly mound the
sea-keep sat on, the low green hills were painted brown in the
light of the setting sun. Along the darkening horizon lay a
darker line, the threshold of the Darkness that lay over the
east. *It's grown*, Marianella thought. *It's taken the White Downs,
and the banks of the Caramath. There'll be no place left in Demoura
any longer where it can't be seen.* She shivered and closed the east
window, and went downstairs where it was warm.

The front door clicked open, and Fred walked in. Instantly the here-and-now closed down on Sue from all
sides, like a fast-settling fog bank or a head cold. Her
hands went on folding dish towels, while Fred aimed a kiss
at her cheek and she wondered how far away the sea-keep
was, and whether one could get an airline ticket.

There was nothing wrong with Fred. He was tall and
blond and reasonably good-looking, and he had captured
Sue's heart in their senior year of high school. Through a
combination of determination, night school, and just a
little bit of native intelligence he had risen in ten years to
assistant manager of the local branch of a gigantic hardware/
variety store. So far as Sue knew, he had never looked at
another woman. And at this moment she wished she'd
never met him. There didn't seem to be any reason.

"Honey, you did a real good job today," Fred said.
"Now, this is how you should keep the place all the time."
Marianella picked up a heavy stone pestle and tested its

weight against her hand. Lady Amalia looked on with faint distaste. "I told you, once I got the kids in school full time," Sue said. " 'Scuse me, I have to go turn the hamburgers. Dinner's almost ready."

"Ah, there you are," Kieran said, not a moment too soon. "I see you've kept busy."

"So I have," Marianella said, pushing a stray wisp of hair out of her eyes with the back of her hand. Her fingers were sticky with pie crust. "It's times like this I wonder if I was meant by Nature to be the chatelaine of any household larger than a shepherd's cot."

"I think you've done splendidly," said Kieran, bristling as though his own ability, not hers, had been called into question. "You've reamed out this place like the fellow in the fairy tale, the one who charmed the river with his flute. With only a little help from Tama and Jacko and your humble servant. Here, let me." He took the heavy pie-dish from her and settled it in the ashes. "Jacko, I think you could lay the board."

The boys had been sufficiently awed by the state of the house, and Mommy's unheard-of determination, to put their room into some kind of order. Kathy finished her homework and set the table, and they sat down to dinner like civilized people.

No one commented on the faintly curried rice, but they ate it, and this surely (Sue thought) was coming out ahead of the game. Fred didn't speak; he was never too hot on table conversation anyway, and he seemed preoccupied. The children were reasonably quiet because Sue had already learned from bitter experience to keep them physically separated by their parents and the length of the table. Mike and Mark tried occasionally to slide down their chairs to kick at one another under the tablecloth, but on the whole the meal was quiet. Sue used the breathing space to try and figure out what she was doing. *Where did these people come from? Out of my mind? Why am I being somebody's servant in a smelly castle? I got married so I could leave home and run my own house. Didn't I? It couldn't have been old Fred.* (But it had been. So we revise our memories, just a little, every time we remember them, and at the end of ten years there can easily be nothing left of them.) *Where did I get them? Did I read about them in school, or see them on television? In the immortal words of Spielberg, who are these people?*

She considered their faces in her mind's eye. Lady Amalia sat alone at the High Table, as was proper. Her beautiful eyes looked out over the Hall as she had looked over the sea, not at it but into the meaning of it. She had laid aside her loose mantle and put on a clean gown, with loose flowing sleeves and a soft hood that fell down her back. It too was made of the soft black silk that said *One with the Sight. Do not touch her, do not speak loudly or startle her, lest you take her wandering Sight unaware and leave her blind and lost.*

Kieran sat opposite Marianella, just below the salt, with the rest of the tiny household to his left. He refilled Marianella's cup, caught her eye, and smiled. "There should be more folk here tomorrow," he said. "Once we pass one quiet night here, and word spreads that her Ladyship is here, they'll come back. And we'll put the keep back in order for her. The gardens are dead, except for the trees, but we can replant them. Would you like that? There's plenty of water in the well."

"There's nothing I'd like better. I thought we were going to stay only till the fall, and go back to Tevrin or the Hill House. But maybe not. I think her Ladyship intends to stay till she finds out where her brother went."

"That's what I hoped," Kieran said, and smiled again. The pale blue of his eyes was like the far mists the Lady saw into, but near at hand and reachable. His smiling mouth was like a flower, not the little pink rosebud of some simpering heroine but a wild flower too rare to have a name. She remembered the softness against her hand. *Kieran, yes, one of the soaps had someone like him once. He was a lawyer or something, little and bearded and charming. But a rat with women, if I remember properly. This one looks a lot nicer. Nice? He's beautiful, dammit. Still, Marianella'd better watch out.*

Amalia—I've seen her in the movies somewhere. Blue eyes, golden hair, high cheekbones, long delicate fingers. Her skin was thin, like ivory stained with rose, like the princess who couldn't sleep on the pea. The sort of fragile, lovely, high-born lady who walked through the pages of fairy tales. She might have been Elaine or Guenevere— except that she looked too honest to deceive her man, and too intelligent to be deceived by him. Maybe that was why she seemed to be still single.

Marianella? It was harder to find what she looked like, she had *been* her most of the day. And there didn't seem to be any mirrors in the castle—maybe they hadn't been invented yet? (*When* were these people?) *How can I see her? Is someone else looking at her?*

She looked through Kieran's eyes and saw a girl like a ripe plum. Her dark hair had been brushed neatly, but little curls were escaping from the restraining ribbons and curling about her forehead and her ears. Her dark eyes were bright, and her skin was like the surface of a golden pearl. Her breasts were like melons, her lips like ripe berries, and if Kieran were only to stretch out his hand across the table he could have touched her. He passed the bread to Arvid at his elbow and wondered if the Lady would indeed stay.

"Honey, are you okay?"

"Hm? Me? I'm fine." *I'm being turned on by the illegitimate offspring of a television set and a—wherever he came from. And they don't make 'em like that around here.* "Come on, Kathy, let's clear the dishes."

After the children were in bed they sat in silence in front of the television set and watched a sitcom and a blood-and-guts adventure team and a suave detective whom Sue immediately pegged as the man with Lord Andri's face. (But this didn't answer the question of where Lord Andri had gone.) Kieran had gone out after dinner to fetch something from the village. Reason said he would come back, but reason ran thin at the shank of a long evening after a long day's riding. Marianella banked the fires in the fireplaces, saw a tough old hen cut up to simmer overnight for tomorrow's soup, and made a trip to the stables to rub Rowan behind the ear and see how well she was housed. Kieran and Rigo had given the horses grain and fresh water and curried them and brushed their manes and tails. Rigo had curled up with Tama in a corner of the Great Hall. But Kieran was nowhere.

"I found out something interesting today," Fred said during the ten o'clock news-and-commercials break. "Oh, and the other thing—we're invited to a party at George Wylie's on Saturday. Can you get a babysitter?" (George

Wylie was Fred's boss, the manager of the Green Valley Road Sav-Mor.)

"I think I can. Kelly just broke up with her boy friend, I happen to know, so she ought to be available on Saturday. What should I wear?"

"Hell, I don't know. Get something new if you like. You'd probably better look nice. The district manager'll be there. That's what it's about, you see. George told us today he's going to take early retirement."

"When?"

"Next June. And he as much as told Paul and Stu and me that we were all welcome to try for the job, and may the best man win."

"Are Paul and Stu going to be at this party?"

"You got it. And some people from the Merton Avenue store and I don't know who else. It's so this guy Bingley can look us all over."

"Well, you can do the work. Remember when you filled in for George for two weeks when he had that gall bladder?"

"Yeah, but that was only because Stu was on vacation and Paul couldn't do it all. I've only been an assistant manager for fourteen months. I don't know what this guy Bingley is going to think. I don't know him."

"Let me get this straight," Sue said. "George can tell Bingley all about your work, or he can look at your file, but just the same we're going to this party so he can see whether you're the manager type—and whether your wife is the manager's wife type. That's it, isn't it?"

"That's it," Fred said. "I don't mind telling you I was worried about the state the house was in—I mean, what if somebody came by?—but it looks better now."

"You let me worry about the house, and I'll worry about the party too. You just keep your mind on your work and we'll knock 'em dead." The sports news came on. "When this is over will you do the garbage? There's no room in the can so you'll have to put it in one of those big plastic bags and seal it up tight." She went into the bathroom and began to brush her teeth.

Marianella saw the Lady Amalia upstairs and covered the bed with the featherbeds that had been warming before the fire. (She still had her own bed to make up. No matter, her feet never got cold.) "I'll open the window a bit, m'Lady. No, not the east window, the south. You sleep soundly." She blew out the candles and went softly down the stairs.

In the room below a single candle burned, and she had left the bedding airing over the foot of the bed. Kieran was there, his brown hair dark in the dim light, and he had made the bed up neatly. The sheets were tucked into the corners, and Kieran was tossing the last feather-filled quilt to float down over the bed, its cover bright red and white. He had set a bowl on the table, and filled it with sweet-smelling roses and pungent lavender. He fluffed the pillows into place like a tidy housewife, and came to Marianella where she stood open-mouthed on the stairs. He put his arms round her and kissed her, softly at first (the curly feathers of his beard and his lips softer than feathers) and then more urgently, and it was long before Marianella remembered to breathe, and to take her hands from the folds of her apron and put them round his neck. His hands stroked her back, curved round and under her breasts. Presently, when they both had to come up for air, he took her hands and led her toward the bed—

"Honey? You about ready for bed?" Fred was leaning against the bathroom door, a sock on one foot, the other dangling from his hand. *Damn*, she thought. *Damn it to hell, what a comedown. I can't, oh, I can't—* She pulled the rags of the fantasy back around her with both hands. "Give me another five minutes, okay? I want to take a quick shower, I'm sticky from shoveling out this house all day." She turned on the shower and stepped in, let the warm water run over her back and her breasts and her thighs.

Kieran, without speaking, sat her down on the edge of the bed, and knelt at her feet. He unlaced her shoes and set them aside. Then he unlaced her bodice and laid it on the table beside the roses, and Marianella obligingly slipped out of the cluster of skirts and petticoats and gave them to him to hang neatly on a peg on the wall. But when he turned back she had skinned out of her shift, tossed it onto the bedpost, and slipped under the covers. Her dark eyes peered at him over the edge of the quilt. So there was nothing for it, he must hang up his own clothes instead. His shoulders were broad, and his body long and straight, and the locks of hair on him like the dark curls of his beard. He blew out the candle and slipped in beside her. He slid one arm under her head, and ran the other hand over her skin as though every inch of her body was precious to him. And when at last he entered her it was as though a door had been opened out of a dark room and the light poured in, only a crack at first and then a great flood of light that filled her whole body.

Above, the window rattled, and Lady Amalia got up to close it. Then she went to the east window and flung it wide, standing long looking eastward where the Darkness beneath the darkness blotted out the stars. At last she went back to bed and shivered for a long while between the sheets before she fell asleep.

Fred rolled over and began to snore. Sue lay on her back in the wide bed, one hand over her breast, smiling into the darkness.

Marianella lay on her back, smiling into the darkness. Kieran's head lay dark on her shoulder, and his hand still cupped her breast. His hair smelled of pine-smoke and the sea, and when at last she slept she lay with him still, holding his mouth against her breast and speaking to him in the dream-language that blows away like the mist in the morning.

CHAPTER 2

Breaking Ground

Sue woke into the cool light of morning and the voluptuous cooing of the pigeons on the power poles. Pigeons and sea gulls flashed through her memory, the Great Hall and the tower, candles and featherbeds and Kieran. She stretched luxuriously, and rolled over on one elbow to look at Fred, who was still ears-deep in sleep. She shrugged and got up, visited the plumbing and washed the crud out of her eyes. There was breakfast to get. She looked over the kitchen, with its buttercup-yellow walls and cutesy print curtains, and thought with longing of the big medieval kitchen with its window over the sea, high ceiling and huge fireplace and honest whitewash on its plastered walls. *That print's got to go*, she thought, *and I could paint the walls white—but would it look right in a kitchen this small? I don't want it to look like the inside of a refrigerator. What a world. Oh, Kieran.*

"Good morning, heart's love," said Kieran, stepping into sight with an armload of kindling. "I brought in your water. You'll want hot water again today? This place hasn't seen the last of the scrubbing-brush yet." He set the stack of kindling neatly under the great cauldron and teased a glowing coal out of the banked ashes into the center of the stack to set it alight. That done, he dusted off his knees and put his arms round her. "Dear heart. You smell wonderful." He kissed her mouth and her hair. "You smell like bed, where I wish I was right now."

25

"Me too. Mmmm—Kieran, wait. Rule yourself. You smell like the sea, where we'll both be if we don't get breakfast ready."

"Hi, honey," Fred said, wandering by in his shorts. "Coffee ready yet?"

"Just perking," Sue said without missing a beat. "Get your clothes on and you can have some. Do you want eggs or cereal?" *I can't, after all,* she thought, *stand around all day in a trance. I've got to be there and here too.* And she brought out the cereal boxes and the milk, and called up the stairs to wake the children.

"So what are you going to do today?" Fred asked, pouring his second cup of coffee.

"Can't you guess? I've got to make a dump run. You can keep plastic bags in your driveway for about twenty-four hours before that dumb dog of MacAllister's finds them and tears them open. Mike, eat with your spoon, not your fingers."

Today I can call myself a happy woman, Marianella thought as she looked over the Hall and her tiny household peacefully gathered to feed itself. Two more women and a half-grown girl had arrived from the village, and Kieran said the staff was now complete. *We shall need more, if we go on living here. If I'd known I'd have brought four or five from Tevrin—if her Ladyship had permitted. She wanted haste and secrecy. I wonder why?*

The Hall murmured with the sounds of talking and eating. Kieran sat beside her on the wooden bench, their thighs not quite touching. His clear blue eyes caught hers, and he smiled over his mug of tea.

They didn't have tea in the Middle Ages. Did they? I could put it in anyway, this isn't real. It's English, and these people sound English, but I don't think they are. She made a mental note on an imaginary scratchpad: *Look up the Middle Ages. Look up tea.*

A happy woman. Or I would be if I knew a little more than I do. Kieran caught her eye again, with a look that made her blood pound. *Absurd,* she thought, *to sit here flaming with passion in the middle of breakfast. If I go on like this, my nether parts will burn a hole straight through this bench.* "Kieran!"

"Madam?"

"In your ear." He moved closer, and she whispered, "I wish

this damned keep were empty again, and we could go back to bed." He smiled, and for answer held up two fingers. "But in the meantime, do you know where the passage is to the sea-gate?"

"No. I asked Uncle Rolf last night, but it seems he's forgotten. I'll make a search. We'll be all over the place today, cleaning and provisioning. I wish the day were over."

With Fred at work and the children at school, Sue tackled the house again. It went slower this morning; she had done more hard work yesterday than she'd realized and her arms and back were sore. It was nearly noon before the last floor was swept, the last bed made, the last box of trash hoisted into the rear of the station wagon.

Let it sit there. Nobody's going to steal it, she thought, meaning the trash, *and I'll take it to the dump after lunch.* She kicked her shoes off and lay down on her bed.

"Madam!" Kieran called, in his formal voice, light and impersonal. "Will you come see this rug? I think it's got the moth." He beckoned her into the tower room, and shut the door behind them. "I found it," he said, and turned back the rug. A trap door had been set in the smooth oaken floor, with a brass ring to lift it by. "The secret's in the rug," he said. "It's so old and shabby that no pillaging soldier would take it." He pulled at the ring and the trap door rose, smoothly enough, but with a loud creak. A flight of stone steps ran downward into the darkness. Kieran took the lamp from the wall and held out his other hand to Marianella. She followed him down into a long cold echoing tunnel whose walls glistened with damp.

The walls of this tunnel were all that remained of the gorge that the stream had cut for itself in its thousands of years' flow to the sea. Once it had been open to the sky, till the ancient builders of the first keep had covered it with a vault of stone and filled it in above the vault with shells and rubble. Now the stream ran underground for more than two miles. A glimmer of sunlight, thirty yards upstream, showed where the wellshaft pierced the stone to reach the water.

At the fortieth step down there was a landing, and a shelf to hold the lamp. Kieran set it down and embraced Marianella in the private half-darkness. They stood there for several minutes, kissing and whispering and touching, till she thought he might have taken her there, standing against the wall. But it was too cold, and she could not keep from shivering. He pulled her away from the wall and warmed her back with his hands. "Next time we'll bring our cloaks."

"And keep them on, I've no doubt," she said. "Next time we'll find a better place. Come on. I want to see the end of this."

Sue became aware of herself, lying face-down on the bed, her arms and legs embracing (so to speak) its flat surface. *Damn*, she thought. *And Fred won't be home till evening and then I have to get the kids to bed.*

Maybe I should get a vibrator, she thought half-seriously, and then violently, *No I couldn't, blast it. Sure as shooting, Fred would find it, or one of the kids, and then there'd be endless explanations. If Marianella has to wait till nightfall, so can I.* She heaved herself up off the bed and went to the bathroom to wash her face in cold water.

From the landing a stone walkway ran beside the stream, down to where fine lines of sunlight outlined the heavy door. Here the stream ran through an ambush-proof grating to pour into the sea outside. Enough sunlight penetrated the water to turn it a deep glowing blue. The grating was made of the dull grandfather-steel, as old as the tunnel and the keep, unrusted after so many centuries. No one knew how to make it anymore.

Kieran held up the lantern, and they looked in silence. No sign of recent passage, no letter tucked in the doorframe, no hasty message scratched into the sooty walls.

"Nothing," Marianella sighed at last. "Let's go back."

"Look." Kieran's voice was like iron. He held the lantern nearer the door, and pointed to the heavy bolt that held it fast. His eyes glittered in the lamplight. He reached past her and seized the bolt, pulled it free with a loud snap and opened the door. The bright sunlight poured in, blinding them for the moment, and the smell of the sea and the loud surf.

The door had been bolted from the inside. "They didn't come this way," Marianella gasped.

"No one came this way," Kieran said.

"The other gate was locked too."

"They didn't leave by any gate." In her returning vision

Kieran's eyes were clear and cold, like centuries-old ice. "They took some other way."

"*What* way?"

Kieran drew her back inside and shut the door again, slammed the bolt home. "We'll ask the Lady," he said, and turned to go up the tunnel to the tower.

A vibrator has no arms, Sue reflected as she drove to the dump. *A vibrator has no face. A vibrator can't kiss, answer the telephone, or drive you to the drugstore, and it's rather difficult for it to earn a living. A vibrator will never get up in the middle of the night and bring you the baby to feed.*

Though I will admit that if all you've got is a vibrator, you aren't likely to have a baby either. . . .

She flung box after box of trash onto the heap that was forming in the dump's staging area, while anxious pigeons swirled overhead and the indifferent workmen stood by with their bulldozers. The sun was high overhead and the smell was indescribable.

A vibrator, what's more, she reflected as she drove back to town, *won't get up before you do and bring in the water and build the fire.*

Neither does Fred.

But then he doesn't have to. Liberty Hill Municipal Utilities does it all for him.

The road ducked under the interstate highway and over the railroad tracks to reach the city. *Where first? The library, or the dress?*

The library, said the Lady Amalia firmly. *You want to learn about the Middle Ages; I want to learn about your Latter Ages. There were some pictures of women's clothing in your magazine, but those were peasants' wives, weren't they? You need to learn how to dress like a lady, and I need to learn how a lady dresses in this land.* Sue obediently turned the car and headed for the library.

She looked up and down the tier of books—*Stuart and Cromwellian Foreign Policy, Gladstone and Disraeli, Henry II, The Economic and Social Foundations of European Civilization*—with dismay. She picked up Volume IV of the so-called *Short History of the English People* and took it back to the librarian's desk. "I must have expressed myself badly. I want to know how people lived in the

Middle Ages, what they wore and what they ate and how they ran their households."

"Aha." The librarian got to her feet. She was a huge woman with a shape like overstuffed furniture and a round face like the moon, but she drifted along the stacks of books as lightly as a thistledown. "This one's about English households generally, but the first couple chapters are on the Middle Ages. Medieval architecture, too. Here's a cookbook, and here's another. This one's on costume. Again, most of these guys polish off the Middle Ages in one or two chapters, so you'll get a lot of Regency and Victorian stuff you don't need. Just be selective. Here's one on the Crusades, with pictures."

Sue checked the books out, and renewed her library card that was on the verge of expiring. She stacked the books neatly and carried them to the periodical section. Here she looked over the fashion magazines, and *Town and Country* and *House and Garden* and other slick pages with compound names. *Amalia, is this what you're looking for?* There was no answer. *How silly I'm being*, she told herself. *There's no such person. I'm expecting advice from something that's an invention of my own mind. Or a part of it.* But in her mind's eye she could see Amalia, her black hood drawn over her bright hair, her eyes misty with distance, her hands folded smoothly as a dove's wings: listening and considering intently, saying nothing, but imposing direction, somehow, guiding the actions of others with her silent will. *That's her Ladyship for you*, Marianella said. *We know she has the Sight, but some of us think she has the Voice too.*

Presently it was two-thirty. Sue put the magazines away and picked up her books. There was a stack of catalogs from the City College by the door, and she picked up one of those too, and went home to intercept the children.

"We've all got homework," Kathy announced as they trooped in. "Good thing the boys got their room cleaned up yesterday. They won't have a chance today."

"You didn't clean up *your* room yesterday," Mark said.

"I didn't have to, because it wasn't dirty," said Kathy virtuously. "So there."

"Cool it, all of you," Sue said. "If you've got homework, do it, and I'll do mine."

"*You've* got homework?"

"I have some books about the Middle Ages to read."

"Why do you have to do that?"

"I don't *have* to, I want to."

The children had nothing to say to this, and the four of them sat down together at the kitchen table to study short vowels, long division, number lines, and medieval household management.

By dinnertime Sue had managed to learn a great deal. She knew more than she had about the Middle Ages, and Europe, and England. She also knew a lot more about Demoura, the Land Beneath the Mountains. It was a lot like medieval England—but how much *unlike* kept flaring up in her face; each bit of medieval history illuminated a contrasting bit of the unknown, the way each match you light in a dark room will show you a bit more of the furniture.

A few million years ago, she supposed, some playful god had taken a triangle of land about 300 miles long and 200 broad, and rammed its sharp end northwards into the mainland. The mountains that rose up as a result had cut Demoura off from the rest of the continent. There were inhabited lands somewhere over the sea, from which trading ships had once sailed to the ports of Tevrin and Landrath, but they were only legends now. No ship had come to Demoura in two hundred years, not since the Darkness came.

In the ninth century, Sue reflected, the Danes had conquered the eastern half of England, and were getting ready to take on the western half when King Alfred of Wessex had rallied the people and driven the Danes back. But there was no king in Demoura; the King's sons had died in battle two centuries ago, when the Darkness took Andarath.

North and south the line of shadow ran, from the foothills of the Weatherwall to the mouth of the Caramath where no gulls flew. Yearly the shadow crept westward, swallowing up little villages and farms. The sun shone colder day by day, the crops bleached and withered, the animals ceased to breed. Bodiless voices wailed round the eaves at night, and over the fields in daylight walked faceless shadows that only the terrified cats could see. The sparrows flew away, the rats set off in defensive groups of five or ten, and at last the men and women bundled up their few goods and fled westward. If not, one night the Darklanders came down like a thunderstorm, and no man or woman was ever seen again.

Good God, I should see a shrink, Sue told herself at this point. *What in the hell is going on in my head? I should forget this whole thing. No amount of housecleaning is worth living in a world full of horrors.*

The thump of the afternoon paper against the door distracted her for a moment. *World full of horrors,* she thought, *I suppose it's no worse than ours.* And Fred was home, on the heels of the paper, and it was dinnertime. She tried to draw a curtain between her thoughts and herself, as Amalia did, but she was new at this and bits kept leaking through.

It's all symbolic, she thought as she handed round spaghetti and herb bread and apple cobbler. *I'm worried about pollution, or disasters like Chernobyl, and terrible things happening to the kids, and so I dream about the Darkness creeping in. Or I worry about crime in the streets, or the next world war, and the Darklanders come down like blitzkrieg on the villages.* She stacked the dishes and washed them and waited for the television to begin. *I should forget about the whole thing.*

But I've got to back Amalia into a corner and find out what's going on.

"Arvid, Rigo," Kieran said when they had risen from the table, "take her Ladyship's chair and put it in the tower room. Thank you. No, you needn't wait." He gave Lady Amalia his arm and walked with her to the tower. Marianella followed with a tray, their cups, and the wine pitcher, and she bolted the tower door behind them.

Kieran saw the Lady seated, and stood before her on the threadbare carpet. He told her in a few short words what he and Marianella had found, and waited. He asked no questions, but he waited, and his cold blue eyes had a power to insist that even Marianella could feel.

Amalia did not speak at once. She sat with her long fingers raised to her forehead, in a gesture Marianella had often seen among the Sighted: fingertips tracing gentle circles over the skin above her eyebrows, as though the eyes of the Sight were there. Between them, the fine vertical lines were already developing in her fair skin.

"Sit down, Kieran," she said, "if you please, and don't tower over me." But Kieran was not a tall man, and the Lady had not opened her eyes to look at him.

"The Lord of Fendarath, my brother," she began, "set off in the middle of spring to come to this place. At Midsummer he sent to me to come to him, and I thought I should go. Living blessedly far from the Shadow as you do, you may not realize how it is for us in Tevrin. The Darkness is now less than thirty miles from the city. It beats upon us like the heat of the sun: it is sand in our mouths, salt in our eyes, thorns against our skin. My brother does not have the Sight, but even he grew tired—tired of me, I dare say. Marianella will tell you how I slept little, ate less, and complained eternally." ("Oh, she did not," Marianella muttered.)

"So when my brother sent for me I was eager to go, but too weary to give the orders for the journey: to call forth fifty or sixty members of the household, gather horses and trappings and provisions and set out in great state. And there was something else that held me back.

"My brother wrote to me that he was staying here with two friends, the Lords Guiard of Holyoak and Zalmar of Northwater. Did you see them when they were here? Can you describe them?"

Kieran glanced at Marianella, and back to the Lady. "I saw them," he said. "Lord Guiard is a fair-haired man, with broad shoulders and long legs. His eyes are blue as flax flowers, and he wears a gold chain round his neck. A very pleasant, cheerful man, or he was when he came here.

"Lord Zalmar is very tall and thin, with black hair. I thought he might be one of the Seers who suffer like your Ladyship from the sendings of the Darklanders. He seemed always to know where one was and what one was doing. And I pitied him, for he seemed to be carrying all the sorrows of the world in his own heart. Have I described them correctly?"

"My brother and I grew up with Lord Guiard," the Lady said. "You have described him well. But Lord Zalmar I have never seen at all. Do you know the House of Northwater?"

"No, Lady. Where do they live?"

"I don't know, and neither does anyone in Tevrin. I asked

everyone I knew. That doesn't mean a great deal any more, after two hundred years of packing up and fleeing from the Darklanders, and settling down and packing up again. Few of us now live in our namelands. Fendarath and Greywell, the homes of my ancestors, have lain under the Shadow for centuries, and instead we hold the Hill House, and Rhadath House in Tevrin, and this sea-keep of Telerath.

"But it seemed strange to me that no one knew Zalmar of Northwater. So when my doorward came to me and said that a servant of Lord Zalmar had come to see me, I let him come in."

"I saw him," Marianella said. "Poor little rat. You said the master was sad and sorrowful? His man was frightened and frightening. He slunk into the room like a beaten hound, and look at each of us in turn as if he wanted to eat us. And then her Ladyship sent us out of the room."

"He said his name was Ruk," Amalia said, "and that hearing I was asking after his master, he came to ask if he could do me any service. He was unwilling to say much about himself or his master, but he confirmed that Lord Zalmar was at Telerath and desired to see me there. Me whom he had never met."

"He could have seen you from afar, or heard your fame sung by the minstrels, and kindled a hopeless passion for you," Kieran said. "The songs of poets are full of such things."

"Maybe," the Lady Amalia said. "Nonetheless, it gave me one more reason not to go to Telerath. I told the man so, but he would not be put off, so I bade him come back the next day.

"That night was quiet. The voices of the Darklands that cry all night, the fingers that scratch against the windowpanes, the wailing winds were silent. It was the night of the new moon, and I thought I might go up to look at the stars. So I left the chamber where I had crouched in hiding for so many days, and climbed to the highest tower of my house.

"But there were no stars overhead. The lamps of Tevrin were bright below me, the air was clear, but high overhead an arm of the Darkness had stretched westward, and I was afraid for myself and for my brother. So I did a thing that I do not attempt often, and probably should not have done then. I rose out of my body and ventured out upon the air. And I thought I would fly westward and see how my brother fared, but before I could begin the journey I heard a cry out of the west, and I knew it was Andri's Voice. And then I heard no more. I sank back down into myself and crouched for hours, cold on the rooftop, while the Darkness slowly drew back overhead and the stars shone again.

"I feared Andri had been taken, I hoped I might still come in time to defend him; but what I knew for certain was that I would not stay in Tevrin one more day to be seen by the man who said he served Lord Zalmar of Northwater. Nor would I let him know I had left Tevrin, nor send him looking for me across the countryside.

"So I crept down the stairs, and woke Marianella, and we saddled the horses in the hour before dawn, and rode out of the city at the opening of the gates. No one recognized us, I saw to that. After that I let Marianella see to everything."

Marianella shrugged. "I had no difficulties. No one bothers a man or woman with the Sight—no one will try to rob her, either, and with a little money most things are possible."

"The night of the new moon," Kieran said thoughtfully. "None of us had set foot in the keep for six or eight days before that. The fear had grown too great. There was nothing to see, and little to hear, only a long sighing in the night. That was the Lord Zalmar, I suppose, or whatever his right name was. He would walk for hours about the hall and the tower, or stand at the wall looking over the sea. The women were terrified of him, though he never went near any of them. He spoke kindly to us, though, when he spoke at all. The new moon," he repeated. "That would have been one of several nights we all kept indoors, Father growling like a bear, and Uncle drinking himself to sleep, and me off in some corner trying to comfort—ah, everybody. It was a night of high winds, I remember that. The Darklanders—dear Heaven, Darklanders flying on the wind as far as Telerath?—they must have gone straight to the keep and back, and not gone near us. Kind of them."

"Treachery," Marianella said softly. "It's the one thing we've never feared. How could any man sell his fellow man to the Lord of Darkness?"

"Not for gain," Amalia said thoughtfully, "nor out of spite.

Out of fear, maybe. Ruk, and Zalmar too, may have lost friends or family under the Shadow, and now are taking a desperate chance to buy them safety—or clean death. I wonder how they speak to the Darklands, and to whom. No man taken by the Darkness has ever been seen again." She rubbed her forehead again, and got to her feet. "Now I've told you all I know, and I can't learn any more till I've rested. I'm going to bed and I suggest you do the same." She went upstairs, leaving Kieran and Marianella looking at one another.

"Far be it from us—" Kieran began with a smile, but he saw that Marianella was shaking and there were tears in her eyes. He put his arms round her and held her close. "There, love. Don't fear. Anything on two legs I'll keep from you myself, and anything else her Ladyship can deal with."

"Oh, don't be stupid," she said, but she rubbed her wet eyes against his collar and let him hold her till she stopped trembling. "What I fear is that you may be right."

"Right how?"

"Her Ladyship," she said. "If the Darklanders have taken her brother, and I don't know what else we're to think, then she's perfectly capable of trying to fight the Lord of Darkness singlehanded. She has no sense of proportion."

"Not much I can do about that," Kieran said. "But come to bed and I'll rub your feet."

"Yes, that will do to start with."

Today, Marianella said firmly the next morning, *we're going to market. Her Ladyship says so.*

If she says so. Sue was sitting on her bed, still damp from showering and washing her hair, wrapped in her clean but shabby terry cloth bathrobe. *It's just as well you're so thin; it's in style there. After three children, you still look like a virgin.* Marinella chuckled. *I never looked like a virgin even when I was one.*

She was sorting through her collection of junk jewelry without really looking at it. Still, some kind of decision was being made: in one pile, a string of fake pearls and a rather plain gold watch with a busted mainspring; in another, a small gold ring and a charm bracelet dangling a dozen silver figures; in the third and by far the largest pile, a growing stack of chains, beads, bracelets, medallions in assorted bright colors and materials, mostly plastic. *Let me guess,* Sue thought, *this pile is the good conservative stuff, right? I'll have to get the watch fixed. What about the ring and bracelet, shouldn't they be in the same pile? They're real gold and silver.*

They're suitable for a young girl, the answer came, *and you could save them for Katherine. Or, if your economy collapses, as it might, and your currency becomes worthless, bits of precious metal will still have barter value.*

Good God, you think of everything.

Somebody has to.

And the rest of it, what do we call that? Sporty and informal?

St. Audrey's Fair.

Garage sale, Sue translated, *or St. Vincent de Paul. Okay, okay. What's this?* She pulled out a long string of heavy green beads. *Oh, yeah, these. They're real malachite, my grandfather brought them back from World War II.* She held them up and admired the swirl of light and dark green within the stone.

Yes. I like those. You're going to wear them, and—Is it warm or cold outside?

Sue glanced out the window. *Coolish and overcast. The weatherman said it might rain.*

Very well. Then you'll wear your black sweater, and your grey coat-sweater, and the beads, and your grey flannel skirt and your good shoes. And if it does rain? Sue pulled out her raincoat, which was white vinyl. *Dear, sweet, gentle Heaven. Susan, if ever you have to butcher a pig, I give you permission to wear that for the occasion. And we'll mark down a new raincoat as your next clothing expenditure after this dress. What about a scarf for your hair?*

Three scarves went on the St. Audrey's Fair pile and one into the wastebasket. *You are better off soaking wet than appearing like that in public.* In her conservative grey and black, and the shiny malachite beads, Sue climbed into the car and went downtown.

Three hours later she had rejected four dress shops. Two of them had been full of ordinary dresses, shirts and jeans and pantsuits for ordinary housewives, the sort of thing Sue would have bought without a second thought if she'd been on her own. But her inner voice had said

something about *peasants' wives* and marched her out again.
The other two were trying to attract the teenage market;
one specialized in plastic and primary colors, the other in
the punk rock look. *Just like half the pictures in those
magazines,* Sue had commented.

*They're trying to sell to those who like to shock the middle class.
And who want to look younger than they are, and the young always
want to shock the middle class. Don't be led astray; you are not trying
to shock anybody.*

Except all my friends who knew me when.

The only thing she had found that both sides of her head
could approve of was a sewing center and yardage shop,
where she bought a scarf in case it rained after all. It was a
big square of cotton, printed in France, with clusters of
flowers in subtle colors. *Yes, some of these are not half-bad,*
Amalia judged as Sue flipped through the pattern books.
*And they have good woollens and a lot of silks. You can sew, can't
you?*

*Yes, and the sewing machine was overhauled last month
when I made Kathy all those new school clothes. But I
can't make a dress in twenty-four hours.*

*No? Then it will have to be Cardwell's. I suspected as much, but I
wanted to exhaust every other possibility first.*

Cardwell's was the local Sak's, the local Nieman-Marcus,
the local I. Magnin's. It was the only place in town that
gave off—or claimed to give off—some of the glamour of
New York, the sophistication of San Francisco, even the
tinsel show of Dallas. Its wares were usually of good
quality and its prices reflected the fact, and Sue had never
bought anything more complicated than a box of bath
powder there. The saleswomen all looked like dukes' daughters, and Sue's knees trembled at the thought of confront-
ing them on their own territory.

In Demoura there are recognized social classes, Amalia said. *You've
seen already the difference between the nobility and the peasantry.
Then the Duke of War, Lord Mark of Hellsgarde, or his Captains
rank me; and Marianella as the seneschal's woman, and chatelaine in
her own right, ranks everyone in the village. You, as the wedded wife of
an assistant-manager (if I understand the term) ought to rank at least
as high as Marianella.*

In your democracy, on the other hand, everyone is supposed to be equal. Either way, I find it hard to understand why you are afraid of a few market-women.

You haven't seen them.

Your egalitarian sentiments do you credit, but I haven't the time to talk you out of them at the moment. Look here, this dress is described as "very easy," only six seams and a neckline and hems. Couldn't you put it together between now and then? Your machine can do the seams in next to no time and we can do the hems during the television. We'll all help.

Between the three of us we've still only got one pair of hands—

—and this is a beautiful silk jersey and very reasonable, the whole thing will cost you less than a hundred dollars. I thought it was black, but I see it's midnight blue. It will look splendid with the malachite. You want four yards. Sue obediently wrote down the pattern number and got up with an exaggerated sigh to get the fabric.

It did feel marvelous under the hand, and her right hand kept creeping into the package beside her on the seat, caressing it. *Mmmm. If I can just get this made up before Fred sees it, he won't complain about the price. And if I can get into it before he sees it, we may never get to that party at all. . . .* And this thought sat much more comfortably on her brain than it might have done forty-eight hours ago. There is, after all, a great deal to be said for sticking with one's familiar old husband, whose habits are known and around whose irritants one had deposited layer on layer of soothing routine. Oysters make pearls by a similar sort of process.

As Amalia had predicted, putting the dress together didn't take long—even though the pattern directions seemed, as usual, to have been translated out of an obscure dialect of French Colonial Mongolian. She bound all the raw edges with zigzag stitching so they wouldn't ravel, stitched the neck facing into place, and tried it on inside out, with the facing lying around her neck like a collar that hadn't quite made it. And the kids came home.

"Mom," Kathy said, "they gave us the PTA envelopes to take home. They gave each of us one but you only have to fill out one. And it's a good thing, because Mark lost his and Mike drew monsters on his. You've got a new dress."

Mark said, "You look neat, Mom. Can I have a cookie?"
Mike said, "Can I have the leftover pieces to make monsters with?" But Kathy said, "It's beautiful. Could I have one like it?"

"When you're older, dear," Sue said. "Give me your PTA envelope and I'll look at it when I have time. I know what it says, anyway; they want money. Would you like a black velvet dress with a lace collar? That's the sort of thing you can only get away with when you're nine years old. You can also help me pin up this one." And between fifteen spelling words and twenty problems in long division, Kathy learned to measure so many inches from the floor and set in the pins neatly parallel.

Sue sat all evening with the pile of silk dark in her lap, rolling the trimmed edge and setting stitch by tiny stitch, through the seven o'clock news and the eight o'clock sitcom and the nine o'clock police show and the ten o'clock news and the eleven o'clock news, and the dress was done. She went into the bedroom and put it on, and came back into the living room to show it to Fred. When she had led him into the bedroom, she told him how much it had cost, and then took the dress off again, and his mind off the subject, and so a second crisis was headed off at the pass.

"Mom, Dad," Kathy said the next morning when breakfast had been eaten and allowances distributed, "can somebody drive me to the Record Barn? I've got enough money now for the record I want."

Sue and Fred exchanged glances. "I've got to mow the lawn," he said.

"Okay, Kathy, I'll take you," Sue said. "When do you want to go? Ten minutes ago? Stop jumping up and down. Go get in the car."

She parked the car in the Record Barn's ample parking lot, and watched Kathy disappear through the door. Slowly she followed. A vague picture was developing behind her eyes, a minstrel sitting with his lute in the castle garden, singing—singing what? Here her imagination broke down.

Inside the Record Barn the air reverberated with rock. The walls were lined with bright-colored albums, and between the racks wandered crop-haired teenagers whose fresh young faces cut the ankles of their punk images out from under them. She caught the eye of a salesclerk. "Do you have any medieval music?"

"Through that door." The door led to a short corridor lined with offices, and the other end opened into a room a quarter the size of the first: the classical department. Only one of the patrons here was a crop-haired teenager, and he was staring with hungry intensity at an album displaying the words GOULD and BACH in ninety-six point type. Clearly it was a different world in here, and the sound in the air was far stranger than rock: a woman's voice singing a strange melody in an unknown language.

The clerk approached, a thin red-haired young man in faded blue jeans and a Mozart T-shirt. "Do you have any medieval music?" Sue repeated.

The redhead gestured at the sound-filled air. "Hildegarde of Bingen, 1098 to 1179. Or would you rather something a little less pure? We just got in the Feast of Fools."

"Gosh. I don't know. I've been reading medieval history, and I thought—but this is a little beyond me. I really don't know anything about music." *Stop apologizing for yourself,* Amalia said sharply.

But the young man was kind, and not inclined to bite. "Well, what have you been listening to?"

"Rock. Jazz. Tijuana Brass. We watch the Boston Pops on TV sometimes."

"Well, that's a good start. Though they don't go much further back than Vivaldi. I bet you know the Four Seasons, and the Guitar Concerto in D. I tell you what—" Crooking a finger, he led her to a corner where a CD player twinkled its mysterious light signals. The song came to an end, and the young man took out the disc. "What we can do is start you out in the Baroque, where you've already been, and slowly work your way backward in time. Do you have a CD player? No? Then we'll stick with LPs for now. For instance, if you like brass—" He let the needle down onto a record, and the music of horns and trumpets filled the air. "That's a canzona by Gabrieli. Lush, isn't it? He wrote it for two choirs of brass at opposite ends of the church, so be sure and sit between

the stereo speakers when you play it at home. Hey, I'm
kidding.

"Hey, I know what you ought to do," he went on
enthusiastically. He picked up a bit of scratch paper (a
flyer announcing a rock concert, torn in four pieces) and
scribbled down a string of letters, the call letters of radio
stations. "There's a limit to how many records you can buy
at one time, unless you've got more money than anybody *I*
know. These are radio stations that play classical music.
This is how to get the breadth of understanding, the
sophistication—what I mean is, you can learn to speak the
language. This one's the best." He drew an arrow opposite
the top one. "They play twenty-four hours a day and they
love music. I mean, they're not just paid to recite the
words, as if it were the stock report. They know what
they're talking about and you can learn a lot from them.
Besides, they're really laid-back. One morning the deejay
put on a flute concerto and fell asleep, and there was a
scratch in the record and it went click, tweet, for nineteen
minutes till he woke up. Did it get him fired? Not on your
life. The listeners depend on that guy to get them up in
the morning. Whenever he goes on vacation they call in to
see if he's sick, maybe they could send in a little chicken
soup? I want to tell you," he finished wistfully, "there's
nothing like being loved."

Sue bought the Gabrieli, and the Four Seasons, and the
Brandenburg Concerti by Bach (in ninety-six point type).
"And when you get used to those," the clerk said, "or
when you can afford it, come back and we'll take you back
another hundred years. I'm here every Saturday and various other times, and my name's Randy."

She met Kathy at the door, clutching her new record.
"What's that stuff for?" she asked, looking dubiously at the
German label on the Gabrieli.

"I'm educating my ears."

"Mom, that's silly. You already graduated a long time
ago."

Fred had cut the lawns, front and back, and trimmed
low-hanging twigs from the apple tree, but the yard still
looked bare and shabby. *We need to do something about
it*, Sue thought vaguely. *Kieran said he'd do the garden*

for me—no, for Marianella, of course. Maybe he'll have a little time left over—Rose trees sprouted in the dark spaces behind her eyes, and emerald-colored lawns starred with flowers, and she put the Four Seasons on the stereo and went to get lunch.

As evening fell, the west wind blew in off the sea, crisp and cold. But overhead, the clouds were streaming out of the east, dark clouds that even the setting sun could not illuminate. "I think it will be tonight," Lady Amalia murmured as she stood at the window with Marianella. "Nothing should happen for a few hours yet. Send down to the village and tell them to bank their fires and go to bed early. There should be nothing to bother them, but I don't want any fires starting from a wind-whipped flame."

She disappeared up the stairs, and Marianella passed her message on to Kieran. "Very well," he said. "It'll mean a bumper crop of babies come Midsummer, but I don't mind if her Ladyship doesn't. The next generation of fighters has to come from somewhere." He glanced up at the glowering sky. "If they get the chance to grow up."

CHAPTER 3

Challenges

"Don't worry about a thing," Kelly, the babysitter, told them as she saw them off. "I know your kids like the back of my hand and I won't let them get away with anything. I'll make the boys go to bed on time, and I won't let Kathy watch *Roseanne*." Thus reassured, Fred and Sue drove away.

"You look nice," Fred ventured as he pulled up in front of George's house. "Actually, you look like a million dollars, so I figure you got a bargain."

"Gee, thanks. How much credit do I get? The living room needs painting, and I'd like to reupholster the sofa, and—"

"Hold it, hold it!" Fred got out of the car, came round to her side, and looked in at the window. "We can't go into this now, but tomorrow night, when the kids are in bed, we'll go over the budget, okay?" He opened the door for her, a thing he hadn't done since their going-steady days. The effect of the silk dress was already beginning to spread out over the world.

It was very plain, with a long straight torso that fell from a round neckline to a smoothly flaring skirt and long straight sleeves that flared smoothly over the wrists. The malachite beads glowed deep green over the dark blue. For Sue's ordinary face there was not a whole lot to be done, but her mouse-colored hair was clean and shining and she had brushed it back and tied it at the nape of her neck. *(Because I say so,* Amalia had said. *I know it isn't fashionable. That's the point.)*

They went to the door and knocked. "We'll knock 'em dead," Sue said. *I'm scared.*

That doesn't matter, Amalia said. *You can be as scared as you like, but you're not going to let it interfere with your duty. You're one of my people. You're not some common housewife, you're Susan Greywell of the House of Fendarath, and you're not going to disappoint me.*

The inside of George and Norma's house was brightly lit, overheated, and crowded with people. In the competitive spirit of the evening, Sue first searched the room and found Stu and Paul and their wives Ruth and Karen. *How do we stack up?* Stu had reached forty, Paul forty-five, and George sixty, in the service of a large corporation that paid their salaries but never really noticed their existence. Three white faces, three heads of thinning grey hair, they looked a lot alike. If George retired and Stu or Paul replaced him, the change would be almost imperceptible to the casual eye.

Fred was a younger man, his color still fresh, his hair still thick and golden. But it came to Sue with a sudden shock that give him another fifteen years and he would look just like Paul, another thirty and he would look just like George. And that was what they wanted, wasn't it? To make him a branch manager, with more money and more prestige? Sav-Mor had good employee benefits and a scholarship fund; with luck, they could put all three kids through college, make lawyers or doctors of them maybe. A comfortable income and a stake in the future, what more could anyone ask?

Stu and Paul, with George, were standing to left, right and center of a man in a white dinner jacket—presumably the Bingley in whose honor the whole thing was being done. He had black hair and broad shoulders and was probably (Sue could not see his face) no older than Fred. And a district manager already; he must be on the fast track.

Ruth was hovering by the buffet, a mistake; there were the usual soggy cheese puffs, the sour tuna dip with wilted vegetables, the little cocktail franks in leathery pastry, the prefabricated potato chips with plastic dip, and Norma's special Swedish meatballs that would bounce on a hardwood floor. Ruth had put on another ten pounds since Sue had last seen her. It was a pity she hadn't been born two hundred years ago, when curves were in fashion; she would have had every man in the room at her feet. With her clear skin and pale-pink jersey dress she looked like a great big baroque pearl, all smooth curves and glowing highlights. Ah well.

Karen had settled by the drinks, a bigger mistake; Sue had partied at Norma's before and knew that all the drinks would be much too strong, with no nonalcoholic alternatives available. Karen looked tired, tireder than usual. After all these years, Sue still didn't know her well; she didn't allow herself to be known. She kept an immaculate house, everything gleaming and not a matchstick out of place. Maybe it was because she had no children. Maybe that was *why* she had no children. She had plenty of money and could have hired a housekeeper, but preferred to do it herself—and she always looked tired.

Norma was nowhere in sight: lying down with a headache, probably. She was a shy woman, who might have done better as a nun in a cloister than a branch manager's wife with parties to give. She always did what was asked of her, but once the invitations were sent and the tables laid, her shyness turned inward on her protesting body and sent it down with migraine or collywobbles or hives. *Maybe that's why her food and drink is so awful,* Sue thought in another sudden flash of illumination. *It all tastes like sawdust to her anyway.*

There were a lot of people she didn't know—candidates from the other branches, she supposed. There was one woman of about forty, slim and tall and elegant in a black sweater and slacks. She had short sleek black hair and a very intelligent face, and her expression was that of one who is concealing boredom behind all the courtesy she can muster. Sue would have liked to talk to her, but couldn't imagine what to say.

Make the effort, Amalia said. *You are here, not only to see and admire, but to be seen and admired. You are here to make social contacts. Also, you will want to invite all these people to* your *party.*

My what?

The rules of hospitality require that you invite George and Norma to your home to thank them for inviting you here. It is appropriate to invite as fellow guests most or all of the people who are here tonight. It's also good strategy, because you can demonstrate to your peers and to Bingley that you can host a party with fewer difficulties than Norma has had.

I would like to point out that it's no kind thank-you to Norma to invite her to another party.

I'm aware of that. Can she take small informal gatherings? Good. Then you will invite her to tea and explain in confidence that if she wishes to send last-minute regrets on account of sudden illness you will understand. Then she can stay quietly at home and be officially, and not actually, unwell, and it will not be to your discredit. Now start circulating and meeting people.

But the air was excessively hot, and smoky, and far across the room were the French doors that led to Norma's side lawn. Carefully sideslipping the other guests— horrible thought to get food or drink, let alone a cigarette burn, on that silk!—she made her way to the doors and went outside.

The air was clean and cold, with a promise of rain before morning, and wisps of cloud drifting over the moon. She drew in a deep breath and let it out, flushing out the stale cigarette smoke. She had never been a smoker, and Fred had given it up several years back on the occasion of a media blitz from the national cancer, heart, and lung associations. "Kissing a smoker," the saying went, "is like licking an ashtray." They had something there. How much better to breathe fresh air than stale smoke.

The clouds drifted across the moon. *Amalia, how's it going at your end? No trouble yet?*

Not yet. They're on their way, I can feel it, but I don't expect any action till midnight or thereabouts.

What will you do then?

Fend them off—if I can. And learn whatever I can—if anything. As you know, I'm fairly certain Andri and his companions were taken by the Darklanders. If I can find out, then—well, then, I'll know . . . .

What if the Darklanders carry you off?

Then I shall know for certain.

Can't you call for reinforcements? Somebody else who has the Sight and maybe a little more Muscle?

Muscle, what a clever way of putting it. Yes, I sent a message around sunset, to Denis the Raven, a very powerful man. But he can't give me any aid from where he is, in Tevrin. He is going to gather his companions and come to me here, but they can't come any faster than another dozen men on the same horses.

I wish I could help. Why can't I help? Aren't you and the Darklanders and the rest of it all inside my mind? Why can't I just make *the Darklanders lose?—or just not come at all?*

Amalia was silent for a long moment. *I suppose*—she said at last—*I suppose that would make it too easy.*

"Hello," said a voice behind her. She turned. The man in the white dinner jacket was standing beside her. He had very black hair, and an expensive tan, and a smile that might have been the gift of the gods, or the product of expensive dentistry. "Hello," he repeated. "I've met everybody else, so I bet you're Fred's wife."

"Yes. And you're Mr. Bingley. How do you do."

Very good. Don't be too familiar.

"My friends call me Chris," Mr. Bingley said, not having heard Amalia, "and you and I are going to be friends. We have so much in common."

"Have we?"

"Sue, what you and I have in common is that we both want to see Fred get ahead. And between us we can do it."

"How kind of you to say so." *He's standing too close.*

"You know there's about ten guys in the running for George's job. And while the decision is made in the corporate office in Detroit, my recommendations will have considerable weight. *Considerable* weight," he repeated, and smiled again, while Sue's mind spun about at high speed.

I know what this is about. He's putting me on the spot. He'll recommend Fred for the job, if—if what? What do you think? I don't believe this. Is it the dress? My God, I should have worn a flour sack—

Be quiet, Amalia said. *Let me handle this.* "Chris," she said, "I know you'll pick the best man for the job. I think it'll be Fred, but that's because I know him better than you do. Is this your first visit to Liberty Hill? I'm afraid we've got a

rainstorm coming in to welcome you; I hope you brought
your umbrella." And she smiled.

"No problem," he said. "I like walking in the rain. Do
you?"

"Oh, I used to love it," Sue said sweetly, "long ago,
when I was single. Nowadays, a house and three kids keep
me busy—to say nothing of the PTA."

"Come on, you must get out of the house occasionally."

"Certainly I do. Why, only today I took my daughter to
the Record Barn. And I got to the library last week. That's
not counting a trip to the city dump after I cleaned out the
kids' rooms."

"You need a real change. That's one of the advantages of
my job, I get to travel. Last week I went to a training
session in San Francisco."

"How nice for you. Did you get to ride on a cable car?"

"No, but after the session was over I rented a car and
drove up to the wine country. Beautiful scenery, wine-
tastings every couple of miles. Only I was by myself, and
it got lonely."

"Yes, that's the other side of the coin, isn't it, leaving
your family behind. But we'll do our best to make you
welcome here." And by special gift of Heaven, the first
raindrop fell. "Let's get inside," Sue said. "I haven't met
half the people here; will you introduce me?"

"Oh, sure," he said, and reached out his arm as if to put
it around her shoulders. If so, he thought better of it and
pulled the French doors shut.

She held him to his promise, and spent the rest of the
evening learning names, faces, and affiliations. When after
the dozenth introduction Bingley melted away from her
side, she let him go. *Pete Rice is thin and pale like a grain
of rice,* she recited silently. *Hope is his wife. Hope and
Pete. They're from Silver Lake. Hope and Pete Rice from
Silver Lake. What time is it?*

Searching the room for a clock, her eyes met another
pair of eyes, cool and grey and luminous: a man in his
forties wearing a tweed jacket with sagging pockets and
leather patches on the elbows. His face was crinkled with
good humor, and although his curly fair hair had been
combed into place earlier in the evening, it was now

escaping from order and discipline in several different directions. He smiled, and gestured toward the kitchen door with a motion of his head. "Hi, there, kindred spirit," the gesture said, as plain as print, "come meet me in the kitchen and we'll talk." Sue smiled at the Rices again, and slipped off through the crowd toward the kitchen.

"Hi," said the man in the tweed jacket, who was investigating the inside of the refrigerator. "You look like someone who could use some real food and drink. What's your name?"

"Sue."

"Hello, Sue. I'm Terry Carmody, I'm Norma's brother. My wife and I are staying here for a week or two—I hope it's just a week or two—till the paperwork gets done on the house we're buying in Bredon Heights."

Bredon Heights was a wooded, hilly suburb of the metropolis, about forty miles north of Liberty Hill, just south of the university, and much favored by university faculty and those staff who could afford it. "What do you teach?"

"Mathematics. Doesn't it show?" He ran his fingers through his hair, making it stand out from his head. He looked, if not quite like Professor Einstein with his halo of white hair, at least like a good enough Mad Scientist for the late night show. "Here we are," he went on, emerging from the refrigerator. "Honest bread and meat and a couple of decent tomatoes, who could ask for better? Do you like beer?"

"Not really. It never tastes as good as it smells. I'll have some coffee; it's getting late."

They sat with the kitchen table between them and made ham sandwiches. "That's better," said Terry after the third bite. "How do you fit into this gathering? You work for the store?"

"My husband does. He's one of George's assistant managers."

"Ah. And he's been called to Bingley's cattle call. You've met Bingley? Dreadful man. He has the single eye, I'll give him that, but it has tunnel vision."

"What do you mean, 'the single eye'?" Surprisingly, she didn't feel shy about asking questions in this man's presence. He took for granted, and made her take for granted, a common ground where everything was worthy of discussion, and there was no such thing as a dumb question.

"Oh, it's in St. Matthew. 'If thine eye be single, thy whole body shall be full of light.' *Ho ophthalmos aplous*—nowadays it's usually translated 'the sound eye—' "

"You speak Greek, too?"

"Aw—" He looked faintly embarassed. "I had to learn the Greek alphabet when I started taking trigonometry, so I went ahead and learned the language; it seemed the simplest thing to do. Now the man with the single eye—the singlehearted man, we'd say—knows what he wants and goes for it, doesn't even see anything that might be a distraction. Which is not necessarily a good thing, I don't care what St. Matthew says. The single eye is a tool, like fire or the gasoline engine or a nicely shaped rock. It all depends on what you use it for. Bingley, now, he knows what he wants."

"Money?"

"Oh, nothing so simple. Money plays a part in it. Bingley wants to be the biggest frog in his puddle. The bigger the puddle, the better, but mostly he wants to be the alpha frog. So here he is, a district manager, which means that in his district he's the alpha frog, all right, but only to those who work for Sav-Mor. He's nobody in particular to the cop on the beat, or the man from IBM, or me. And he knows it, and it galls him. So he has to magnify his little spark of limited power, any way he can.

"Look at this party. I'd say the odds are nine to one—did I mention my field is probability and games theory?—the odds are nine to one Bingley has already looked over the files on all the assistant managers, and already knows everything he needs to know. Fifty percent probability he's already decided whom to recommend, maybe forty-five percent he'll just pick one at random when he's had his fun."

"What about the other five percent?"

"Oh, he *might* consider the cases on their merits and make a rational decision. I'm not betting on it. Have another sandwich. A craving for power is a pitiful thing."

He took another swallow of beer. "And like all evils it comes of a good that has been distorted out of proportion."

"How?"

"A living creature needs its share of the world, enough of the land or sea to let it make a living and reproduce." He had slipped into his lecturing voice. Sue found she didn't mind. "So most living creatures have a strong desire to get, and keep, their share of the goodies. Because if they didn't they wouldn't have survived, and somebody else's kids, that *did* have that desire, would inherit their turf. Follow me?"

"Sure."

"Okay, in man—let's say, in human beings, we still have this desire for a share of the goodies. That is, I want my little chunk of land that'll keep me alive—or, because I'm a social animal, I want my tribe to have *its* share that'll keep us all alive. And then I want to have my share of the tribe's turf, which means status. And, as it happens, I particularly want it because I'm male. (Females are usually content to take their status from their menfolk, though not always.) I need this to stay alive, so I want it, so I need it to make me happy."

The evil begins, said Amalia suddenly, *when someone begins to seek more land, or more power, than he needs.*

"The evil begins when someone tries to get more than he needs," Sue echoed.

"Hey, you do understand me. It begins, doesn't it, when power stops being a means to an end and becomes an end in itself. It's right, it's *a* right, for a man to want and try to get the power he needs, power over his own life. It's wrong for him to want power for its own sake. It becomes sadism; as Auden put it, it will always be irrationally cruel, since it is not satisfied if another does what it wants; he must be made to do it against his will. Hence—" he gestured with the remains of his sandwich "—torture chambers, nuclear buildup, and Bingley."

"I see," Sue said thoughtfully. "So when he was making passes at me out on the terrace, he was trying to establish ownership over Fred and Fred's belongings."

"Did he, though? Typical. And inexcusable. What did you do?"

"Talked about the weather."

"That's the fight. I hadn't realized Bingley was into that kind of sexual confusion."

"Confusion? I got the impression he knew what he was doing."

"What he was doing was confusing the symbol with the thing symbolized. Did you ever watch two monkeys—"

"Batten down the hatches, he's starting in on the monkeys again," said the black-haired woman, who had come in unnoticed. "Between an ape and that turkey in the white jacket, I unhesitatingly affirm my preference for the ape." She pulled up a chair.

"What, you too? Sue, this is my wife, Claire."

"Hello," said Claire. "Pass me the beer, there's a good fellow. Thank you. Me what, too?"

"The bounder's been laying siege to Sue's fair name," Terry said. "But she routed him with a look of cast-iron virtue and some talk about the weather." His eyes met Claire's, and suddenly they burst into song:

> "How beautifully blue the sky,
> The glass is rising very high,
> Continue fine I hope it may,
> And yet it rained but yesterday,"

and broke up into giggles.

"No, he wasn't interested in my virtue," Claire said, "but he offered me the branch managership of the Green Valley Road Sav-Mor."

"What, offered it? Or just dropped hints?"

"Offered it, flat out. He must have known I'd say no. I told him how much I make at the Entworks, and he turned pale." They laughed again.

"She writes software for supercomputers," Terry explained.

"What about the monkeys?" Sue asked.

"Oh. Well, consider two little monkeys, up in their trees, defending their territory along some invisible boundary line, each of them displaying—how shall I put this—oh, what the hell, you're a married woman. Each of them reared up on his hind legs, displaying his erect penis. Or depending on the species, turning his back to display his pale-pink testicles. Then there's the mandrill, who's got his whole set of equipment decorated in fetching tones of red and blue, and his face done up to match, so that you see him coming and going.

"Now what are these monkeys saying to each other? Is the monkey gay? Is he saying 'Let's do it'? No, and no. Is he even saying, 'Screw you, buddy?' Not exactly. He's saying, 'Look at me. I'm not a female, I'm not a juvenile, I'm not an oldster, too tired and feeble to stand up for myself.' (None of whom participate in power struggles, you see.) 'I'm a healthy young male, ready to fight for my share of the turf.' And the other monkey says, 'Me too,' and after they've made their point they go away. What started as an organ used for sexual purposes only has become a battle flag, a symbol of power.

"Unfortunanly, the symbol has become confused with the thing symbolized. Even before you leave the animal kingdom; among the social apes, one male will pretend to mount another, to show him who's boss. He's saying, 'Compared to me, you might as well be a girl.' No actual sex act takes place.

"Among humans it gets steadily worse. Your average human male may sense there's a difference between his organ as something to make love to his wife with and as something to show off to the boys in the locker room with. But he couldn't put it into words.

"Nowadays, psychologists speak of swords and guns and bombs and high-rise corporate headquarters as 'phallic symbols.' But as Jung pointed out, the phallus is itself a symbol, a symbol of power. And too many people can't tell the difference between the organ that symbolizes power and the organ that really confers power—which is occasionally the fist, but usually the brain. They assume, to put it crudely, that anybody who can't get an erection can't pilot a spacecraft, write a symphony, or make a killing on Wall Street. *Quod erat absurdum.*"

"It's where I part company with orthodox feminism," Claire said. "Because I don't mistake the human traditon of male dominance for something recent, and culture-based, and transitory, I don't fool myself into thinking it can be done away with by waving a wand and chanting 'Sisterhood is beautiful.' "

"It's widely theorized," Terry said, "that men who commit rape do so because they haven't the confidence to compete with other men. A women doesn't have a flag to wave, she's a safe environment for him to glut his grubby little ego with stolen power. Conversely, I'm convinced many men choose homosexuality because they disdain to waste their power symbols on someone who doesn't have one of her own." He drained his glass. "Of course it's hard to prove any of this. It's not like mathematics."

"I've done some work on the recent history of male-female relations—say, the last ten thousand years," Claire said. "We appear to have two traits running side-by-side, like recessive genes: one for egalitarianism, one for male dominance. And the switch seems to have happened at the agricultural revolution of the Neolithic, when for the first time people amassed large amounts of property. Before that it wasn't worth it. Hunter-gatherer cultures are egalitarian, but farmers and herders are male-dominated. I could go on for hours, but do you realize it's ten minutes to midnight?"

"Then I've got to make like Cinderella," Sue said. "We have to get back and take the babysitter home. I'm delighted to have met you two."

"Oh, the pleasure is all ours," Claire said. "Do keep in touch—you can always reach us through Norma. Or—" she reached into her pocket, and raised her voice just a trifle— "remember what I said; if Fred is thinking of making any career changes, do have him call us. We can always use brains." She gave Sue a card that said ENTWORKS, Software to Order; and Claire's name, and an address and phone number. All this was so obviously for someone else's benefit that Sue was not surprised, when she turned to go, to find Chris Bingley standing in the kitchen doorway.

"Good night, Chris," she said, trying to brush past him. But escape was difficult; the living room was crowded with people and their coats, to-and-froing (Fred and Sue weren't the only couple who had to get home to their babysitter).

"What were the Carmodys talking about?" he asked. His expression, if not his tone, implied the Carmodys' conversation was way over her head, and possibly his own.

"Anthropology, mostly, and math. Probability theory."

"Did you understand them?"

"Oh, the anthropology was very interesting. The math was too, but a little hard to follow in places." *There's the understatement of the week.*

Bingley frowned. "Look, I think you and I should have lunch," he said, "and talk over Fred's chances." His eyes were on the Entworks card in Sue's hand.

"That would be nice," she said. "But I'm hoping to have you all to dinner one of these days. How long will you be in Liberty Hill? But there, I suppose you'll be coming and going. I can always get your schedule from George. Good night!" And she made her escape, into her coat and out the door.

"What'd Bingley have to say to you?" Fred asked as they drove home through the gusts of rain.

"He said you were among the front-runners," Sue paraphrased. "I think he was just trying to make me feel good." *And* there's *the misleading statement of the year!* "He seems to be very nice." *Nice, if you like wolves. Amalia, thanks for your help. I couldn't have done it without you.*

Yes, you can, once you learn. It's called, "To the pure, all things are pure." You are so virtuous and respectable that you don't even know where his words are leading. And you don't permit yourself to be led.

Sue was already in bed when Fred, yawning, returned from taking Kelly home. "I think we sleep tonight," he said. "It's late."

"Mm-hmm." The east wind had risen, and sang a thin cold song across the battlements and through the windowframes. Amalia had not attempted to go to bed. Instead she had dressed warmly and sat on the hearthrug, staring into the dully glowing coals and waiting for the attack to begin. For some time the desire had been rising in her to go up to the tower roof and see what was approaching; she overcame it and stayed where she was.

It was cold. Her fingers were so cold she could not feel them. She held them over the fire, but it too was cold. The orange light was fading to red, dimming to black. Tiny splinters of ice sparkled on the dead coals; icicles were forming on the firebrick and creeping outward to cover her body.

She looked again, and it was gone. She took a deep breath,

and let it out slowly as she had been taught, and held out her hands to the warmth. *A feint, no more,* she thought. *Testing me.*

The wind sang. Something tapped at the window. A tree branch? None of the garden trees grew that high. A stray leaf or broken twig, caught up in the wind? Something tapped again. She would not turn to look, but in the corner of her eye something fluttered, hovered, waved: it was a hand, a fleshless hand of white bone. It reached for the latch and turned it. The window swung open, the hand was creeping inside. *Go away,* Amalia said calmly. The hand was gone. The window was closed. It had never been open. *Children's tricks. Do you think you have an untaught peasant here, to be frightened out of her farmstead? I am the Lady of Fendarath!*

"Lady of Fendarath," a voice said softly.

Amalia turned. A manlike creature was sitting cross-legged on her bed—but no, "cross-legged" implied straight-boned legs that flexed at hip and knee. This creature was boneless; its fingers were like ribbons. And it had no face.

"Amalia, you're mine," it said. Its voice whispered from a hollow in the base of its throat. "Give up your foolish Lightlands concerns, your palace politics and children's games, and come to me. I shall possess you, and you will serve me. For I am Imber, Lord of Darkness."

"You and my grandmother's cat," said Amalia. "You haven't the smell of power. You are no more than a glove on his hand." And she took up a brand from the fire and thrust the glowing end toward the creature's body. It vanished.

She turned back to throw the brand into the fire. The creature was standing there, curving arms outstretched to her. "Amalia," it said, "my choice, my desire, my jewel in the darkness. Come to me."

For a moment Amalia was so furiously angry that she could neither speak nor act, and the creature moved closer. Then her training reasserted itself, and she reached for the techniques she had learned as a girl: the naming of names, the recitation of powers, the gathering of forces. The creature stepped backward, raised its hands to its eyeless head, faded from sight. It had been only a handshee, a sending of the outward accidents of some creature, under the power of the Lord of Darkness. It had looked real to the outer eye and to the Sight, but anyone who knew if for what it was could dispel it with an act of will.

But the handshee could not be made out of nothing; somewhere the creature had a real body, and she had never seen one like that before. The Darkness was breeding new creatures, preparting for some new attack. She would have to let Denis the Raven know about this.

The wind fell silent. There was a presence, hovering just at the edge of her awareness: a shape, no, several shapes, dull brown to her mind's eye, bitter to her taste, dust-dry to her touch. Servants of the Darkness. Behind them, something that shone with a dull black radiance, a hint of power, a commander surveying his armies, an enemy to reckon with. She breathed again, and waited.

The wind sprung up again, blasted against the window and blew it open. That was real, and she got up to close it. Tendrils of smoky air, like long arms, swirled round her, but they dared not stay long in the room with the fire and Amalia. She drew the window shut and secured the latch. In the outside air faint shadows were dancing, but to her Sight they took on shape: shapes out of legend, shapes out of two centuries' combat.

Like flakes of ash, the rishi swirled in the air, beasts as large as wolves, as lithe as cats, riding the wind on the membranes that stretched between their legs. Their eyes shone with cold fire. Their riders clung to their backs, little manlike warriors no bigger than children, the Shadowlings. Flatfaced and eyeless, they saw through the eyes of their rishi and through the power of their master. Their short curved swords were as sharp as razors, and they had to be hacked to pieces before they stopped fighting.

But tonight they did not approach; they had only come along for any harm the sight of them could do. Slowly they rose and fell on the wailing wind.

Behind them hung other shapes, huge dragonlike forms with slowly beating wings. Two of them, Amalia thought, circling and waiting behind their front lines: they must be two of the mysterious Shadowknights that came to the wars from time to time. No man had ever defeated one, but always after a space of years they vanished again. Now there were two more.

And then, faint behind the windrush, she heard, *Amalia, help me!*

Andri's Voice, thin and desperate. Amalia thrust her hands toward the window, palms out, as if pushing the terrible summons away, then clapped them over her ears, which did no good. *Amalia, help! Ah, mercy!* and a long descending cry. Amalia snatched up her skirts and ran for the tower stairs. She climbed them to the ceiling, fumbled at the latch, and pushed open the trapdoor that led to the tower battlements.

She stumbled onto the flat stone roof and fell to her knees. The wind was like a bludgeon. She got to her feet and searched the sky. Summoning all her power and casting her Sight outward, she caught a glimpse of her brother, his face pale, his eyes black-rimmed, riding the back of a leathery-winged worm. Then he touched the reins, and the creature banked and turned away. The other gathered the air beneath its wings, rose, and swooped down on her.

She was enveloped in darkness. Her Sight went blind, and left her only the feeble senses of the body: whistle of wind, taste of dust and sulphur. She stretched out her hands and touched skin, human skin, and human hands touched her and drew her into an embrace. Someone's mouth came down on hers, and she tasted salt: sweat, or tears perhaps, or blood.

It was as if the heat of his kiss burnt through their clothing and they stood naked together, skin against skin. She felt his flat-muscled body under her fingers, and shivered as his hands moved down her back and over her flanks. Soft hands, a scholar's or an artist's, maybe, not a minstrel's or a warrior's. His mouth was water to her thirst, air to her drowning, food to her hunger; but his touch kindled in her a greater hunger, a flame she had never known and could not name.

And he was gone. The dark wind rose up like a high-crested wave and fell back toward the east, and the small cold stars shone overhead, and the sea air came creeping in with a taste like tears.

There were hands touching her, ordinary hands: Marianella's hands that lifted and turned her where she had fallen along the rooftop in a crumple of black robes; Kieran's hands that picked her up and carried her down the stairs and put her into her bed. She lay prone, blind with tears, not heeding their questions, until at last they went away. She lay weeping till the grey dawn. The fire went out and the room grew cold, but her mouth and her body and her heart were afire with longing. The cool air poured down the roof hatch that Kieran had forgotten to close, but it was no matter. She knew they would not come back.

CHAPTER 4

Setting Forth

The storm that had played cat-and-mouse with Liberty Hill all night pounced just before dawn, and the rumble of thunder and rattling windows woke Sue out of a confused and uneasy sleep. It took her a few moments to realize what was bothering her. The last time she had felt like this was just before Mark was born. The baby had descended like a rock into her pelvis—a sign that his arrival was imminent—and he had seemed to gain ten pounds overnight. Sue had walked splay-footed, like a duck, perpetually exhausted with two toddlers to care for. Whenever she managed to lie down she had been like a beached whale, or a snake that had miscalculated and swallowed a lead weight instead of a mouse. It had been a major effort just to turn over in bed. It was the same now, except that what weighed her down was not Mark kicking and squirming in her belly but Amalia lying inert in her heart.

Amalia had not slept at all. She had lain with her head pillowed on her arms during the night, not weeping any more but finding it a job of work to keep herself breathing. From time to time she would look outward, past Kieran and Marianella lying in each other's arms, past the castle folk asleep in the Hall, past the village and the rabbits running over the grass and the owl floating under the moon, searching. And finding nothing, she would fall back into herself in despair. Land, sea, and sky were empty.

Poor Amalia. Haven't you ever been in love before?

Is that what it is. A cloud of names and things named swirled up in her mind and settled down again, rearranged. *I'm obliged to you for telling me. I might have taken days to figure it out. O dear, yes, I find new meanings in all the songs of the poets. Particularly the tragic ones.*

Amalia, who was he? He was with Andri. Was that Guiard?

No, of course not. I should have known. Guiard has kissed me once or twice. Poor man, he has loved me since we were children together, or said he had. I always thought of him as a brother. But if this is what he endured all these years on account of me, I wish I had understood sooner. I'd have wedded him at once, and one of us could have been happy. No, that was not Guiard.

Zalmar?

Maybe. As Kieran said, the poets sing of such things: a wandering knight who falls in love with a lady on first sight, or even sight unseen, hearing others speak her praise. Do you suppose it could be so? Her thought was wistful. *Why would he have gone to such effort, come such a long way, unless he loved me?*

Maybe.

Sudden bitterness. *But then why did he go away?*

Maybe he's not his own master. Silence. *Because—you have to face this—either he's a prisoner of the Darklanders, or he's working for them. And the same goes for Andri.*

Oh. Amalia turned over in bed, lay staring into the icy darkness. *Yes, you noticed that; I wish I had not. His hands were not bound; he held the reins and guided his beast. He was my little brother; when he fell into the fishpond I pulled him out; when he got lost in the hills I brought him home on my pony. And now it would seem he's gone into a place where I can neither reach him nor bring him back. I shall have to think about this.* She turned over again and hid her face in her arms.

Why don't you get some sleep? Sue hauled herself to her feet and found her bathrobe, made a quick tour of the kids' rooms. They were adequately covered and their windows were closed. She snagged another blanket for her own bed and crawled back into it. Fred slept on, and his back was agreeably solid and warm. She curled up against it and went back to sleep.

Sue, I need to tell you something, Marianella said the next morning. Sue had just gotten the family home from church

and put lunch on the table. *Something the Lady said last night.
She said twice yesterday you'd made claims you couldn't back up, and
would have to make them good.*

Claims?

*You told the music merchant you had been reading medieval
history, when you have only skimmed a few books for interesting bits of
household management. And you told Christopher Bingley that the
PTA kept you busy, when all you have ever done with the PTA is to
send it money. Mind you, her Ladyship is not objecting to small social
falsehoods as such. She says they are the grease that keeps our lives
from squeaking like the wheels of oxcarts. But if you were caught out
in a lie—if someone who did know about medieval history started
discussing it, and you didn't know how to answer, you would lose
honor. Or if someone who did go to the PTA said, "That's funny, I
don't remember seeing you there." You see? To protect your own good
name, her Ladyship says, you're going to have to make your word good.*

And study medieval history and get involved in the PTA.
"Oooh."

"What's the matter, Mom?"

"Nothing, dear. Eat your lunch." *I'll do it, Marianella,
but you don't know what you're asking. The history I can
take—in fact, I expect I'll enjoy it. But have you ever been
to a PTA meeting?*

I don't even know what a PTA is. A religious brotherhood?

*Religious? No. Sisterhood, maybe. It's a group of
parents—in practice, that means mothers—who get together with their kids' teachers to decide how the school
should be run.*

*But that's very important! You should have been involved in it all
along.*

*It's nothing but palace politics. The mothers don't really
have any say in how the school is run, unless they can
influence the school board who really run it. I've always
suspected the women who are really active are the ones
who have to stay home because they have kids and would
rather be out becoming president of General Motors. When
their kids grow up, they abandon the PTA and get a job or
run for City Council. I am going to be way out of my
league.*

I am understanding about one word in three of all this, Marianella said, *but if I can manage even a small castle, you can manage the PTA.*

I'm not going to be running it, give me a break! But she retrieved the envelope from Kathy's bookbag, and wrote a check and put it back in the bag for Monday morning. Tucked into the envelope had been a little slip of paper announcing the first meeting of the school year, next Tuesday evening, and she tacked this on the kitchen bulletin board and marked it on the calendar. Then she washed the lunch dishes (there weren't many of them), put the Fifth Brandenburg Concerto on the stereo, and sat down to read about that long history of wrong things done for the right reasons and right things for the wrong reasons, the Crusades.

Amalia lay in bed till midday. Marianella brought a tray of food and wine up to her room, but it was after noon when the Lady finally rose and ate it. Then she dressed and came downstairs, and asked for her horse to be saddled.

There was a place, about five miles from the sea-keep of Telerath, where the River Medon divided into two parts on its way to the sea. The southern and by far the larger part kept the name of Medon and flowed into the sea just above Point Roun. The northern branch had been given the name of Medufar, the Medon's Little Brother, in a language that was no longer spoken in these parts. It reached the sea just north of Telerath Village. So much everyone knew.

The middle branch had no name any longer, so long had it been vaulted over by the long-dead stoneworkers who had made it the water supply for the sea-keep. They had concealed their handiwork so subtly that anyone who was ignorant of the history of the country could stand at the place where the Medon split in two and never realize that it had split in three. The overhanging bosom of a granite knob concealed the place where the third channel dropped into darkness, and the rushing rapids of the Medufar drowned out the roar of the underground waterfall. The canal, as old as the oldest tower of Telerath, had been dug by arts lost to Demoura now, and fed the castle's well before it flowed out the dull steel gate into the sea.

Amalia urged her horse to the top of the knob and looked around her. To her right the Medon, forty feet wide and the color of polished jade, curved through a shallow valley dark with oak and moss and out of sight to the south.

To her left the Medufar broke over shallow stones and sparkled in the sun. Further on, Amalia knew, the rocky ground rose and the little river had cut itself a trench three fathoms deep and a bowshot wide, and ran that way four miles before it flattened out into the shallow, fordable stream that bordered the village. Except for that last mile to the north, the place was remarkably defensible, if one had the men. A good commander would fortify the village, no doubt, and put a garrison there.

Twenty-five square miles, she mused, more or less. The soil was not enormously fertile, being mostly chalk, but it was well-drained and there was peat in the Medon valley and marl to be dug near the village. Hard work could build a good-sized settlement there.

She brushed her fingers across her lips, and sighed, and looked long into the east. *Kisses are like goblin fruit,* she thought, *once tasted, forever craved. If I could drown in those kisses it would not be enough, and I shall go hungry and in sorrow forever.* And her next thought was, *Lies! That kiss was the elixir of life. It has transformed me: I have steel now in my marrow, my flesh is illuminated. I could live a thousand years in the memory of that kiss, and if I live a thousand years nothing can take it from me.* And both these things were true.

At last she descended from the knob and began to explore the area, looking for paths and obstacles and hiding places. When the sun had fallen low enough to cast long shadows, she rode back to the keep and asked for pen and paper. Kieran brought them to her, a new-cut quill and a bottle of black squid's ink and a crackling curling sheet of lambskin, not the finest of vellum, but adequate. "Dinner will be on the board in a few minutes, my Lady," he said.

"I'll dine in my chamber—no, I won't. I'll dine in the Hall, as I ought. Dear Heaven, but I am weary. Kieran, give me your arm."

Marianella had marshalled her wits, and Tama's too, to concoct dishes that would tempt her Ladyship to eat. She remembered the night Denis the Raven and five of his companions had come to Rhadath House worn out from an encounter on the Downs that they would not discuss. They had been "too tired to eat," they said, "just a little mutton broth, I thank you, Madam." The chatelaine had bound up her sleeves and consulted with her cooks. The end of the story was that Denis and his companions had demolished a haunch of beef among the six of them, along with bread and fish and deep-fried aubergines and apple tart and quite a lot of wine, while the pink had crept back into their cheeks and their earlobes, and their voices ceased to drag like wounded snakes and began to chirp like well-fed canaries. This gave Marianella a model to imitate, something to live up to.

She began with a fish course, calling on some of Kieran's kinsfolk for a selection of the day's catch. There was a plate of stuffed crabs, and an eel pie with herbs, and one big shiny fish stuffed with spinach and egg yolk and mushrooms, steamed in the act of catching a little fish in his mouth. The rest of the catch went into a spicy fish stew with cream and leeks. There were three or four kinds of bread, and a sweet custard with raisins, and apple tarts. The second course began with broiled pigeons and chicken in spicy syrup, and a rabbit pie in which four tough old coneys had died and gone to a heaven of garlic and wine under a crust gilded with egg yolk. There was a salad of the last of the summer's lettuce, with flowers of nasturtium and pot-marigolds, and a salad-for-show with vegetables carven into flower shapes. There were the usual barley and rice and potatoes, and those two all-time favorites, spinach fritters and stuffed turnips. Finally there were honey cakes and cream cakes from the sideboard, and cheese and biscuits and the last of a barrel of wine dated ten years back—the year of the long summer, the year Kieran had caught a salmon in the Medufar and met his first girl behind a haystack.

They didn't have potatoes in the real Middle Ages, Sue reflected. *Nor rice—did they? I don't care. If Marianella had them, she'd cook 'em.*

She might have spared her trouble. Lady Amalia set to her meal with as much determination, and as much enthusiasm, as if it had all been barley bread and sour beer and she had a battle to fight in the morning. She was dutifully refueling her body, and this was what Marianella had wished her to do. But her professional pride was piqued. (However, the rest of the household was mightily impressed, and when Kieran proposed her health they drank it standing and with loud cheers. So the evening was not a total loss.)

After the meal the Lady retired again to the high chamber, and after a few minutes Kieran and Marianella followed her. They found her sitting at her small table, drawing with a near-dry pen on the vellum, lines so fine that from where they stood they could make out nothing. She had weighted down the four corners with the inkwell, her seal ring, her candlestick, and a smooth granite pebble she had picked up during the course of the afternoon. These she removed, and let the parchment curl up on itself again, and folded her hands and waited for them to speak.

Kieran was in a dangerous state of annoyance and frustration. He could not be expected to carry out his duties, which included the defense of this keep against attack, without up-to-date information on what kind of attack it was likely to be. But the rules of his society prevented him from extracting this information from Amalia at the top of his lungs. She was his liege lady, and he owed her respect and obedience; this, plus her seeming fragility, prevented him from taking her by the shoulders and shaking her, as he longed to do. So he, too, waited.

Marianella suffered from fewer inhibitions. "Lady, for heaven's sake, what happened?" she demanded. "What were those that howled in the wind last night? Did you find out anything about Lord Andri? Who struck you down?"

Amalia looked at her hands. "Andri and his companions are surely taken by the Shadowlings," she said. "For your other questions you deserve answers, but I am not in a postion to answer them. Tomorrow night—no, the night after, I will tell you everything I may."

(*May*, not *can*, Kieran noted silently, and fisted the hands he had folded behind his back.)

"Kieran," said her Ladyship now, "do you have a horse?"

"Yes, Lady. The three-year-old by-blow of a passing destrier, ugly but dependable. His name is Speedwell, and he is in the stable." (No one was going to accuse *him* of withholding information.)

"How appropriate," Amalia said, almost smiling. "The blue speedwell is the badge of our house; did you not know? Then you will ride out with me tomorrow. I want someone who knows the countryside. Until tomorrow," she said, and inclined her head by half an inch.

"Very good, m'lady," said Kieran, and bowed, and set his teeth.

"All right," said Fred after the children were in bed. "Let's take a look at the budget." He brought out his check register, and a sheet of scratch paper covered with numbers. "Not being a fool," he said, "and knowing you like I do, I know you haven't started all these projects all of a sudden because you're bored, or want to show off. Even the dress. Especially the dress. You're spending money on making us look like manager material. It's an investment."

"That's right."

"So the question is, how much can we afford to invest? Now, I've been putting three hundred—" he pointed to a row of figures "—three hundred a month into the credit union. I don't want to cut that out altogether, that's our emergency money. But I could cut it down to one hundred for the time being, and you can have the other two hundred. Okay?"

"That's great, Fred. Thank you." Sue was touched, and proud of him. She hadn't realized he'd been saving that much.

"And anything else you can save out of the household money is extra."

"Mother's sugar bowl."

"Right. And you've already spent a hundred on that dress—you'll be able to wear it again, won't you?"

"For years and years."

"Good. So you can have another hundred for the rest of September." He pushed the check register toward her. "Have fun. What are you going to work on next?"

"The living room and the front garden. They're what people see first."

"Right. I dug up those old bushes, like you wanted, and mowed the lawn. Ooof!" He stretched and arched his back. "God, I'm stiff. I'm not used to digging any more. Whatever happened to Sunday being a day of rest?"

"Poor fellow," she soothed. "You've got to get back in shape. I'll let you dig some more next week. Saturday, if you'd rather. For the time being, if you'll take a shower and come to bed, I'll rub your back."

"And not watch the news?"

"And not watch the news."

Fred smiled. "You got a deal."

Kieran in a rage was not a comforting sight. Admitted, this was not a flaming hot explosive rage, shouting and beating on tables and throwing things against the wall (*I should hate to be on opposite sides from this man in a war!* Marianella thought). This was only a dark icy rage that lay like a cold damp blanket of sooty cloud over every attempt at merriment, or even conversation. The gathering in the Hall broke up early.

"I know," Marianella told him when they were in bed. He was lying on his belly, his chin propped on his folded arms, his cold eyes staring at the headboard. Her fingers moved over his back, smoothing the dark ruffled feathers and kneading the hard knots out of his shoulder muscles. "She's an exasperating woman. She always was, even as a child. I've served her all my life, and I'll probably serve her all the rest of my life. So will you, I expect, and she will go on being exasperating to the end."

"You have a rare talent for understatement," Kieran growled. "Blast the woman! Why won't she tell me what I need to know?"

"She may not know herself," Marianella said. She rocked her knuckles back and forth over his skin, a technique borrowed from breadmaking. Inch by inch she worked down the long rigid back muscles, and felt them soften. "The Sight, so I'm told, is fuzzy and capricious. It'll show you the tree, but not the forest, or t'other way round. And sometimes it shows you what you want to see, or what you fear most, never mind if it's real or not." She turned her attention to his legs and feet. The calf muscles were hard, and she dug into them with her knuckles and the heels of her hands, and ran her thumbs along the insteps. His toes were white and well-shaped, not distorted by tight boots. The village must have a decent cobbler. She worked her knuckles up his thighs, and kneaded the rounded buttock muscles. The man seemed not to have an ounce of extra fat on his body. "But if it's any comfort, she keeps her promises. She said she'd tell you all she can, two nights from now, and she will. Whether it'll be any use to you, I can't foresee."

She ran her fingers over his body, long and firm and pale and smooth. The shadows were dark and soft between his thighs. He appeared not to notice. Curse the man! What was needed to shift him, a rap over the head, or fire set to his mattress?

"Damn," Kieran said, and turned over in bed and stared up at the ceiling. Marianella started in on the muscles of his chest. The little useless nipples were like flowers of helebore, pale winter roses in their wreaths of dark hair. "Damn her and all mysterious scheming women! The ones that don't talk are worse than the ones that talk too much. Present company excepted," he said, and pulled her down to him.

"You're an old bear," she mumbled into the side of his beard, and poked her thumb into his ribs.

"Don't do that!"

"Bless and save us, the man's ticklish! How did I get this far without finding that out?" She thrust her fingers into his armpits, and he roared like a bull and seized her. But she was too quick, and her hands not to be confined. It was as well that the bedframe was a sturdy one. It took him ten minutes to pin her down. Their bodies came together like a small explosion, and he did his best to peg her to the bedslats under the mattress. When the air cleared they lay together for a long time, unwilling to separate or even to sleep. After a time Marianella became aware that Kieran was murmuring fragments of poetry into her ear:

> "Minnow in the basket,
> twist and turn, wouldn't be caught;
> you tonight are like a minnow in my hand."

Sue found herself, next morning, in the supermarket, reading the fine print on a loaf of bread. Divide the price by the net weight, it came to . . . umm . . . about ninety cents a pound. (*Get a calculator*, she noted on a mental shopping list. *Sav-Mor has some real cheapos, even before the employee discount.*) The whole wheat came to ninety-five cents a pound, the buttercrust was just over a dollar. *Demoura has the Shadow, and we have inflation. The annual rate of creep appears to be about the same.*

Down at the end of the next aisle, the white flour was about twenty cents a pound, the whole wheat a trifle less. *Right!* She hefted a sack of each into her cart, and added a jar of yeast. Cookies? She reached for a bag of chocolate chips, and stopped, and drew back her hand, and went to the produce section instead and bought raisins in bulk and walnuts that she would have to crack. Another five bucks saved, and less sugar into the bargain.

Her path to the checkout stand led her through the soap-and-detergent aisle. A young couple stood there, a dark-haired man and woman with troubled eyes. They stared at the bright-colored ranks of dishwashing detergents and did not speak. Their cart was empty.

Sue hated to start conversations with strangers, and the American ethic of "don't get involved" was carven into her brain in letters an inch deep. But the young couple looked so woebegone that Sue hesitated, and cleared her throat, and finally said, "Excuse me, but could I help you find anything?"

The young woman said something in a foreign language, but the man spread his hands and said despairingly, "Soap!" She couldn't place the accent. "So many different kinds. What's the difference?"

"Sometimes there's no difference at all," she said. "What kind of soap were you looking for?" They looked blank. "Were you planning to wash dishes, or clothes, or yourselves?"

"Dishes," the woman said, at the same moment that the man said, "Myself."

"Well, for dishes—where are you from?"

"We came from Poland last month."

That explained a lot. "Yes, America is different from Poland. We have a different kind of economy." (*Don't say "capitalist" or "communist," why upset them.*) "All this stuff in bottles, from here to over there, is for washing dishes. The different brand names are made by different companies, all competing for your money."

"In Poland there's one kind, maybe two. It comes in big grey bars and you stand in line for it. If they have any."

"We only do that with gasoline. Now the first thing you have to learn is to ignore all the commercials. All the manufacturers are going to try and convince you their dishwashing liquid is better for your dishes, softer on your hands, and cheaper than any of the others, but they're really all alike. The one thing you *can* do is to save a little money by buying the house brand." She picked it out. "See? The brand name's the same as the store. All these other guys spend millions on advertising their brand names. The store does all its advertising in one piece, so they don't spend so much just on detergent, so they can pass the savings on to you. Aside from that, there's no difference."

"What about the colors?"

"The colors? They're just colors. Which would look best in your kitchen, pink or blue or white or yellow or green or—oh, look, somebody's brought out one in lavender. But they won't sell it to me, I don't have a lavender kitchen."

The Poles settled for white. Sue showed them the hand and bath soap, and the shampoo, and the powdered laundry detergent. She told them about that great old American institution, the commercial laundromat, and hoped they weren't living in too crummy a neighborhood. Still, people who had coped with Russian soldiers ought to be able to handle American punk kids. She showed them scouring powders, and bleach, and steel wool pads, and cleaners for windows, tile, and floors. "And everything else is the same," she finished. "Sometimes one brand name really is better than the others, but you'll never know it from the commercials. Ask your neighbors." She said goodbye, and wished them luck, and hurried away to the checkout stand. *Before I start telling them about toothpaste, and confuse them completely.*

As she drove to the library, she remembered the summer before she was married, when she had worked as a file clerk for a large soap manufacturer that also made, among other things, toothpaste. It had had one brand that was heavily advertised for its "fresh, clean taste." The stuff tasted awful, and left a tingling sensation in the gums that might or might not be associated with freshness and cleanliness, depending on your point of view. One day she had finally asked the sales manager what was in it.

"Chloroform," he had said.

"*Chloroform?* What for? How does that help clean your teeth?"

"It doesn't," the sales manager had said frankly. "It tastes so strong you think your teeth must be getting cleaner." Sue had never used the stuff again.

At the library she picked up four cookbooks, and some of the basic English and European histories she had skimmed over last week. There was a poster on the wall that she hadn't noticed before, announcing the fall semester at the City College, whose catalog she had picked up last week and hadn't read. Evening classes started this week; day classes had started the week before. There was a photograph of a roomful of students listening to (or at any rate, being lectured to by) a clean-cut young instructor, and another photo of the same or similar students doing arcane things with a roomful of little computers. Something very like a computer began ticking and purring inside Sue's head, and she thought of Claire Carmody, and her little business card, and her tactics for confusing Chris Bingley. This very day, she vowed, she would read over that catalog. And she took her books and went home.

By eleven o'clock she had chosen four bread recipes. By one o'clock the first batch was in the oven. It was a sour and dismal failure—too little kneading and too much yeast—but the other three succeeded: an adequate white, a spectacular white, and a nice crunchy whole wheat. While the loaves were baking she cracked nuts, and the cookies were coming out of the oven by the time the kids came home.

Amalia rode out on Pathfinder, with Kieran on Speedwell beside her. He showed her sheep paths, and foxes' burrows, and shortcuts. He showed her where the rivers could be forded, and where they ran unexpectedly deep, and he tried to draw her out. She answered in monosyllables, when she spoke at all.

Amalia, in fact, was aware of Kieran for the first time as a man, an exceptionally virile man at that. It disturbed her. She had never taken notice of such things before. The Sight looked away from the things of the body. The lords and gentlemen she had known, even poor Guiard, had forborne to break in upon her quietness. The passages between Marianella and her lovers, though she had usually been aware of them, had not touched her.

The unseen visitor of two nights back had broken down too many barriers. She longed for the mysterious mouth and the hands that had touched her like fire. Her body was uneasy in the saddle. The passion between Kieran and Marianella had kept her awake most of last night. She was aware of the shape of his hands, and how proudly he sat in the saddle, and the long straight lines of his back and limbs. While he showed her tall trees suitable for keeping lookout, and banks of heather where one or two might hide ("a good place for an ambush, my Lady"), she thought of lying with him in the heather, and what would happen if she asked him to make love to her, not to take him away from Marianella, but only to ease her burden a little. *But what if he said no? But how would it be if he said yes?* And she kept silent, and her heart grew heavy.

Sue's afternoon was made no easier by the radio's afternoon choice of programming. They began with the Songs of a Wayfarer, by Gustav Mahler, sung by a baritone with a rich dark disturbing voice. Sue could not understand the German words, but the announcer gave a brief explanation before the songs began. It seemed the hero's girlfriend, who had beautiful blue eyes, had married someone else. He had wept on her wedding day. When he walked across the fields, all the little birds had sung, "Isn't this a great day?" but he could only answer, "It's no good for me." For a while he thought of killing himself, but eventually decided the best way out of it would be to leave town. He packed his knapsack and sneaked out in the middle of the night, and camped under a linden tree that showered its blossoms over him like snow. There he forgot everything, "love and pain and world and dream."

The music was beautiful, but it did no good for Amalia, with her heart as heavy as that first inedible lump of bread, nor for anyone who had to listen to her. But now the announcer explained how the composer had adapted some of the wayfarer's songs for his First Symphony, sometimes called "The Titan," which they would now play. She listened in fascination while the music played, almost forgetting to stir her cookie dough. Yes, there he was walking across the field, and the cuckoos singing. Here was a merry peasant dance, suitable for somebody else's wedding. The next piece was the children's round, "Frère Jacques," but set in a minor key, and terrifying. She had a mental picture of the forest in Hell where the bodies of the suicides hang from the branches of the trees that hide their miserable souls. Above it all an oboe played, sweet and clear and heartbreaking as the bird who sings in the gallows tree. The symphony ended eventually in triumph, but by now Sue was plunged into depression. The children's return home lightened her only a little.

"Hey, cookies! Neat!"

"One apiece, that's all," she warned them. "They're for your lunches this week."

Amalia sat all evening sketching with fine dry lines on vellum. A rough map of the land between the rivers was beginning to take shape. She wished for half a dozen soft pencils from Sue's world, with erasers. *I'll send you some,* Sue offered. *What's your ZIP code?* But Amalia didn't think this was funny.

"I want you to look at this," Sue told Fred, and shoved the City College bulletin under his nose. "See? *Computer Science 2, Introduction to Microcomputers.*"

"I don't know anything about computers," he protested.

"I know. That's why. It doesn't cost much, you can get your paper and diskettes cheapo in the Computer Department; it's every Wednesday and Friday from now till Christmas."

He looked at her, and at the catalog. "When does it start?"

"Day after tomorrow. Eight o'clock."

"I'll see what I can do." He folded the catalog back, and put it on the coffee table. Then he reached for the TV knob, but Sue's hand was there before him. "I feel depressed," she said. *And horny,* she did not add. "I think it's *your* turn to rub *my* back."

Fred looked her up and down. "You're just trying to turn me off TV," he said. "Okay by me."

Amalia took pen and parchment out with her the next day, and amended her map in light of what she could see from the big granite knob where the river split. She made notes of water supplies, and lines of sight, and soil types, and how the hillsides sloped. Then she rode back to Telerath and inked it all in with clear black lines, and made many notes in the margins. She wrote a letter, and folded letter and map together, and sealed them with her ring: the tall speedwell of Fendarath. Then she went down into the Hall.

Fred had done his best, and his best was far from bad, but Sue woke up depressed nonetheless, heart-heavy with Amalia's frustration. So her first stop was the Record Barn. She found the bin marked MAHLER and read the backs of record jackets. She found translations of the wayfarer's songs, and read them over. It was tempting—and here was a recording of the symphony by the same conductor who had recorded the songs with the velvety baritone—but no. She put the records gently but firmly back in their bin.

"No Mahler today?"

"Oh, hi, Randy. No, I'd better not. I listened to this yesterday with a friend who—put it this way, her heart got broken so recently that some of the pieces are still bouncing. She got terribly depressed, and that depressed *me*."

"Aw-w-w," Randy said. "Look," he said, plucking at the fabric of his shirt. "Pure cotton, highly absorbent, great for crying on. Why don't you introduce me?"

"I don't think that would be possible. Couldn't you just recommend some music that's good for a broken heart?"

"Oh, sure." He took her elbow and guided her across the aisle to a bin marked RENAISSANCE LUTE. "John Dowland," he said. "These lute songs are the saddest things in the English language. 'In darkness let me dwell; the ground shall sorrow be, the roof despair, to bar all cheerful light from me.' 'Flow, my tears, fall from your springs; exiled forever let me mourn.' Give your friend this and a bottle of wine and let her have a good cry. Then, when she's ready to start getting better—" The bin was one of several that said BACH. The album said "The Art of the Fugue."

"This is the greatest piece of music ever written," Randy said seriously, "and it is unfinished. Not because God would be jealous of a perfect human creation; not because Bach was dying; not even, as my composition professor used to say, 'because he left it as an exercise to the student.' The music doesn't stop, it goes away, into the other world. The last recorded of many conversations between the mind of J. S. Bach and the mind of God. This is the cure for all passion, because it is passionless. This is the medicine for melancholy." He shook himself. "Whew! Why doesn't somebody stop me when I get wound up? No, seriously. Play this for your friend, and she'll get well. And I still want to meet her."

Sue shrugged. "Give me your address, and I'll see what I can do." *Now, why did I do that?* she asked herself as she paid for the Dowland and the Bach. Obviously she couldn't introduce Randy to Amalia. There was something in the back of her mind that she couldn't quite lay her finger on. Oh, well, it would pop up when she was looking for something else.

"No, I don't want beige," Sue explained patiently to the clerk at Standard Paints. "I don't want off-white, I don't want antique white, and I don't want ivory. I might settle for oyster-white, but what I really want is the plain old white that comes out of the can."

"It'll look *cold*," the clerk said persuasively. "Now, this Apache White—"

"Have you ever seen the inside of a medieval castle?" Sue broke in. "Well, it's been painted for the last thousand years with plain old whitewash. That's what I want it to look like. Anyway, the rooms face west and south, they're plenty warm enough."

"But you don't want—"

"Don't you try and tell me what I want. I know what I want. And I want three gallons of the flat and two of the semi-gloss enamel." (She had measured the walls, and a conversion table, square feet to gallons, was posted right behind the clerk's head where he chose to ignore it.) The man sighed in defeat, and stacked cans of flat white paint on the counter.

Over lunch she played the Dowland record, which was a heartbreaker, and wallowed in melancholy while she caught up on her bookkeeping. On the one hand, she had had two hundred dollars plus a few corners cut on the grocery money. On the other hand, between the dress and last week's records, and this week's records and the paint, she had about twenty-five dollars left. That would be for the garden.

There were almost no flowers at the nursery—it was September, after all, and frost was not so far away. There were pots of stiff bronze chrysanthemums, and bulbs to plant for spring or to force indoors, and a sign promising bare-root roses in April. Sue picked up the bulb of a paper-white narcissus, and put it down again. Next month, maybe. "What I want," she explained to the elderly man who ran the place, "is something to make a hedge with, for a windbreak on the northwest side of my house. An evergreen, I suppose. Something tough. Yew, maybe?"

"It's awful slow-growing," he said. "And the berries are poisonous. You got little children in your neighborhood?"

"Hordes of them. I see what you mean."

"Besides, yew would get windburn in a real cold winter. I got some barberry out back, though. That'll live through any winter in the United States. You clip it into a hedge as it grows. How long a hedge you want? You need about one plant every couple of feet."

"Gosh, it's about sixty feet, and I've only got twenty-five dollars. Maybe I should come back after the beginning of the month."

The old man grinned. "Tell you what I'll do. We've got some in four-inch pots out back that are getting rootbound. They ought to go into bigger pots, but my son's on his honeymoon and I'm shorthanded. I'll sell 'em to you for your twenty-five dollars and you can save me the trouble of transplanting them. Not at all. Not at all. I like people who like plants." And he helped her load them into the back of the station wagon.

Liberty Hill, like many other communities in the state, had been laid out in the land grant days on a grid provided by the U.S. Department of the Interior, neatly north-south and east-west. But the suburb Sue lived in had been built in the late 1950s, and the developer had taken the contour principle to heart. The streets ambled around the curves of the region's gentle hills, and the little creeks had been incorporated into storm drains that almost always worked.

So when Sue had said she wanted a windbreak on the northwest side of her house, it was no more than the truth. But the side in question was the front of the house, where the scruffy lawn lay between the street and the living room wall with its oversized picture window. Sue had always had the feeling it would be nice to have some privacy, but the thing was not to seem "unfriendly." The steadily growing hedge ought to do the trick, creeping gradually upward year by year, without shocking anyone's sensibilities. Meanwhile, she would have more flowers and less grass, more of a garden and less of a lawn. *Bare-root roses in April.*

The huge sheet of glass was a terrible energy leak as well, and Sue had started scanning the magazine ads for double- or triple-glazed windows or maybe even a little solar greenhouse. But they all appeared to cost an arm and a leg, and would have to wait a while.

She broke the little barberries out of their pots, and set them in place around three sides of the lawn. Now she had, not a hedge, not even a border, but a dotted line where one would someday be. She left one three-foot gap opposite the front door, for an entrance; eventually they'd put a gate there. She sat back on her heels and looked over the space she had defined. There was still nothing there but threadbare grass, but her mind's eye could see flowers bright as jewels, maybe a weeping willow, a marble bench for a minstrel.

Just as she was straightening up to go inside and relax, an inner voice suddenly rumbled, "TUESDAY. PTA," and the bottom fell out of her interior; it felt like the kind of Flash Gordon/Indiana Jones adventure where you fall thirty feet to land on sharp spikes or hungry crocodiles, or both. *You don't have to do anything,* she told herself.

While dinner was in the oven she took a long hot shower, and laid out the decorous sweaters and skirt and the malachite beads for luck. *You don't have to do anything,* she repeated. *Just sit in the audience and applaud the speakers. You don't have to be a leader, just part of the chorus.* But the rocks were rumbling under her feet; hidden machinery was moving into place to squeeze Flash or Indy through a keyhole or shoot him down the rapids. The vultures were gathering. She took a deep breath and let it out, as she had seen Amalia do. It didn't seem to help.

While the board was being cleared, the Lady Amalia remained at the High Table. She called Kieran and Marianella to her. "When we were attacked three nights ago," she said, "I was touched by a finger of the Darkness. I am no longer able to govern this fief of Telerath, nor to defend it from further attack. So I have sent for aid. Tomorrow, Captain Lord Randall of Tower Lost will arrive to take command of this keep.

"I hope he will take you into his confidence, Kieran, for you would make him an able assistant, but he must be left free to make his own decisions.

"With him is coming Denis the Raven, and his companions, and many other people who will need shelter of some kind. Lord Randall is bringing such provisions as he can, and I hope building materials as well, but you may have to find other things for their needs. In any case, he will be in command, and you must obey him as you would me. Now I am going to bed. When Lord Randall arrives, send him up to my chamber. No one else is to enter it till then." She got up from her chair and turned to go, but blundered against the table (there were tears in her eyes).

Marianella took her by the shoulders. "Lady, are you all right?"

"No. I am *not* all right." But she held Marianella close for a moment, and gave Kieran her hand to kiss. Then she went upstairs.

"Well, and what do you think of that?" Kieran said, sitting on the edge of the table.

Marianella shook her head slowly. "I don't know what to think."

"She's not told us everything."

"I don't suppose she has. I don't suppose she can, for she is turning everything over to Lord Randall. What worries me is the change in herself. Something touched her, she said. Some poison of the Darkness? And she does not expect to be able to take any further part in our defense. Except for that, I would feel confident for the first time in weeks. If we can't be safe with Lord Randall defending us in the physical realm, and Master Denis in the spiritual, then we can't be safe anywhere."

* * *

The meeting was held in the Silver Hill Elementary School cafeteria, a white-enameled room that stretched out into dimness in two dimensions under a low ceiling. It smelled of soap and cold baked beans and refrigerators. The glass and tile and stainless steel of the food service area looked painfully empty, and reflected the faces of parents and teachers like forlorn ghosts.

There were about forty women there, and two lone men. One of these Sue recognized as Mr. Hoskins, the assistant principal; the other must be some child's conscientious father. He looked lonely and uncomfortable, a man out of his element, an intruder into the mysteries of the Mother Goddess. As she watched, he tugged at his tie, and readjusted it, and ran his finger around the inside of his collar.

"Not a bad turnout," Sue murmured to the woman sitting next to her.

"Yes, but half of them will be gone by next meeting. Their initial enthusiasm dies out very quickly." She did not look like one whose enthusiasm ever died out, once kindled. She had the same look of competence and good sense as Claire Carmody. Her camel-colored suit was neatly tailored, her purse and shoes were good leather and carefully polished, her long auburn hair was smoothed back into a secure knot at the nape of her neck. "I wish we had a better meeting place; this cafeteria is so depressing."

"Isn't it? The ghosts of our vanished youth—" But the chairwoman was calling them to order, and Sue found herself on her feet, hand over heart, reciting the Pledge of Allegiance. It gave her an incredible sensation of *déjà vu*, as though they had slipped back down the arrow of time to the fourth grade. The feeling was not relieved when the meeting began, all strictly according to Robert's Rules of Order. Sue's attention wandered.

Amalia lay awake in her bed, behind her barred chamber door. Below her, Kieran and Marianella were slowly falling asleep. Rigo and Tama, who had a flaming falling-out earlier that evening, were being reconciled in the deep straw in the stable. Outside an owl flew by on silent wings. *I'll wait till midnight,* Amalia told herself. *By midnight they should all be asleep.*

"Here it comes," Sue's neighbor whispered. She came back to the here-and-now and played back the last few minutes in her head. The chair had just asked for new business.

"Madame President, I have some new business," a woman well into middle age was saying. "I had lunch last week with Bob Shafer, the president of Shafer Construction. For some time he has been considering making a donation to the school district for new facilities. It's a tax break for him, of course, and he has to get confirmation from his tax lawyer, so it may be nearly Christmas before we get confirmation from *him.* But what Bob intends is to donate the construction of a new gymnasium, to replace the old one, at a cost to him of about $900,000. I would like to move a vote of thanks from this organization to Mr. Shafer for his generosity."

Another woman popped to her feet. "I second the motion."

Through all this, Sue's neighbor had been sitting with her feet drawn under her, like a cat ready to spring. The vote was taken; the ayes had it. The redhead shot up her hand. "Madame President!"

"Mrs. O'Hare."

Mrs. O'Hare rose to her feet. "Madame President, I would like to move that a study group be formed to consider this matter. There is no question of our gratitude for Mr. Shafer's generosity. There is some question whether it is being applied in the direction that will be best for our children. The current gymnasium and its equipment are not spectacular, but they are adequate. I think we should consider whether these funds could be better applied to something the school lacks altogether." A fraction of a second's pause. "A microcomputer facility, for example. I move a committee be formed to study the question." She sat down.

Sue stood up. "I second the motion."

"Of course, Mrs. O'Hare is a computer expert," said a spiteful voice. She made it sound like a conflict of interest.

"Order, please."

"Well, I am no computer expert," Sue said. (She was still on her feet, didn't that mean she had the floor?) "I can't tell a bit from a byte. But I read in last week's paper that twenty years from now—when most of our children will just be settling into their careers—the ability to use a computer will be as necessary as the ability to drive a car is now."

"Oh, come on. Do you really think everyone is going to have to get a college degree in computing, just to get a job?" (The same voice? a different one, she thought.)

"Address the chair, please."

"Oh, no," Sue said, "any more than we all take three-year technical courses in auto mechanics now. But we all know how to drive, don't we?" She glanced to right and left. "Think how out of it you'd be if you couldn't drive. Well, that's how far out of it our kids will be if they can't use computers. In any case, all we're talking about doing tonight is forming a committee to study the subject. I second Mrs. O'Hare's motion. Madame President, will you call the vote?" She sat down.

Madame President did so, a tad reluctantly. The motion carried, just. "We need to consider the committee's membership, then."

Mrs. O'Hare asked for, and got, the floor. "I have a suggestion. Since it appears that most of us are able to get out of the house on Tuesdays, let's meet next Tuesday, same time, anyone who is interested, and put the committee together on the basis of interest."

Sue raised her hand. "Why don't we meet at my house? I have room for a gathering this size, or nearly. If the school can lend me some chairs. It's warmer, and we won't rattle around so much."

"Madame President, that is a very good idea," said Mr. Hoskins, "particularly since the Little League Steering Committee was planning to meet here next Tuesday. I can arrange for some chairs."

"Very well," said the president. Her mouth was pursed. Perhaps she had expected her term of office to be smooth and simple? She had just encountered a lump in her custard, whether a rock or a chocolate truffle she could not yet tell. "Is there any more new business?"

There was none. Adjournment was moved, seconded, and carried, and instantly a buzz of talk broke out.

"Thanks," said Mrs. O'Hare under cover of the din.

"You're welcome. What's your other name? Mine's Sue."

"Shevaun," the redhead said. "Spelled S-i-o-b-h-a-n. Mother was a traditionalist. I do appreciate your support. I was beginning to think I wasn't going to get any."

"Oh, I'm great on support," Sue said. "But you're going to have to run this committee, because I really do not know a bit from a byte. Just blind luck I read the newspaper last Sunday."

"Where is it we're going to meet?" a voice shouted above the hubbub.

Sue raised her voice. "Five-twenty-five Lincolnshire Drive. It's about six blocks from here. If you don't know where it is, see me and I'll draw you a map."

The crowd parted, and the middle-aged woman bore down on Sue. Her hair was a puff of ginger-flavored whipped cream, and more of the same had settled into her hips, though her face and upper body were thin. Her eyes were cold and hard. "How do you do," she said, smiling with her mouth. "I'm Myra Stone. So nice to have you with us. I don't believe I've seen you here before?"

Sue drew herself up about three inches, and put on Amalia like a robe of ceremony. "How do you do," she said. "Will you be with us next Tuesday? Oh, but it would be so nice if you did. We need to bring different points of view to look over the situation. It doesn't matter if you don't know computers; I don't either. None of us is ready for the old rocking chair as long as she's ready to learn. Let's get some coffee."

Mrs. Stone lost about a quarter inch of her smile, and looked at Sue with something like grudging respect. "All right."

Six maps, two cups of coffee, and some cookies later, and having made arrangements about chairs, Sue said goodnight to the group and left. Siobhan O'Hare walked with her to her car. "Well, good night," she said. "I'll see you Tuesday."

"Can you drop by on Tuesday afternoon?" Sue asked. "Say, three or four. We'll have tea and plot our strategy."

"Thanks, I will. By then I should have my act together. I'm teaching a class starting tomorrow night."

"CS 2? Microcomputers, at City College? Far out," Sue said. "I think my husband is going to be one of your students."

Just after midnight, Amalia rose from her bed and put on her robe again. She had set out a few bits of clothing and other necessaries, and now she rolled these in a pair of blankets and secured the bundle with a leather strap. She slung it over her shoulder, unbarred her door, and closed it behind her.

In the room below she paused for a moment. Marianella lay on her back, her mouth half-open, snoring faintly. Kieran lay beside her, his head on her shoulder and his hand on her breast. *It comes out right for some of us*, Amalia thought. *Maybe they will have children.* And she crept down the stairs.

She visited the silent kitchen, and passed through the sleeping Hall to the door. She had no light, and needed none. In the stable she took sacks of grain and loaded a packhorse, and saddled Pathfinder, and led them out across the draw-bridge into the night. Tomorrow Captain Lord Randall would set a sentry.

She crossed the Medufar by one of the fords Kieran had shown her, and headed east and north. The moon, waxing toward the full, was falling into the west. The Darkness lowered in the east, but the stars shone brightly overhead. After a while Amalia began to sing, in a tongue unknown in those lands:

> "I set out in the silent night,
> in the silent night,
> straight over the darkened fields.
> No one even said farewell to me,
> Farewell! Farewell! ..."

CHAPTER 5

Corporal and Spiritual Works of Mercy

Captain Lord Randall rode up in the morning, with Denis the Raven at his side. Behind him rode fifty knights, and behind them marched three hundred men-at-arms. A red poppy flowered on the white banner above their heads, and they wore scarlet and black and touches of silver.

Marianella stood in the middle of the drawbridge, watching them approach. Behind her, the castle folk fluttered back and forth between Hall and well, kitchen and stable. Even Kieran was ill-at-ease, and had thrice suggested going up to rouse the Lady Amalia—once to offer her breakfast, a second time to advise her that someone had left the drawbridge down, a third time to tell her the Captain's banner had been sighted crossing the ford of the Medon. Marianella had sat on all these suggestions, tactfully but firmly. Her Ladyship had said she was to be visited only by the Captain and Master Denis, and so she should be. Kieran had retreated to the stables, to fuss over grain and bedding with Rigo. Now he came out, dusting chaff from his clothing, and joined her on the drawbridge.

The Captain was in his thirtieth year, tall and broad-shouldered. With his blazing blue eyes and his mane of black hair he looked like Kieran writ larger and darker. His scarlet cloak fluttered bravely about him, but its hem was frayed, and his black tunic was spattered with mud. He had come from battle beside the Caramath.

Master Denis could have been nineteen, or fifty. He had

thin hair like pale gold, that had deserted the top of his head and fallen as far as his shoulders. His grey eyes were calm as he looked over the procession, but the lids were red and swollen. He too had been fighting. His body seemed to float an inch or so above his saddle; it was an illusion, but Marianella knew the signs. "Tama!" she called over her shoulder. "Go kill that old grey hen, and pluck and clean her, and put her in the pot to seethe for broth. Then send the boy down to the village for the new milk, and save it for me, and three or four eggs." It would take all her skills, both of cookery and of tact, to get Master Denis to take his needed rest.

Behind the neat ranks of soldiers came the supply train, long lines of wagons and pack animals. Thank heaven. Kieran had sent messages north to his kin in the other villages, and they would send what provision they could, but it would have been hard on them, to be asked to feed an army—

Behind the wagon train, other figures climbed into sight: a great crowd on foot, carrying bundles, a few of them pushing or pulling carts. They were the people who had lived along the banks of the Caramath, under the deepening Shadow. They had fled in the Captain's train, and probably by his orders. And what was Telerath to do with them?

"I feared this," Kieran said. "We can feed them, if I send to the north, but I shall need her Ladyship's authority. Will she see me after she's seen the Captain?"

"Probably," Marianella said. "If not, the Captain will. The man you want to talk to now is Michael the Red, his sergeant-at-arms. See him, there, riding down the line on the dusty bay? Catch him when he comes back, and he will unravel everything. You may be sure he knows the provisions in those wagons to the last sack of meal, and the numbers of soldiers and farmfolk to the last man and woman."

"Michael the Red," Kieran repeated, watching the sergeant-at-arms turn his horse about and come cantering back. He was a cheerful brown-bearded man, past his first youth but only just, with a scarlet tunic and a gold-buckled belt round his plump middle.

Captain Randall and Master Denis were upon the drawbridge now, and Kieran and Marianella stepped forward to receive them. Rigo held the bridle for Master Denis to dismount, but the Captain stayed on his tall horse, looking over the courtyard and the people in it.

Master Denis's eyes were looking at something else, as they usually were, soft and cool as mist on the sea. Then with sudden sharpness they focused, and his spirit flashed over Kieran and Marianella for an instant with the eyes of an eagle. "But it's the little Marianella," he said gently. "My dear child." He put his arms round her neck and kissed her softly on the cheek. "Tell me now, where is your Lady? I have had no word or sign from her since she sent to me three nights back."

"Master Denis speaks for me also," the Captain said. "I need to see Lady Amalia at once, and ask her what happened here. If I know that, maybe I can explain what happened on the Caramath."

"She is in her chamber, my lord Captain," Marianella said. "She left orders none was to see her till you came."

The Captain swung himself down from his horse. "I'll see her now. Come, Denis. And then, mistress, you can bring us some tea. A bucketful deep enough to drown my head in, that should be adequate. When was it I last left the saddle? Midsummer?" He unfastened the scarlet cloak from his shoulders and tossed it to the servant who had trailed behind his horse. "Take this, Ulrico, and get it cleaned. Get yourself some breakfast first." His voice trailed away as he vanished inside the Hall. Kieran left Rigo to tend the horses and went in search of Michael the Red.

Marianella led the guests up the stair to the Lady Amalia's door. She knocked, but there was no answer. Lord Randall pushed her aside, not ungently, and opened the door and went in. Master Denis followed, and drew the door closed behind him. Marianella retreated down the stairs, where the boy stood with the milk pail. "There you are, Jacko," she said. "Take that milk to the kitchen, and tell Tama to heat a pint of it in the ashes, and to beat in honey enough, and an egg, and nutmeg, and—never mind, I'll see to it myself." She lifted the pail out of his hands and took it into the kitchen.

And then? And then? Sue thought impatiently. But *then* wouldn't come. She couldn't see through the closed wooden door, any more than Marianella could, nor tell how the Captain and his wizard were reacting to Amalia's absence. And where *was* Amalia? (Out on the road some-where to the east; Sue didn't know nearly enough about Demoura's geography.)

In the early hours of the morning Amalia had made her way through the hilly Chaldon Downs, letting Pathfinder choose their road so that she need not use the Sight. By the time the sun rose they were out of settled country, climbing up into a high flat moorland that extended far to the north, but was only some forty miles wide east to west. One day's travel should bring her to the Caramath; a second day, and she would find a place where it could be forded.

The moor was covered with twisted grey heath and patches of dark green bracken, the last growing things to be found in lands under the Shadow. There had been grass, and a few tough old oak trees, but now they were dry and dead. The birds had flown away, the mice and rabbits had escaped to the west or died. The wind was out of the northwest, clear and cold; it pierced to the bone, and Amalia huddled deeper into her cloak. They covered another five miles before she saw any living thing.

She almost missed seeing it: a furry scrap lying motionless by the side of the road. Then she saw its eyes, dull, not shining, but more alive than anything else in that drab moor-land. She reined in Pathfinder and dismounted to take a look. It was a cat, a young striped tomcat that had fled the Shadow hovering over some farmstead and tried to cross the moor before it starved. It had almost made it; another ounce of fat under its hide would have meant another day of travel, and a chance to reach the settlements in the Downs. Now—well, it wasn't dead yet. But Amalia needed urgently to continue her journey into the east; she could not justify any delay. She stood for a minute or two in the road, deliberating, trying to persuade herself to go on.

Finally she picked up the cat in the crook of her arm, mounted into the saddle, and settled the lightweight little body in her lap. What she could do without stopping, that she would certainly do; and there were a few fresh eggs in her saddlebags. She had planned to roast them in the ashes of her campfire when she must stop to let the horses rest and graze. Now she fumbled in the bags behind her, found one with her fingers and pulled it out. She felt again and found a drinking cup and cracked the egg into it. As the horses' hooves steadily ate up the miles along the road, she coaxed the cat to take notice of the egg and slowly lap it up. Before they had finished five miles, he was beginning to look like a tomcat again; she brushed the dust out of his soft striped fur and named him Boots for his white paws. The sun rose slowly out of the Shadow and the mists along the valley of the Caramath. The road stretched onward.

It was like waiting impatiently for next week's *Dallas*. The story had found a natural place to take a break, and would not advance till it was time. It was like being caught in the groove of a stuck record; she went round in circles, slipping back each time to where she had been with a click she could almost feel.

Records. She scooted the stereo cabinet out of the living room into the dining room, found a corner for it by a wall plug, and plugged it in. That was the last piece of furniture that needed to be moved; the living room floor was bare except for a pile of newspapers and the paint cans and brushes. The curtains, faded and sunstreaked but fortunately still in one piece, were in the wash. *Get on with it.* She put *The Art of the Fugue* on the turntable and began spreading out newspapers to protect the floor from the paint. Her hair was bundled into a clean, soft old diaper, she was wearing her very oldest shirt and her disreputable blue jeans, and nothing was lacking but the inclination. Grimly she mounted the stepladder and put her brush to the wall.

The music was cool and tranquil, an agreeable contrast to her state of mind. It was the song of one who has solved life's problems and put them behind him. The different instruments were playing the same melodies, but at different times, like children singing a round, but much more complicated. If she tried to follow any one line she quickly got lost, so she concentrated on turning grimy fly-specked cream-colored walls into smooth, glowing white walls and let the music wash over her like the waves of a cool sparkling sea.

(Where was Marianella?) In the kitchen, brewing her sleeping potion for Master Denis, which looked an awful lot like a warm eggnog—saving those powdered herbs she was sneaking into it—and would probably do him good. Tama watched with respect. With a Captain in the courtyard, a Master Seer up the staircase, she was moving in rarefied circles these days.

(Kieran?) He was in the stables with Michael the Red, talking masculine shop—no doubt they would get to the business of getting the army and the refugees fed and sheltered soon. So far it had all been fishing, and hunting, and the adventures of gentlemen who were known to them both.

And Amalia was somewhere along that damned road, and the Captain and Master Denis behind a closed door that she could not see through. Sue put more paint on her brush and attacked the second wall. And the doorbell rang.

It was Kelly, her sometime baby-sitter. "Hi," she said. "Do you by any chance need me to sit for your kids this Friday? Or Saturday? Or maybe both nights?"

"Well—I hadn't planned on it." Kelly's face fell. "But now you've put it in my mind," Sue added quickly, "—come in and let me think about it. I warn you, the place is upside down. I'm painting the living room."

"Sounds great. Can I help?"

"Umm—yes, you can. Take this little brush and this can of enamel and do the baseboards. Start on the other side of the room, so I don't drip on you."

They painted in silence for a few minutes. "What's the feminine of Tom?" Kelly asked suddenly.

("Boots," Sue almost said.) "Thomasina, I guess. Sometimes shortened to Tamsin. Why?"

"I was thinking of Tom Sawyer getting his friends to paint his fence. Remember? 'Work consists of what a body is obliged to do—' "

" '—and Play consists of what a body is *not* obliged to do.' "

"So how about me sitting for your kids this weekend?" Kelly persisted.

"Okay, okay, I'll get Fred to take me to the movies. What's the matter? Are you short of money?" Kelly had graduated from high school the past June, and had shown no signs of getting a permanent job.

"Yes." She painted an inch-wide strip of baseboard. "No, not really. I just don't want to sit at home. You know Andy and I broke up."

"Yes."

"I thought I was going to be married by now. Only he kept stalling, and then he just came out and said he wasn't ready to settle down. So he's going into the Air Force." She painted another inch-wide strip.

"At least he decided that before you got married, not after. Breaking up is messy; but not as messy as a divorce."

"Yeah, I guess you're right." She dipped the corner of her brush into the paint and ran it delicately along the top edge of the baseboard. "What's that music?"

"*The Art of the Fugue.* Like it? It's supposed to be good for hurt feelings."

"Who said?"

"Friend of mine."

Kelly listened for a moment. "Kind of old-fashioned, isn't it? It doesn't have a beat. But I like it. I think your friend was right. That guy didn't have any problems."

"Not any more. He was dying."

"Yeah."

Marianella loaded her tray and carried it through the Hall. Captain Lord Randall had asked for a bucket of tea and he would get it, not quite a bucketful but the largest pot in the kitchen, big enough for three even when one of them was the Captain. Then Marianella had added bread and butter and cream and jam and boiled eggs and stewed fruit and, of course, Master Denis's posset. She carried the heavy tray up the stairs and balanced it on her hip to knock at the door.

The Captain opened it himself. "Ah, food ..." he said in an abstracted voice, as though bread and milk had only just been invented and their possible use for the benefit of mankind was still being worked out. He stepped back and let Marianella enter with the tray, and put it on the table. There was a folded paper lying on its surface, and the Captain moved it aside. He had been sitting at the table, reading it, a paper sealed with the blue speedwell of Fendarath. Master Denis was lying on the bed, leaning on one elbow, his soft boots kicked off and dangling from the footboard. *Really, in a Lady's bedroom* ... Marianella looked around for the Lady Amalia. She looked around twice, three times, before it dawned on her that the Lady simply was not there.

Booted feet on the stairs. Over her shoulder Marianella saw Kieran come into view, with Michael the Red behind him.

"My Lord Captain," Kieran began as he came into the room, "I think I ought to report at once...." His voice trailed off as he, too, looked round the tower room and discovered that the Lady was not in it.

"Report, yes?" the Captain prompted.

"... that the drawbridge to this keep was found down this morning, and the gate left unlocked," Kieran said, comprehension spreading over his face with no sign of pleasure in it. "Will that have been her Ladyship?"

"Too right," the Captain said. "She left things in order as best she could, I'll give her that, but she's slipped out from under our noses, she's diddled Master Denis as if she'd been doing it all her life, and she's left me holding the baby. Ah, well, man proposes and woman disposes. What have you for me, Michael?" He sat himself at the table again and poured out mugs of tea.

Marianella rescued the gently steaming bowl of milk-and-things and brought it to Master Denis where he lay on the bias across the bedcover, his eyelids red and heavy. She knelt before him with the bowl, and he smiled.

"Where has she gone?" she asked him as she lifted the bowl to his lips.

Master Denis drank, and sighed, and shrugged one shoulder by way of answer to her question. "What's in this?" he asked in his turn. "None of your herbs and potions, Marianella; I've work to do."

Marianella turned innocent eyes up to him. "Just milk, and egg, and honey, all beaten together, good for someone who's been up all night and is too tired to chew," she said. "If you were her Ladyship, where would *you* go?"

"I'd stay right here where I'm needed," he grumbled. "Or if not, I suppose I'd go north, out of the thick of things, not as far as the foothills of the Weatherwall, but some deserted place where I could rest. She took a very bad attack three nights ago." He drained the bowl and licked the dregs of honey from his lips, slowly, like a man remembering his beloved's kisses. "I don't know any details, which is why I wish I could talk to her. But I felt it, that night, I felt her like a bruise as she built her shield up around herself. Blast it." He shifted his weight onto the other elbow. "By spring there'll be battle on every foot of ground between the Caramath and the Medon. I've got to find her, I've got to start searching. She can't be far away yet, and she can't leave her shield up forever, it's like walking in the night. I shall work outward in rings, over the otherworld, going over every wave of the ground till I find her." He yawned. "My back aches."

"Lie back, why don't you," Marianella suggested. "You can search just as well that way; it isn't as if you were going to fall asleep."

"Not likely," Master Denis murmured, as he fell back against the pillows and let his eyes shut the last tenth of an inch. His breathing grew slow and regular. Marianella drew the bed curtains round him and picked up the empty bowl.

Four notes out of the cello, the ones that in European notation (so the record jacket had explained) spelled B-A-C-H. The dying man's signature to his work and his life. The violins took it up and wove it into a smooth rich fabric, a mesh made up of all earthly memories, all heavenly hopes, and spread them out for the ear to see, and unraveled them again to run like ribbons straight into the other world.

The otherworld was quiet when Amalia dared to take a look at it. Like a frightened animal peering out from between blades of grass, like a battered warrior putting aside the stones of the fortress he had built over his head, she set aside the fragments that had shielded her mind from Master Denis and any other searchers and found the surroundings very quiet. Good.

She had left the road a few miles back, where it turned toward the south to lead down to Hudelsford, and crossed overland to the edge of the high moorland. From here she could look straight downward from the cliff's edge to the western valley of the Caramath, and the river itself like a line of hammered silver inlaid on the brown earth. On the eastern side of the river, the Shadow rose like a wall. It felt strange, after all these years of the Shadow creeping imperceptibly over the land, to have a real boundary between the two kingdoms. Of course, it would only last until the Shadowlings consolidated their hold on the Caramath and began to creep westward again.

She peered over the edge of the cliff again, till Pathfinder stepped uneasily backward. No one could get down that way, but there were streams that crossed the moor and slid downward through channels of their own making to the river. She would simply have to find one.

There remained the question of which way to turn. Northward, out of her way, and thus lengthening her journey? Southward, to the stone-paved ford where the road crossed the river—and nearer the Hudelsford garrison and the possibility of capture? "What do you think, cat?" Boots rested his chin on her forearm and surveyed the scene. Clearly he did not like what he saw—a cat could see the Shadow and its creatures more plainly than a man could—but whether from weakness or from trust in Amalia, he didn't try to run away. He rubbed his chin against her knuckles and said something in Cat in a hoarse whisper. It sounded noncommittal. Very well, they would compromise: north to find a canyon that led down to the Caramath, then south till they found a place to ford it. This would put off her decision for another day.

"Let's have some lunch," Sue suggested. "We won't be able to tell whether this room will need a second coat till the first one's dried." They went into the kitchen and invented soup and sandwiches, and because Kelly had had enough Bach for one morning they put on an old Gilbert and Sullivan record.

When Michael the Red had finished reporting to his Captain on the progress of making camp, and taken a look at the Lady's map, he loaded a plate with food and filled a mug with tea and took it all to the eastern window where he could keep an eye on the camp. Kieran filled another mug and joined him.

For the better part of a mile to east, north, and south the ruins lay: little more than foundation stones now, where once a trade city had stood. The farmfold were choosing sites to settle in. The wall-stubs of one old building could be built higher with the stones from another, and leave clear a bit of land for a kitchen-garden.

"Ah!" Michael said, when he had sent the second slab of bread, cream, and currant jam to its destiny. "That's more like it." He caught Kieran's eye and smiled. "'Tisn't as if we weren't eating out there," he said, and emptied his mug of tea. Kieran laid hold of the teapot and refilled it for him. "Thank you, brother. No, our supplies kept up with us most of the time. But it's unchancy work, fighting the Shadowfolk— our hearts were in our mouths, as the saying is. Half the time the men couldn't eat, and the other half they couldn't digest it." He despatched an egg and drowned it with tea. "You wouldn't think, until you'd seen it, that what made strong fighting men sick, these farm folk have been living with for *years*." He put paid to another egg and surveyed the table for fresh victims.

"There's not much to see," he said, after finishing off another slice of bread. "Nothing you or I could see, at least. Just the silvery Twilight sky and the rishi floating overhead like dark stars. They hardly seem to move, they fly so high. Not a whisper of a wind, not a living thing in sight, and you think nothing's going to happen.

"And then something you can't see lays its cold breath on your neck!"

He polished off his plate with a crust of bread. "Then Master Denis will tell you, after the fact, that it was a silverbellied what-d' ye-call-it. *He* can see them all right, but a fine lot of help that is."

"He's asleep," Kieran remarked.

"Good. He's had it worse than we did." Michael glanced out the window. "What's that fool doing?"

"Digging," Kieran said, "and right over our watercourse!"

"You there!" Michael bellowed. (The crockery rattled on the table.) "What do you think you're doing with those spades?"

"Digging a latrine trench, Sergeant," the voice came back, small and far.

"Not there, you son of a drab, that's the water supply!" Michael tossed his plate with a rattle to the table. "Come along, Kieran, and help me find him a site that won't put us all down with the galloping gripes!"

The Captain held up the teapot. "Michael! You can kill this before you go. And then you can refill it for me, mistress, because I shall probably be here all day." He picked up Amalia's letter and unfolded it again. The sounds of the men's footfalls echoed down the stairs and died away, and as the silence crept back into the room they could hear the little sound of Master Denis snoring. And the phone rang.

"Honey, I'm going to have to work late," Fred's voice said. "So I'll grab a hamburger or something and go straight on to the class. Hey, the Computer Department's going to have a sale on microdisks."

"That's nice, dear, but don't buy anything till you've checked with Siobhan. Make sure your Kumquat disk will work on the school's Mango."

"They're not using those," Fred said patiently. "They're using PS/2s. And they all use the same three-and-a-half-inch diskettes."

"Whatever. See you later." She hung up the phone and returned to the dining room. "Fred won't be back till late. Would you like to stay for dinner?"

"Thanks, but I promised my mom I'd be home for dinner. Could I come back this evening? I don't like staying home. My mom is so sympathetic it makes me itch. She's always doing something or other to try and take my mind off it." She picked up her soup spoon and stared at it. "Sometimes I think I'm okay, and then when I'm not looking it hits me like a ton of bricks. That's the trouble with taking your mind off it, it takes you off guard."

"Well, let's try the opposite approach." They cleared the dishes and washed them while the angelic counter-tenor sang.

In darkness let me dwell: the ground shall sorrow be,
The roof despair, to bar all cheerful light from me,
The walls of marble black, that moistened still shall weep,
My music hellish jarring sounds to banish friendly sleep.
Thus wedded to my woes, and bedded in my tomb,
O let me living die, till death shall come.

"Gosh." Kelly blew her nose. "I see what you mean. After that there's nowhere to go but up." While the walls finished drying they baked cookies and a pound cake, and then put on a second coat.

Amalia led the horses down a steep bank, toward the cover of the trees and brush that lined a little stream, under a cloudy sky. When she reached the bottom she found, as she'd hoped, that the river that had cut it had left sediments enough behind to provide a flat place to stand, a smooth place to sit and rest, a level place to ride one's horse, all along the bank of the river. Perhaps she would stay in the valley and follow it as far as the Caramath.

Already the shadow of the western rim of the canyon was creeping up the eastern rim. The sun still shone overhead, but its light was not bright enough for afternoon, nor warm enough for September. The Darkness was not so far away.

She dismounted, and took the saddle from Pathfinder's back and the bridle from her mouth. Grunting and cursing, she took the load from the packhorse's back, and the hacka-more from his head, and hobbled him. There was no need to hobble Pathfinder; she would not wander. "Some of us may as well eat in comfort," Amalia told the horses, and spread out oats for them, and broke out another egg for Boots. She sat herself on a fallen log to eat flat bread and an apple, and drink water from a wooden cup. Pathfinder paid no attention to her words—no matter what the folktales said, the horses of the Seers could not *really* understand human speech—and settled down to crop the grass.

I should make the Caramath by nightfall, Amalia mused. *Then, unless I'm badly out of my reckoning, an hour or two southwards should get me to Hudelsford. But that was still inhabited, the last time I heard. I'd rather not be seen.*

Master Denis is right, Sue thought. *She ought to get back to the keep and make herself useful. Can't I make her go back?* She imagined Amalia turning round and riding home again. She could visualize it, just. But it didn't seem real. It didn't fit into the plot, whatever it was, and it was clear that the plot had her in its grip. She got down from the stepladder for the dozenth time, moved it over the strewn newspaper, and climbed onto it again.

The Shadow had not yet touched this valley, small as it was, at all. No Shadowlife grew here, no glimmerworts, no flitteries hovering over the water, not even the greenish as-phodel that alone grew in both worlds. But they would come.

Amalia finished her apple and buried the core in the soft earth at the river's edge. Maybe from its seeds a tree would sprout, to grow tall in the rich soil—and to be overrun by glimmerwort and spiderlime. How soon?

The children came home and goggled at the bare white living room, until Sue chased them upstairs to do their homework. The next thing was for her and Kelly to move some of the living room furniture back out of the dining room, so that dinner could be eaten in it. They pushed the sofa and chairs and tables to within a cautious six inches of the still-tacky paint, but there was no point in putting the bookcase back until it could be pushed up against the wall and refilled.

"Time to call it a day," Sue said.

"Right. I'll be back after dinner, and help you shove the kids into bed."

Some things don't change, Sue thought, as she washed dishes for the fourth time that day while Mark splashed in his bath. *No matter how far I go, I still have to come back down to earth and wash the dishes.*

It's true, said Marianella from her own kitchen. She had six helpers now, but she was cooking for over a hundred. *Nothing's certain but birth and death and dinner. Talking of dinner, don't forget you have to give that dinner party for Christopher Bingley. Her Ladyship said so.*

Okay. Let me get the kitchen painted, and the dining room prettied up, and I'll get back to the library again.

The house rules laid down that if the children had finished homework, baths, and toothbrushing before 7:30, they could stay up another half hour and watch the evening magazine on television. Once all three of them had been cleaned up and parked in front of the tube, Sue ran fresh bathwater, climbed in, and stretched out. The hot water stung her back, and the soap bubbles tickled her nose. She rubbed lazily at a splash of paint on her writs and saw it crumble away. She stretched again, and felt her muscles loosen inch by grateful inch. And the phone rang.

It rang a second time while she was struggling to her feet, and then stopped. There was a murmur in the hall, while she stood dripping, and a tap on the bathroom door. "Mom, it's Kelly," Kathy said. "She says can she come over in half an hour, and are you going to do any more painting tonight?"

"Tell her yes and no." There was a blank silence on the other side of the door. "Yes to the first question, no to the second. Okay?"

"Okay. She said in that case she'd wear a dress."

Sue sank back into the warm water, but the golden moment had passed, not to return, and she applied herself to scrubbing. When her unwanted layers of paint were swirling down the drain, she got into clean jeans and moved the bookcase back against the wall. The books went in at random: she'd sort them tomorrow. They were a miscellaneous lot anyway: old textbooks and paperbacks and collections of fairy tales, and a pile of novels that had once been best sellers.

Idly, she thumbed through one of the books of fairy tales, and stopped between one page's flip and the next. There, almost, was Telerath sea-keep. There was more space between the Hall and the tower, and the curtain walls were higher, but the shape was the same. The banner-bearer conducting the knights up to the gates had a cross on his banner, not a poppy, but the bright armor was the same, and the red cloak of the knight in the lead. *Sonovagun*, she thought, *that's where I got it.*

After a bit of thought she pulled the novels off the shelves and stacked them in the laundry room, along with clothes Kathy and Mike had outgrown, ready to give to the Salvation Army or the St. Vincent de Paul or whatever charitable agency next knocked on her door. The fairy tales she put back on the shelves, next to her library books. Then she washed her hands again and put on a dress and made coffee. *Now I'll be the lady.*

Kelly arrived, nicely dressed and carefully make up. Sue assumed she had been vague with her family as to where she was going—and if they cared to think she was out with a young man instead of sitting home moping, that would do no harm to her image. She put the kids to bed with the efficiency of a young Mary Poppins, while Sue raided the dryer for the living-room curtains. They pushed the furniture back the last few inches, hung the curtains, and sat down to listen to the Bach again.

"I never thought I'd like this stuff," Kelly said while the stereo changed sides. "I thought those guys were old and stuffy. This isn't stuffy at all, but it's—distant. He isn't reaching out to grab you, you have to follow him."

"I think some of his pieces are more accessible than this; I'll get my friendly music expert to find me some. Yes, this is remote." The needle descended onto the disk. "He's already halfway into the other world."

"Damn it," Amalia said softly. She took a few steps away from the light of her tiny campfire, and stared southward where a dozen other tiny lights shone across a great starless darkness. Very small they seemed, and few and far away, but they meant a human habitation, and they were only about five miles distant.

Was it the village of Hudelsford, or had that been evacuated, and the villagers replaced by soldiers or scouts? For Amalia's present purposes it didn't matter; they were her own human kind, and they were a nuisance and a considerable complication.

There was nothing else to be seen, not a spark or a star, but Amalia knew that the bank of the river Caramath lay only twenty feet from her campfire. The smell of the river-water was strong in her nostrils, rich with life and mud, not clear and thin like the rivers of the Shadowlands. Not yet.

Somewhere along those five miles, Amalia was fairly certain, there would be a place where she could ford the river. In spring, when the water was high, there was nowhere safe to ford but at Hudelsford, where the road ran to the river's bank. At this time of year, though, there would be many shallow spots: she need only find one. But if she tried it in the daylight she would be seen, recognized and detained perhaps; certainly they would try to keep her from going into the Shadow. And if she tried to find the place in the dark, she would likelier than not overshoot it and find herself in Hudelsford before she knew what she was about. Unless she went out-of-body and searched thus above the riverbanks, invisible to her fellow men and dangerously visible to others.

"I could easily fail to find what I sought, and find what I didn't seek, like the poor fellow in the song," she said aloud. Pathfinder snorted and resumed grazing. Boots, curled up on a nest made of her blanket, raised his head from the remains of his third egg and mewed softly.

Then he raised his head higher and stared into the darkness. His fur bristled, and he got to his feet. Stiff-legged, tail bottling, he backed away. When he was a dozen feet from the fire he bolted and ran, vanishing into the darkness in the direction of Hudelsford. Amalia stood looking after him for a moment, then returned to the fire and sank down into the nest he had left in the blankets.

It was for the best, she told herself. She couldn't have taken him much further in any case, and with three eggs inside him and a day's rest he'd easily make it to Hudelsford. They would take care of him; cats were valued in the Twilight lands, because they could see the Shadowthings—but it was hard to persuade them to stay, because they could see the Shadowthings. Boots would be all right. But his going made the night a little darker, and she rested her hands on the little spot of heat his body had made, until it faded away. When it was quite gone, she wrapped herself up in the blankets and stared into the fire. There seemed nothing for it but to wait for the first glimmer of dawn, to look for the ford before any watchers were awake, and it would be a long, cold night.

After a while she began to sing softly, a ballad older than the Shadow, for it spoke of lands no man now living had seen.

> It was the second night of May,
> and stars were budding in the sky,
> when I rose up from where I lay
> and left my body in its bed,
> and left my bed and house behind,
> and mounted quiet and unseen
> the evening like a winding stair
> and ventured forth upon the air.
>
> And not to chase the fleeing day
> into the kingdom of the dead,
> nor birds of paradise to hunt,
> nor gather flowers of the rain,
> but it was you I meant to find,
> O white and black, O dark and fair,
> to see you for a fragile hour
> asleep and dreaming in your bower.
>
> I flying tasted every land
> along the thin skin of my soul:

I soared above the snowy peaks,
the badlands dark and harsh as lye,
the grassy plains where horses drum,
and worn green hills as old as sleep,
and even to the bitter sea
that long has parted you and me.

And over golden Ambarey,
that tastes of spices and the sun,
and over Glar whose wine is sweet,
and over Mellan's chilly sound.
Above the plains that taste of chalk
I flew beneath the sleepless Bear;
to rugged Markrath thus I came
where flowers tremble with your name.

Descending through the spicy air
I swooped along the Rath's dark banks
and found your village on the hill,
and in the village found your house,
and found your window in the wall,
and through the window to your room
like moonlight thin and cold I flew,
and lastly through the bed to you.

I saw you lying in the sheets,
with darkness hidden in your eyes,
your open fingers spilling dreams.
The moon fell white across your arms
and lost itself within your breast,
and starlight sparkled on your lips
and night upon your hair lay deep,
and all your body soft with sleep.

And all my pains had been for naught:
Your body you had left behind.
And ventured out upon the air,
And you were gone, I know not where.

And the doorbell rang. Sue and Kelly looked at each other, and Sue left the Bach playing and went to open the door.

Amalia had come to the last line of the song before she

realized that she was not alone. Just at the edge of the fire's dim light, half-hidden in a clump of trees, there was a shape that was no tree, a watcher and a listener. And it knew also that she had become aware of it.

Chris Bingley stood on the doorstep. His eyes were bright, his smile white as enamel, and he was wearing clothing he must surely have bought in California: skintight jeans, and a bright blue shirt open at the throat, and a gold chain around his neck. He looked like prime-time television brought to life. She glanced sidewise to look for an earring in his ear, but no such luck. "Hi, Sue," he said, and smiled again. "Is Fred home?"

You snake, you know he isn't home, Sue thought, and smiled back. "No, he has a computer class tonight. Won't you come in anyway, and have some coffee?" She stepped back and let him in. *Look at him grin; he heard from Pete or somebody that Fred had a class. If I stand here, I can watch his face.*

It was worth watching. His jaw didn't drop, not really; no sound escaped his lips; but he stopped dead for an instant and his eyes glazed when he caught sight of Kelly.

"This is my neighbor, Kelly Sikorsky," Sue said. "We get together every now and then to listen to music. I have a new recording of the *Art of the Fugue.* Let me get you some coffee."

It was the shape of a man, outlined by his very stillness against the trembling of the leaves. Now he stepped forward, and the moon shone on his face, pointing up his strong bones and hollow cheeks. His eyes were deep shadows.

She hurried out to the kitchen for another cup, and hurried back before Bingley could recover the use of his voice. He sipped in silence, his glance switching back and forth between Sue on his left and Kelly on his right. Sue cut him a slice of pound cake; Kelly offered him cookies; if ever a man could be killed by kindness, Bingley should be.

He stepped closer. The fire flickered in his eyes. "A good night to you, Lady. May I share your fire?"

"Of course, be welcome," Amalia said as she must. He was tall, she observed, and thin, with strong cheekbones and a nose like a hawk's beak, and great dark eyes hooded by their lids.

When the second side ended, Sue was ready to manage the conversation. "Chris, I'm so glad you dropped by. Fred will be sorry to have missed you, but it gives me the chance to ask you about your schedule. Are you going to be in Liberty Hill long?"

"I have to go to Detroit tomorrow," Bingley said. "District managers' meeting. I won't be back in this part of the district till the end of the month. Say, the 30th."

"So you'll be here two weeks from Friday," Sue persisted. "Then won't you come to dinner? We'll have George and Norma and a few other people you know. Do say yes."

Bingley said yes—he could hardly avoid it—and drank his coffee as though it were poison, or as though he hoped it was. He seemed about to speak, and Sue got up to turn over the Bach and start the stereo again.

"I must be going," Bingley said quickly, and got to his feet. "I'll see you, Sue. Nice to have met you, Kelly," and made his escape.

Sue shut the door behind him, and raised her fists over her head like a victorious athlete. "One for our side. Kelly, you were perfect!"

"He was hoping to find you home alone, wasn't he?" Kelly said. "What a stinker. He is awfully cute, though, in a plastic sort of way."

"I know he's good-looking," Sue conceded. "He knows it too, that's half his problem. The other half is that he's on a power trip." They fell silent, and listened.

The man knelt by the fire and held out his hands to its little warmth. He was wrapped in a black cloak that covered everything above his muddy boots, and its hood stood dark about his face. He looked like a man dressed up to pass for one of the Shadowfolk, or at least to pass unnoticed among them. Yet he was clearly a man. His mouth was wide and full, and his hands large and graceful in the firelight, and the long fingers had the right number of joints.

"And now I'm going to have this guy to dinner," Sue said ruefully as she said goodnight to Kelly. "What was it the fellow said when he'd crossed the river?"

" 'The die is cast.' "

"Well, it certainly is. Want to come over again in a day or two and help me pick out recipes?"

"Sure. Listen, my mom says the one thing you absolutely have to do with recipes for guests is to try them out at home first. Otherwise you can come up with a horrible mess and not even know it till it's too late. So you and I need to do some practice cooking. Mom's also got about a million cookbooks I can look in."

"Okay, you do that tomorrow, and I'll try the library. Then come over on Friday with your list, and I'll bring out my list, and we'll mix and match. Then, if you like, Fred can take me out to the movies and you can sit with the kids."

"Great!"

"And next week we'll start cooking."

"You're out late tonight, Lady," the tall man said after a long silence, "and the wind is cold." (Sue shivered, and snuggled deeper under the blankets.) "I thought everyone had been led out of these parts." His voice was deep and resonant, but husky, like a viol played upon its lowest string by a frayed bow.

"I believe they have," Amalia said, and bent to stir the fire. The pot of water she had set in its coals was beginning to boil. She reached into her pack and found tea and a second cup. (There were rules about how you treated a chance visitor to your fireside, however you disliked his company or distrusted his motives.) She washed the cup Boots had eaten from with a little of the hot water, and when the pot boiled she took it from the fire and threw in the tea leaves.

"Those lights are the village of Hudelsford, only five miles from here," the man said. "The farmfolk are gone now, but there is a garrison there, watching the Shadow. They would give you shelter."

Again Amalia said nothing. She put bread and smoked meat on a broad leaf and offered them to him, but he shook his head. "Thank you, I have eaten." But he accepted a cup of tea when it had steeped, and held it between his hands and sipped slowly as if he were grateful for the warmth.

"My name is Ulf," he said presently. "I used to have a bit of land on the other side of the river. It's gone now, so now I wander."

And if you believe that, I've got a bridge I'd like to sell you, Sue commented sleepily. Amalia did not believe him either. Whatever this man's proper trade, he was no farmer. He sat straight-backed upon the ground, and held his head like a nobleman. His stillness, and his alert glances into the darkness about them, spoke of a soldier—or at least one who had long hunted and been hunted in the wild. And his speech was strange; his resonant voice lingered over its vowels, as though he had been a singer once, or at least trained to speak in public. She could not guess at his birthplace from his speech, but that didn't mean a thing: Demoura's original regional accents had been so mixed and sifted by two centuries' flight that it was nothing out of the ordinary to hear Edran's whine and Markrath's trilled Rs dwelling side-by-side in crisp-spoken Tevrin.

"My name is Mali," she said. (Not so far from the truth, that; it was a peasant's homely version of her own name, and back at the Hill House there were two little maidens with the name, called after herself.) "I live to the north of here, or I did."

"And now you are making for Hudelsford, or further south? To Tevrin, maybe?"

Amalia shook her head, and poured more tea. Her hands were trembling, and some of the hot liquid fell onto his hands. "I'm sorry," she said, but he said, "No harm," and smiled. The smile lit and changed his face; he might have been a pleasant man once, even a handsome one, before some hardship had drawn lines on his face and thinned the flesh over his bones.

"You didn't answer my question," he said now. "That is your privilege, of course. But I tell you frankly, Lady, that I do not like the idea of your traveling alone in such an ill-omened place as this riverbank. Will you go to Hudelsford, and let the commander give you an escort?"

Amalia turned away to put another branch on the fire, and said nothing. Taking this to mean "no," Ulf went on, "Then I myself must be your guide."

"I can guide myself, I thank you, and protect myself as well."

"In the courtyards of Tevrin, maybe you could, or in the safe places of the West. But honor and law are crumbling here, among the last unhappy few to flee the Shadow. Do not think that your robe will protect you. Oh yes, I know: you are one of the Seers of Tevrin. But unless you are one of the greatest, and I do not think it, your powers will not protect you here. How long could you stand, do you think, against two or three men with long knives, whose plan was to strike off your head now so that they might search your saddlebags and your body at their leisure?"

Once more Amalia had no answer.

"Lady, be gracious, and accept what must be," Ulf said in a softer voice. "My desire is to keep you from harm. I cannot let you travel alone."

" 'Cannot?' What prevents you?"

"My honor, such as it is," he answered, "and the foreboding of my heart."

"Somewhere between here and the village," Amalia said at last, "there is a ford across the river. If you will guide me there, I shall ask no more of you."

But Ulf stared at her with great distress. "A ford across the river!" he cried. "Have you lost your wits? Are you seeking your death, or worse?"

"I haven't lost my wits, only the privilege of choice," Amalia said sharply. "And so have you in this matter. I go into the Shadow to find my brother, and bring him back, or to die in the attempt if need be. And I do not believe you can stop me."

Ulf bowed his head and seemed to struggle for a moment with his own thoughts. "Then I must surely go with you," he said.

"Thank you, no."

"Do you know the lands on the far side of the river? Do you know the roads? I do," he said. "If I cannot prevent you, no more can you prevent me. Come, we'll cross before the moon goes down." He whistled, and from the grove came trotting a horse as thin and dark as its master. "And at every quarter-mile I'll beg you to turn back, till at last you heed me."

"Oh, sorry, honey," said Fred as he got into bed. "I was trying not to wake you."

"You didn't," Sue said. "I wasn't asleep, not quite. How was the class?"

"Oh, it was great. I'll tell you in the morning. G'night."
He reached out and touched the nearest part of her, which
happened to be her breast. She patted his hand, and they
both turned over and were silent.

Ulf led the horses over the soft mud of the riverbank, so
that their hooves would make no noise. The cold moonlight
on the water swirled around his boots. Amalia walked a pace
ahead and just above the waterline. The lights of the garri-
soned village drew steadily nearer, and the rooflines began to
show against the stairs: uncounted houses, many of them in
ruins now, and two inns that now were barracks.

"Here," Ulf whispered. "We can cross here." He led the
horses into the shallow water and held out his hands to
Amalia. "Mount now, Lady," he said. "This water will rise to
your waist." His hands lifted her to the saddle as if she
weighed nothing.

The die is cast, Amalia thought as they crossed the river, and
wondered for a moment where she had heard it.

CHAPTER 6

To Travel Hopefully Is Better Than To Arrive

The next morning Sue stood in the middle of the living room and gave it a hard look. The paint was smooth; she and Kelly had left no streaks or patches; and in the morning sunlight it shone with a cool fresh glow. Through the picture window she could see the lawn, still scruffy but neatly trimmed, and the little barberries spreading out their twigs around three sides of a square, with the promise of a hedge to come.

But with the window she came to the next problem, or the first of the day: the curtains. She had washed them carefully, and they had neither torn nor faded (being Fiberglas) but they had lost any zip they'd ever had, and hung like limp pale yellow rags on either side of the window. She took them down again and considered. Did the window look better without them? Almost—except for the naked hardware, all the little metal hooks and eyes clustered at the corner of the window like corsages for robots. She put the curtains back up. They weren't much but they would have to do, at least for the time being, and if she kept them open people would see as little as possible of them.

Her back to the window, she looked over the rest of the room. The furniture was borderline, not as bad as the curtains, and would do till she could do something about it (maybe new covers, maybe next year). She had polished the bookcase and the coffee table till the wood gleamed,

and the rows of books made the place look fairly respectable. The floor would need polishing in time for the dinner party, but maybe not in time for the PTA meeting,
and . . .

The room didn't look too bad, she decided. It looked
bare—which was not necessarily a bad thing. She hadn't
realized how much junk had collected in that living room
over the years, till she had had to put it all in carton boxes
and stow it in the dining room. Souvenirs of past vaca-
tions, kids' school pictures, third-grade art projects. It
would all go into the basement, not to be brought out
again unless somebody asked for it—and she was willing to
bet nobody would ask for it because nobody would remember it.

The place did look bare. Should it, if she was trying to
make it look like the castle of her inner vision? *Not necessarily*, Marianella said. *This sea-keep is bare because it's been neglected.
In Rhadath House there are tapestries on the walls, coffers and chests
and all the pewter and silver set out in the Great Hall. They don't
seem to make tapestries in your world, but you could put some pictures
on the walls, maybe a vase of flowers on the mantel. This is a house,
not a monastery.*

Do you have monasteries?

*The Great Keep of Hellsgarde is a little like one. I'm told they have
no hangings on the wall, nothing laid away in chests, because in every
shadow the Darklife could take root. Everything is laid out on shelves
and turned daily—or sealed up in crocks.*

Pictures on the wall, well, she would have to hunt up a
print-and-poster shop and see if she could find something
good, but cheap. There were one or two good vases in the
cupboard, a big white stoneware one and a smallish round
blue bowl, but no flowers. It was October, after all. After a
bit of thought she took her clippers out in the back yard
and snipped some bright-colored twigs off the sugar maple
and filled the vases. The big one on the mantel, the little
one on the TV set, that would do for the time being.

The dining room, now. That had been painted only
about three years ago, and though she no longer cared for
the warm rust-colored walls and yellow curtains, they
were still fit to be seen and would get her through the
dinner party (the dinner party! sudden touch of cold in the

pit of the stomach). She got another carton box and cleared off the top of the side table. She might not have any pewter, but there was no point in displaying eleven juice glasses with oranges painted on them.

A pity she didn't have a real built-in sideboard, like her grandmother's house—thank God this house was just old enough to have a dining room at all, though the architect had already been drifting toward the "nook" and "family area" concepts, and there was no real wall between the living room and the dining room, just a sort of arch. That would come in handy for the PTA, though; the meeting could spill out into both rooms. If she took all the leaves out of the dining-room table and put it in front of the TV, everybody in both rooms could see it and that's where she'd put the speakers.

The walls here could use a picture too—a still life, maybe, something that looked like food? Ah, and if she had a sideboard she could set out her pewter and silver too, if she had any pewter and silver. She laughed and picked up the box of glasses. They could live in the kitchen cupboard where they belonged.

And the kitchen . . . well, that was the next step. She spent the next couple of days working her tail off, getting the kitchen ready to be painted. It was not a question merely of covering old paint with new paint; there was serious grime involved here. So she climbed ladders, perched precariously on countertops, scrubbing the kitchen walls free of the greasy ghosts of hamburgers past, with a soapy phosphate solution that did its best to take the skin off her hands. It was the kind of stuff you mustn't pour down the drain or it would choke Lake Erie to death on its own algae . . . or something like that. It took her twenty minutes to explain the process to Marianella, but after that she had the solution in moments. *If it makes plants grow where you don't want them, put it somewhere you do want them,* Marianella said practically, and Sue diluted it down and watered the garden with it.

In between times she cleared out the cabinets and scrubbed them, and added new shelf paper to her list of things to get on the next grocery expedition. *And I could use a hood over this stove,* she thought, *to keep the hamburgers off the walls in future.* But that went onto the growing list of things to be done someday, somehow, when she had the money.

Here on the edge of the Darklands, the sun still rose. They could not see it, but the starless black vault of the sky slowly paled and flushed into a beautiful burnished pewter. From the west, where the sky overhead was still clear, came a stronger light. They had only traveled a quarter-mile last night, to get out of sight of the Hudelsford garrison across the river. Down the river, around a curve, and sheltered behind an outcrop of rock, they had made a fireless camp and settled down to sleep.

Now, turning her eyes away from the light in the west, Amalia saw that the horses were cropping the dead, dry grass. "Should they be eating that?"

Ulf was standing against the rock, his black cloak wrapped about him, his hood fallen back from his head. "It won't hurt them." He bent and plucked a blade of the yellow grass, and examined it. "This is not long dead. There's nourishment in it. They can safely eat the grass for as long as they are willing to. In time the Darklife will grow over it and spoil the taste. But even then it won't poison them. The Darklife is too different."

"Then I must save the grain I brought, and let them graze as long as they will."

She expected Ulf to contradict her at once, but he only leaned back against the rock and closed his eyes. After a long silence, he said, "Lady, go back across the river, I beg of you. Let them take care of you at Hudelsford. You do not know what awaits you here."

"I have a better idea," she said as she rolled up her blankets. "I'll go on, and you go back to Hudelsford."

Ulf shook his head. "I'm no use to them." And he sighed, and walked slowly to his horse and began to inspect its feet.

Even in this stronger light, Amalia could make no sure guess at his age. In time of peace, he might have been forty; in these troubled times, he might be thirty or less, tired and worn after much watching and difficulty. His brown eyes were large and luminous, and his pale skin was lined with cares and pocked with some disease (or perhaps it was only the scars of adolescence). His black hair and beard were short and sparse, but neatly trimmed for one who had been wandering in the wilderness. His horse was thin and old, and its head drooped, but it had been a fine animal once, with the short neck and rounded head of the chargers in old paintings. Man and beast, a pair of unhappy fugitives; and yet they seemed uncommonly tough and enduring, and Amalia must keep reminding herself that she should trust neither of them. In the second hour of the silvery twilight they saddled the horses and rode into the east.

Sometimes Sue would stand in the center of the floor and dither, unable to decide what to do next. The more projects that got done, the more that appeared, springing out of the floorboards like mushrooms out of the forest floor. She felt at times like the shipwrecked sailor in the poem, the one who could never decide whether to look for food, water, or shelter first and wound up spending all his time at the beach. *You'll never get it all done,* Marianella would remind her. *It's endless, by the very nature of it. If you had this house spotless this minute, your dinner cooked, your guests at table and yourself in a velvet gown, watching a dozen pipers lead in your seneschal with the roasted boar's head, you would suddenly say to yourself, "Damn it, I should have had a spiced crab apple to put in his mouth instead of that plain old lemon." Do what you can and forget about what you can't. No one else will notice.* And Sue would mutter, "I must first get some chickens, and, No, I mean goats," and tackle whatever seemed to be closest at hand. Somehow, it all got done.

Around Friday noon, when her arms were ready to fall from their sockets from weariness and her stomach ready to turn from the smell of solvents, she left it all in a jumble and drove to the library.

The variety of cookbooks available was fairly impressive; either this branch library was set up to cater to ambitious housewives, or else the chief librarian had once been a frustrated Cordon Bleu. There were no medieval cookbooks, but on the basis of her other reading Sue decided she didn't really want to introduce onion salads, stuffed pigs' stomachs done up to look like hedgehogs, or sugar sculptures in the shape of full-rigged ships, onto her dinner table. Not in Liberty Hill. Not just yet. So she picked out some Julia Child classics, and a Chinese cookbook and some other odds and ends, and got them home in time to meet the kids coming home from school.

"I'll put it this way," Michael the Red said to Kieran as they walked through the camp. "We have provisions enough, between what we brought and what's promised from my Lord Captain's estates at Southern Shores, to feed these people for five, maybe six months." He paused to let a cart go by, laden with wild hay the men had been cutting along the banks of the Medufar. "Or, we have enough to feed them for, say, two months *and* to plant a crop of winter wheat that could feed them next year. If there's decent farming land here."

"These uplands are good enough land," Kieran said, "but they don't hold water. The winter rains will water them, and you can start your wheat, grow onions, lettuce, winter cabbages. It never snows here. But come the spring, it dries up except along the rivers."

"That's what your Lady's letter said."

"If you were to rig a crane, now, or a gang of cranes to work along the river and hoist water into irrigation channels—"

"You'll have 'em," Michael said. "We've got good engineers with this army. We're short of draft horses, though. Maybe I can send to Telerath for them. No, the question here is what you're going to feed these people on till their first harvest comes in."

"I already said I can send to the North," Kieran said. "We've got kin at Becksford, who owe us favors. They'll send grain, vegetables, a few cattle, maybe some horses for the plowing. You said you had two months' provisions not counting the seed corn. Mostly grain?"

"Mostly grain. Some vegetables."

"Well, there's the sea at out backs, and there's fish in it. We've always taken as many fish out of it as we could eat or salt to send away. If we had more men—"

"How many men do you need?" Michael said. "We've fishermen's sons in the ranks; all I have to do is find 'em."

"Find me some boatwrights while you're at it," Kieran said. "We've only got the six boats and one of 'em's past her prime."

Michael stopped in his tracks, and a blissful smile spread over his face. "Could you use a sixty-foot sailing ship? If you had the men to crew it? Some of those supplies are coming around from Southern Shores by sea, on the *Golden Apple*. She's old, but sound, and no one in Tevrin is going to need her back till the war's over."

"How long is that likely to be?"

Michael lost his smile. "Let's get inside." He led the way down the main street that was rapidly taking shape as the camp formed around it. Big square tents were springing up like canvas mushrooms, roofing over the rebuilt walls. Before some of the tents stood rows of weapons, smooth-polished and ready for use; nervous women and tired-looking men peered out of others. But they looked happier already than they had yesterday.

Seven hundred and twenty and two men and women: all that had remained on the two banks of the Caramath. A brick-faced man was building a bread oven out of clay and small stones, and between two of the tents a rope had been stretched to hold somebody's washing. The military camp was becoming a town before their eyes. But something was amiss, and it took Kieran some time to realize what it was. There were no children.

Michael led Kieran to the command tent in the center of the camp. A pair of bright-helmed guards stood to either side of the canvas door-panel. Inside they found a folding table and two chairs next to the folding camp-bed, and the manservant Ulrico hanging out bedding to air. Michael spoke a word to him, and he picked up an armload of blankets and slipped away.

A roll of vellum lay on the table. Michael took it as they sat down, and unrolled the crackling skin. It was a map of the southern part of Demoura, with a fine red line drawn in along the Caramath. Kieran could see where similar lines had been drawn in further to the east, and erased again as the Shadow advanced.

"You see how we stand," he said. "The Shadow is now only forty miles from the gates of Tevrin. If it falls, then of all the Land Below the Mountains we shall still have almost half. But if Tevrin falls, the heart will go out of us, and our end will not be long delayed."

"I don't know a great deal about it," Kieran said. "I have never been out of my own county in my life. But I should have said that we will never fall so long as Hellsgarde hangs on." He laid his finger on the map, to the north of Tevrin, where the red line suddenly zagged eastward around the mark of a sharp rocky outcrop with a point like the prow of a ship.

"Truly, Hellsgarde will hang on so long as one man remains alive on it," Michael agreed, "and so long as that one man is the Lord of the Council. But how long can Hellsgarde endure if Tevrin falls? It can't provision itself, and must soon be starved out. But here is what I wanted to tell you." His stubby finger traced a line across the map from west to east. "Master Denis has been watching over his shoulder as we rode, watching them building up behind our backs. He says he can't see half a mile past the Caramath any more, they shadow the air so."

"Readying for an attack?"

"Nobody knows. He's never launched a campaign this late in the year. But whenever he does, he'll find us standing ready to fight him"

"Unless this is a feint, to draw your forces away from Tevrin."

Michael shrugged. "My Lord Captain says not, Master Denis says not, the Lord of Hellsgarde says not. How are you with a sword?"

"Not much. I can use a bow."

"Then I'll train you," Michael said cheerfully. "Come, we have all winter. I'll make a fighting man of you, and more—you'll make a Captain of yourself." He grinned at Kieran's look of disbelief. "I can always tell. Men will follow you."

Before Kieran could answer, a strange sound cut through the air, a high, indignant wail. *A cat*, Kieran thought first, and then, *a peacock*? So quickly had he grown used to this strange village where the youngest inhabitant was at least twelve or thirteen years. It was no cat—! Michael joined him as he peered out the tent flap. In a tent across the way stood or knelt half a dozen women, crowding round another woman who sat on a three-legged stool, holding a bundle in her arms. It cried out again, and waved a tiny pink fist. *Impossible*, Kieran thought. *They've been living under the Shadow—*

Then he saw the other woman, standing off to one side, her expression equal parts pride and relief. She would never see nineteen again. Her face was lined and sunburnt and her long tawny hair streaked with grey, but her eyes were elaborately painted and her cheeks rouged. One of the army's camp followers: fond of her child no doubt, but glad to be rid of it and free to get about again. Her worn black velvet gown was cut very low in front and looped up high on each side—to avoid the dust perhaps, or to display her dimpled knees. Her bare feet were dirty.

"The child will have fifty foster mothers by nightfall," Michael murmured.

"One of yours, Sergeant?"

Michael gave the mother a disdainful glance. "Heaven forbid. I have *some* pride."

O, I've been there, Sue mused. *When Kathy was that size, how I loved the middle-aged ladies who wanted to hold her! They had the touch and I didn't. "Take my child—please!" I'd have handed her over to Lady Vader if she could've kept her quiet.*

Evening came, and just after sunset Kelly arrived with a load of cookbooks for her evening's entertainment. Fred and Sue went to the movies. Within Liberty Hill there was a choice of a Clint Eastwood western, a borderline-science-fiction rock epic, and a terribly sensitive slice-of-life about people with contemporary sexual problems, so instead they drove twenty miles north and saw a Lucas-film in its third re-release, and enjoyed their evening.

They had only ridden a few miles when the horses' hooves fell silent. Thin strands of plant tendrils, oyster-white and tiny-leaved, were creeping over the stones of the road, muffling them. "Stoneweed," Ulf said. "It grows over the stones and cracks them with its roots. In time all this stone will be cracked to gravel, and then to dust. But the stoneweed will still grow here, and the roads will be visible for hundreds of years. At that, it's easier on the horses' hooves."

Something suddenly clarified in Amalia's mind. Ulf, kneeling beside his horse, inspecting its unshod hooves. He had found some trifling irregularity, a chip made by a stone perhaps, and carefully filed it smooth. But how could that horse have gone weeks or months, ridden over rough country and stone-paved roads, without cracking and splitting its hooves? Either it had stepped out of some hidden stable or sheltered pasture only yesterday, or it had been walking over something very soft. Amalia looked down at the muffling white stoneweed, and did not speak her mind.

"Is it always so quiet?" she asked instead, for the whole country was completely silent. The breeze that had been blowing at dawn had died away, and there was no sound at all but the horses' breathing and the faint creaking of their harness.

"This is a place of transition," Ulf said. "The birds and insects have flown away or died, and their Darklife counterparts have not yet arrived. Have you ever seen how life comes back into a forest after a fire? First the ferns spring up, and the molds and rots, and those insects that live on dead wood. Later the green plants come back, and the birds and animals that live off them. So here the stoneweed comes first, and the spiderlime, and the other colonizers. Your western lands, Lady, are to the Darklife like forests where the fire still rages, which they seek constantly to quench and invade. Further to the east, yes, other creatures will come; there are lands where their voices are heard, where I do not intend that you should go."

They were traveling now through what had been farmsteads. The fields were deserted, full of dry weeds; the dead trees were thick with spiderlime whose pearly strands, scarcely thicker than cobwebs, crept over the wood and crumbled it to dust almost as they watched. The wooden houses and barns were already slumping, their roofs collapsing under their own weight. A plow lay at the side of the road, where some unhappy farmer had abandoned it when it proved too heavy to bring along. Its wooden parts were already quite crumbled away, and in the soft earth where it had lain the first luminous blue shoots of the long-leaved glimmerwort were sprouting. But the iron plowshare lay untouched, beginning to rust—no, that was too deep a red for rust. "Ironcrop," Ulf said. "The Darklife does not use iron, but iron will not poison it; that is only a fable. But there is nothing that eats iron, so the ironcrop likes to take root on it where nothing will disturb it. In time every piece of iron that was left will be thickly coated. And look there." He pointed. Along the edge of the road, close to the ground, grew clusters of a tall flower, a stiff spike with many greenish-white flowerets.

"Asphodels," Amalia said.

"Yes," Ulf said. "The only living thing that grows in both worlds."

"How well do you know these lands?" Amalia demanded. "And how long have you been roaming them?"

"Too well," Ulf said, "and too long." And he would say nothing further.

On Monday Sue woke up with the kind of unreasoning panic that she had once felt on the morning of a math test. *I have invited Bingley and a dozen other people to dinner and I don't know what to do with them, and I haven't even invited them yet. . . .*

Get hold of yourself, Marianella said. *You are trying to deal with too many unknowns at once; remember how ill you always fared with your algebra. Let us start with two solid facts: you have a dinner service for twelve, and your table can seat that many, just, if you put in all the leaves. But you don't have to have all twelve. How many do you need? Yourself and Frederick, that's two. Bingley himself, that's three. Is there a Mrs. Bingley?*

I'm sure there must be, but I don't know her. Anyway, she probably lives in Detroit.

No matter, we can handle odd numbers if we must. We are bringing these people together to feed them, not breed them, no matter what Christopher Bingley might desire. George and Norma, that's four and five. This fulfills the obligation you owe them; what's more, you met Bingley under their roof so you must invite them the first time you invite him.

Where do you get these bits of information?

You read an old book on gentilesse when you were in school. Emilia Post, I think. Now, those five aside, you have six or seven more places. The best choice to fill them would be the other assistant managers, who are your peers and Fredericks' rivals for the office. If you left them out, it could be said you feared their competition.

There are too many of them; there must be ten or eleven assistant managers from four branches just in this district.

Then Stuart and Paul and Karen and Ruth, that makes nine; they are your husband's closest associates. That leaves one more couple, and I suggest the Carmodys. They are intelligent and can keep the conversation moving. Besides, we have already seen that Bingley respects Claire Carmody.

He's afraid of her, you mean. Be careful she doesn't frighten him into recommending somebody else.

That's a risk I'm prepared to take, and that makes eleven. Do you know any unmarried woman who might make a twelfth?

Nobody but Kelly, and she's too young.

I agree, and I have other plans for her. What about Siobhan O'Hare? Is there a Mr. O'Hare?

There must have been once. I'll ask Fred.

Good. See how simple it all is? Now get up and take your shower and go paint your kitchen.

Kelly reappeared after breakfast, and they started in on the kitchen, swapping recipe ideas back and forth as they worked. By the time the first coat of paint was on the walls, they had settled on a crown pork roast ("Mom says October's a good month for pork"), stuffed with something to be settled by future debate; but they were agreed on the grenadine glaze and the little crab apples on the points of the crown. Potato crullers, to show off. Escalloped eggplant, to continue to show off. Green beans, for those who didn't care for eggplant, and a chance to relax from nonstop elegance—with slivered almonds so they mightn't relax too far—"and besides," Kelly said practically, "they taste good. Sunflower seeds taste even better, only you don't want them to think you're a hippie." A green salad would follow the main course, European-style, and what the dessert would be was still up in the air. Kelly was pushing for a croquembouche, which was a pile of cream puffs, stacked pyramid-fashion, while Sue kept thinking wistfully of a baked Alaska. "But it has to be *baked*," Kelly insisted. "Who's going to bake it and bring it to the table quick-before-it-melts? You? You're supposed to sit there and soak up compliments, not jump up and down like Kermit the Frog. In fact, I think you need a parlormaid to wait on table. I hereby volunteer."

"Oh, Kelly, that's awfully nice of you," Sue said, and meant it. "Is there anything I can do for *you*?"

"You could introduce me to a nice butler," Kelly said. "Somebody like Mr. Hudson, only maybe a little younger. Do you think I should have a black dress and a little ruffled apron?"

"I've got a ruffled apron," Sue said. "White organdy, no

less. Christmas present a couple of years ago. The butler may take a little more doing. Do you have a black dress?"

"No," Kelly said. "I've got that green jersey I wore on Wednesday, and—" But Sue was not to hear about the rest of Kelly's wardrobe, because an idea was opening up inside her mind with the brilliance of a speeded-up flower on a PBS science program. When they stopped for lunch, Sue went into the bedroom and called the Record Barn.

"Hi, Randy, this is Sue. Do you work Friday nights?"

"No."

"Good. Do you work *Wednesday* nights?"

"Usually not."

"Great," she said, and described her plan. When she had finished, she heard a low, respectful whistle over the telephone.

"You are one clever lady," Randy said. "You can count on me." Sue hung up and went out to her lunch, humming.

Mile after mile, silent on the soft white road. The Shadow seemed to deepen as the sun rose higher above it, and on the darkening ground the blue glimmerwort shone ever thicker, like drifts of blue stars. Without sun or shadows to give her a sense of time, Amalia had no idea how long they had been riding, nor how far she had ridden before she looked up and found that she was alone. Ulf had fallen back somewhere and ridden away. Amalia rose in her stirrups and craned her neck this way and that, but neither to her eyes nor to her Sight was there any sign of him.

The sky arched overhead, dull-black and glowing like charcoal, or diamond dust. The air was warm, but a tiny breeze had sprang up, to blow coolly against her right cheek: the last breath of a south wind off the far-distant sea. The ground was a deep ash grey, as smooth as the breast of a dove. The air was clear, with no fragrance and little moisture, but away to the north the first ranks of hills lay veiled in their mist, their curved shapes overlapping like fishes' scales, deep on deeper grey on deepest grey pearl. The land was as silent as death, but it was not dead. Life of a kind was moving in and settling down in its own way. Like the ferns and insects after a forest fire, as Ulf had said—and where in all this glimmering wilderness *was* Ulf, anyway? *Absurd,* Amalia thought. *I didn't want him along in the first place; why should I complain if he goes away again?* And she urged the horses forward, under the empty sky.

Pathfinder was the daughter of war-horses, a beast of the House of Fendarath. She had yet to meet the Shadowbeast that could frighten her, though maybe that would come. She held her head high, and carried her mistress boldly. But the packhorse from the village of Telerath had not been bred to the borders of the Twilight, and though he did not seek to turn back, not yet, his head drooped and his ears lay back and his eyes rolled from side to side.

The little breeze had changed its direction, and blew now almost straight into Amalia's face. It whispered in her ears, a whisper she could almost resolve into words: subtle, alluring, almost affectionate—but in no language that she knew.

To her Sight the land was less empty, for the ground was riddled with small burrowing things like bright specks of warmth that left pale burning narrow tracks behind them: like beetles, perhaps, but doing the work of earthworms. The ash-colored land at this level was like a mesh of glowing lace. And there was something else going on, some busy cluster of creatures making their living just the other side of that hill. She came over the brow of the hill and saw it. The packhorse stopped short, trembling from head to foot, and even Pathfinder snorted with dismay. Before them lay the body of a horse, or what remained of it, and a man who crouched nearby, watching it out of eyes dull with fear. Above the horse a cloud of flitteries rose and fell, little many-winged specks of gauzy white. The air was thick with their wings as they drifted up and down, darting away and returning like bees above a field of flowers. But the horse was already flayed, and here and there the white bone showed through the flesh. And the crouching, rat-faced little man was Ruk, who had come to Amalia in Tevrin, Ruk the servant of the mysterious Zalmar of Northwater.

"What's the matter?" Kelly asked. "You look like you've seen a ghost."

"Not quite," Sue said. "I think I'm getting an idea."

"Don't scare it," Kelly said. "Can I top off your coffee?"

"Yes, please."

Flitteries, Amalia thought. *I always thought they were harmless.* One saw them along rivers and streams in the Twilight lands, hovering over the calm water in the evenings. As soon as the gnats and mosquitoes deserted a bit of water, the flitteries moved in, and very pretty they looked, shining above the dark surface. Yet there was the saying that they could bite. And as she watched, the miserable Ruk clapped a hand to his face and howled as though he had been struck by a live spark from a forge.

"Get away from there, you fool!"

Amalia turned sharply. Ulf had returned, soundless over the white road. His hoarse voice rose to a harsh half-shout. "They prefer dead food, but they won't say no to live meat if it's stupid enough to hold still for them! Get across the road!"

Ruk rose slowly to his feet and backed away. The flitteries continued with their meal. Amalia looked over her shoulder at Ulf, dark on his dark horse, and back at Ruk. "Ruk! Do you know me?"

The little man stared at her, and swallowed, and stared again. "Ulp! Yes, Lady, I know you."

"Then tell me: do you know that man? Is that your master, Zalmar of Northwater?"

Ruk was silent for a long moment. "No, Lady," he said at last. "No, that's not my master. I never saw that man before."

"Well, then," Ulf said, "what are you going to do, man? You can't go on. You can't go back, come to that, unless—" He reined in his horse close to Amalia. "Lady, the man's a poor wretched scoundrel," he said in a low voice, "but yet you may wish to save him. Will you give him your packhorse, to ride back into the Lightlands? Garwin can carry some of your packs."

"Until you ride away again," Amalia murmured. "Where did you wander off to?"

"Looking around," Ulf said. "It's too quiet here, I don't like it. We should be seeing more action this deep into the Dark, but there's not so much as a shouf overhead. But do not fear, Lady, I shall always come back to you. Well? What about the horse?"

"Give it to him," Amalia said.

Ulf rode forward. "Ruk!" he said. "Would you save your life? And maybe your honor if you ever had any? Then take the Lady's other horse and ride straight back along this road to the ford. Go to the garrison commander at Hudelsford and ask him to put you to service." His voice was harsh. "Work and fight for your own kind, and make yourself a man again." Without waiting for an answer, he dismounted and walked straight into the cloud of flitteries, which rose up like smoke to avoid him, and pulled Ruk's saddle from the carcass. Perhaps because the leather was old and dry, the creatures had not yet touched it. He tossed the saddle to Ruk, who followed slowly after him and began to saddle the packhorse.

"Will you not go back with him?" Ulf asked Amalia. "His company is not what I'd choose for a Lady, but it's better than none, certainly better than mine."

"Why don't *you* go back with him," Amalia snapped, "go to the garrison commander and fight for your kind, two scoundrelly brothers-at-arms."

But Ulf only shook his head, and seemed to take no offense. "It's too late for me," he said, and said no more. He had not paused in dividing Amalia's packs between Pathfinder and Garwin, and she supposed that his suggestion had been only for form's sake. They set Ruk on the other horse and watched him dwindle into a small dot in the west before they mounted their own horses and set off in the opposite direction.

They rode now side by side, their horses nose to soft nose, their booted feet almost touching in the stirrups. "What is your proper name?" Amalia demanded.

"I have none," Ulf answered calmly. "It's been too long. Once I had land and kinsfolk and a proper name. Now I am Ulf, son of Nobody."

Amalia set this aside as a dairymaid sets aside a pan of cream, to be skimmed later when it's ripe. "And what is a shouf?"

Ulf looked thoughtful. "If the rishi is the sparrowhawk of these lands, then the shouf is the great mountain eagle. Its body is one great wing, and its mouth is always open, sucking in the tiny life that feeds it. It soars through the sky-cover, black underneath, creamy-white above. It's a bowshot from wingtip to wingtip, and it could pick up a horse with each claw. But it won't alight on the plains; it could never get off the ground again. It roosts in the mountains, and on the tops of towers. The shouf are the eyes of Agniran over all this land."

"So, did your idea come home to roost?" Kelly asked as she stacked the dishes in the sink.

"I think so," Sue said. "Where's that country cookbook —no, not the French one, the American one. It occurred to me that the traditional thing to go with pork is apple-sauce—but you usually make a stuffing with breadcrumbs— pumpkin pie, banana bread, here it is." She looked the recipe up and down. "If I take this apple Betty and reduce the sugar and increase the spices, to make it more savory and less like a dessert—"

"Go for it," Kelly said. "Only try it out first. Do stuffed pork chops for the family and see if your husband'll eat it."

"Right," Sue said. "Here, if you're going to wash I'll dry . . . ohmigod, the PTA committee is going to be here tomorrow night. Every time I think I'm all set I remember that."

Stop worrying, Marianella said.

"Stop worrying," Kelly said. "The paint'll be dry by then and you can bake banana bread."

"You preheat the oven," Sue said; "I'll mash the bananas."

Amalia crouched in the middle of their campsite, picking every shred of plant fiber out of the two-foot circle Ulf had scribed on the ground with the toe of his boot. "We dare not build the smallest fire," he had said. "Even a spark would attract . . . unwelcome attention. But if you can clear that circle, we can bake some camp bread. I shall be back in a bit." The dough was mixed in the pot and the bakestone lay beside it. The horses munched their grain, and Amalia's thin fingers picked out half-inch stems and quarter-inch stems and tiny crumbs, and threw them all away.

They had camped in the lee of one of the crescent-shaped hills that were becoming common over the landscape—gently sloping on their outward side, falling steeply within the horns of the crescent—the shape of a creeping sand dune, but hard as brick to the touch, and covered with a stiff growth like petrified moss. An the "wind" that had shaped them, so far as she could tell, blew straight out of Agniran.

"Here we are," said Ulf, reappearing as usual without the sound of a footfall. He was holding a dozen short plant stems—she supposed they were plants—separated by his fingers, bristling in all directions, so that none of them touched the next. Near the tip of each stem was a thick swelling, like a fat cattail (or a corn dog on a stick, Sue commented from her alien viewpoint) each glowing with a dull red light.

"Shape your bread," Ulf instructed, "put it on the bakestone, and set the pot over it like a bell." When Amalia had done this, Ulf laid the stems over the pot so that each could touch the next. They began to glow much more brightly, almost to an orange heat, and their warmth radiated outward till Amalia had to move back or be scorched. "It's not a fire," Ulf said, "but a process like the pollination of plants. As the heat dies down, they'll set their seeds and blow away on the wind. The process ordinarily takes place in the belly of a ... well, another creature I hope you're not to meet. Not that it has any lasting hatred for your kind. But it's a nearsighted beast that prefers to charge first and ask questions afterward."

Presently Ulf tipped the glowing stems from the pot, and they retrieved the hot bread and ate it. Then Amalia sat without speaking, watching the stems break into fragments, one by one, and darken a deeper and deeper red.

Something slipped past the corner of her eye, something white. She looked down and saw a line of flowers lying on her breast, a garland of the narrow-petaled asphodels, each floweret threaded through the split step of the next, chained together as children chain daisies. They shone on her breast like dim stars. Ulf must have walked far for them, for neither the glowing reeds nor the asphodels had been visible from the road today. "Thank you," she said, her voice soft with surprise. Ulf did not answer. He had vanished into the night again.

He returned when the stems had died down to white seed-fluffs like ashes, and were blowing away. Without a word he took her blankets from her pack, gave them to her, and gestured toward the shelter of the hill. Obediently she went where he pointed and lay down, and he wrapped himself in his black cloak and lay down beside her, sheltering her between his body and the hill. In spite of her anxious mind and her uneasy body, she slept as well under his protection as ever she had in her life.

Amalia assumes a lot, Sue reflected as Tuesday night wore on, *assuming that everyone is going to respect her black robe and let her alone. And yet they do. Even Ulf:*

he may look like a Hell's Angel with a horse instead of a Harley, but he's behaved like a perfect little gentleman. She had leisure to think of things like this, because the committee's discussion had washed over her like a tidal wave and left her behind. As Siobhan O'Hare had probably counted on, the women who had take the trouble to come to the meeting were those who were already fairly enthusiastic about computers (or maybe the opposite camp had all gone to the Little League meeting being held the same evening). Siobhan had brought one of the microcomputers from her class and a program called Logo that taught children to draw pictures by writing programs. So far the ladies had drawn a house, a cat, and a Christmas tree, all about the same size, and their enthusiasm knew no bounds.

"I think you convinced them," Sue told Siobhan after the meeting, while they picked up the last crumbs of banana bread, macaroons, and brownies, and folded up the chairs for Mr. Hoskins to take away.

Siobhan nodded. "I hope I wasn't just preaching to the converted," she said. "Because this bunch has got to go and convince the rest of the membership, and *they've* got to go and convince Mr. Shafer that we don't need a velvet-lined sports palace. I don't object to the sports; I just object to the velvet-lined palace. Oh, no more coffee, thanks, I've had too much already. That's the trouble with being a single parent, you try to do it all and end up doing too much."

Aha, said Marianella. "Well," said Sue, "I would hate to make your life any more complicated. But would you like to come to dinner a week from Friday? I warn you, my motives aren't pure. We're entertaining the boss's boss and we could definitely use another intelligent person to help carry the conversation. We already have a few, so you won't be all alone."

Siobhan smiled. "But that is a compliment," she said. "I'd love to. Sue, you never got a chance to play with the computer, did you? You were too busy pouring coffee. Come and test-drive it before I shut it down and take it apart." So Sue sat down and learned how to define "TO MOUNTAIN" and "TO STAR" and to make a whole mountain range, dark blue, with a field of stars glittering above it, pure and clear as the icy water trickling down from the snowy peaks. *Visit scenic Demoura,* she thought, and watched in silence while Siobhan saved it into a file and copied it onto a diskette. "Next time I'll bring a printer," she said. "Good night."

"Good night," Sue said, and went into the bedroom where Fred had hidden from the PTA and was waiting for her.

"This place," Ulf said, raising his head, after a long silence. "This place was once Kindarie."

Kindarie! Amalia looked round her, trying to catch a glimpse of anything that might be left of the fabled city. There was nothing but a heap of crumbled stone away to their left, thickly hung with sheets of the white stoneweed. The towers had crumbled, the pillared halls of which so many songs had sung. The walls had fallen into the streets, filled in the Wide Way that had divided the city in two like a berry. A marble stairway had run from the Almond Gate to the Hall of Flowers, and over its white stones the musicians had wandered with their harps and vielles in their hands and laurel leaves in their hair. Now they were gone, and the Wide Way was gone, and the city was gone. The air was warm, but Amalia shivered and drew her cloak closer around her. Ulf watched her.

"I know," he said. "It was very fair, this city, and the music more wonderful than words could tell. They used to say the singers had voices like flutes, and the flutes had human voices. And the air was like pale gold, and white doves sat upon the roofs. The Darkness took it in one day." And he too pulled his cloak around him, and pulled his dark hood over his face, and spoke no more that day.

By Wednesday the house was spotless, the groceries bought, the cooking carefully choreographed for Thursday and Friday. Kelly phoned up mid-morning to say that she would come over if needed, only she hoped she wasn't needed because she was busy sewing. Sue took off her apron and threw it into a corner of the bedroom, changed out of her grubby jeans into her decent jeans, and went in search of a print-and-poster shop.

She found it on the third floor of a large bookstore, a

room like a gigantic hayloft whitewashed inside and hung with samples of picture frames. The top forty prints jostled for space on the walls, but most of them sat in huge plywood bins, interleaved with sheets of plywood like file folders.

In front of her was a bin marked "A-B." It was six feet deep from front to back. But since the alternative was to find a clerk and say, "I'm looking for some prints for my house—what kind? I don't know, something for the living room and something for the dining room," she pulled the first sheet of plywood toward toward her and started leafing through, hoping the lightning would strike.

It didn't take long. Under B she found a still life full of grapes, each one as bright and clear as a drop of glass, with tendrils twining in all directions like a little girl's hair in a high wind. It was the work of Osias Beert, the caption said; well, she had never heard of him but there was no time like the present. She pulled out a copy of the grapes from between the plywood sheets with one hand and continued to flip them over with the other. Botticelli—Bosch and Breughel, a bit too raunchy for the living room—a panel of pale gold, tall and narrow, and her hand made a snatch for it before it disappeared again behind the plywood. A group of young women, wearing white pleated gowns and carrying medieval musical instruments, their hair a dozen shades of blonde and auburn, their heads crowned with laurel, their eyes pure, their faces calm. They were descending a steep curved marble staircase under a pale rich afternoon sunlight that turned marble and skin, white gowns and silver flutes alike a delicate clear gold.

It was a picture of Kindarie. But how could it be? There was no such place. . . .

I've seen it before, she told herself firmly. *I saw it years and years ago and it's stuck in my mind till now. This guy was a Victorian*—Sir Edward Burne-Jones, 1880—*and they probably made millions of copies of it.* But how could she have seen anything so beautiful, and not remembered it? Shaking her head, she took her prints to the checkout counter.

"Can I get these framed?"

"Yes," the clerk said, handing her a price list. "But it usually takes about two weeks. Right now, more like three."

"Darn! I haven't *got* three weeks. I wanted them for Friday. Can I put them up with push pins now and bring them back later to get framed?"

"Sure you can," the clerk said. "I'll get you a mailing tube to carry them in." He sold her a packet of glass-headed push pins along with the prints, and threw in the mailing tube for free.

Clinging to her package, Sue walked back to the parking lot deep in thought. If she were to start thinking of Demoura as a real place, she would be well down the path to the funny farm. Nor was she willing to buy the science-fictional idea of an opening between worlds, the sky cracking open to let through the unguessable. If she *hadn't* seen the picture before, then—then, she and Sir Edward simply had similar tastes and liked to imagine the same things. When you thought of it that way, it was obvious. If they hadn't liked pure-eyed musicians wandering barefoot down golden marble steps, he wouldn't have painted them and she wouldn't have bought them. She took the prints home and pinned them in place, and they looked so *right* that she found it hard to remember what the walls had looked like without them.

Day after day, the sky grew darker and the land stranger. There was no longer any trace of human habitation. Even the land had changed: instead of the long ridges built up by years of plowing, the fields were divided into irregular blocks six or eight feet across, like plates of shell on the back of the tortoise that holds up the world. Thin streams of water trickled between the plates, and strange crops grew inside them, grey and black and whitish stems. Some of them bore strange fruit, tiny shining blue-green crystals like undying sparks, or great melon-sized globes that shone with a dull red light. Amalia had not realized that the Darkness would be so *very* dark, nor that there would be so many unexpected sources of light. "Light is a waste-product for these things," Ulf explained. "They put out light to get rid of it, Lady, the way a Lightlander sweats. The part that shines is the part the farmer throws away."

For there were farmers here, but not human farmfolk. They

looked akin to the Shadowlings Amalia had seen on the frontiers of the Twilight, small and black and eyeless. They stepped from field to field on feet with delicate long toes like a rail's, and paid no attention at all as Ulf and Amalia rode by. "They belong to the worker, not the soldier caste," Ulf explained. "We're not among the things that interest them. They're not lacking in intelligence, but it's their way to attend to what's down there in the fields, not what's up here on the road."

For the road had risen, or the fields had sunk, till it ran between them on a high causeway, six feet or more above ground level. Things like soft feathery reeds grew at the base of the roadway, where it sloped down into the fields, and from these rose a smell like mint, and a musty-sweet smell like the inside of a working beehive.

And the shouf soared overhead, dark in the dark sky, but now even Amalia could make them out. They flew at random, it seemed, and paid no attention to strangers on the road; but Ulf looked upward often, his thin face anxious, and what he saw or thought he did not share with Amalia. Daily he asked her to turn around and go home, but only out of habit, it seemed, or a sense of duty. She always refused, and he continued to guide her onward.

It was in the middle of the day, when the warm damp air was at its warmest and dampest. They had stopped to let the horses rest under the shelter of what might perhaps be called a tree: a tall slender pole that rose forty feet out of the feather-reeds, with flat leaves like gigantic lily-pads emerging all round the stem in a lazy spiral. It was cooler underneath: not that there was enough light for the leaves to cast a shade, but they seemed to absorb some of the heat.

Amalia walked forward along the road, stretching her legs. Something flickered away to the north, where the dark hills rose almost invisibly toward the Weatherwall. Heat lightning? Some trick of the Darkness? She heard Ulf's voice behind her, calling out softly with words she did not quite hear. Then his hands were on her shoulders, and bore her down, and they tumbled down the bank together into a clump of the feathery reeds that nodded over their heads and filled the air with the scents of mint and honey.

Ulf's long body lay atop Amalia, his hands still clutching

her shoulders, his head turned backward to look into the sky. "Rishi," he whispered. "They may have seen us, I don't know."

They lay together, silent and rigid, for some minutes while the rishi, at least forty of them, passed slowly overhead. A patrol? An expedition against some Twilight frontier garrison, or the constant challenge of Hellsgarde? Ulf would not venture a guess. When the last of the rishi had vanished into the west he let out his breath in a long sigh, and his body relaxed against Amalia's and his head rested on her shoulder, his breath warm against her throat. Amalia lay still, not daring to move. If she had moved, it would have been to put her arms round him, dark mysterious to-and-froing rascally wretch as he was, and open her mouth and her knees to him. *If not for the war, and the Sight, and the training,* she thought, *I should certainly have been one of the great harlots of legend. This is like being on fire.* And she lay motionless in the sweet-smelling reeds, hardly daring to breathe, until it was safe to climb up the bank and continue on their way.

Poor Amalia, Sue thought as she poured the coffee Wednesday night and set the needle down on the First Brandenburg Concerto. *She should've gone through all this at fourteen or fifteen, the way Marianella did, when she was still young and green and her mother or her duenna or somebody was around to keep an eye on her. To have to discover sex all at once, fully blown, with a mature body is hardly fair. And I'm not convinced old Ulf is the best person for her to do her discovering with; though I suppose he's got the experience, and he seems to like her.* And the doorbell rang.

"Oh, my God," Kelly said. "Not him again! I thought he was out of town!"

"I think so," Sue said, and opened the door. On the doorstep stood Randy, with a bundle of records under each arm and a guitar slung over his back. "Come on in," she said. "Kelly, this is Randy Jamison, who's agreed to buttle for me. Randy, this is Kelly Sikorsky. I didn't know you played the guitar."

"Oh, Segovia I'm not," Randy said, "but I thought I'd bring it along." And when the First Brandenburg was over, he played Renaissance and Baroque music, Bach and

Vivaldi and Granados and Satie, and the twelfth-century Songs of Our Lady by Alfonso the Wise, King of Spain. It was an education, and a considerable ego-boost for Kelly, to whom Randy directed all his glances and most of his best notes. It was plain that for two devaluated new pence he would have gone on one knee before her, playing serenades and zarzuelas while clutching a rose in his teeth.

The evening broke up at ten-thirty when Fred came home, bringing the printout of Sue's mountain range. Randy insisted on driving Kelly home, all of three blocks away. "I think I've made a match," Sue said as they watched his taillights dwindle into the darkness.

"Women," Fred said, but he said it kindly. "Why don't you leave well enough alone? Or concentrate on the husband you've already got?"

"It's only a quarter to eleven," Sue said. "I'll toss you for first crack at the shower." And they locked the door and turned off the porch light.

The land and sky were now very dark indeed, and the only light came from some of the growing things, the little crystalline fruits of the stoneweed that crunched under the horses' hooves with a sound like tiny bells, and the white shapes out on the black lakes that shone like great water-lilies of illuminated milk glass, and the campfire-reeds that grew in big rings like mushrooms. And the little glowing thistledowns that followed Amalia wherever she went.

These had appeared first, only half a dozen of them, on the day after they had seen the rishi. They hovered round Amalia's face at first, like moths round a candle flame, but as the hours wore on they descended to cluster around her breasts. "Like bees seeking flowers," Ulf said. "They sense the sweetness of your flesh. But you need not fear them; they will do you no harm. Those are the soft ones."

"There are hard ones, then?" Amalia asked. "What do they do?" But Ulf made no answer. He had shown great alarm, almost despair, at the first appearance of the things, but he would not discuss them further. Hour by hour they gathered, and swarmed around her, till she was cloaked from head to foot in a halo of soft light. She could not touch them; they darted away before her hands like fireflies. Gently they touched her lips and her throat and her breasts. At any moment she could shake a dozen of them out of her skirts, and when she dismounted they swooped down under her hems and drifted slowly upwards under her robes, touching her body softly like butterflies' wings or the shy kisses of a ghost. This did no good for her peace of mind or body; but otherwise she found the things comforting, as though something were taking care of her. (But caring for her with what purpose?) Her only fear was that their light would draw attention to their presence on the road.

"We've already attracted attention, I'm sure of it," Ulf said. He had become despondent, and he no longer troubled to urge her to turn back.

Sue stood in her kitchen at a few minutes after seven, eyes closed, running through lists in her head. Fateful Friday. The air was full of the smells of cooking, but nervousness had driven away Sue's appetite. All the recipes had been field-tested, and Randy (pointing out that the original meaning of "butler" had been "the man who pours out the bottles") had insisted on picking all the wines. He and Kelly were out in the living room, checking out the last-minute details. They had solved the problem of dress by going out and buying fabric and constructing a dress and matching shirt out of wine-colored jersey. Kelly's dress looked decorous and competent under the organdy apron, and Randy's shirt had a Russian collar buttoned up the side with little crystal buttons. It didn't look like *Upstairs, Downstairs*, but it looked good. All that was lacking was the hostess, who was hiding out in the kitchen in a fit of panic.

The doorbell rang, and she heard Randy saying, "I'll get it. You go get the sherry." Kelly came into the kitchen and looked Sue up and down.

"Well, you look great," she said, "if you'd stop being so scared. Come on, they're going to bite the crown roast, not you."

"Does it show?" Sue asked feebly.

"Let's say, if I had another two minutes I'd put some blusher on you. But no time now. C'mon, lady, pull your socks up and go out and meet your guests."

It was the word "lady" that did it. Sue took a deep

breath, pulled Amalia around her like a protective cloak, and went out to do her duty.

"Hey, it's *The Golden Stair*," Terry Carmody said. "I like the Pre-Raphaelites, they've gone so far out they're coming back in again. I didn't know you were a Burne-Jones fan."

"I don't know yet if I like *him*," Sue said, feeling as usual that you could say anything in front of Terry. "I know I like this."

"Where are they going?" Chris Bingley asked, trying to squeeze in between Sue and Terry.

"Your guess is as good as mine," Sue said. "Down to the Hall of Flowers to give a concert. . . ."

"Or back," Terry suggested, "after the concert, back home for high tea. Look, it's late afternoon, and singing's thirsty work. Oh, thanks," he added as Randy deftly changed their empty glasses for full ones. Bingley drained his in one gulp, and Randy caught Sue's eye and drifted discreetly away.

After a while it became easy. The wine was good, Siobhan and the Carmodys kept the conversation moving along, those guests who were too dull for conversation could concentrate on the food, and Randy kept a stack of Mozart on the phonograph all through the dinner. The pork was crisp, the stuffing savory, the eggplant rich and creamy; Chris Bingley had worn his white jacket again, but Terry Carmody had honored the occasion with a real dinner jacket with satin lapels and black tie. The evening was a success. Sue began to relax, quarter-inch by quarter-inch.

The causewayed road had risen to an unguessable height, and now it formed a bridge that stretched across a wide river. Amalia's attendant lights were reflected faintly in the dark water, between drifts of the floating white lilies.

"Where are we?" Amalia asked.

"Mmm?" Ulf said, raising his head like one rousing out of a dismal dream. "This place? When the sun shone on it, this river was called the Kendal, and these waters beneath our feet were the Fords of Murion."

"Murion?" Amalia said. "That place is still remembered in song. There the knights stood off the Lord of Darkness, while the people fled across the shallows, after the fall of Andarath, and there the King's son Aumery fell, the last of the royal line."

Ulf snorted with contempt. "Do they say so?" he said. "You must not believe everything you hear." They began to descend the eastern slope of the bridge, into a darkness unrelieved even by flowers. "You are now closer to Agniran than to Tevrin," he said. "Lady, I hold you to witness that I did what I could to keep you from this place."

"No one could deny it," Amalia said. *But if he had been set to bring me here, what better way could he have chosen, to stiffen my back and shore up my resolve, than to bid me at every mile to turn round and go home? How well does this man know me?*

"Ulf," she said after a dozen breaths, "what happens to the lilies when they drift out to sea?"

There was no answer, and she turned round in the saddle to look for him. In the dim light from her flittering companions, she could not make him out. "Ulf?" she called again.

Silence, and now her lights began to rise from about her and drift away, like leaves in the wind or birds that suspect the hawk. Behind her, on the bridge, she heard a faint pattering sound, like running hooves upon the soft stoneweed. "Ulf!" she cried, but to her Sight five shapes appeared, three small figures like Shadowlings and two shapes as large as men, mounted on great cats eyed with fire. Across the bridge at the gallop they came, while Amalia waited in the darkness, not daring to flee in any direction. She heard Pathfinder scream, once, and then a flat shape like a cloak of seamless leather caught her up and wrapped her close, cutting off air and consciousness together.

Sue sat decorously at her dinner table, watching the candles burn with a little shifting flame. Beyond them, a shape moved, and she blinked and brought it into focus at Kelly, standing behind Bingley and making urgent faces behind his back. *Smile!* she mouthed, and Sue smiled, and Kelly leaned forward and put the croquembouche on the table, tall and noble with its little rivulets of chocolate sauce. Randy stepped forward to pour the sweet golden wine, and the little bubbles danced in its depths. Tiny sparks, dancing in limitless darkness.

CHAPTER 7

The Bottom of the Well

"Your dinner went great," Fred said. "I don't know what you're so depressed about."

"Just reaction, I guess," Sue said. Amalia in the darkness, carried along on the back of something without a name. "I worked hard on it, and it did go well, but now I'm tired. In fact, I think I may have picked up a touch of the flu."

"Don't give it to me," Fred said cheerfully. "Where'd these little cookies come from? They're good."

"Leftovers," Sue said. "I had Siobhan over to tea again, since it's Tuesday, and she brought over Mrs. Stone, too. At this rate I'll soon be having regular Tuesday afternoon At Homes, like my great-grandmothers."

"Fine," Fred said. "I'll sing them a chorus of 'I'm My Own Grandpaw.'" He picked her up off the sofa and led her into the bedroom. He fed her a couple of aspirin, tucked her into bed, and turned off the light. Then he crawled in beside her and made love to her with such gentle but persistent enthusiasm that hardly anyone could have helped feeling better.

"You're smiling," he said presently, peering at her in the moonlight. "You can't fool me. This is probably the best time to tell you that we need to give another party, say, by the end of this month."

"Oh, good God, Fred," she said. "*Another* party, *this* month? You'll have to bribe me with something better than a roll in the hay. How about a trip to Europe?"

"Take it easy," Fred said. "This one'll be bigger, but simpler. I want to throw a bash for the people in the Computer and Camera Department, for having had the top sales this quarter. If it were warmer, I'd make it a barbecue, and even in October, they'll probably spill out into the back yard if it isn't raining. Anyway, all you need to provide is beer and hamburgers and stuff. No champagne, no Mozart, and Bingley won't be there."

"We can probably do them a little better than just beer and hamburgers," Sue said, warming to the idea against her will. "But how *many* people? Where are we going to put them?"

"Only about thirty," Fred said. "Just as well Computers and Cameras won the prize, and not the hundred-and-fifty people in Housewares."

"Thirty people, yeah, they'll fit," Sue said, "if I do a buffet and let them all balance their plates on their laps. And Randy can play his guitar, and if it's Mozart, they won't know the difference."

"Wonderful, how they've held up," Kieran said to Michael the Red. It was one of the bright warm days of late fall, false summer they called it; and the transplanted farmfolk were plowing, and sowing cabbages and wheat. They sang as they worked, the women beside the men—though already many of the wives were begging off and lying abed in the morning.

"Peasants are tough," Michael agreed. "I could have told you that."

"I could have told *you* that," Kieran said. "I'm a peasant myself."

"How well you conceal it," Michael remarked. "You ride like a nobleman and you give orders like a Captain. Perhaps your father—"

"Not that I've ever heard," Kieran laughed. "And I still hold a sword like a salmon-gaff, you said so yourself. I've been working with Teel of Hudelsford, though; now, there is a canny fighter. He's been showing me some of the tricks his lot used, to keep the Shadowlings off their backs. If he could teach some of the other men, and we could learn to work as a group—"

"Do it," Michael advised. "We'll need them, before this bread is baked. I'll tell the Captain." Michael glanced back over his shoulder toward the keep, and sighed. "If he ever comes down out of the tower."

Kieran was staring into the east. "I wish the Lady hadn't left us," he said. "My girl misses her."

"We might see her yet, come spring," Michael said. Kieran shook his head.

"If Master Denis can't find her, then she's dead, or gone into the Shadow," he said. "And if she's gone into the Shadow, then I hope she's dead. Ha, there's Teel." He and Michael walked down the slope to meet the grim-eyed smith with the heavy hands.

The phone rang next morning, around eleven while Sue was shoving pans of bread into the oven. "Hi, Sue, this is Chris. Have lunch with me?"

"Gee, I suppose so," Sue said, holding the phone with one hand and trying to brush flour off it with the other. "You mean you're coming here?"

"I mean I'm taking you to the Pavilion," Bingley retorted. "Your kids are in school and your husband's doing inventory, and you have no reason to say no."

The hell you say, Sue thought, and said, "I suppose so. I can't go anywhere before ten to twelve, that's when the bread comes out of the oven."

"Fine," Bingley said. Sue hung up and surveyed the situation. The Pavilion was the classiest place in town: expensive, posh, and said to have exceptionally good food. Obviously the silk dress was called for. She considered the malachite beads, then put them back and coiled her French scarf into a thin rope to tie round her waist. She brushed her hair and put on a little makeup. *What am I doing this for? I don't want to* encourage *this turkey. I suppose I'm trying to look good enough for the Pavilion, never mind good enough for Chris Bingley.* The doorbell and the kitchen timer rang together, and she answered the door with a potholder in her hand. "Hi. Thirty seconds." She pulled the brown loaves from the oven, shook them out of their pans, and stacked each one crosswise on its pan to cool. "All set."

Bingley had been watching with open admiration. "I

think you're wonderful," he said. "Baking bread and programming computers too—that takes a very special person."

"Oh, I don't know," she said vaguely, not bothering to
correct his misunderstanding. "Siobhan is talking about a
database system for her PC, putting all her recipes online.
But I can't do that till Fred decides what kind of system
he's getting."

The Pavilion was dim and velvety inside, with soft carpets, soft seats, little candles flickering on the tables. If
Bingley had chosen this setting for its soothing qualities,
he had put his foot in it: the place reminded her of the
Darklands, and put her on her guard.

To crown it all, the headwaiter looked—no, he didn't
look like Ulf, not really, but he was tall and thin and
serious-looking. *But if that's Ulf,* she mused, *who is Bingley?
A Shadowling farmer, padding through the paddies? No,
he must be the beast that eats the fireweed, the one that
charges first and asks questions afterwards.*

"I love the way you smile." Bingley said when the headwaiter had stalked away (on long delicate toes?), leaving
them to contemplate the menu.

"I was thinking the waiter looks like a heron," Sue said.
*And you are a Darklander rhinoceros that eats cattails
and drops seeds.* And she opened the menu to conceal her
face. Fortunately, the menu was a large one, stiff and
showy in red and gilt. Unfortunately, it was in French. *And
to think I took two years of French,* she thought, *and it
might as well have been Egyptian for all I remember of it.*
But "boeuf" must be "beef," and "sole" was a fish, and if
she kept her mouth shut as much as possible she ought to
be able to avoid disaster.

"You're silent," Bingley said, which was so close an echo
of her own thoughts that it made her lower the menu to
look at him. He was fiddling with the tiny candle in its red
glass bowl, trying to fish its wick out of the puddle of
melted wax with a matchstick. "I never knew a woman
who could keep her mouth shut." He levered the wick
into the air, and both wick and matchstick burst into
flame, nearly catching his fingers. "That's better," he said.
"Soft lights are all very well, but I'd like to be able to see
you." Sue hastily looked elsewhere.

The waiter was returning. His frosty eye whisked over them, a little less disapproving it seemed of Sue than of Bingley. Perhaps her French scarf rated more Brownie points than his Midwestern tie. "Are you ready to order, madame?"

She glanced over the impenetrable menu once more. *Fall back five yards and punt.* "What would you suggest?"

Bingley started to speak, but the waiter said, "The sole Meunière is very good today." Bingley shut his mouth again. The waiter raised an eyebrow, and Sue nodded. "And for you, sir?"

"I'll have the same."

"Very good, sir. May I recommend a half-bottle of—" but Sue really was not up to listening to wine talk, not today. She would ask Randy for pointers later on.

Amalia had lost all sense of time in the endless dark. She had woken to find herself on the long back of one of the big cat-creatures, sitting sidesaddle before the rider. The animal was long and low in the body, with more joints in its legs than a real cat, and its pace was gentle. Its feet were very large, soft-padded, but splayed out and webbed, as if the cat's mother had had intimate knowledge of a gander. Its fur was soft, and its body was warm, but the air was cold and the land almost entirely dark.

It seemed they were out of the farmlands, or at least far from places where the crops gave off light as waste products. The dark river flowed alongside the road, a stone's throw to their right. Towards the northern horizon there was a dim glow over the ground, but not enough to see by. She could see nothing of the rider whose right arm held her in place, nor of his companion, and to her Sight they were masked and veiled in a web of impenetrable power. They seemed to be men; perhaps they were the Shadowknights she had seen from the tower keep of Telerath, so many nights ago. She had lost count.

She wondered idly whether they were still on the road. The glow of the stoneweed's tiny fruits had vanished, and the cats' feet would be silent on any surface.

But she knew they were still heading southeast, and she supposed their way led to Agniran. *I am going where I intended to go,* she thought, *perhaps by a faster road.* But she had not

planned to enter Agniran so openly, but to come stealthily
and learn what she could before acting. *And with what action?*
she asked herself. *I thought once that I could sneak in, find Andri,
sneak out again with him. Heavens, how simple I was.* The fact was
that no one had penetrated so deeply into the Darkness, none
that had ever come out to tell of it. No one but Ulf.

And what had become of Ulf? Very likely he had been
working for the Darkness all along, and the Shadowknights
had paid him off and sent him about another errand. Good
riddance, she should say—but she missed the only human
companionship she had had in this strange place, however
obscure and treacherous he might have proved to be.

But he tried to make me go back, she reminded herself. *But he
could have found no better way of making me go forward, and very
likely he knew it,* she answered. *O strange enigmatic shape of
darkness.*

The cats were climbing again, as if there were another
bridge beneath their feet. There were no lights, no shining
lilies, but Amalia sensed the river had spread out into a flat
sheet of water far below. As far as her Sight could reach, not a
leaf lay upon its surface, not a breath of wind disturbed it.

Now something began to sing, far off across the water: deep
and resonant, like the harsh-sweet voice of a harried mother
of giants. Amalia thought of a mother shouf crooning like a
great-bass shawm to its babies. If shouf had babies.

Presently another voice began in a higher range, cold and
sweet. It might have been a bird, or a few birds, perched in
the lilypad trees and chirping over the fields of sparkweed.
The nightingale sang last night, the ballad went, *On the branch of
the gallows tree*— But there were no trees, no fields, and no
living thing but themselves between the bridge and the horizon.

They rode onward through the music, a soundscape of
unseen creatures. Still the water stretched out on all sides in
the darkness, empty but for the few gentle ripples, tracks of
creatures invisible even to the Sight.

Something was rising up before them to the southeast, a
sheer smooth wall like a cliff. Smooth, nothing clung to it; it
could not be stone or the stoneweed would have attacked it.
Their path led directly toward it, toward an irregularity in its
blank face that resolved itself into a gate. The gate of Agniran.

Now, when there is nothing I can do about it, Amalia thought, *now, I learn what Ulf might have told me at the outset. I could never have come unseen to Agniran. The watchbeasts would have been aware of me, and sung my way to the gate.* And this last realization, which made no practical difference one way or the other at this stage, plunged her into the very bottom of the dark well where despair was. She pulled her hood over her face.

"Sue? You okay?"

"Oh, sure." She became aware that Bingley had been speaking for some time, and that the waiter had returned with their lunch. "I'm sorry," she said, "I was wondering whether I'll have time to make cookies this afternoon. I don't think I will, but it's no matter. I have some in the freezer."

"You really are a surprising woman," Bingley said. "Cookies, computers, anthropology, mathematics, and you don't look like a professor, just a beautiful, beautiful girl. I remember the first night I met you, everyone was milling about like a herd of steers, and you were standing there like a gazelle, so fresh and cool. . . ."

Be modest, Marianella prompted. *It's all illusion.*

"It's all illusion," Sue said. "We were building up to a thunderstorm, as I remember, and everybody was sweltering."

"You weren't."

Sue said nothing, and turned her attention to her fish. The sole Meunière turned out to be sautéed in butter with a lemon sauce, and the wine the heron-man had chosen for it was light and fragrant. *But watch it,* she told herself. *If you got smashed with this guy around, all sorts of things could happen. None of them pleasant.*

Inside the wall there was light once again: glowing mounds lay here and there at the side of the dark structures. Middens, Amalia realized: piles of garbage thrown out by the city-dwellers, slowly decomposing into fertilizer and light.

There were no individual buildings, houses or shops or palaces, such as one might have seen in a city of men. Instead, the ground was covered with great tubes of the same smooth stuff as the city wall, tubes that coiled apparently at random upon the ground, like worm castings or the shells of the caddisfly. But she could tell they were hollow, because occasionally one opened into a doorway through which the Shadowlings were emerging.

She remembered what Ulf had said about the different castes of the Shadowlings. Here, in the citadel of Darkness, would these be the warrior caste?

Whatever they were, they did not behave like men. Plainly she was a very uncommon visitor, but where a crowd of men would have shouted, shaken their fists and spat at the enemy in their midst, these only gathered along her path and whispered. Their eyeless faces turned to follow her as she passed. Their small mouths whispered constantly, like wind in the grass. Here and there the tubes turned upwards suddenly, like mushrooms, and opened out into low-rimmed platforms, crowded with more of the Shadowfolk. These were smaller creatures, some only just able to peer over the parapets. Nurseries? Schools? Hatcheries? Cadet barracks?

There were no streets, but there were open spaces here and there. Some of them connected into paths that wound between the tubes, tracks just wide enough for one cat to pass. Their path twisted and turned, switching back on itself and passing under coils that rose off the ground like bridges over a canal. Yet they were steadily working their way into the heart of the city. A shape was becoming apparent before them, a structure of coiled tubes like the rest of the city, but raised up in itself, turn upon turn, sprouting into balconies like strange flowers and towers like tall poisonous mushrooms. Here was the heart of Agniran, the citadel of Imber, Lord of Darkness. The city looked as if it had been, not built, but excreted, as perhaps it had been. Amalia held her head high, not acknowledging the whispering attention of the little Shadowlings, but she felt increasingly weary and sick. *What waits for me here?* she wondered. *Death, or a dark cell to moulder in? Little do I care, if only I can lie down and rest.*

"It's getting late," Sue said. "Quarter to two already; I'd better get home." They had finished the sole, and the wine (or Bingley had), and the Pavilion's justly infamous walnut pie. Even after Sue had pulled her attention away from Agniran—with all the determination of one who has been burrowing in the freezer for the last package of peas and will *not* go on till her fingers get warm again—she did not feel like talking. Neither did Bingley, it appeared, for he simply sat and stared at her.

"Okay," he said, "okay, I'll take you home."

"And before that I'd better find the ladies' room. That pie was sticky."

The ladies' room was large, and lined with red cut-velvet wallpaper like a Victorian bawdy house, and at this hour of the afternoon it was empty of human life. Her face washed and her other needs attended to, Sue stood for a long moment staring into the mirror. Hers was not a beautiful face however you looked at it, least of all under these fluorescents. She looked neat and respectable, even upper-middle-class, but no sane man would make a sex goddess out of her. *No, what it comes down to, and I must not forget it, is that he still thinks he might be able to push me around. Some people take a lot of convincing.*

Right, Marianella said. *You might not think it, but I have had troubles of that sort, growing up a servant in a great house. I had no real difficulty, because I always had her Ladyship to appeal to. If I wanted to. Now, you, if I found you had decided to want to go to bed with Christopher Bingley, I should send for the exorcist, I beg your pardon, in your world it's the little men in the white coats. If you really want to cuckold your husband, I give you leave, so long as you find someone worthy of your attention.*

Bingley was waiting for her in the hall outside. It too was deserted except for themselves, its walls blank but for a public phone and the decorous little doors marked *Mesdames* and *Messieurs.* "Hi!" Sue said. "Are we off?"

For a moment Bingley didn't answer. Then he took her by the arms and backed her up against the wall and started kissing her. "Sue, my God, Sue, I can't stand it," he murmured.

Neither can I, Sue thought, but with an entirely different meaning, and bent her head, digging her chin into her collarbone till he could get no closer to her mouth than the corner of her eye. "Stop it," she said between her teeth, and when he stopped it she said, "Mr. Bingley, I am a respectable married woman and not something you picked up at the drugstore. Also my heels are not round at all. You think being a district manager gives you *droit de seigneur?* Take me home right now."

Perhaps it was the "Mister" or the French, or the look in her eye. At any rate Bingley dropped his arms quickly, and said again, "Okay, okay," and led the way out the front door and into the parking lot. He opened the car door for her, he closed it for her, got in on his own side and put the key in the ignition. "I'm sorry," he said.

"I'm glad to hear it."

He guided the car out of the parking lot and into the street. His driving left something to be desired, because half the time he was looking at her (stealthily, out of the corner of his eye) instead of the road. It was nerve-wracking, but she set her teeth and did not comment. They were halfway home before Bingley asked, "What's *droit de seigneur?*"

"It's where the lord of the manor was supposed to take all the peasants' wives to bed."

"Oh." He digested this. "And did they?"

"According to what I've read, no, they didn't. It was a story invented in the Renaissance, when they wanted to get away from a medieval way of thinking. The way people in the twentieth century would sneer at the Victorians. It was the same Renaissance writers who called the medieval churches 'Gothic,' meaning crude and barbarian."

"I guess I fell for you the first time I saw you," he said. "Maybe it's just a matter of good taste. You're such a different sort of person from anyone else here. How'd you come to marry Fred? Where did you come from originally?"

"Wrong again," she said. "I was born and grew up right here in Liberty Hill. And I married Fred right out of high school, because I loved him, and I still do. And I won't waste breath discussing your taste, but your judgment is lousy."

Bingley fell silent again, and returned his attention to the road. Sue allowed herself a very small, unobtrusive sigh of relief.

He pulled up to the curb in front of her house and set the handbrake. "Sue, I love you," he said. "Do you believe me?"

"No, I don't. Thank you for lunch." She got out of the car without waiting for him to open the door, and went into the house.

What do you think? she asked. *Did I blow it?*

I don't think so, Marianella said. *You're still being the pure one to whom all things are pure. You had no idea he had such intentions. You're shocked and horrified, you're so full of righteous indignation that you said some things that . weren't polite. Your character is maintained. On the other hand, you must tell your husband all about this as soon as possible, and I don't know how he's going to take it.*

Fred will take my side of it, Sue said. *I think.*

The year was falling fast toward winter, and the days were growing short. "That's all right," Kieran said to Teel the smith. "By the time we run out of daylight to practice in, we'll be ready to practice at night."

"Probably," Teel grunted. "The rishi move fast, though. By the time you aim at them they're somewhere else."

"I am hoping that won't be a problem," Kieran said. "We don't have to hit dead-on with these things, just get near."

In the open field before the keep—a place full of rock and rubble, not fit even to grow weeds—several small groups of men were throwing stones at targets suspended from tall poles. Their aim was not so very good as yet, but they were working at it steadily. Some used short throwing sticks, or long sling-staffs, to lengthen their casting range. None touched the stones with his bare hand. Some used shepherds' slings, and these were the best shots, having had the most practice.

When a stone hit a target it spun it round like a windmill, and the marksman and his fellows cheered. Each team was made up of two or three men casting stones, partnered with a tall lanky youth with straw-colored hair. Seven strawheads: seven teams. "It's going well," Kieran said. "I wish we had more Helglings."

"With Helg gone to his fathers you'll find that difficult," Teel said. "When do you want to start night practice?"

"Whenever you have the stuff."

"Next week," Teel said.

Sue had not overestimated her husband. When she had told him her adventures of the afternoon, he simply said, "What a bastard. Do you think he'll give you any more trouble?"

"I hope not," Sue said. "He seemed to be willing to take 'no' for an answer. He talked a lot of garbage about love, of course. But if I wanted to believe that, I would be ready to buy the Brooklyn Bridge."

"Fine," he said. "But if he does show up again, please keep in mind that I never asked you to make it with Bingley to get me a promotion. I don't need it that badly."

"That's what I thought too." They smiled at each other, and Fred folded up the newspaper and dropped it on the coffee table.

"Oh, yeah, wait a minute," Sue said as they got up. "What about your party for the Cameras and Computers gang? Have you set a date for that?"

"A week from Saturday. That okay with you? And the Employee Relations budget is springing for the chips and dips and everything we can get from stock; all I've got to buy is the hamburgers and hot dogs, and the beer."

"*Everything* we can get from stock?" Sue asked, a gleam developing in the back of her eyes. "You mean I can go up and down the aisles with a list and a shopping cart and charge it all to Employee Relations?"

"If it's for the party, sure," Fred said. "What've you got up your sleeve? Maybe I'd better find out how much they're prepared to spring for."

"You do that," Sue said. "Mike, what do you think you're doing out of bed?"

"I had to go to the bathroom," Mike said with an air of injured innocence. "Why can't you buy the Brooklyn Bridge?"

"Because it's not for sale," Fred said. "Like your mother. Go to bed."

The moon was down, and a thin light cloud cover had shut out most of the starlight. Kieran crouched, back pressed against the rock that split the Medon and the Medufar, eyes and ears straining into the blank darkness. ("Haven't you even a *little* of the Sight?" one of the Helglings had asked him in exasperation. He had not. But he had ears, and a nose, and he had been exploring these rivers and woods all his life.) Just ahead of him was a cleft in the rock where a rabbit could hide, or a Shadowling even, but not a man. A man could hide his bow and arrows in it, though, and Kieran had done this during the day. Now, if no one had found them . . .

Below him the water surged around the rock, a modest muffled sound like ten or twelve men whispering together. The smell of the water was rich in his mouth and nostrils. Further off, a cricket chirped slowly—the air was damp and growing cold—and all the way across the river a nightingale was singing on the highest branch of a tall beech tree that Kieran had climbed as a boy. But the loudest thing in his ears was his own feet upon the gravel, the grating whisper of his leather jerkin against the rock as he slid closer to the cleft and his hidden bow. Another foot traveled, and his hand found the place where the granite cracked. He thrust his arm deep into the cleft, and his fingers touched the rough sinews that backed his bow. He smiled.

The bow strung, the arrows slung over his back, he turned his back toward the rock again. He took a pair of thin leather gloves from his belt, and pulled them on. The song of the nightingale was clear and brilliant in his right ear. The river murmured beneath him. He stood for a moment, taking earshot on his landmarks, being sure of his bearings. Then he bent his knees and leaped into the darkness.

The cool air whistled past his ears, and for a heart-stopping moment he feared he had misjudged and would fall into the river or worse, onto the rocks. Then his outstretched arms slammed against something hard, and before he could fall further his hands gripped the branch and held it fast. The supple branch bent under his weight, but did not break, and he hooked one knee over the branch and held on for a moment while he caught his breath.

Below, someone cursed under his breath, and the murmur of the waters was drowned out by the voices of indignant men. Kieran smiled again, and swarmed down the branch, down the parent tree to the bank on the far side of the river where his own team was waiting for him. Across the water came the sounds of indignation, and Teel's bellowing laughter. "Kieran, you clever bastard, I should've known better than to fight you on your own ground!"

"You owe me a quart of ale," Kieran called back.

"You won it fairly," Teel said. "Meet you at the water."

Now the dark woods were full of the sounds of people, rousing from under the shields that might have hidden them from the eyes of the Darkness and trooping down to the edge of the water. A light glowed briefly, and vanished again as someone shouted, "Cover that light!" On both sides of the Medon, the teams were assembling. Forty feet of smooth water, more felt than seen under the scanty starlight; somewhere far from shore a fish leaped and fell back with a splash.

"Arm," a voice whispered behind him. "They're bringing up the hoops." Kieran took an arrow, one of the strange arrows he had fashioned this morning out of Teel's "stuff." It was head-heavy, and he felt carefully for its balance before he set it on the string. Then he raised the bow, without drawing it, and pointed the arrow's blunt head into the middle of the air. "A little higher, and just a point to your left ... ah, up, up, shoot!"

Kieran drew the bow and loosed the arrow, and as it left the string its head burst into fire. A dull red glow for one heartbeat, a white fireball for the next, and then a flowerhead of brilliant sparks, red and white, high in the air above the river. By its light they caught a glimpse of a thin willow-hoop, thrown high and falling again; Kieran's arrow had not gone through it, but it had come close. All around them other hoops were flying, other fireballs cast by sling or staff to meet them high above the river. The brilliance was painful in their dark-adjusted eyes. All the fire of the stars had come down to earth, falling with steamy hisses into the river. One hoped the fishes had had the sense to dive for cover.

All too soon it was over; both sides had run out of hoops and fireballs alike. No one had been able to keep score, Teel's four teams against Kieran's three, and nobody minded. A cheer went up from both sides of the river. Dark lanterns were uncovered, bottles uncorked. Kieran sat himself on a mossy stone a few yards from the riverbank, and Sala the Helgling came to sit beside him.

Sala was the youngest of her family, born a scant dozen years ago when the Twilight was closing down on Hudelsford. She had the pale hair and long arms and legs of all her kin, and the great dark blue eyes that seemed not to see what was in front of them, to be looking always somewhere else. She knew most of what went on around her without looking at it; she had a little of the Sight, a little of the Voice, and like all her family she was a firestarter. The children of Helg the wheelwright of Hudelsford, the daughters as well as the sons:

each of them the core of one of Teel's teams, the heart of Kieran's strategy to throw light into the faces of the Darklanders. Sala drilled with Kieran's own team, and manlike he was sure she was the best of the lot.

"That was wonderful," she said. "I wish we'd had more firepowder, I was just getting warmed up." And she shivered.

"Don't let yourself get cold," Kieran said. "Where's your cloak?"

"Up the hill. I'm not cold." She sat down next to Kieran on the rock. "When do we get to go and really fight? When do we got back to the Twilight?"

"When the Captain decides it," Kieran said. "Or when they attack, if they do, and bring the Twilight here. I confess I'm in no hurry."

"Oh, I am," Sala said. "I'd like to go now, get our land back. I'm not afraid of the Twilight, I grew up in it. I never saw the sun till I came here. Though I'm not afraid of that either."

"Anything you are afraid of?"

"Only to be left behind like a little babe," Sala said. Her eyes seemed to flash, even in this dim lantern light. "I would have hated that. But you prevented it."

"I'm not the fool who's going to leave one of our few firestarters home milking cows when there's a war to fight," Kieran said. "Though if you were much younger I would have had to. I daresay even a little maid could have thrown fireballs from the curtain wall. It's a pity there are no more of you."

Sala shrugged. "It could be done. Just find Mother a new husband."

"What?"

"It's from her we get it, not from father. Didn't you know? No, you didn't. That's funny. You're a bachelor, Kieran, after all; if you want more little firestarters, you could wed my mother and beget some." She giggled. "Or Meredy, even. She's all of sixteen and would like to settle down."

"If I laid a finger on Meredy, Kai would bend me into a hoop and throw firepowder through me," Kieran retorted. "If anyone's going to start begetting little firestarters it's those two, though I hope they won't settle right in the middle of the war."

"Then there's the lads, only they're too shy to speak to women; the woman's got to speak to them. I shall have to put the word round."

They were silent for a moment. She moved closer to him, and he could feel her thin shoulders shivering. "You are cold."

"No, I'm not! Kieran, could you do something for me? Will you promise?"

"Not before I know what it is. I'm no such fool as I look."

She took a deep breath. "I'm tired of being a virgin, Kieran, will you lie with me?" And she bent her fair head, slowly, and laid it on his shoulder, as if the deed took much courage.

Good Heavens, no! was on the tip of Kieran's tongue. He bit it back just in time, and sat staring at the lantern, feeling like a clown who has wandered into the wrong play by mistake.

Was this his fault? Was it something he had said or done? Suddenly his life was filled to bursting with eager women. There were the village girls, of course, most of whom were his cousins, which made it difficult; and then there were the farmwives and their daughters and their mothers sometimes, yes, and even some of the army camp-followers who had approached him in broad daylight and suggested a special discount on their rates, just for him. He had said "no" to some, "yes" to others, and been confirmed in his opinion that none of them could hold a candle to Marianella. And no doubt he was an ungrateful rat to complain; but what seemed like any young man's delightful fantasy was downright embarrassing sometimes as reality.

Aw, poor baby, Sue thought as she loaded hamburger, buns, and another quart of pickle relish onto a tray. The late October weather had turned unusually mild and they were having the Cameras and Computers party outdoors after all. *Don't worry, kid, it ain't nothing you did. You haven't been leading them on. All you have to do is stand there in plain sight and be Kieran.*

"You'll probably knock me into the river for this," he said at last, "but you are too young. Even Marianella waited till she was fifteen. Her friend Susan was eighteen, and betrothed. Then there's our Lady Amalia, still a maiden at twenty-three, and there's no lovelier lady anywhere. Besides, what if I got you with child? How could you scramble down cliffs and up trees if you were carrying a little firestarter? Why, the war might be over before we could get any use out of either of you." Sala giggled again, and he began to feel better. "Now, I'm going to ask you to wait till you are fifteen, and the war is over. After that, why, it is my duty as your team leader to see to it you have what you need, eh? But I bet you'll have a man of your own by then, and won't need me." So he hugged her round her narrow shoulders, and smiled, and they got up and made their way back to the sea-keep. And all the way back Kieran thought, *I am using the same tongue to talk my way out of young maids' laps that I used once to talk my way in. Farewell, spring; farewell, youth. I'll never see nineteen again and I fear I'm about to settle.* But he thought of Marianella and smiled.

The party was beginning to come together, like well-blended Hollandaise. The guests had started out in little clumps, men here, women there, the men drinking beer too fast and talking about the World Series, the women clutching their elbows and not talking at all. Sue had had to make a half-dozen trips through their midst, breaking up the little clusters and mixing them together. She felt a bit like Ulf, setting the fireweed going—or maybe she was the Darklander rhinoceros now, crunching up the stems and mixing them thoroughly in its gut! She smiled at the thought, and Fred called from his place at the grill, "What's funny?"

"Tell you later." At any rate, the party was catching fire—not in a shower of brilliant sparkles like that last one, but with a steady warm glow that would easily last out the evening. And they had only had—she stopped by the refrigerator and calculated—about two beers apiece. Good; she didn't want her party's fire fueled on alcohol. There were only about two men there who could be counted on to drink too much; she and Fred would have to keep an eye on them, take away their car keys if need be.

Meanwhile, there was plenty of potato salad, chips and dips, hamburgers, hot dogs, beans, and coleslaw out there, not to mention the beer. There was also a huge green salad, raw vegetables for the dip, a platter of exotic pickles (but those were almost gone; she should have gotten more), and a cauldron of hot clam chowder—just to keep it a notch above your standard-issue cookout. And it wasn't time yet for the fruit salad, the cookies, the pound cake, and the gallons of hot coffee that would take the edge off the beer and send them all home.

She shut the refrigerator door and leaned against it. All of a sudden she was feeling awfully tired, and there wasn't anything for her to do at the moment. Maybe that was why. Her eyes itched and her feet ached. *Next time I'll have the wits to make sure Kelly and Randy aren't busy before I let Fred announce the date!* Nobody needed her at the moment. She went into the bedroom, locked the door, kicked off her shoes and lay down.

The nearness of the fortress was overpowering. Fifty feet tall? A hundred feet? She could not sense its top, only its towering height above her head, and its smooth bulk before her beat upon her like the heat of the sun on her skin—for her dulled brain remembered the sun now as an invisible source of heat, and the memory behind her eyes could not remember light any more.

So it was a surprise to her when the gate rose like an eyelid and showed them a long tunnel-like corridor with a glimmer of light at its further end. The three Shadowlings fell back, as if even that faint whiff of light was offensive to them. The two Shadowknights dismounted, and lifted Amalia down to the tessellated pavement, and allowed their cats to be led away. They closed up on either side of Amalia and guided her into the mouth of the tunnel. The gate closed behind them.

The tunnel wound this way and that through the fortress, like the path through a maze. Few doorways opened to right or left, and all of these were dark. The Shadowknights pressed on steadily toward the faint light.

The air was growing cooler and drier, a relief from the warm mugginess outside, and it held a faint fragrance, not quite that of flowers, but sweet, and like something out of the Lightlands. The light was growing.

There were sounds in the air, sounds like the ringing of deep gongs and little bells, and something that sang like a flute (or a bird?), and something that ticked and clicked like a cricket (or a wood block). If they were living things, they were happier, livelier creatures than she'd met anywhere in the Shadowlands; and if they were musicians, then she wished she might learn something about their music before she died.

Ahead of them the tunnel ended in a soft wall—or was it a curtain, or a screen, made up of long velvety ribbons that hung from the ceiling. Thin vertical stripes of light, red-tinged, leaked out between the ribbons. The light shifted and flickered, as if something were moving about on the far side of the curtain, and the Shadowknights halted.

The ribbons burst open, and instantly the light faded; the creature pushing through the curtain shook the last glimmers of light from its body like a seal shaking off water. It was smooth and supple, like a seal. It was the boneless, faceless creature whose handshee had confronted Amalia in her tower.

"Amalia, my jewel," its voice purred from the slit in its throat. "You've come to me at last."

"Not for you," the Shadowknights said, speaking for the first time and almost with one voice. Their voices were human, but no more than whispers. Hard to recognize a whisper, but Amalia feared she recognized these.

"No, not for me," the creature agreed, with something like sadness in its voice. "Not for you either, but for the Lord Imber. And he's waiting." It glided up to Amalia and laid its boneless hands on her shoulders. "Jewel of the poisonous West," it said. "May he have joy of you, and keep his talons off me the while." It slipped between Amalia and the Shadowknight and drifted off down the tunnel.

They led her through the curtain into a great hall, round-vaulted like a bubble or the interior of a snail's shell, large and echoing and very dark. Here they stopped again. Amalia's senses, revived by the cool air and shocked awake by the sudden reappearance of the boneless Shadowcreature, began to explore the place. A high smooth vault overhead. An open floor many yards across, smooth-paved, with here and there a mound of something soft, like a heap of grain or a pile of furs. Further on there was a double line of man-high pedestals leading off across the room, to where a shape rose against the wall. An angular shape, like a stack of stone blocks, the first square-edged thing she had seen in this place. It rose upward like a throne, and something was gathering and taking shape on it. And the light was returning. Far into the bowels of this fortress, deep under the cover of Darkness, a cluster of stars was beginning to shine high atop the throne.

Amalia glanced to either side, to the faces of the Shadowknights beside her. She saw what by now she had expected to see: pale-eyed Guiard, and Andri her brother, wearing the black spiky armor of the Darklanders. By now it was no shock to see them, only a great sorrow.

Many old stories made sense now, tales of valiant men swallowed by the Darkness dovetailing with tales of terrifying Shadowknights. What power the Dark Lord had over their souls Amalia did not care to speculate.

"Andri, can't you speak to me?" she ventured.

Her brother's eyes glanced toward her, and away again. "You wouldn't understand."

"It's hard for him," Guiard whispered. "Our Lord Imber's desire for you colors all that we see. For me—" for a moment his eyes seemed really to see her— "Amalia, for me it is what it was before, except that I can no longer escape in sleep. But Andri still remembers being your brother...." His voice died away.

The lights above the throne were growing in number, as if a bank of mist were drawing away from a starry sky. A hundred, five hundred starry sparks hanging in the air, taking a man's shape against the darkness, a shape with arms and shoulders and a glittering crown on its head. But there were no features in the oval beneath the crown.

How strange, and how marvelous, that the great enemy of mankind should be so beautiful, that the Lord of Darkness should be made up of light. *But light is a poison to these creatures,* she remembered, *it's like dung to them. So their Lord is a center of foulness to them, a source of poison in their lives. It must be hard for them.*

The shape outlined in stars raised its right arm (trailing a cloak of inky black fringed in light) and waved its hand in dismissal. Sparks scattered. Andri and Guiard stepped back. Their footsteps retreated, and Amalia knew they had gone beyond the curtain and left her alone.

The Lord of Darkness stepped forward, descended the steps of his throne. As he passed between the pedestals he stretched out his hands to either side, and two by two the dark tips burst into flame. Real flame: a thin oil burning with a well-trimmed wick, Amalia judged. Why would such things be wanted or needed here?

Between the last pair of lamps he stopped. Tall and dark

and shining, a shape of terror and power, the stars shining in his crown and about his body, he bent his head down to look at Amalia. Almost she could see a face, strong cheekbones and eyesockets, dimly seen in darkness, like the mountains on the dark side of the moon.

Here he stands, Amalia thought, *my conqueror and my doom. I am sorry about Andri, and about my people, and the last of the light going down under the Shadow. But I am tired; I cannot fight any longer; I am going down into death or worse, and all I can feel is to be glad that my destroyer is so beautiful.*

The dark figure raised its left hand to its starry breast, and took out a little vial of some deep red liquid. The invisible fingers unstoppered it, and held it to the invisible lips. And the bright stars took flight, drifted away like the soft lights that had followed Amalia across the Darklands, dispersed like a swarm of shining bees scattered by a tossed pebble. They expanded into the air and were gone. And the dark figure steeped into the light of the nearest lamp, and his face was the face of Ulf.

"I'm sorry," he said. "Lady, we have only a little time. The drink I took will dispel him for only a few minutes. Please believe me: if I had had my own will in this you would never have come here."

"Oh, I believe you," she said. "You're not the first I've seen who's not his own master. And I am too weary to care." But when he held out his hands to her in silent appeal, she took them in her own.

"Tell me," she said, "since we have so little time. How did I get into this? I never meddled in the war, not till I was dragged into it. Why was it me that he sought? Where has he seen me, even?"

"I saw you," Ulf said, "for my sins, and to my lasting regret. I walked through Tevrin under many names, seeking what I might find. I heard you spoken of, your wisdom and hidden strength. I went to Rhadath House and waited at the gate until I saw you, high upon your tower. And where I saw only your beauty, he smelt power, a power unknown perhaps even to you. He will have you for his use, through me, alas! and there is nothing—" he caught his breath, as if he had been struck; "nothing you or I can do—to prevent him. . . ."

He jerked his hands out of her grasp. The lamps were

burning low, their flames no brighter than red coals, as if something was choking the air out of them, and out of Amalia too. She drew breath with an effort. The crown of stars lay upon Ulf's brow, and his sorrowful face disappeared into the darkness that was his master. "Amalia, forgive!" he said softly, as if from far off. "I forgive you," she cried, but could not be sure he had heard. Imber was gathering like a storm cloud full of silver rain. The sparks of light that outlined him were more brilliant than all the hidden jewels of the real night, white and burning blue and fiery red.

Imber raised his hands, and the inky cloak parted to reveal a body full of light. A noble shape, a figure full of power, a cluster of stars in the form of a man. He grasped her shoulders, and his touch flashed through her cloak, through her flesh to kindle fire in her bones. He drew her to him. Lips that were stars burnt her with their kiss; arms that were flames bore her down to the ground; flesh that was light possessed her, not with one thrust but with thousands, each separate starblade piercing her like a single note of the great music that he was working upon her. And she knew the touch: she knew the hands within the flames, the lips beneath the stars. The light blotted out thought and memory; as she sank into its depths she thought, *This is likely to be my death. But if not, then I shall live forever.*

But I won't last out the evening, at this rate, Sue thought as she lay on the wide bed, listening to the random party noises outside the bedroom window. *And is that how Imber gets power over his Shadowknights? Somehow I doubt it; they seemed to be pretty straight. I suppose he matches the tool to the task at hand, and when in God's name is this party going to be over?*

"Great party, Fred," said a voice outside the window. Jerry Forrester's, she thought. Fine; Jerry was a hardened cynic and pessimist, and if even he was having a good time the rest of them must be ready to go up like skyrockets.

"Thanks," Fred said, "but it's mostly Sue's work. I just said 'party,' and she got out her shopping lists and made it happen."

"My sister sees her at the PTA," Jerry said. "She says Sue and her friend have just about turned the place upside down. She's turned into a real wheeler-dealer."

"Uh-huh," Fred agreed. "Want another beer?"

"I guess so. Doesn't it bother you, her going out and messing around in school business like that? Next thing you know, she'll be getting a job. And then she'll be 'too tired' to make it in bed. I say, keep the women at home where they belong."

"Now, you listen to me," Fred said. His voice was a trifle thick, and Sue could tell the beer had been taking advantage of him. "The first week she had all three kids in school, Sue got the house cleaned within an inch of its life. The second week, she took the PTA in hand. The next thing after that, she put together a party that impressed the hell out of the district manager, which might get me a better job than I've got. And let me tell you something else. Ever since the same time, she had been *fantastic* in bed. You wouldn't think it was the same woman. So I say more power to her, and if she wants to get a job she can get a job, and I'll drive her to her interview and buy her a briefcase. Where's that beer? There it is. And if she wants to run for Congress, I'll vote for her."

Amalia raised herself on one elbow, as best she was able; she was lying on a heap of soft dark little spheres that sank gently under her weight, but clung together like bubbles of foam on the surface of a brook. Overhead there was a sound like thunder, but not thunder, a deep musical rumbling that threatened at times to resolve itself into words.

The lamps were burning brightly again. A dozen paces away, scattered cloaks, boots, tunics lay dark on the dark floor; somehow Imber had snatched her body, and his body, out of their clothing and laid them on this bed of dark foam.

That body lay beside her, the shape she had learned to love so desperately. His skin was very pale, and his waist was long and narrow, and the flat thin muscles lay like lily petals along his bones. His dark head was pillowed in his arms. He had been weeping for a long time.

"It doesn't matter," she said. "Come; be comforted. I hadn't planned to bed down with the Lord of Darkness, it's true. It's you I wanted to lie with." She took a lock of her hair and dried the tears that streaked his face. "Whoever you are."

CHAPTER 8

The Enchanted Sleep

I knew it, I knew it, I knew it, her heart sang. *Or I should have known it, anyway. Amalia is a one-man woman; I might have known that all these guys would be him. Why didn't she guess? Put it down to lack of experience.*

"So who are you?" Amalia asked.

He raised his head a little, and sighed. "That would take a long time."

"Are you Zalmar of Northwater?"

"Yes, among others."

"Ruk lied, then."

"As he was under orders to do." The thunder rumbled overhead, the murmur that was almost words, and he sank back into the black bubbles with a moan.

Amalia dug into the foam and put her arms round his shoulders. "What is he doing now?"

"Ruk? I've no idea . . . oh." He turned over and stared into the dark vault overhead. The inky foam swirled around his hips. "While you were riding through this city," he said, "the autumn sun was shining high above the cloud cover, shining with a heat and brilliance that you perhaps remember. While you stood before him, the sun was setting in a lake of fire. Much of the cover has burnt off; it must be replenished. While we lay here, he rose out of this place, high above the world. Now he drifts overhead, making new clouds to preserve the Darkness and protect all that lives here. That is his thunder that you hear."

"When will he come back?"

"Not till dawn."

"Good," Amalia said. "That gives us time to talk." She sat upright and clasped her hands round her knees; the black foam adjusted itself beneath her. "Can't you look at me?"

He glanced at her, and away. "You are too fair. Remember that my eyes are accustomed to the dark." Then bitterly, "How can you bear to look at *me*?"

"I love you," she said. (Now he turned his eyes toward her, warm dark brown eyes full of disbelief and despair.) "And I want to know your name."

"A long time ago . . ." he began, and let his voice trail off. He stared up into the darkness for several seconds. Then he said, "I was Aumery, the King's son of Andarath. That was my name. So you see that you must not believe everything you read in the epics."

"You mean you didn't fall in the battle of the Kendal. Were you there at all?"

"I was there," he said. "I was there, and fighting for the Lord of Darkness. I was the first of the Shadowknights. I do not *think* I slew the King my father, but I have never been certain."

"The ballads say the King was struck down by the Shadowknight," Amalia said, "but history records that his horse reared and fell on him, and that he died of a broken back in his own tent, the next day. Not an easy death; but not your doing."

"It's all my doing," Aumery said.

"Then you were there from the beginning," Amalia mused. *Which would make him over two hundred years old. Not that I care.* "You remember the days before Imber came into the world."

"I remember that Imber came into the world through me."

"That's the second time you've said that. What did you *do*?"

Aumery drew a deep breath and let it out in a sigh. "North by west of here, in the foothills of the Weatherwall, there is a pass called the Notch of the Kendal. Do you know the place?"

"Only by hearsay. The spring that feeds the Kendal rises there, it's said, but the walls of the gorge are so steep that no one can walk there, and the spring has never been traced to the source. It's all under the Darkness now anyway."

"Only under the dim Twilight," Aumery said. "The creatures

of Darkness fear to go there. And when I was a boy there was indeed no way to enter there, for the gorge is steep, as you say, and the only path between the sheer walls of stone is the water's own channel. That was only a little stream, clear and very cold, that ran out of the mountains into the Downs, to join with many other streams to make the Kendal River. And the water was sweet, and men said it had a virtue to cure headaches, and sleeplessness, and sorrow.

"Men also said that there was some strange thing at its source, something mortal eyes were not meant to see, and so the place had been made inaccessible to men. And because it was so, no one had ever gone up there to look.

"Then, in the spring of my twentieth year, the stream dried up. Word came to the King my father in the palace in Andarath, where we sat in the garden, under the great plum tree. There the sun shone, and the birds sang in every branch!

"My father's counselors searched the archives, and found no mention of another time the spring had run dry. They feared it meant some evil thing. And the King sent messages to all his knights, calling them to attend him in Andarath at midsummer, when he would hear all their counsel and determine what he should do.

"But I was young, and proud, and impatient, and I had no desire to wait till midsummer for a council, till next year maybe for anything to be done. I saddled Garwin, and in my pride and folly I told no one where I was going, but rode alone into the north.

"In the foothills I found the streambed, and it was dry as they had said. The hills were green, with drifts of flowers white and gold along their flanks, but there was a shadow over the place, as if the sun had gone behind a cloud. But there was no cloud, only a thin haze high overhead. I rode along the streambed, smooth pebbles filmed with dust. On either side of me the walls of the gorge rose higher, and the sky became a narrow ribbon overhead, ever a deeper blue, and the air grew cold. I climbed shallow stone steps that had been waterfalls, and crossed rockfalls that had been rapids, places so rough that I had to dismount and lead Garwin by the bridle. And at last I came to a place so steep that no horse could climb it, a ladder of stone smoothed by the falling water. But there were still handholds, and leaving Garwin at the foot I climbed up the stone face. The mist deepened overhead, and when I reached the top and climbed onto level ground, I was surrounded by fog. The ground was thick with frost, and treacherous underfoot. And above me the gorge widened out into a little valley, and there I saw a building without walls, only white pillars to hold up its roof. Even in that dim place it shone, and the fog poured out between its pillars to fall and freeze upon the ground. It is the House of the Mists, Amalia."

"That place! The resting place of heroes in the morning of the world. But a living man would lose his soul if he set foot in there. You did not go in?"

"I like to think I should have had better sense," Aumery said. "But it was not left to me to choose. As I stood there staring at it, the mist round about me began to move, as if stirred by the wind. But there was no wind. For a moment I saw, or seemed to see, a pair of glowing eyes—and then it swirled round me, it pounced, like a snake upon a mouse, and overwhelmed me.

"I thought, I can't breathe. But I was breathing. I could not speak, or move, but he moved me. I walked deeper into the mist, or my body did, and it grew very dark around me. But ahead of me was a deep red glow, and presently I came to its source. It was a small thing, no bigger than a hazelnut, hanging in the air in front of me, glowing red as blood. It was the Heart of Imber.

"Do you remember, or has the tale been lost in the centuries, how the cruel wizard Kasthei chanted his heart out of his body to keep it safe?"

"I remember," Amalia said. "He hid it in an egg, inside a golden bird, and set the bird in a tree of thorns, inside a great castle—"

"On a mountain of glass, surrounded by a lake of fire," Aumery finished.

"But the hero got the thing anyway, and when he took his sword and pierced the wizard's heart, a thousand miles away the wizard dropped down dead."

"So would Imber fall, if the Heart were broken at his feet," Aumery said. "But Imber has surpassed Kasthei. My hands took up his Heart and carried it out of the darkness, onto the plain. Then the mist all blew upwards as if with a sudden gust of wind, and I saw the House, fair and shining, carven out of the living rock, and the mist pouring out from between its pillars. And I walked toward it. I set foot on the steps, walked between the pillars into the forbidden place, and laid the Heart down in it. And at first I did not realize what was happening to me.

"I went out of the House again, and stood on the plain outside. I raised my hands above my head, and through the circle of my arms a dark wind blew, and on the wind flew the fathers of all the Darklanders. Shadowlings on rishi-back, carrying their young and bundles of seeds; spores, larvae, little dragonets. Through me they poured down into Demoura, to grow and multiply under the growing Darkness, to take Kerkerri and Markland and push their way down into Andarath itself. I followed after them, the vessel of Imber.

"And now I realized the change that had been wrought in me. I had gone into the House of Mists a prisoner in my own body. I came out of it a prisoner *outside* my body. From inside the House I watched myself walk away. What was said is true: a man who trespasses there gives up his soul. Mine is still there."

Amalia leaned over him, eyes wide in horror. "But you're *here*. You're speaking to me!"

"A part of me," he said. "My body is here, and the animal spirits that move it, and it does some part of my will, when not overshadowed by Imber. I can send forth its accidents and appearance at his bidding, or when his attention is elsewhere. Thus I rode with you as Ulf, or with your brother as Zalmar of Northwater, and let the Shadow into Telerath. I have walked in Tevrin as his spy, and led his battles, and I have been Hodur, and Arkiel, and other names that you would know if I named them. And still I stand removed from myself, a soul prisoned in the House of the Mists, frozen in ice. And his Heart lies at my feet."

Amalia brushed her fingers across his lips. "Can you feel that?"

"Of course I can feel it."

"Good," she said, and bent down and kissed him. After

a moment his arms rose and curved round her, held her close with a strength born of desire and despair.

This was the place she had longed to be: in this man's arms, his fingers soft upon her skin. In this dark and evil place they had come together, each finding in the other a spark of light and warmth. They fitted so well, not only in body but in kind. A woman with the strength and courage of a man had found a man with a woman's endurance under hardship and capacity for love. As his body filled her body's needs, so his loving kindness fulfilled her spirit, warming what was cold, cherishing what was storm-battered, illuminating what was dark. He made her aware of herself.

But—as the man had said, his soul was elsewhere. Amalia, with no experience of her own, had known but little of the solid bond, stronger and deeper with time, that grew between a wedded pair with the Sight. Even less did she understand the complex relationships that linked the warrior-wizards of Hellsgarde. But even a virgin with the Sight must have a vague idea that lovers among her kind experienced something more than the simple coupling of the flesh.

But the flesh was still new to her, and his touch set her blood on fire. His last penetrating thrust exploded within her like a bursting star, and her awareness fragmented like a starshell. Her mind, unable to reach Aumery's, spread outward like ripples in a pond, and for a few brief moments she felt and loved every living thing in the fortress, from the smooth-skinned, golden-voiced musicians seated at their gongs, to the boneless creature shivering in its cell, and the smallest Shadowling wallsweepers playing at odds-and-evens under a table.

"You never did that before," Fred said.

"You complaining?"

"Hell, no."

At last they lay quiet again. The lamps were burning low and dim, but Amalia could see that he was smiling. "Do I please you?"

He lifted his hand to touch her cheek. "You are my heart's core, the only thing I love. But I smile because I have an idea. I'm going to get you out of here."

"Without you? I won't go."

"You shall go," he said firmly. "I won't have you staying here to face him. But we have till moonset, when the shouf rise. Stay here till then." The music began again, clear ringing tones like great bells, or drops of water falling in a green rain forest where every living thing is fresh and new. Aumery's long fingers brushed Amalia's hair away from her face, and brought her head to rest in the hollow of his shoulder. "Just Heaven," he murmured, "let me never forget again what human skin feels like."

There is a lot to be said for lying around in bed with your own husband—not doing anything in particular, just resting the head on the shoulder and marking time. There is even more to be said for having an extra hour to do it in, such as happens the morning they switch off Daylight Savings Time. By lifting her head just a trifle, Sue could peer through a lock of Fred's hair and catch sight of the clock on the bedside table. Seven forty-three, it said. She let her head drop and tried to get her memory out of neutral. *Did we set the clock back last night? No, we did not. So it's really only 6:43, we have lots of time.* She snuggled closer, and Fred held her closer and said "Mmmm . . ." into the top of her head: affectionate and all that, but not anything like awake. *Amalia has her man—under whatever peculiar circumstances—and I've got mine.* She reached up and touched the "snooze" button of the clock radio. At this hour they would be playing some nice quiet Bach or—

"While Brunnhilde is sleeping in the magic fire," said a dry British voice, "the progression of chords that represents the workings of Fate is turned in on itself—" A piano played two chords, repeated over and over. *Oh damn,* Sue thought, *it's the opera lecture on delayed tape.* "When Brunnhilde is awakened, she sings, 'Long was my sleep,' and the suspended Fate music is repeated. Then, as she sings, 'I have awakened,' the music begins to move forward again, suggesting that fate is again at work." *Cheers.*

"Next, the third act of *Siegfried.*" Fred rolled over and pulled the pillow over his head.

The music rose up like a storm, quick and urgent. Riding music, it sounded like—she had no idea what *Siegfried* was supposed to be about. But this was music for a desperate ride across wild country, a ride into danger

with deadlier danger at the back, under a black sky loud
with thunder.

"Now," said Aumery. He leaped to his feet (the black foam
surged like a wave of the sea) and strode across the floor to
the pile of garments Imber had left behind them. Amalia
followed. "You are going now—here are your boots—and I
will have no argument."

"Very well," she said, so meekly that if he had known her
better he might have taken warning. He led her across the
room, blowing out most of the lamps as he went by them, and
picking up the last out of its stand. He stopped by a curtained
doorway, and gave her the lamp. While she held it, he stepped
through the curtain—to protect, she supposed, some unhappy
Shadowling from the worst effects of the torchlight—and
spoke briefly in the whispering Shadow tongue. Returning, he
led her into a tunnel whose mouth opened behind the throne.

Perhaps the Shadowlings had never invented staircases—or
perhaps some Shadowcreature that frequented the place could
not climb. The tunnel coiled upward like a vine, round and
round, gaining perhaps twenty feet with each slow turn. Aumery
climbed it eagerly, half-running like a youth, dragging a bewildered Amalia who soon became short of breath. But before
she must call a halt, he stopped and led her out onto a
platform that was open to the dark sky.

Overhead the sky was black as pitch from horizon to
horizon. Below, the wasteheaps of the city glowed like piles of
rotten fish. The air was still and warm, with a closeness that
in the Lightlands would have meant a thunderstorm. "I saw
you first," Aumery said, "leaning from a terrace such as this,
but bright in the morning sunlight. It was Midsummer's Day,
and the streets of Tevrin were full of people, dancing with
roses in their hands. But I was seeing troops and fortifications,
looking for weaknesses. For you know, I think, that Imber
plans to take Tevrin in the spring. I walked among them like a
ghost, seen but unremarked. The flutes, the roses, the fresh
salt wind passed over me untouched. Then I looked upward,
and it was as if there was a second sun in the sky. One strand
of your hair shone upon the wind, like a flash of sunlight on
a gull's wing. Your arm made warm the stone parapet it
leaned upon. I saw, and I knew I loved you.

"Once I should have climbed the stones of Rhadath House

to reach you. But that was long ago, and my soul lies frozen in stone in the House of the Mists. I could have held your image in my heart forever, never daring to come near. But Imber saw you through my eyes, saw something more than your beauty and your grace. Some power he saw, and something more: a strength of will that, if it were channeled, could perhaps resist Imber himself. If I had such strength, maybe, Imber would never have gained entry into this world."

Amalia laughed. "I've often been told I'm a stubborn, obstinate woman, but never so pleasantly."

"Perhaps he meant to destroy you," Aumery continued, "or worse, to use your strength for his own. But he shall not do it. This once I will defy him."

"What will he do to you?"

"Nothing, my heart, that he has not done before. He cannot kill me; I am his foothold in this world. Here is your horse."

A soft-footed Shadowling emerged from the archway, leading Pathfinder with her eyes blindfolded. Each seemed to dislike the other's smell, and the horse kept dancing and tossing her head, and the Shadowling ducking and shying away from her hooves. Aumery took the bridle, and the Shadowling hurried away. He checked the saddle-girth and the stirrups, and the buckles on the saddlebags. "You have provisions for four or five days," he said, "and that should be enough, till you come into the Lightlands again. Go back to Telerath, Amalia, and stay there. There he cannot reach you; great ones have made their fortress there, whose power will last your lifetime. Live there in peace, beloved, and if you can, remember me." He lifted her and set her on Pathfinder's back, and put the reins in her hand.

Amalia did not speak, but she bent down and kissed him many times, like one making provision for a long journey. "My dear love," he said, and stepped back. Amalia pulled her hood over her head, and set her feet in the stirrups. She felt a shifting overhead, as if the featureless darkness had broken loose from the vault of heaven. And with no more warning she was seized from behind and lifted into the air.

Her hood blew back onto her shoulders, and the wind whistled in her ears. Pathfinder screamed in terror, and all Amalia's skill was occupied for some minutes in gentling and reassuring her. The horse's body was wrapped round by two long shapes like leaves, or fingerless hands, that held her suspended beneath a velvety membrane stretched wide above their heads. Amalia had known the shouf were large, Aumery had given some warning; but this must be a very captain of flyers, and its wingtips stretched almost out of sight in the thin haze through which it flew. It was all velvet black on its undersurface, all creamy white above, and its mouth gaped open to strain the motes of its food from the air. And close behind the mouth, between the roots of the gigantic wings—Amalia's thought probed, delicately—yes, there was its dear tiny little brain, with room for only one thought in it, the thought Aumery had set in it before they parted. *Fly straight into the west as far as you can, and leave your burden atop a cliff where you can pause and set it down gently.* Probably he had had in mind that cliff above the Caramath, where she had paused so long ago and looked across the river into the wall of Darkness. Amalia smiled, and gave it a new command: *Fly straight north until I tell you to stop.* The shouf leaned into the wind, and banked and turned.

(Far away, in the high tower room at Telerath, Master Denis turned over in his sleep, and smiled.)

For the first time in many hours, Amalia remembered her brother. Poor valiant Andri, who had met a power greater than his own, and Guiard who had loved her, now thralls of the enemy of light.

Shadowknights. The annals of Tevrin and Hellsgarde were full of them, though there had only been—how many? eight, ten?—in the two-hundred-year history of the war. Each had appeared out of nowhere and without a name, led the forces of Darkness for a time, and disappeared again without any man having counted a blow against him. Whatever powers the Dark Lord had given his Shadowknights, Aumery's unending life was not among them—to their benefit, Aumery would have said.

And there was nothing Amalia could do for them. She turned her mind to the task at hand. Far beneath her, the darkened landscape was passing swiftly by. Tessellated farms and settlements were thinning out, giving way to high rolling hills covered with fireweed and asphodel, patches of glimmerwort, and at last even tufts of real grass.

The air was growing colder, blowing out of the west with the scent of hail on its breath. Her skin prickled, every small hair standing on end. Pathfinder whinnied uneasily, and then a gust of wind took the shouf under the wing and sent it up a thousand feet, keeled over on its side like a galleon in a gale. Amalia had enough to do to keep Pathfinder on the near side of panic, without trying to soothe the shouf's anxieties; fortunately, it seemed to have none. It turned its big feathery jaws into the wind with the stubborn endurance of a dog in a cold rain, and banked its wings to send it north again. It was used to flying, after all; though not perhaps through thunderstorms.

Once Amalia had stood in the highest tower of the Hill House, watching and listening as the thunderheads boomed and crackled together in the sky. Then the slate-colored anvil shapes had built up above her head; now they were all around her, a mass of boiling turbulent moist air that if it rose much higher must toss them out of the cloud layer altogether, into sight of the stars. Ah! And into the sight of Imber? *Down!* she told the shouf, and obediently it plunged over the brim of the wind into the bubbling soup of gale and rain below.

It's all right, perfectly all right, Amalia insisted. *We are running, running with the wind.* Pathfinder shivered, and tucked her feet under her. Her opinion of running with the wind, if it could have found words at all, could never have found decent ones. Fortunate that her eyes were still covered.

Amalia could see only fitfully with her outward eyes; billows of cloud like inky seas under the brief light of distant lightning bolts. To the Sight it was all bubbles and swirls of hot and cold air, dry and damp, and the dangerous contrasts of electrical charges between earth and sky. She could not even tell how high they were any more, but the shouf seemed to know where it was, and it was still heading north.

Crack! A jagged arm of lightning reached up from earth to heaven, close enough for a whiff of scorched air to reach Amalia's nostrils. At this sudden attack of light the shouf jerked its wingtips upwards, and fell head-downward with a silent scream of pain. Amalia felt the shock of the fall, not in the pit of her stomach as the poets liked to say, but in her groin: a touch less welcome than Aumery's, less alien than Imber's. She wrenched her mind away from the memory. They were now only a few thousand feet above the ground, and the rain was falling on them in torrents. She coaxed the shouf, still whimpering in her mind, to rise a little higher. Even in this turmoil it could probably detect a hillside or cliff-face in time to keep from plunging into it—but there was no harm in being sure.

Ahead of her, a pale glow was developing upon the air, telling her that the Shadow was thinning out, the sun was rising, and the great Weatherwall was before her.

By the time the sun was fairly up, the granite roots of the hills had broken through their grassy covering and were pointing sharp-edged fingers into the sky, and the shouf was in distress. Its white back reflected the worst of the sunlight away from it, but it was taking in diffused light from the air and reflections from the granite, and its gill-baskets were wheezing like bellows with increasing irritation. Clearly Amalia must descend and let it get away as quickly as possible.

There was a scarp in front of them and a little to the west, where a huge dome of granite had split under the uneven stresses laid on it. Half had fallen in splintered rubble into the valley below; half had reared its head into the sky. Two ravens were wheeling in the air high above it, till suddenly they caught sight of the shouf and decided their own best interests probably lay in being somewhere else. There must be powerful updrafts above so great a cliff, enough for even a shouf to hover long enough to set them down. She guided the beast's tiny attention in that direction.

The shouf curled its wingtips inward, delicately, just enough to reduce its lifting surface, and slowly drifted downward toward the rim of the cliff. Like a butterfly laying an egg, it set them down. Once Pathfinder's hooves were firm on the ground, the shouf released her, spread its wings, and rose on the updraft. Amalia urged the horse forward; she took a few steps and stopped still, shivering. So Amalia dismounted and led her forward by the bridle, well away from the cliff's edge.

The disc of the sun had just cleared the topmost layers of Darkness to the east. (Imber had returned to his fortress by now. What had he found, and what he done? Amalia thrust the thought aside.) The world lay spread out below her eye, hundreds of miles at a glance. To the south the hills tumbled downward into once-fertile lowlands, now hazy under the Twilight. The dry streambed that once had been the

source of the Kendal traced across the land like a thin grey
pencilmark. To the north, the narrow valley cut upwards
through the mountains, rising even to the level of the great
half-dome where she stood. Behind her, the thin grass was
crisscrossed with the trails of deer and mountain sheep, leading up into the heart of the mountains.

The mountainside was beginning to waken under the sunlight. Real plants spread their leaves to catch the light; real
birds peered out from under their wings and began to twitter
like penny-whistles; real animals, lizards and bugs and ground
squirrels, started about the business of making a living. It was
such a pleasant change from the lives of the Darklanders, who
had no internal clock and seemed never to sleep at all.

Amalia would have liked to sleep herself, for the sun was
warm and she was weary. But no chance for that; she had a
long way to go and no time to waste. She reached for the
stirrup again, and stopped. There, a dozen feet away; there,
under the half-shelter of that spur of rock—

Any Lightlands animal as dead as this would have reeked of
decay, and the white bones would be showing through the
rags of flesh. But the rishi had no real bones, and there was
no smell of corruption. The flesh was crumbling into dust
under the rays of the morning sun, and every little breath of
wind carried away a drift of grey powder. That was all. Little
was left of the rishi but the tough membrane that had covered its belly and wings. And beneath the membrane lay a
huddled Shadowling.

Amalia stepped closer and considered. The Shadowling was
still alive, shivering and ill as a man might have been after a
night in a snowstorm or a day on a featureless desert. The
membrane was wearing thin under the onslaught of sun and
wind, and soon it would begin to let the light through. The
Shadowling's thin-fingered hands clutched at its head, as if
the light hurt it where a man keeps his ears.

What could she do for it? Was there a cave anywhere near,
where it could hide? Not atop this chunk of granite, surely.
She searched upward. Yes, the shouf was still within range,
high above her, circling to gain altitude. She called it down
again. While it descended, slowly and reluctantly, she wrapped
up the Shadowling in the remnants of the membrane. It
whimpered when she touched it, and she thought it would

probably die anyway. But she bundled it up and gave it into the tentacles of the hovering shouf, and sent them away into the East. Maybe its fellows would be able to cure it; maybe Shadowlings ate their sick and injured, like termites. She could not help it any further.

She brushed the fragments of dead grass from her knees, and looked up to see Ulf standing there.

"Amalia," he said. "You should not have come here."

"It's you who should not have come," she said.

"I told you to go back into the West and live out your life. Do you think you can match your mortal strength against the power of Imber?"

"Whatever I may think," she said lightly, "Imber thinks so."

"You don't know what you are doing!" he cried.

"You're mistaken," she said. "I know exactly what I am doing, and I don't think you can stop me. You are only a handshee."

There was no answer. He was gone. The wind whistled over the granite, through the short tufts of grass. The last crumbs of dead Shadowlife had blown away. She mounted into the saddle and found a path that led down the rounded slope of the granite dome, a path that crept along the mountainside till the dry cleft of the Kendal rose to meet it.

Now, like Aumery and Garwin two hundred years before them, they must climb through the rough channel cut by the vanished stream. A few scrubby bushes had taken root among the rocks, but the sand and gravel was too clean, almost sterile, for much life to live on it. Most of the granite had been worn smooth by long centuries of flowing water; only a few great boulders had fallen recently enough that their edges were still sharp. Amalia dismounted near one of these at midday and they rested in its shade to eat—a bit of bread, a bag of grain—and to drink some of the pure, tasteless Darklands water from their waterskins. Then they went on.

The sun passed over their heads from east to west, and the sky was red by the time they reached the base of the last cliff. This had been, once, a waterfall sixty feet high. It must have been beautiful when the water ran, falling in a long stream through the shining air or breaking on outcrops of rock in a halo of mist. But now it was dry, and the air was dry and very cold.

I'm strong, Amalia reminded herself. *I'm obstinate*. And if Aumery had been able to climb this cliff, it stood to reason that she could too. (But he was a foot taller than she was, and his arms and legs longer in proportion. Never mind.) There were plenty of rough places and projections to put hand or foot into, and the rock was dry. It was growing dark, but never mind that either; the Sight could tell her where to step as easily in the dark as in the light, and she was anxious to be finished. She poured out more water for Pathfinder, and tucked the skirts of her gown up round her knees. Then she took hold of an outcrop of rock and began to climb.

At first it was surprisingly easy. There were plenty of places to catch hold, and she made it halfway up the cliff before the light died. After that it went much slower; there were still places to catch hold, but they were cold as ice under the fingers. Several times she had to pause on a foot-wide ledge or boulder and blow on her hands till they could feel again. The plain above her head drew nearer, and she sensed that it was even colder than the rock where she clung, covered with ice and white under the moon. She set her elbow on the parapet, found a new setting for her foot, and heaved herself up onto the plain.

The moon was only a few minutes from its setting, but under its light the whole plain glittered as if encrusted with diamonds. Every rock wall, every boulder, every dead twig was coated with ice.

The House of the Mists was free of ice, and it too shone under the last rays of the moon. It stood near a vertical wall of rock, almost touching it, as if it had indeed been carved out of the solid granite. It did not look like a house that people would live in; a temple, perhaps, or other public building that no one slept in, with no need of keeping out the cold. Smooth white pillars rested on a platform of four or five steps, and held up a shallow pitched roof. From between the pillars the mist poured out, and condensed on the rock all around to freeze into another layer of ice. Perhaps this explained where the source of the Kendal had come from—and the freezing cold explained why the stream had gone dry; no water remained liquid long enough to flow down the cliffs. But what explained the cold? Some spell of Imber's? It did not really matter; she knew what she had to do. She drew her robe closer round her, wishing it were heavier, and crossed the plain to the steps of the House of Mists.

Inside it was entirely dark. There were shapes to be sensed, more pillars she thought, and some larger blocks of stone whose purpose she could not guess. She gathered up her courage and stepped inside, took two steps over the polished floor.

And went blind.

Far away in the tower keep of Telerath, Master Denis sat bolt upright and cried, "Amalia! Ai, ai, she's gone!"

And after that, Sue had to get up and cook breakfast.

CHAPTER 9

The Eye of the Storm

Now what do we do? Sue asked as she washed the breakfast dishes.

I don't know, Marianella said. She had been up most of the night, soothing Master Denis back to sleep. Hot milk and herbs had failed in their purpose, and she had finally poured a cup of aquavitae down him and left him to sleep it off. It had been raining since before dawn, and still the drops dripped from the tiles, ran along the gutters, and puddled in the courtyard. *I know what you should do. It is raining here and will soon be raining there; look out the window—you need to go to market and get that raincoat her Ladyship told you about, the one that is suitable for better than a pig-killing.*

And the phone rang. "Sue? Siobhan. Are you free today? Something's come up and we need to talk."

"I was going to go downtown and get a raincoat," Sue said, "but I can fit that in sometime else. What's happened?"

"Some kid was playing on the bleachers yesterday afternoon; his foot went through the plank and he fell through."

"Good God!"

"Fortunately, he only fell three feet. Scraped his shin. But I think you and I need to take a personal look at those bleachers. Maybe the school really does need a new gym for safety's sake, in which case—"

"We have to forget about the computer room. You're right, of course. Darn it."

"The other thing is sort of at cross-purposes to that,"

176

Siobhan said. "My dad was in the construction business, and when he died some of his people went to work for Shafer. I've got eyes and ears in Shafer's office, and one of them thinks Shafer's up to something. She thinks he's thinking of spending maybe a hundred thousand on the gym and telling the IRS, say, five. You follow me?"

"Oh, brother."

"So we need to talk, and we need to look at those bleachers. I have a class from nine to ten and then I'm off till three. We can get your raincoat and have lunch and look at the bleachers and generally put our heads together. Okay?"

"Sure."

"You know Cardwell's has a branch of Burberry's now? On the fourth floor. That's the place to go if you want a *real* raincoat, not just a cheap plastic imitation.'"

"Gosh." Even Sue had heard of Burberry's, the original trenchcoats, all hung about with straps and D-rings so that you (you being a British army officer in World War I) could hang your binoculars and grenades from them. But they must cost an arm and a leg. "I don't know—"

"Oh, come on," Siobhan said. "They've got a little nook on the fourth floor and you step inside and think you're in England."

Yes, Marianella said firmly. "All right, I will," Sue said. "I'll pick you up at the college at ten." If you couldn't lick 'em, you could join 'em with grace.

Amalia rose to hands and knees, stumbled to her feet and clutched her robe round her. The stone was cold and clammy, and her hands were numb. The House was dark, pitch darkness not relieved at all by the little glimmer of moonlight outside. She could see the outermost row of pillars, outlined against the moonlight, but none of the pillars inside. But that was ridiculous, any Seer could see in the dark. But she couldn't. Panic took her, and she put her hands to her head and screamed.

The echoes of her scream rolled through the House, hollow and cold. Like a wave of the sea the sound rippled against the stones, falling back into a muddle of damped-out wavelets in the shallows. She saw them, dimly lit, falling into ripples around her feet, where the cold hovered like a vulture

over the smooth stone floor, where her body stood screaming like a wild animal. Come, she must do something,
the echoes were a disturbance in this quiet place. Did she
still have anything to do with that loud-lunged body
across the floor? It appeared she did. . . . She caught her
breath, covered her mouth with her hands, let the sound die
down around her. She looked round, and still saw nothing.
But over there to her left, maybe twenty feet away, *herself*
stood, seeing and unseen. Ah, it was what Aumery had said.
Her soul was taken, frozen solid in this place. And had she
expected anything else? Could she have held out when a
great-hearted hero had fallen victim? Never mind; she must
carry on as best she might. And if her prisoned soul could still
see. . . .

She considered the layout of the place. Before her
visible feet there was a pair of columns with a structure
like a table between them. Lines of power curved round
that point, like dark twisted rainbows. Yes, *there*. . . .
Upon the flat surface something shone dully, a darkness
less than absolute. *There, before you.* Amalia took a step
forward, another, and stubbed her foot against the base of the
block in front of her. But now she could see something, a
faint reddish light radiating from a small object in front
of her, an egg-shape, smaller than an egg. The Heart of
Imber.

She reached out and took it in her hand. It was neither
warm nor cold, and very light in the hand, as if it were empty
inside. And that faint reddish light. It made her uneasy to
look at it, and she tucked it into a pocket of her robe. She
watched herself turn away and stumble toward the outside, and then looked up. Aumery; Aumery's spectre
standing on the other side of the pillared hall, frozen like
herself. Only his eyes lived, dark in his pale face. Amalia
turned back between the pillars to look at them: nothing. His
shadow and her own, prisoned souls invisible to her mortal
eyes. There was nothing she could do there, and she turned
back and started to pick her way across the frosty ground. It
was harder now for her to keep her footing; dependent upon
her eyes, she could not *know* where the hidden pits and
hollows lurked to twist the foot.

Amalia. It was not sound, and it came painfully slowly,

more laggard than speech. *My beloved. Forgive me that I am glad to see you here.*

I am too, she projected across the cold, still room. *I wish we were closer together. If I had taken those two steps to right, not left! But it can't be mended now.*

Your outer part. Will she not fall from the cliff?

I think not. There is still moonlight outside, she can see the cliff's edge. Perhaps she should wait till day?

But in Amalia the panic still lay close under the surface, and she would not remain on that open moonswept plain any longer. And it was very cold; she had not noticed before how cold, but now her teeth were chattering and her whole body shaken with uncontrollable shivering. Twice she fell in the snow, breaking her fall with her left arm while her right strove to protect that deadly, lightweight burden in the fold of her robe. What if the Heart were broken elsewhere than at Imber's feet? Would that destroy him in any case, or make him safe forever? She had no way of knowing, and only one chance to find out.

She followed her own footsteps in the frost to the cliff's edge. Because of the angle of the westering moon, the cliff face was in darkness. But there was no point in waiting; it was going to be darker before it was lighter. She turned her back to the cliff and knelt on the edge, awkwardly felt for the foothold in the rock. Lower, lower still, till her tendons threatened to crack, fumbling across the smooth stone with her booted toe. *There.* She lowered herself onto it, and found the place beside it for her other toe. For one moment she looked again at the House of the Mists, white and cold and stainless in the last rays of the moon. Then she slid down the rock away from the sight of it, and found her next foothold.

It was not as difficult as she had thought it might be, not at first; she no longer had the Sight to find her the hand- and footholds, but they came readily to her grasp. Fear still lay heavily at the pit of her stomach, but it was dull and unfocused, not enough to make hands shake or knees buckle. Common sense would have expected a tired woman with neither light, Sight, or experience in climbing to have fallen to her death almost at once, but somehow she clung to the rock's cracked face and lowered herself inch by inch.

They entered Cardwell's by the Center Street door,

since that was where Sue found a parking place, and made their way through the menswear department, between tall piles of shirts folded as neatly as morning papers. Cleancut salesclerks in immaculate cuffs went to and fro around them, preparing for a sale scheduled for next week. Sue made a mental note; if she didn't blow her wad this week . . .

The elevator was one of the standard automated variety, with lighted telltales and heat-sensitive floor buttons; but its walls were lined with mirrors and its ceiling subtly textured.

They stepped out of it onto the fourth floor of another world. The Cardwell building, constructed in the late 1960s before energy shortages, was all steel and concrete and glass; but the Burberry shop was paneled in pale golden wood and had Oriental rugs on the floor. On the wall before them hung a dozen prints illustrating the works of some nineteenth-century author— Dickens? Yes, there was Ebenezer Scrooge telling the messenger boy to go and buy the turkey as big as himself—and the air smelt of civilization. It looked like the entrance hall of a Stately Home of England, or perhaps Alastair Cooke's parlour on Masterpiece Theatre. The raincoats began in the next room, neatly lined up, sleeve to sleeve, like the regiment awaiting the colonel's inspection—some of them with binocular straps on the shoulder.

Between their ranks a woman was approaching, a sleek elegant blonde wearing a dark brown tailored dress with a silk scarf twisted through her collar. "Good morning," she said. "May I help you?" Her voice was cool, and she reminded Sue a little of a dog or cat sizing up another of its own kind, to determine who was to be top dog (or cat)—and a little of Mrs. Stone.

"I think so," she said. "I want a raincoat with just enough insulation that I can start wearing it now and go on wearing it into the beginning of the snow season."

"I think we have what you want," the woman said. "Will you come this way?"

That's right, Amalia said. Pure swirling mist making icy lace upon the pillars, leaf by leaf. *She's nothing but a human being, trying to earn her living; you are the higher-ranking, so you must show her courtesy. That's all it takes.*

Sue tried on five raincoats, delicately insulated under their tartan linings, and the third one was the right one. Crisply tailored, sleek (but not plastic-shiny), it made her look two inches taller and as though she had just stepped off the evening Concorde from London, and it cost sixty dollars less than what she and Marianella had agreed was the most she could afford. So she bought an umbrella to go with the coat, and put it up over her head and Siobhan's as they stepped out of Cardwell's into a torrent of rain.

It must be now near dawn, and the wind had sprung up. Hundreds of miles away, at the mouth of the Caramath perhaps, a little breeze had risen, that ruffled the whitecaps on the waves and the sleek feathers on the sea gulls' backs. Further north, along the edge of the Twilight, the moving air made the dim grass ripple like wheat, and stirred to wakefulness the last few birds on the trees. But here in the dry gorge of the Kendal there was nothing for it to stir but a little sand, and nowhere for it to blow but up the narrowing channel, like the spout of a funnel or the nozzle of a blacksmith's bellows; no gentle breeze but a sharp-edged inquisitor, it howled around Amalia's ears and blew sand into the back of her neck. Her eyes, blind with stinging tears, could not tell if it was day or still dark. Her hands were numb. Her toe groped downwards, found a crevice; but when she put her weight on it the rock gave way. Her feet scrabbled against the rock face; her fingers clutched and slipped, and she fell: fell three feet and landed with a breath-squashing thump on the drifts of sand at the foot of the dry channel.

"There's where the kid fell through," Siobhan said. It was just before noon; the eleven o'clock gym class had been sent off to get dressed and the lunchtime crowd had not yet arrived, and the two women had the gym to themselves.

The building dated from the early fifties; there was a plaque on the wall outside the main entrance, dedicating the place to the memory of the school's alumni who had fallen in World War II.

Before I was born or thought of, Sue thought, *or Siobhan either.* But the building seemed sturdy enough; it had been maintained with innumerable coats of pale gym-green paint and a new set of daylight-colored fluorescent lights sometime in the seventies. Someone had managed to keep the hardwood floors reasonably smooth, and a great variety of colors in the frost-painted windows showed where a long series of broken panes had been replaced promptly with whatever color was available at the time. The place seemed admirably sturdy; and yet there was that hole in the bleacher seat, with a pair of orange traffic cones set out to try to keep the curious away from it. They crossed the floor to get a closer look.

The wooden plank that formed the seat had been, not simply broken, but wrenched backwards, and a long splin-tery corner broken off to leave a three-cornered hole. It looked a lot more like deliberate damage than accidental; still—

"Hi, Mom!" and "Hi, Mom!" she heard at either side: Kathy at her elbow, and on the other side of Siobhan a tall boy with his mother's bright hair even further brightened, like a radioactive carrot. They made introductions, Sue's Kathy and Siobhan's sixth-grade Sean, and invited them to go about the business of eating their lunch. But of course whatever the parents were doing was more inter-esting than any business of their own; and if it was none of their affair, so much the better. They settled down beside their mothers on the bottommost, or unbroken bench, and began to unwrap their sandwiches.

"What brings you here?" Sean asked chattily, "and would you like half a peanut-butter-and-bologna sandwich?"

"No thanks," Siobhan said with just a slight shudder. "I'll make 'em for you, but I draw the line at eating them. Anyway, Kathy's mother and I are going to go out and have lunch. We wanted to take a quick look at this broken bench, and see if there are any more bits around that are likely to collapse."

"Aw, shit, there're hundreds of them!" Sean said cheerfully.

"Watch your language! Please," Siobhan said.

"Sorry, Mom. I declare by the Great Horn Spoon and the twenty-four nostrils of the Twelve Apostles—is that OK?"

"It's borderline. Go on."

"—that half the benches in this gym are ready to go the way this one did. It isn't because the wood's gone bad—not mostly, at least—it's because the nuts've come off. Can you see from here? I guess it's too low. Look up here!" Ignoring protests from both mothers, he scrambled over the broken bench and under the one above it. "Look under here. See where this support dingus is? There's supposed to be three bolts on each corner, holding the plank to the supports. Only the kids fiddle the nuts off while they're sitting here, and then they lose 'em. After a while the bolts work loose, and when all three bolts are gone then the plank is loose on that corner, and then you can rock it. You gotta have something to do while you're sitting here watching Silver Hill lose its fourteenth game in a row, right? And when you rock it, then the bolts on the *other* corner work loose. And so on and so on. This corner broke off because it hadn't anything under it and because it was being walked on by Petey Vanderhof, who is not exactly lightweight." He finished his last bite of lunch and crumpled his paper bag into a compact lump. "Watch this, underhand." He tossed the lump under his left elbow in the direction of the nearest trash can. It missed by six feet.

"Pick it up," Siobhan said. "You know of anything else around here that needs fixing?"

Sean looked thoughtful. "The hot water in the boys' showers is never hot enough," he said, "but I thought they did that on purpose. I'll make a list and let you know. You going to report it to the PTA?"

"Something like that," Siobhan said. "Go pick up your bag."

"The hot water in the girls' showers doesn't work either," Kathy said. "You want me to make a list too?"

"Yes, please," Sue said. "Only keep quiet about it; we don't want to make a big fuss."

"We'd better get going," Siobhan said. "We want to meet Miss Anderson at twelve-thirty."

Amalia got to her feet. One elbow had struck a stinging blow against a pebble and was still humming with pain, but (a hasty rummage in her pocket with her good hand) the Heart of Imber was undamaged. It glowed richly in the near-dark, the color of fire, the color of blood. It seemed to pulse softly, like a flickering lamp or a demon star; it drew the attention. She averted her eyes and put the thing back in her pocket, and settled down with her back to the wall to wait for the sun to rise.

Now that she had gained a little distance from the House of the Mists, strangely enough, she had lost the feeling of being split in two. Instead, she felt that just as her body, huddled in its cloak, was wrapped round in the shroud of night, so within her heart the House of the Mists stood, cold and beautiful, and herself within it.

And the whole thing inside my head, Sue finished. *I am beginning to feel as many-layered as an onion.*

The dark sky overhead lightened by slow degrees. Staring into the mist for minute after minute, she could see no change, but if she closed her eyes and opened them again the sky had paled a little: a few more drops of milk in the dark soup. Gradually the rim of the canyon became visible, deeper against a scarcely paler dark. She rose and took a few steps away from the foot of the cliff, looking upwards into the hills. Rank upon rank they rose, clean curved line above line, each ridge paler than the last with mist and distance. Crushed onyx, and behind that charcoal, and then slate, and wood-ash, and paper-ash, and milk, and pearl: she counted seven ranks of hills before they faded into the sky, the unguessable peaks of the Weatherwall, their snowy tops not to be told from the clouds. No man had ever climbed them; none knew what lay on the other side.

And the pale light poured in through the mist, touching the marble pillars, the crystal floors, the strange murals on the walls—all of them obscured beneath the sparkling leaves of the frost. Amalia's footprints were still visible upon the floor, and the smooth place where her warm hands had snatched up the Heart of Imber. Amalia looked into Aumery's eyes and smiled in her heart, but did not speak. Just as well that she could still conceal her thoughts from him.

The sun must have risen now, far to the east of the Darkness, and the mountains took on a color of pale rose. They were made all of the new granite, and flecks of mica glittered across their sides, and their snowcaps blushed like a bride in the dawnlight. Above her head Amalia could see a line of brilliance, the very rim of the crystalline frost peering over the edge of the cliff. As she watched, a single drop separated from the edge and fell, changing shape and glittering through the air, to land with a tiny plop!, a mere whisper of sound. It left a little fingermark of dampness on the sand.

At last she could see Pathfinder, standing a dozen yards away, eyeing her nervously. As she approached, the horse backed away. "Come, Pathfinder. It's all right." But she still backed away, till she came up against the wall of the gorge and could go no further. The white of her rolling eyes flashed in the half-light, and Amalia approached at a snail's pace, hand cautiously extended.

Does she no longer recognize me? Have I changed so much? Do our horses truly have the Sight, as it's been said? Surely I look the same, smell the same.

Now she became aware of sounds overhead: some small thing, or many small things, were whistling through the air, invisibly, like gnats. Not close in around the ears, though, but a few feet overhead. What could they be? Some Shadowbeast that she could no longer see? Something that could live in light, as flies live in dung?

Pathfinder tossed her head, and rolled her eyes again at the strange things in the air, and Amalia took the opportunity to move in quickly and take hold of the bridle. She stroked the smooth damp plane of the horse's jaw and murmured soothing noises, while she sorted through her memory of the Darklife, creatures she had seen and creatures she had been told of. Nothing seemed to fit. Ah well, new Shadowthings cropped up from time to time, particularly when—ah, and Aumery had said, had he not, that Imber was planning a new offensive against Tevrin in the spring? "Come, Pathfinder. Let's be on our way." She could not mount yet, there were too many banks of stone and dry rapids to be crossed; she took a better grip on the bridle and persuaded Pathfinder to turn and pick her way down the gravel slope.

Pathfinder needed no great persuasion; she wanted to get away from the things overhead. But they followed, whistling faintly through the slowly brightening air, never getting too close and never showing themselves to the mortal eye.

"Basically, I'm a sneaky person," Miss Anderson said, and let a few drops of milk fall into her second cup of coffee. She did not look like a sneak; she was a small, dark, sleek-looking woman who might have been designed by Agatha Christie to be Colonel Bantry's housekeeper or Miss Marple's lady companion. Her dark eyes were downcast: shy, not sly. But she was Shafer's secretary, and Siobhan's private wire into his office. "I suppose it takes one to know one," she said, and speared a tomato out of the heart of her salad. "I know Shafer's pussyfooting, because I pussyfoot myself. I'm curious to the point of nosiness; wherever I am, I want to know whatever's going on there. And I can't find out what Shafer's up to, which means he's been hiding it very carefully."

The cafe where they had met was a far cry from the Pavilion: brightly lit, waitresses in ruffled aprons, the walls stencilled with cute little girls with watering cans. Tables, chairs, and menus were all plastic, and the food was too. If a secretary wanted to meet a few fellow-conspirators with no fear of being seen by her boss or her boss's friends, here was the place.

"Do you mean—this sounds silly," Sue said, "—do you mean he's keeping two sets of books, like in the movies? One for himself and one for the authorities?"

"He easily could be. I seldom see any of the financial records, and in any case I don't speak accounting. I can't recognize a dirty deal from a glance at a few figures. Pity. I suppose—" she looked thoughtful "—I suppose it started last year when he let his accountant go. I don't mean he *fired* him; he said he couldn't give him a raise, and the accountant, who was a good one, went out and got a better job elsewhere. Since then Shafer's been doing his own bookkeeping; claims he can't afford another accountant. But he pays his workmen union scale, which is a bundle, and he gave *me* a healthy raise. Either he thinks I'm not very bright, or else it's some of the very best butter."

"What's he going to do if he gets audited?" Siobhan said.

The secretary shrugged. "Maybe he is keeping two sets of books, and thinks he can bring it off. I don't know. But I can tell he's concealing his wholesale materials costs, and his stocks on hand, and his net worth. And I wouldn't trust him as far as I could see him, and I'm very nearsighted."

They fell silent while the waitress set their sandwiches on the table. "I haven't any children of my own," Miss Anderson remarked. "Just the same, I would really hate for Shafer to build a piece of schlock and somebody else's children get hurt in it. So I'll keep an eye on him, but as I said my eye's not trained to spot a dirty deal either in the books or out in the yard. I think you're going to have to find some special talent."

Below the last dry waterfall, Amalia mounted and rode south. The Weatherwall shone behind her, white in the sun, blue and purple like a bruise in the shadows. It would light her way south, halfway to Hellsgarde perhaps.

Before she had gone more than a few miles, a little stream came flowing down out of the foothills on her right, and another, very pure and clear, out of the Twilight on her left, and now the Kendal had water in it again. It foamed and gurgled over the stony bottom. Every stone was a different color. Every grain of sand was a different color; she had never seen these things until she lost the Sight! She guided Pathfinder to the western bank. Here the moss was smooth, unmarked by any hoof for hundreds of years, and it was the color of emerald. A few long-legged waterflies danced over the rippling surface of the water with rainbows in their wings; a little golden sweat-bee nosed its way out of its hole in the bank and buzzed importantly away.

There was no other sign of life; but the Shadowthings whistled and hummed overhead. Pathfinder quickened her pace, and Amalia had to rein her back. If once she were given her head, the horse would run till she dropped, and there would still be a long distance to go. That was why horses had riders: to keep them from yielding to the impulse of the moment and running themselves to death. "Easy, there, that's a good girl," she said. "They're making funny noises, aren't they, but they can't do anything to us or they'd have done it. Maybe they're just keeping watch. You keep walking, one hoof in front of the other, there's a good horse, and we'll have you under a stable roof by nightfall." *I hope.* Escorted by faceless whistlers, they moved steadily downstream, fording little cross-brooks and keeping to the western bank. It was nearly noon before they saw the sun.

"Where do you want to go," Sue asked, "home, or back to the college?"

"I'd better get back to my office," Siobhan said. "I have a three o'clock class and I want to make sure my material's ready. The department secretary was supposed to see to it that my photocopying got done, but the department's grown so in the last couple of years that she's awfully overworked. I may have to do my own copies. Good God, who's that?"

"Who's what?" Sue asked, trying to see what Siobhan was looking at, and hastily returning her attention to the traffic before she could be squashed by an oncoming truck.

"My God," Siobhan said. "No, keep driving; I'll tell you later." But at this moment the light turned yellow, and Sue was pinned in place between a city bus, a dilapidated Volkswagen van, and the light which was now red.

"Look over here," Siobhan said. "It's raining buckets, they won't see us. Look over at the portico of the Pavilion. All those poor souls, huddled under the awning, coming out of the warmth of a three-martini lunch into the rain. Who's that in the grey suit?"

It was not really a question. "It's our boy Bingley."

"Right. Now look at the other one, even taller than Bingley, tall and rather thin. Got him?"

"Yes—" but at that moment the light changed and Sue had to drive on. "Who's he?"

"That's Robert Shafer of Shafer Construction, the guy who's causing us all this trouble. Did you know he and Bingley knew each other?"

"No. Are you sure they do? Maybe they just happened both to be there."

"No, they were smiling and chatting together. You didn't see. And shaking hands goodbye, till they realized it was raining and they were stuck there." Siobhan had turned round in her seat, peering as best she could out the back window. "There they go, making a run for it toward the parking lot. Poor babies. You know, if we had a *really* high-toned restaurant in this town, it'd have a covered walkway between the door and the parking lot."

"Oh, no," Sue said, with a confidence born of much reading. "They'd have their own garage, and a garageman or two to bring your car to the door, and what's more they'd have a doorman at the door to call the garageman, and to lend umbrellas to people who needed them."

They drove in silence for another three blocks. "Well," Siobhan said, "what are we going to do? You know everything I do now."

"No, I don't," Sue said. "Isn't there some way of fixing those bolts so the kids can't fiddle them loose?"

"Oh, sure," Siobhan said. "I can find out suppliers and prices, if you like. They've had them all along, of course, only when that gym was built they didn't need locking bolts; in those days Liberty Hill school kids didn't go in for petty vandalism."

"Well, they do now," Sue said. *The Darkness closing in.* "Okay, get me your list, and when Sean brings you his list of things that need repairing, I'd like that too as soon as possible. You realize the committee meets tomorrow night, and the whole PTA meets *next* Tuesday?"

"Good grief, so they do." Siobhan said. "I'll phone it all in to you, or else drop it at your house. What are you going to do with it?"

"Dunno. I'll have to think of something."

Master Denis lifted one heavy eyelid and looked suspiciously at the cup in Marianella's hand. "More of your vegetable flavorings?"

"Only a hair of the dog that bit you," she said. In fact, it was some of Captain Lord Randall's private store of brandywine, abstracted for the purpose along a chain of intrigue that stretched from her through Kieran and Michael to the Captain's servant Ulrico.

Master Denis drank it as if it were medicine and made a face. "What's the hour?"

"Just after one."

The Master Seer put his feet to the floor and reached for his robe. "I must go upstairs. Marianella, will you have some of the men bring up a chair with arms and a high back? And find my warm cloak, there's a good girl."

"Upstairs?" She glanced toward the room's shallow, vaulted ceiling. "You mean you're going on the roof?"

"Yes. And I suppose I'd better have something to eat. A bite of something sweet, and some meat." He sounded less like a hungry man ordering lunch than like a rat-catcher choosing his poisons before descending into the cellar.

Kieran and Rigo hauled the great chair from the Hall to the roof, swearing and grumbling as they guided it up the narrow stairs. Master Denis sat on the edge of the bed, chewing his way through honey cakes, bread, and boiled ham with a dogged determination that would have hurt Marianella's pride if she hadn't realized he was not even tasting them. Then he took his warm cloak, close-woven and lined with dark fur, and climbed the stairs to the roof. He had the men turn the chair towards the northeast, and sent them away. He wrapped the cloak tightly round him, though the sun was shining brightly overhead, seated himself in the chair and pulled his hood far down over his face. "Thank you, child. You may go now. If I haven't called for you by sunset—" the black hood tilted, as if to glance at the sun "—no, by full darkness, then you had better come up for me. Speak my name once, and if I don't answer, then on no account speak again, but send for one of my companions, Ryan or Lucas or whoever you can find."

"But Master Denis!" Marianella cried. "What are you going to do?"

"I'm going to Hellsgarde," he said. "My body will be safe enough while I travel, I think. I must ask if they've had any news of Amalia, or what they've seen on the borders of the Darkness. I felt her go, cut off like a short thread. And yet my heart tells me she is not dead. I must know. Go now, dear child. I shall be all right."

You think, Marianella finished for him as she went slowly down the stairs. Kieran met her at the foot of the tower, questions in his eyes; but she only shook her head and passed by him into the kitchen. The fragrant loaves were cooling on the kitchen tables, and it was time to get the pies into the oven.

All told, Sue calculated on the back of an envelope, she had saved about forty dollars since she started baking bread and things instead of buying them. Of course, she had blown it all on records, but this simply meant that she now had both better bread and better records. She had still not wet her toes in the mysterious waters of the Middle Ages, but she had worked as far back as the Renaissance with a record of marvelous rhythmic dances with strange names like "Washerwomen's Brawl" and "Basse Dance 'Without a Rock.'" She was also easing cautiously forward into the twentieth century; if anyone had told her six months ago that she would be listening to Hindemith and Stravinsky, she would have thrown a shoe at them. Her method for choosing what records to buy was fairly simple: she listened to the radio until she heard something she couldn't live without, something that wrung her heart, something that spoke of Demoura—and then if she had the money she went out and bought it. The clerks in the front of the Record Barn, the ones who sold the rock that kept the Barn in business, never looked at her any more; they had her pegged as one of those strange people who hung out in the back of the building.

As the day wore on, the road followed the bank of the Kendal south by east, deeper into the Twilight. By midafternoon Amalia could see no further than a stone's cast ahead, the dim grey of the road just visible between dun-colored hills. But surely the rock and fortress of Hellsgarde must not be far ahead.

The day was nearly gone, and far away in the west she saw the sun set below the edge of the Twilight, deep and somber. Pathfinder's dark mane, stirring in the wind of her own passage, was coppery; the fine soft hairs that tipped her ears gleamed like fresh blood. Those ears were set back, alert and nervous. Amalia too strained to listen, but there was no sound save the faint stirrings of the wind and the steady beat of hooves.

Then the horse's left ear bowed, the cartilage bending downward under the weight of some unseen thing. Pathfinder snorted and raised her head, but before she could do more Amalia had leant forward and batted the invisible creature away, an automatic gesture like swatting a mosquito. It had been a small scaly thing, she decided after the fact, weighing about a pound, scaly and with many small scrabbling feet. She must have killed it, or at least knocked it silly, for it did not come back.

"Walk," she told Pathfinder sternly, reining her in just a

trifle. "I don't like it here any better than you do, but we can't run for it till we see Hellsgarde."

Strange, so strange, to be riding along the borders of these things and no longer able to see them. She tried to remember if anyone had mentioned a small scaly creature among descriptions of the Shadowthings' latest entries into the war. (Even noncombatants like Amalia picked such things up in casual conversation and shoptalk.) Nothing came to mind. Maybe it was something new, only recently bred under the Shadow for Imber's spring offensive. It was now growing very dark, and there was still no sign of Hellsgarde. If she had not lost the Sight, she could have called ahead for guidance from the Duke and his people, but as things were she was on her own. Warm breaths of wind fanned her face. Against her better judgment she allowed Pathfinder to increase her pace to a trot.

By mid-afternoon Sue's thinking had jelled. When Fred got home she took him into the kitchen, out of the children's earshot, and told him about what Miss Anderson had said. "Yeah, well, it doesn't surprise me," he said. "I never met Shafer but I've heard a few stories. What are you going to do?"

"I think I have an idea. Can I bounce it off you this evening?"

"Sure, honey. Is that your spaghetti boiling over?" Sue turned hastily to the pot and turned the heat down.

Master Denis had spread himself thin upon the air—cautiously, and not too thin. He could travel more swiftly this way; but there was always the danger of losing his human shape altogether, forgetting his identity and the body that sat cloak-wrapped in the great chair far behind him.

His toes trailed along the warm surface of the Kendal, among lilies that tasted of honey and forgetfulness; gradually, gently, his feet unraveled and drifted behind him like pale ribbons. It was warm and close about him; in the Lightlands there would soon have been a thunderstorm. He tasted the shapes and surfaces of the riverbank, the ripples in the air, the pale and deeper shadows of the Darkness—ah! there beyond him, there something moved. He drew back in haste like a snail tasting salt.

He remembered his hands, his feet, the long thin back that

ached after a long day's riding; and he slowed his flight and felt the air whistle silently around him.

There, and there, three shapes of the enemy, closing in. Silverbacks? Denis thought so: smaller than the shouf, swifter, and with a deadly cunning. He gathered himself for battle.

They struck like a fiery wind, tossing him tail-over-top into the clouds. He recovered himself, stooped like an eagle and plunged toward the river, passed within blinks of one of his attackers and stabbed out with a dart of pure light, a tiny lightning bolt. The silverback screamed, faint and high, and reeled backward. Denis pulled out of his dive just above the river's surface, and rose again like a falcon. The two remaining silverbacks swooped in upon him, one from the left and one from the right, and spun him like a top. He struck out, but had no way of telling whether or not his darts found their targets. The heat of the attack was suffocating. His senses dimmed. He began to think of the possibility of defeat, of bringing together his memories before it was too late to say farewell to them.

Then from a great distance he seemed to hear a voice, a human voice, no, many voices. *Hold on. We're coming. Hang on. Watch your flank. (Delma, your bolt; quickly, there overhead.) We're coming.*

He drew his tattered knees to his chin and plunged like a meteorite. The silverbacks pursued him. He fell without a splash into the river, spread out and slipped between the layers of warm water; emerged man-shaped onto the bank a dozen yards away. The silverbacks had seen him, maybe, but they were too busy to attend to him. High above him, they swirled and twisted, harried by smaller shapes with the slender bodies and merciless beaks of doves. They swooped and soared, cartwheeled, stabbed and stabbed again. Laughing, Denis bent his head to the ground, just to rest for a moment.

He came to himself in a great illuminated space, smooth and glowing like the interior of a huge pearl, the Great Hall of the Keep of Hellsgarde. The air was brilliant with the light of lamps that hung on every wall, and with the mighty spirit of the Duke of War, and with the love and loyalty of his people.

Denis. Welcome. Rest and be easy. Someone get out the wine; now that Denis is here the war can start. Martin, don't be silly. Welcome, Denis. All of them his friends and brothers. Delma, a small and delicate spirit in a mountainous body, with skin like swans-down and a sting like a scorpion's. Martin, a jester and a sharpshooter, drinking for Denis's benefit the wine he could not taste for himself, not being there in the flesh. (Tiny bubbles drifting along his nerves.)

Marina, *the mother of us all*, old now and frail in her body, but full of skill and guidance, the linkmaker, the circlemistress. Adrianna, an oasis of strength, robed in silver and fiery velvet, flung a long-tendriled wing around Denis and fed him power as Marianella might have fed his body food. Genevra, a soundless voice like the deepest note on the bottom string of a viol, her pale eyes seeking the dark vault overhead while her hands sheltered his like seeds in a pod. And others who had not shared his own days at Hellsgarde, known to him only in the otherworld: tireless Pavel, bitter Mayling, Donal the merciless.

Over them all reached the sure strength of the Lord of Hellsgarde, the warrior-wizard, the Duke of War, in whose line was bred power unequalled in the two worlds. *Welcome, Denis. What brings you such a distance?*

I'm seeking news of Amalia of Fendarath, who went into the Darkness. She came out of the Shadow yesterday; she was in the foothills of the Weatherwall. Then in the stroke of a moment I lost her, but I think she is not dead. I thought she might come here.

There's a horse and a woman on the road well to the north of us, heading this way; but I should not have said it was Amalia. The woman is not gifted. But she bears some unchancy thing, and now the creatures of Darkness are massed above her. Shall we go to meet them?

That was a rhetorical question; the folk of Hellsgarde lived to strike back at the Shadowlings whenever they came near. To north and south the Shadow crept slowly westward, but Hellsgarde remained, white on its spur of rock, a sharp blade pointed into the vitals of its enemy.

They brought out more lamps and set them alight, burning in all the brackets around the Hall. Throughout that fortress there was no room without lamps, no corner where the light could not reach, except for jars and boxes that had been sealed in the Lightlands. They gave the Darklife nowhere to take root. It followed that of the supplies brought to them in wagon-loads out of the West, a great part consisted of lamp oil.

In the center of the room was a great pile of rugs and cushions. Donal and Genevra stood here already, shaking and turning the cushions so that their dark sides might feel the light. The others joined them, settling themselves in a rough circle; it was not necessary for them to join hands, but many did. Lord Mark took his place in the center, his hand upon his sword hilt, his other arm around Marina. Delma lay at his feet, and Adrianna behind him, her cheek against his shoulder. Opposite him Genevra sat, her hands folded in her lap, her mind reaching out to her companions. One by one they linked in, gathered their strength, and rose together out of their bodies into the battlefield of the otherworld.

Imagine an eagle, a tremendous warrior-bird, sleek and deadly. The Duke of War its body, Genevra its brain, Marina its spreading wings, Denis its eyes to search for Amalia; he dared not do battle so far from his mortal flesh. The rest made up the bird's beak and talons, its daggers and bludgeons —to vary the metaphor—its crossbows and catapults, its lightning bolts. Adrianna kept its heart beating, and the hearts of those who made it up.

Sue had spent much of the day in polishing up the house—there was no point in not impressing the hell out of the committee, and the idiot-level scutwork kept her body busy and encouraged her brain to think. From time to time she would lay down broom, duster, or box of miscellaneous-junk-to-put-somewhere-else, sit down to a notebook on the coffee table, and write down another few words or add up some figures. (Siobhan had come through with Sean's list of the gym's needs—he had even pumped the school custodian about rusted fittings and weary gaskets—and her own list of suitable fixes.) Finally she wrote MEMORIAL in large letters at the bottom of the page, and drew a circle around it.

Yes, Amalia said. She had contributed ideas throughout the day; a noblewoman could not help growing up familiar with palace politics and the art of persuasion, and she had had little to occupy her mind as she stood frozen in the House of the Mists. Even those who love as she and Aumery loved cannot stand gazing into each other's eyes forever. Sue looked the page up and down, then folded it up and tucked it into her bra. The timer rang to announce a batch of cookies, and she got up and went into the kitchen.

Marianella too filled much of the day with housework. The cold weather had set in, and the pig-butchering, and Marianella had the kitchenmaids to supervise in salting and smoking and sausage-making, and the spices to measure out. That once done, there were the chimneys to be cleaned out, and chinks to be stopped and windows mended against the winter wind.

Once she slipped up to the top of the tower, crept up the stairs and peered over the edge of the trap at Master Denis. He did not move, and she dared not go to look at him. She crept downstairs again and ordered new rushes for the floor.

Eight o'clock saw most of the committee in place around the dining room table. Siobhan as chairman at its head, Sue in the middle where everyone could see her.

("I talked to a couple of people," Fred had told her. "I put together what they all said, and I think your plan's going to work. Just don't let them fast-talk you out of it.")

"First off," Sue said, "I've learned how it happens that Mr. Shafer was able to make the school such a generous offer. You'll remember that when Mrs. Stone brought up the topic originally, it was still tentative. I've managed to find out why. Shafer Construction put a bid in on a contract to build a new state prison—"

"Not around here!" one woman cried out.

"No, no, up at Hallford," Sue reassured her. (_It's always like this; "build it anywhere except in MY neighborhood!"_) "Well, he got the bid," Sue went on. ("And he ought to make a decent job of it," Fred had said, "considering that if he doesn't he may find himself living there.") "It's going to bring him in a bundle of money—which is why he's looking for a tax break—and he's going to be paid a chunk of it up front, to cover his materials and labor costs. But the state, as you probably know, works on a July 1st fiscal year, so Mr. Shafer won't get his startup funds till summer. But the IRS works on the _calendar_ year, so he has, theoretically, nearly six months to do his project for us and get his tax loss." Mrs. Stone was glowering, probably because of having her monopoly on Shafer intruded upon. "I think it's very clever of him, to figure out a way to benefit us and himself at the same time," Sue said innocently, and watched Mrs. Stone's face relax by maybe a quarter of an inch.

"I said 'theoretically,'" Sue continued. "Because you can imagine how much luck he'd have trying to break ground in January. So he's really got only three months, maybe a little more; that's *if* he goes ahead with his original plan—" And the doorbell rang.

"I'll get it," said Fred, who for once in his life was sitting in. He went to the door while the members of the committee murmured and whispered. "Hello, Chris," Sue heard from the door, and her heart skipped a beat; and another when she saw Bingley stroll into the dining room, followed by Robert Shafer.

Fred made introductions—all the committee except Siobhan and Myra Stone were meeting Shafer for the first time, and none of them but Siobhan knew Bingley. Fred found them two more chairs, while Sue and Siobhan exchanged worried glances.

"I heard about this meeting this afternoon," Bingley said, his eyes on Sue, "and when I ran into Bob a little later on I felt I really ought to bring him along. He has some news for you." He sat down without another word and took a cup of coffee, and went on watching Sue over its rim while Shafer spoke.

Shafer was tall and lean, and elegantly dressed (for Liberty Hill, anyway); he had once been incredibly good-looking and was still not bad at sixty or so, with his mane of silver hair and his bright blue eyes. He didn't look like a building contractor; he looked like a duke, or an actor, or (if you looked closely enough) a con man. He always looked you carefully in the eye when he spoke to you, as if to gauge how you were taking it.

His news, of course, was that he had gotten the state prison contract and was in a position to need a tax loss. Sue was proud of the committee: not one of them (not even Mrs. Stone) betrayed by the flicker of an eyelash that she had heard it all before, not five minutes ago.

"And this means that we can get started with the designs for the new gym," Shafer went on. "Now, I have some preliminary sketches here—"

Now, Amalia said out of silence and darkness. *Quickly, before he can get his hand into his briefcase.*

"Actually, Mr. Shafer," Sue put in, "we had a couple other points on the agenda. Perhaps we should refer it to the chair—"

"Yes, go ahead, please," said Siobhan, "since this is something Mr. Shafer will want to hear."

"Mrs. O'Hare put together a small task force," Sue said, not naming names, "to check out the state of the gym. We were delighted, as you can imagine, to discover that the structure of the building is sound and does not need replacement. There are various items that need repairing —we have a list—the bleachers need a couple new seats, for example, and locking bolts—"

"That gym was built in 1950," Shafer interrupted. "It doesn't have a tennis court, or a pool, or—"

"But it has a sound framework and a perfectly good roof and a new heating system," Sue said. "It does need some plumbing work and some other details, as I said. But it also has something else that we shouldn't discount, and that is tradition. Have you—" her voice choked off, more from a sort of stage fright than from sentiment, a feeling of having stuck her neck out entirely too far.

Go on.

"Have you been in the gym recently? Have you read the plaque inside the front door? It dedicates the building to the memory of the alumni of this school district who *gave the last full measure of devotion* in World War II. Most of us don't remember that war; it was before our time. We never knew those people. But I don't think we should forget them—"

"Well, I can't argue with that," Shafer said. Myra Stone had tears in her eyes. (But she was old enough to remember the war, just. Certainly Shafer was.)

Sue swallowed hard. "However, I can understand Mr. Shafer's wish to give the school the very latest and best," she went on. "But the gym isn't where we most need to be up-to-date. The committee has concluded that what we really need—" the committee hadn't concluded anything of the sort, chiefly because Mrs. Stone had kept on stonewalling, "—is a computer facility, that is, a classroom unit equipped with up to thirty or forty microcomputers."

There was a dead silence for one, two, three heartbeats. Then Shafer said, "I think that's a *good* idea."

Sue's eyes met Siobhan's again. *Bingo.*

The unseen things were thick around Amalia now. The Darkness was so total that even above the Shadow the sun must have set. The road was thick with stoneweed, and by its tiny lights she could guide Pathfinder along the road; otherwise they would have been unable to move. Far ahead she thought she could see a faint pale smudge upon the blackness that just might be the white fortress Hellsgarde atop its tall crag. But until she was certain she dared not let Pathfinder run; and meanwhile the Shadowlings hummed and whistled about her head.

There was something on her shoulder. Quicker than thought, she reached up and slapped it away; it crunched beneath her fingers. Once when she was twelve, lying thinly covered in bed on the hottest night of summer, a spider had come and crawled on her leg, and she had slapped the tickling thing away. One of the big long-legged full-bodied ones, it had crunched juicily under her hand; and Amalia, who ordinarily liked spiders and protected them from the broom, sat up in bed screaming for lights. So now the invisible Shadowling crunched damply, and Amalia screamed and shook it from her hand.

"The only trouble is," Shafer went on, "that I don't know anything about computers."

"Well, thank goodness; there's two of us," Sue said in mock-relief, and reached across the table to shake his hand. (His palm was smooth, and his fingernails neatly manicured.) "But don't worry, we have people who understand computers, beginning with Mrs. O'Hare. Why don't we appoint a small group, maybe just two or three, to act as liaison between you and the PTA? Then they can find out whatever you need to know. Will that be all right?" There; she'd said it.

"Why, of course," Shafer said genially. "I've known Siobhan all her life. Her daddy was my best competitor." If there was an edge in his voice, nobody could have pointed it out. There was a bewildered half-smile on Myra

Stone's face; her plans for Shafer's bounty had been thoroughly reshuffled, but she couldn't very well complain about it if Shafer himself didn't. Sue brought out more coffee and another plate of cookies. Chris Bingley was still watching her; he caught her eye and winked.

Something on feet was paralleling her course, something on the far bank of the Kendal. The river must be thirty or forty feet wide here, so she was safe from the creature unless it could swim. But now her memory, unbidden, brought up the tale of a Lord of Hellsgarde of an earlier day, one who had fought a dozen unnamed things along the bank of the Kendal, held them off at the ford, the ford just to the north of the fortress ... and was it only her overactive imagination, or was she truly hearing something splashing through the water, heading toward her across the shallows?

Something crackled overhead, and she looked up in sudden hope. Yes, high over her head lightning flashes were cracking like distant whips, lighting up the clouds with fitful brilliance. It *could* be a real thunderstorm, of course. But there was no thunder. Or it could be the warriors of Hellsgarde, fighting high over her head to drive off the Shadowlings and cover her flight to the castle.

A great flash close overhead, and a thin quavering scream that never came from a human throat. A moment later something fell heavily to the ground, not a dozen feet to her right, with the faint crunching sounds of ruined cartilage—big enough for a rishi and its rider, maybe even big enough for a silverback. The footsteps hastened, closing in on her, and peering behind her in the lightning flashes she glimpsed the outline of what was following her: tall, upright, two-legged, but with something trailing after it—a cloak, a train, a tail? She drew her robe closer around her and shivered, and allowed Pathfinder to go just a little faster.

Then the moon, far away to the west, fell below the cover of the Shadow to flood the banks of the Kendal with a pale cold light. The two-legged thing hissed like an angry cat, and raised something like hands to shield something like a face; and in the dim light Amalia saw a white shape in the distance. A little triangular shape, like the very tip of one of the snowy peaks of the Weatherwall, or a single pavilion off the tournament field in the half-forgotten days of peace. The crag and castle of Hellsgarde, thickly whitewashed to keep off the stoneweed. Amalia shouted, "Go!" and let out the reins, and Pathfinder laid back her ears and leapt forward in a burst of speed. Amalia clung to the saddlehorn and gave the horse her head. Their chances of reaching Hellsgarde, before Pathfinder collapsed or the Shadowlings caught up with them, were about even—if luck was with them and nothing was waiting for them on the road ahead.

"The only snag I can see," Fred told Sue later as they got ready for bed, "is that while Shafer can fix the gym and build the computer room at cost, so to speak, and credit himself with what he would have sold it for, he's going to have to pay real money for the computers, and I don't know how much he's going to be willing to spend."

"We thought of that too," Sue said. "Siobhan says a lot of the companies will donate computers to schools; it gives *them* a tax break. She's going to plug into some electronic mail networks and ask around—and I thought I'd ask Claire Carmody too. So we're set—if the liaison committee can just keep Shafer honest. It'll be Siobhan, of course, and me I suppose, and one other person. I'm hoping we can find someone who knows accounting, without letting Shafer know she does till after she's officially in!"

"Oh, yeah, Fred—did you know Bingley was planning to come to the meeting?"

"He said he'd try to make it."

"You didn't warn me. I just about had a heart attack when he and Shafer walked in together."

"You didn't warn *me* that he and Shafer knew each other!"

"I didn't know I needed to. Oh, well, it all worked out."

She pulled off her pantyhose and tossed them into the air; they landed atop the bedside lamp and Fred hastily snatched them away before they could scorch. "You better come to bed before you float away."

When night fell, and Denis would not answer her call, Marianella had gone obediently to find his companions. Ryan, who was just Marianella's age and looked fourteen, perched himself on the arm of Denis's chair and touched his cheek with the back of his hand. "Ah, he's all right," Ryan said. "His heart is beating and he should be back with us shortly."

They waited and went on waiting, while the cold moon rose over the Shadow, till at last Denis opened his eyes. He glanced upward at Ryan and raised one eyebrow, and yawned and stretched and finally focused an eye on Marianella. "Hello," he said.

"But what about her Ladyship?" Marianella burst out. "Did you find her? Is she all right?"

"Alive," Denis said. "But maimed." And his eyes closed again, and he fell asleep against Ryan's arm.

CHAPTER 10

The Nature of the Beast

The day had begun badly for Marianella, after a night full of unpleasant dreams. Even after she had shaken Master Denis awake long enough to explain that Amalia had not lost her arms or legs, but only the Sight—"Is *that* all!" she had cried, and the Seer had glared at her and answered "Isn't *that* enough?"—she had lain uneasily, and woken to find that Kieran had already risen and gone. Something about sword-practice with Michael the Red. Then one of the kitchen maids had had a quarrel with her young man and was so distraught that she had let the porridge burn; Tama had sprung to its rescue and saved most of it, but the stench of the burnt pot filled the kitchen. By midmorning Marianella had a raging headache, and had to go in search of some of her own herbs.

The day began no better in Liberty Hill; something had gone obscurely wrong with Fred's car, and he had spent an hour tinkering with its insides, snarling and barking at his innocent wife and children, and generally behaving like a bastard. Most other things he could take in his stride, but if something went wrong with his car, his very own personal automobile, why then Fred (ordinarily the most reasonable of people) felt it as an attack on his masculinity and snapped and thrashed about like a wounded alligator till the thing was fixed. What's more, he was beginning to act the same way about the computer. *Men*, she thought with resignation, and phoned in to Sav-Mor to explain that he would be unavoidably late, and got the children out the door and off to school while his back was turned. At last he gave up, called the auto repair shop—the moral equivalent of the defeated general surrendering his sword—and took Sue's station wagon to work. It was like having a thunderstorm, full of noise and electricity, finally move off to throw its lightning bolts at some other town.

Amalia woke late—the sun was already high above the Shadowcover—but not as late as the Hellsgarde folk. In the flickering light of the lamps she could see them, or most of them, still dead to the world, curled up in amorous twos and threes among the rugs and cushions. *Just as well I lost the Sight before I came here*, Amalia thought; she had never been easy in her mind about the methods the Hellsgarders employed to renew their psychic energy.

Genevra, however, was already up; she had her own sources of strength. She had stirred up the fire to boil water, and was filling the lamps with fresh oil. Now she saw that Amalia was awake, and stepped across slumbering bodies to reach her. "Good morning," she whispered. "Would you like some tea? I was just making myself some. They'll all be out for a while yet, I'm afraid."

"Tea! That sounds wonderful." Amalia rolled out of the nest of soft blankets and got to her feet. "I haven't been able to boil water in—oh, ten or twelve days."

"Where have you *been*?"

"Under the Shadow."

"And fighting the army of the Darklands singlehanded?"

Amalia looked down at her clothes, ripped and muddy, torn to shreds around the hem. "Something like that. In addition, I've been marching through the undergrowth, riding cat-back, and climbing mountains."

"I believe you," Genevra said, and poured out mugs of tea for Amalia and herself. "I'll get you some fresh clothes."

"Thank you," Amalia said. "But not black; I'll never wear the black again."

"As you like," Genevra said. The Hellsgarde folk did not trouble to wear the identifying black among themselves; they dressed in such clothes as would amuse themselves and their companions. Genevra this morning was a tall pale lily in blue and cloth-of-silver. But Amalia had lived all her life till now in the protective cloak; now she felt she no longer had the right to wear it, and must begin as she meant to go on. After they finished their tea Genevra took a pitcher of lamp-oil and led her down the hall to a storage room used mostly for clothing—some new, some well-worn, most returned to the common stock when everyone had become tired of the sight of them. There were no doors on the rooms, no curtains for the alcoves, no covers to the chests; most of the things lay singly on shelves, exposed to the lamplight. While Genevra refilled the lamps Amalia looked along the shelves. Twice she reached without thinking for a dark brown or charcoal grey, and resolutely drew her hand back. Here was a pile of brilliant red that shimmered under the lamplight; so bright that she blushed to think of herself in it; she shook it out and found that it consisted of a long loose tunic and divided skirt, suitable for riding. That would do very well. She hung it over one arm and continued her search. "Oh, that will look splendid," Genevra said. "Let me find you a cloak. You look cold."

She selected a white cloak lined with heavy fur, and leather boots to replace the ones Amalia had worn to the insoles, and layers of warm underwear. After she had dressed Amalia stopped shivering, and began to remember the work she had before her. Turning over trifles of jewelry in a brass tray under the lamp, she picked up a big silver medallion on a chain, in the shape of a crowned heart—surprisingly light, it must be hollow. Yes, it opened here, like a locket; a thing to carry a lock of someone's hair, perhaps, or some other token. Amalia smiled, and carefully unfolded the rags of her old gown. She took the Heart of Imber from the pocket and put it into the medallion. The fastening was tight enough to be safe; it pinned securely with a silver pin.

"What is that thing?"

"I'll tell you later." Amalia put the chain about her neck and fastened the white cloak over it, hiding it from sight.

When she came back into the Great Hall, the rest of them were awake and busy emptying the teapot. At first they were silent, but one by one, as they remembered she could no longer hear their thoughts, they murmured "Good morning" and moved away. "Good morning, Amalia," the Duke said courteously, but like one who is speaking a foreign language.

"No one before has gone more than a few miles under the Darkness, and returned to tell the tale."

"Nor ever will again, I think," Amalia said. "I was guarded and guided." The dark eyes of Ulf/Aumery appeared before her inner eye, and she squeezed her lids together hard to block the tears.

"Who is the man in your thoughts?" the Duke went on, "and what is that thing at your breast?"

"What does it look like?" Amalia countered. "I'm not making a joke, I really want to know."

The Duke of War considered the Heart, invisible to Amalia inside its silver casing. "It's a thing out of the Darkness, certainly; but it is not alive. Or I don't think so. It bides; it does not act. Power is in it, and a darkling light. It feels bitter. It tastes dark red. It's fragile."

"Yes," Amalia said after a few moments of silence, breaking into the Duke's musings. "It's all of that. Do you remember the story of the wizard Kasthei who protected his body from harm by hiding his heart far away? So with the Lord of Darkness. This is the Heart of Imber."

The listeners stirred uneasily. It was not the custom in Demoura to name that name openly. "Yes, I dare to speak his name. I have stood in Agniran; I have lain in the arms of Darkness; I have beheld Imber face to face. There I learned of this Heart, and I sought it; at a terrible price I brought it out of the north. And if I can break the Heart at Imber's feet, he will die."

The listeners glanced at each other, and nodded. "That *feels* right," Adrianna said. "But do you mean to go back under the Shadow to do it?"

"Of course not," Amalia said. "The Shadowknights would catch me and take the Heart from me before I'd gone a mile, and someone would take it back to its hiding place. No, I shall need your help.

"And I bring you an end to your lives as you have known them. Lord of Hellsgarde, I must tell you now that your long fight has been fruitless, and your defense of this keep to no purpose. Yearly, behind your back, villages and farms fall under the Shadow, and you can do nothing to prevent it. Your fortress is a thorn in the side of the darkness, no doubt, but the Darkness flows westward to either side of you, and you cannot hold it back."

"This I have known all my life," the Duke said with dignity. "But what other thing was there for me to do, than the task my fathers gave me?"

"This, now," Amalia said. "I need an army to protect me on my road to Agniran, that the Heart may not be taken from me. I need the power of all this company, and the power of all the Seers that walk under the sun in Demoura, to fight off the attacks of things unseen." The words surged out of her, tiredness and shyness consumed like twigs in a wind-whipped flame. "I need the provisions to feed them, and the horses to carry them, and the weapons to arm them. I need all our resources, with nothing held back; because if all our strength cannot win our way to Agniran, then we are already defeated." She stopped, and drew in a long breath, as the fire died down within her. "And just now I need another cup of tea," she said, and sank down onto a cushion. Adrianna went to get it, while the others looked at one another.

"She's right," Marina said aloud. "I foresee it. Either we will conquer now, or never; and die into the dust, and our children be pushed at last into the sea." She seemed suddenly very old, and her voice trembled, but her will was firm. "Mark, my lord, this is a hard thing for you. But you are the Duke of War, and you must give the command. We must leave Hellsgarde now, and go back to rouse our people for battle."

"The Lord of Hellsgarde glanced round the circle of his people. "Make ready," he said. "There's a supply wagon setting out now from Light's End, that will reach us by noon. We'll ride back with them."

Amalia's speech had left Sue with a flea in her ear, a stumbling fragment of memory that would neither lie down and go to sleep again nor stand up and identify itself. Something she had read in high school, and it might have been Churchill during World War II, but somehow she didn't think it was. After tearing around the house all morning, cleaning it like someone trying to drive out devils, she threw her duster into a corner and took a bus to the library.

The fragment in Sue's memory turned out to be part of

a poem. While the librarian was hunting it up, Sue looked
through a collection of Churchill's speeches.

> "We shall go on to the end, we shall fight in France,
> we shall fight in the seas and oceans, we shall fight
> with growing confidence and growing strength in the
> air, we shall defend our island, whatever the cost
> may be, we shall fight on the beaches, we shall fight
> on the landing-grounds, we shall fight in the fields
> and in the streets, we shall fight in the hills; we shall
> never surrender. . . ."

*That's what Mark's been doing. What about Amalia's
war?* And then the librarian returned with a thick book of
poems. "Here you are," she said. "It's 'The Ballad of the
White Horse,' by Chesterton. There's the bit you want.

> "I tell you naught for your comfort,
>   Yea, naught for your desire,
> Save that the sky grows darker yet
>   And the sea rises higher."

Yes, Amalia said. *That is where we are.* It was full day
over the Weatherwall, and the frosty ground beyond the
pillars was full of brilliance. The mist swirled and sparkled like diamond dust. *How beautiful it is.*

*You mean to take the Heart to Agniran, and break it at his
feet,* Aumery said. *At my feet. Or to attempt it, at least. Do
you think you will succeed?*

My heart's love, Amalia said politely, *do you think I would
tell you? Whatever you know, he knows.*

Almost all, Aumery agreed. *He cannot understand why I let
you go. He never would have done it. I have still a few secrets
from him.*

Sue skimmed the rest of the poem, which was very long
and appeared to be about Alfred the Great, king of a small
part of England, fighting off the Danes in the ninth century. *Very appropriate,* Sue mused as she checked the
book out to read at her leisure, *but there is still no king in
Demoura. By heredity alone I suppose it ought to be
Aumery, but he's on the other* side, *it really wouldn't suit.*

She had lunch in a coffee shop near the bus station,
reading "The Ballad of the White Horse" while she ate her

chef salad and drank cup after cup of hot coffee. The day had turned bitterly cold, and what had threatened to fall as rain this morning would probably be snow by evening. One other passage caught her eye:

> "For the great Gaels of Ireland
> Are the men that god made mad;
> For all their wars are merry,
> And all their songs are sad."

She would have to show that one to Siobhan—if Siobhan didn't already know it.

She had an impression of unhappy eyes somewhere at the edge of her field of vision. She lowered her book and caught sight of a woman sitting in a booth in the corner of the room. She was probably no older than Sue herself, but she looked sick and old and tired. There were dark shadows under her eyes, and her thin fair hair was drifting away from the ponytail at the back of her neck to fall in straggling locks around her face. She looked ready to drop from exhaustion, and scared to death to boot. She had a four-year-old and a two-year-old with her, and—yes, she appeared to be pregnant with another, which would be enough to exhaust anybody; still . . .

The four-year-old had a glass of milk in front of him, but he seemed more interested in trying to get hold of his mother's coffee. His eyes too were shadowed. He looked bruised all over, though there were no marks on his skin. The toddler still had the clear eyes of babyhood, but there was a fading brown-and-purple mark on her cheek. The whole thing was as straightforward to the eye as a painting by Norman Rockwell, except that Rockwell would never have painted such a sight, probably would not have admitted that such things happened.

Intolerable, Amalia said. *This is not to be borne. What do you think you are doing, sitting placidly there on your undamaged rump? Get over there and do something!*

What can I do? Sue protested silently, while all of late-twentieth-century America rose up and shouted, DON'T GET INVOLVED! *She'll tell me to mind my own business.*

It'll do you no harm if she does. You are a lady of the House

*of Fendarath. (I am?) Has no one ever told you that nobility
carries obligations? Get over there.*

Sue picked up her book and her coffee and took them
over to the booth. The woman looked up, startled. "Hi,"
Sue began. "You look pretty upset. Anything I can do to
help?"

The woman looked away, and shook her head slightly.
(See?)

Sit down and persist. What is it you say? "Hang in there."

Sue sat down, while the children stared, and let a few
moments pass. The woman was staring at her coffee cup;
her hands were trembling. "Do you want to talk about it?"
Sue said.

Again the woman shook her head, but the four-year-old
spoke up, "Daddy hit her."

"I thought it was something like that." The woman did
not answer. "Does he hit you often?" A little nod. "Well,
you know there's only one thing you can do about it."

"Pray, and be patient." The woman's voice was hoarse.
"That's what my mother said."

"Excuse me, but your mother was absolutely wrong.
What you've got to do is leave him, because he'll never
stop until you do."

"It's my duty to stay with my husband."

"No, it's your duty to help him get well." That got a
reaction; the woman stared at Sue as if she were speaking
Greek. "Any man who beats his wife and children is *sick*.
Just as sick as the man who's on dope, or the one who
thinks little green men from outer space are living in his
ear. And if you're going to help him try to get well, you
have to let him *know* he's sick. By *leaving*. Because until
you do, he's going to go on thinking he's all right."

"But—" the woman began, and broke off with her mouth
hanging open.

Her four-year-old broke into the silence again, saying
calmly, "He kicked her in the stomach."

While she was pregnant, Sue thought. *That's what they
always do in the magazine articles*. In fact, almost everything she was saying was culled from one article or another, but the fire in her heart was Amalia's. "Did your
father beat your mother?" she pursued. The woman nod-

ded. "And she put up with it. And she told you to put up
with it too. Not just in words, because you grew up seeing
him beat her and thinking that must be right. Did your
husband's father beat *his* mother?"

"I guess so. I used to see her with black eyes and
things."

"Uh-huh. And he grew up watching him beat her, and
thinking that must be right. And he's going to go on
thinking so, until you teach him different. And you know
what will happen if you don't?"

The woman shook her head once more. "Unless you
leave him now, and send him word that you won't even
see him again till he agrees to get help—and I mean a
marriage counselor to start with, and probably a psychia-
trist after that—why then, he'll just go on the way he's
been going, and your son will grow up to think it's all right
for a man to beat his wife, and he'll beat *his* wife. And
your daughter will grow up thinking it's all right for a
woman to be beaten, and she'll lie down and let her
husband beat *her*. Maybe he'll kill her. Maybe he'll just
make her life hell for sixty years. And your grandchildren—"

"But there's nowhere I can go," the woman said. "I've
got no money, I couldn't get a job. I never finished high
school, and anyway there's the baby coming."

"Are there any relatives you could stay with, who'd have
the guts to keep your husband away from you? No, I
suppose not. Never mind, there are places you can go,
safe houses run by women who've been in the same boat;
they're so careful (*you might even say "paranoid"*) "that
no man even knows the address. Neither do I, but I can
find out. If I find you a place to go, will you go there?"

The woman had been looking at the bruise on her
daughter's cheek. "Yes," she said.

Sue felt a surge of triumph, but she concealed it. "Great,"
she said. "You stay *right here*, don't move till I get back.
I'm going to phone." She found a pay phone within sight
of the woman's booth, and kept an eye on her just in case
while she called Siobhan's office. "Hi, Siobhan. Do you
have the address of a safe house for battered women?"

"Good God, Sue!"

"No, no, no, not for me, for somebody else. You know Fred better than that."

"Well, I like to think I do, but people have been fooled before. Safe houses. I don't know of any myself, but I bet I know those who do. Can I call you back?"

"Sure. It's a pay phone, I'm not at home." She gave Siobhan the number.

"Okay, give me a couple of minutes. Don't go away."

"Don't worry, I won't." She hung up and went back to the booth. The little boy had spilled his milk down his front, and was crying and resisting his mother's attempts to mop him up. "Cool it, kid," Sue said, and took him in charge.

"He wants to go home and get his new space gun," the woman explained. "And I don't have any clean clothes for them, or anything—"

"You don't go home," Sue said firmly. "Does your husband work? Is it *absolutely certain* that he isn't at home right now? What do you think he'd do if he saw you packing up to move out? Anyway, the women at the house probably wouldn't approve of toy guns. And they'll find the children clothes and things, they probably have a stock of things other people's children have outgrown." *Rather like Hellsgarde.*

The phone rang before the woman could argue any further, and Sue went to answer it. An unfamiliar woman's voice said, "Are you the woman who needs shelter?"

"No, but she's right here," Sue said. "Shall I get her?"

"Yes, put her on." Sue sent the woman to the phone. It was a long conversation. Sue sat in the booth keeping the children quiet.

"I want to run away," the little boy volunteered.

"That's exactly what you're going to do," Sue told him. "You and your mother and your sister are all going to run away to a place where it's safe. But once you get there, you mustn't run away any more, or somebody might find you." *Listen to me.* Still, she probably couldn't make the poor kid any more suspicious than he was already. After a while his mother hung up the phone and came back to her seat. "I'm supposed to take the Number 65 bus," she said. "She said it stops right out in front here."

"Okay," Sue said. "Do you have bus fare?"

"Yes, I've got the grocery money for the week. Do you think I ought to take it all?"

"I think you should," Sue said. "He's got the paychecks, hasn't he?" She looked out the window. "Is that bus the 65? I think it is. You run and catch it, quick. I'll pay for your coffee. Good luck." The woman picked up her purse and her children and hurried out the door. Sue watched from the window, and when the woman actually got on the bus and drove away she let out a long sigh of relief.

At this point the waitress returned, glancing in confusion between the table where Sue had been sitting and the booth where she was now. Sue raised a finger and called her over. "It's okay," she said. "I'm paying for her."

"Uh, okay. That was a chef salad and coffee over there, and another coffee and a milk over here." She did arithmetic while Sue got out her wallet. *Very well done*, Amalia said.

By noon, Marianella had things in hand again. The kitchen maid had dried her eyes and recovered some of her composure. The other women, in the process of trying to comfort her, had offered advice out of their varied experiences, and the morning had turned into an orgy of reminiscences. (After all, when *they* get together, don't they spend their time talking about *us*?)

"I suppose they come in all sorts," Marianella summed up. "Are we ready to serve out? Tama, get that kettle, would you. Now mine, he has a frightful temper sometimes, but he's neat and tidy and he always picks up his clothes, so I think I'll keep him."

"Please don't trouble yourself." The words could have been chiseled out of ice. Kieran was standing in the doorway. (The man did have the damnedest talent for showing up unnoticed.) His blue eyes were blazing, and before Marianella could speak he turned sharply and stalked away.

"I see what you mean," Tama said.

"Men," Marianella said, and shrugged. "I'll talk to him later. Let's get lunch on the table." But Kieran did not take his lunch in the Hall—no doubt he had gone to join the soldiers in their mess tent, as he sometimes did—and when Marianella finally got a chance in the middle of the afternoon to look up in their bedroom, he had taken his clothes and other belongings and left the room empty of any hint of his presence. Marianella began to feel cold. He was not in the Hall, not in the courtyard; when she fabricated an excuse to go into the stables, he was not there either, nor was his horse Speedwell. *I'll have to talk to him*, Marianella repeated to herself; but just now she wasn't certain where she was going to find the opportunity.

Damn, Sue commented. *Where is he?*

The supply wagons reached Hellsgarde around noon, and the Duke came down himself to explain the change in plans to the drivers. They took the news quietly, and only asked what part of their cargo should be abandoned, and what taken back to Light's End. The Hellsgarders had already filled their packs with their most necessary possessions, only a few pounds apiece. Many of them had horses, and rode them; the rest sat in the wagons among the cargo. They offered Amalia a seat in the wagon, but she preferred to ride Pathfinder; the horse was dancing nervously in the path and glancing overhead at nothing Amalia could see. *Now even my horse has more of the Sight than I have.* But the thought did not distress her much; she had seen enough of the Darklife to last her a long time.

A strong wind had blown in out of the west, pushing even the Shadow back a little, so that Amalia could see, if only dimly, where they were going. But the wind was cold, and promised rain or worse by nightfall, so they loaded up in haste and set off.

Amalia, turning backwards in the saddle, could see the outline of Hellsgarde, silhouetted against the Shadow like a mountain of snow. She could even see the faint black line, thin as a spider's thread at this distance, where a bosun's chair had been left to dangle down the wall, half through the yearly task of whitewashing the faces of the castle and the rock. There was no need to finish it now. No one would ever paint the sides of Hellsgarde again; either when they returned to the castle there would be no need, or else no one would ever return. Amalia pulled the warm cloak tighter around her, and bent into the wind.

The pass through which they rode was called the Lifeline, and the rocky shapes it wound through were called the Heller

Hills. Once they had been called the Hollow Hills, before the Darkness came, and the tale run that elves had lived beneath them. If you wandered into their halls, you might dance for an evening and come out hundreds of years later. But now all Demoura was sunken into a two hundred years' sleep, and no one believed in the elves any longer; there were too many Shadowlings abroad already. The first few hours of the ride were pleasant, even though the wind was cold. The Shadowlife of the transition zone died back quickly, leaving only the tall asphodel to cover the ground with its low-spreading leaves. By the time they were well into the hills, there was grass growing again, and little scrub oaks that hung onto the ground with clenched roots, their backs bowed against the wind. And the rain blew in, falling sideways into their eyes; Amalia drew her hood over her face.

A bitter north wind chased the bus all the way home, and caught it just as Sue was getting off. It stung her face with the first snow of the season, tiny crystals that melted as they touched the ground. It blew her along the sidewalk and up the front steps, and tried to bluster its way into the house with her, till she put her shoulder to the door and shut it out. Five minutes later it blew the children home, excited and shivering, their eyes like stars and their hands like lumps of ice. She made hot chocolate for them to take the chill off.

"Mom?" Kathy said. "Is Daddy still mad?"

"Oh, I don't think so," Sue said. "I think they'll have his car fixed before he gets home. He wasn't mad at *us*, you know, just at the car. But the car doesn't care if you get mad at it or not, so it tends to spill over and make you yell at your family." *Fred's father used to do exactly the same thing*, she recalled, *and where have I heard that before? Yelling at them isn't a tenth as bad as hitting them. Just the same—* "So listen, Mike and Mark—when you're grown up and have cars and families of your own, you remember what it feels like, and don't yell at the wrong people. Okay?" The boys nodded solemnly, and Sue hugged them all hard before sending them off to do their homework.

In Telerath the rain fell heavily out of a northwest wind that would have borne snow further inland. It hung over the sea like a mane of straight grey hair, and the fishermen stayed close to shore and came in early. There were plenty of fish, crowding close to the surface as if they could no longer tell the difference between water and air. *Neither can I*, thought Kieran, who had taken a turn on the nets—not in the *Golden Apple*, but in one of the little boats—as an effective means of getting away from the keep; *the air is so full of water that if I stay out here much longer I shall grow gills.* A big grey pugfish leaped out of the water almost under his nose, and Kieran had his handnet under it before it knew what was happening. Yes, the fish were plentiful, but the weather was too wet to dry them, and there were no more barrels to salt them down in. "That big pug'll look good on the high table," the boatmaster said, and Kieran nodded without speaking. *I don't like pug anyway. It cooks up too dry.* (But not under Marianella's hands, with an egg sauce and stuffed with herbs and the bread she baked.)

When they returned to shore Kieran avoided the keep and went into the camp. It looked as if it had been stirred with a stick. Men were trotting back and forth with armloads of weaponry, carefully wrapped in oiled cloth against the rain. Wagons were being loaded with barrels of flour and casks of wine and barrels of Telerath's best salted fish. In the middle of it stood Michael the Red, bellowing orders in a voice like a crosscut saw, and in front of the Captain's tent (which Ulrico and two men-at-arms were about to strike) stood Denis the Raven, wrapped to the cheekbones in his warm cloak. He saw Kieran, and raised a gloved hand in greeting. "Not the best day to set out," he said, "but orders are orders. "That's what they say in the Army, you know. Orders are orders."

"You're *leaving*?" Kieran asked, his wits still waterlogged. "Today?"

"Alas, yes," Denis said. "At least, I am staying, and a few stout fellows to police the camp. Not that it needs much policing. But the Duke of War sent a message; they are abandoning Hellsgarde and going into the west, and they want the army around them for protection and support. I believe they're going to gather their forces up around Meadingham, fifty or sixty miles north of here, and then to Tevrin to spend the winter."

"May I go along?"

Master Denis looked sharply at him. "Can they spare you here?" he said. "I know the Captain planned to take some of your fire-throwing teams along, but I thought your lot was going to remain. Seemed to me your firestarter's a young thing and cannot leave her mother."

"Not she," Kieran said. "Just ask her. She's all afire to go off and take back the Shadowlands singlehanded, and I'd better go along to keep an eye on her."

"Well, well," said Master Denis. "Perhaps you'd better." He was still looking closely at Kieran, as if he could look *through* him and understood more than Kieran would say. "Go collect your people, and make them dress warmly and pack spare hosen in their bedrolls. You'll be going through a sea of mud if this lasts. Just as well *I'm* not going."

Why, the little so-and-so, Sue commented. *He's going to sneak off without even saying goodbye? I'd better warn Marianella.* But Marianella was rolling out pastry with singleminded concentration, and Sue could not get through to her.

The phone rang, and Sue went to answer it, feeling a sudden dread that it would be Fred or perhaps the auto shop with the news that Fred's car would need X days and Y dollars to put right. But it was only Bingley.

"Hi, Sue," he said. "How're you doing?"

"Oh, hello," she said. "What's up?"

"Nothing," he said. "I just wanted to say hello. You handled Shafer very nicely last night. There were *tears* in the old bastard's eyes. You had him wrapped round your little finger."

"No thanks to you," Sue said. "I practically had a heart attack when he walked in. Couldn't you have given me some kind of warning?"

"I would've if I could've," Bingley said. "We were together all afternoon, ever since lunch; he was trying to pick my brains. Needless to say, I wouldn't be picked. Anyway, I knew you could handle it."

"Gee, thanks. It's nice to know somebody has such confidence in me."

"Oh, I do," Bingley said fervently. "I appreciate you if no one else does. That husband of yours doesn't know what he's got going for him; just sits back and takes you for granted." ("Oh, he does not," Sue muttered, but Bingley plunged on unheeding.) "Listen, does he treat you all right? You know what I mean. Are you safe with him?"

"Of course!" Sue said indignantly. "Good God. He never even raises his voice, except when the car won't start."

"Except when the—" Bingley broke off and laughed. "You are funny. I suppose that's as good an excuse as any. I've gotta go. Talk to you later." He hung up quickly; perhaps a secretary or someone had wandered into the room. Sue returned the phone very gently to its cradle, a substitute for throwing it against the wall. Bingley had revealed an area of unexpected innocence in himself; he clearly didn't know a battered wife when he saw one. Perhaps somebody had brought him up properly. Perhaps he was the type who tended to say "I'm a lover, not a fighter"—caring not how many hearts he broke so long as no bones went with them. *Oh, I could easily have done worse. Fred not only doesn't beat me, he doesn't chase after strange women and he practically doesn't drink. If I could cure him of the Great American Car Fetish he'd be practically perfect—and probably die young.*

There were plenty of people to tell Marianella that Kieran had gone off with the army—after the fact. "Oh, yes," she lied, "I knew that," and pasted a smile onto her face, a smile as thin as the mushroom slices she was stuffing the pugfish with—for Master Denis, since no one else was around to appreciate it. It was just as well, she told herself over and over; this would keep them from realizing that she and Kieran had quarreled, and by spring it would be ancient history. *Kieran,* she thought, and *My dear love,* with an earnestness that surprised her. *O Kieran.* And *It doesn't matter,* she told herself fiercely. *It doesn't matter because it is over; I shall never see him again and so I needn't worry about him. O Kieran. It doesn't MATTER!*

Oh, the poor kid, Sue thought. *Amalia, can't you do anything?*

I couldn't change people's minds even when I had the Sight, Amalia said. *When we all get to Meadingham I could command him to return to her, but I doubt she'd have him on those terms.*

No, I suppose not. Damn.

Now the rocky banks rose steeply on either side of the road, with little shrubs growing out of the crevices. The road looked as if it had been carven out of the hills, by some power no man commanded nowadays, by the grandfathers of heroes who had built when the world was young. There had been a few minutes' worth of red sunlight in their faces as they rode up the crest, but the sun had set beneath the distant sea and by now it was quite dark. The riders from Light's End lit their lanterns, and the light spilled out on the rocky ground and lit up the misty breath of men and horses. Outside the lanterns' reach the night seemed even blacker. The horses of the Hellsgarders had drifted together, walking shoulder to shoulder while their riders slumped as if in weariness, and when Amalia spoke to Genevra she made no answer. Only Adrianna turned her head a little on her breast, and said softly, "Things overhead. You know. Sssh." And Amalia was silent, and drew her cloak a little tighter around her, as if she might conceal the Heart from watchers overhead.

He is attacking with every force he has so far to the west, Aumery said. *But the Hellsgarders are keeping them at a distance, and his confidence is turning to puzzlement. He thought his attacks had driven them out at last, but they fight not like a defeated rabble fleeing, but like an army covering a strategic withdrawal to better ground. What did you say to them? How were they persuaded?*

How should I know? I can't hear them speak any more.

You— Very well, don't tell me. Be content that you have worked great confusion in your enemy.

It must be nine or ten of the clock, Amalia reckoned, but there were no clocks. As they began to descend the western slopes of the hills the Darklander attack must have tapered off, and the Hellsgarders one by one returned to their bodies and looked round them and shivered, and drank of the jug of spiced cider Adrianna carried on her saddlebows, still hot by some art of hers that Amalia envied more than her lost Sight. When the jug came to her she held it for a while to warm her numb hands. The crowned medallion was cold and prickly between her breasts.

The wind had died down to a whisper, and the rain it bore fell softly, like a thick mist. It drifted past the lanterns like an army of ghosts. There was no more Shadowlife on these hillsides, and the trees rose up on all sides with their leaves shiny as wet oilcloth and their trunks looking as if they had been waxed. Remembering the dark landscapes she had rid-

den through with Ulf, Amalia looked on these dark wet
thickets of trees with pleasure; they were her own kind of life.
But she was growing very tired, and her greatest concern now
was not to fall asleep, lest she fall off the horse before they
reached shelter. She rode in a dream through slow-moving
forests of mist, while lines of marching trees filed past her on
either side, and scarcely knew where she was until a huge
shape with a voice at once harsh and tender, like a jaybird
sitting on eggs, lifted her from the saddle and tucked her into
a hard warm welcome bed.

Fred came home early, in Sue's car, bringing with him a
little red-and-white box in a little paper bag. The starter
solenoid to fix his car with, he explained, and he'd better
get it installed while there was still some light. So he
spent half an hour huddling over a pile of cold metal in the
middle of a snowstorm (some of the flakes were sticking to
the ground now), but he didn't mind at all because the car
was responding to treatment. (*Men!*) There was no cider in
the house, but Sue heated mugs of tomato soup to hold
everyone till dinner, and put cider and cinnamon and
cloves on her shopping list. When Fred finally got inside,
his nose red and the light of triumph in his eyes, he was
properly appreciative.

"I'm sorry about this morning, honey," he said as they
got ready for bed. "I shouldn't take it out on you."

"No, you shouldn't," she agreed, "and the next time
you try it I'm going to yell back. Just the same, I've seen
worse. You don't get drunk, you don't beat us—"

" 'Mr. Fields, do you approve of clubs for women?' "
Fred quoted. "Mmmm, yaas, but only when kindness
fails.' "

"I think I'll keep you," Sue said.

"Well, that's a relief. Let's go to bed."

Marianella delayed going to bed as long as she could; she
knew what she would find. Empty room, cold bed, no Kieran.
She checked over the inventory of the spice cupboard, and
went back twice to make sure she had locked it. She went out
to the stables to check on the horses, and down into the
cellars to check on the barrels of fish. Finally she climbed the
stairs and crawled into bed in the darkness, hoping she would
be tired enough to sleep. But she lay awake between the cold

sheets, her feet icy and her body uncomfortably warm. *Kieran.* Her heart would not let her rest, and she feared she would have to take another lover, if she could find one in this wilderness, just to be able to sleep. She could not lie still, and tossed back and forth like a fish in a net. Suddenly she flung off the bedcovers and put her feet to the floor. This was not of her own doing; she realized with a shiver that there was some compulsion on her. This fire in her body was no fault of Kieran's; something had hold of her as if it had set a hook in her flesh and was pulling her along by it. She took a step, and another step, across the floor. She put her weight on her heels and tried not to move. *Come,* she felt in the depths of her body, *come to me.* She shook her head violently, and took another step. What thing was calling her? Some creature of the Darkness, the thing that had touched Amalia?

Then her foot set itself on the first step that led up the tower, and she knew. She laughed from relief and delight, and ran lightly up the tower stairs. She flung open the door, crossed the room quickly (for the air was growing very cold), and slipped under the covers and into Denis's arms.

To lie with a great Seer such as Master Denis—and she had done the like a time or two before—was to be not a woman tumbling with a man, but a handmaiden serving before the altar of a god. She felt overpowered, swept off her feet by something greater than man into a torrent of passion that left her breathless and trembling. (The fact that Denis was able to know exactly what she was thinking and feeling, and conduct himself accordingly, had something to do with it.)

What's more, when word got to Kieran (as it undoubtedly would) of what she was doing in his absence, he would be given to know that she wasn't wasting any tears over him.

CHAPTER 11

The Night the Sun Turns

By morning the sea, sky, and air were all equally grey, and almost equally wet. A ferocious wind had blown in off the sea, and for three days it whistled round Telerath tower like a family of idiots with flutes. The farmfolk were uneasy about their crops, but as it turned out the vegetables were old enough, and the wheat still young enough, to spring up again once the wind and rain had passed. Meanwhile they kept inside their shelters, huddling over carefully rationed fires and watching the big drops of water slowly form on the underside of the canvas and roll downhill into the green turf of the walls.

Marianella's original intention, once she learned that Amalia was in Meadingham, had been to go to her as soon as possible; but then the weather turned foul. It was easy to persuade herself to stay on a little longer, just to make sure Tama would be able to run the keep by herself. By the time the storm blew out, Tama was running the keep by herself and Marianella was keeping to her bed with the quilts pulled up to her chin; her bones ached and her stomach was queasy. If anyone had asked Tama, she would have diagnosed one part cold weather and three parts Kieran; but nobody asked her and she kept her mouth shut. She fed Marianella broth and bread and brought her a basin or a chamberpot as needed—or saw to it that somebody did. And she told her the news, at first, till it became plain to Marianella that Tama could handle all without her advice, and plainer to Tama that Marianella was feeling too wretched to give a damn.

One part cold weather and at least three parts Kieran,
Sue agreed, not knowing how close to the truth she spoke.
She was feeling fairly rotten herself; her usual pre-Christmas
cold had her throat between its teeth and she could hardly
speak for coughing and croaking. She would have been
glad to crawl into bed herself, but there was nobody to
wait on her; maidservants were long gone into the past
and household robots still part of the misty future. She
would have given years off her life for R2–D2 to wash the
dishes or C–3PO to make the kids get dressed, but they
weren't on the market yet. The stores were filling up with
radio-controlled monsters, death rays, vortex blasters, and
the giant moth that sat down on Tokyo, but nothing useful,
nothing beneficial, not this Christmas. It was a sad comment on the misdirection of human ingenuity.

At that, she was better off than most people, because
Kelly came in twice, once to help with the house and once
to help with the baking. Sue had a fruitcake recipe so
stuffed with fruit that it looked like stained glass when
sliced, and it would take more than a cold to keep it from
being made this Christmas.

"Two broken legs and the plague at least," Kelly agreed,
holding a slice up to the light and admiring the clear red
and yellow and green. "The water's boiling; you get into
bed and I'll bring you some tea." She brought Sue a tray
with a little teapot they had found at a garage sale, and a
cup and saucer, and a slice of stained-glass fruitcake. "Now
I've got to go; I promised my mom I'd run her some
errands downtown. Anything you need?"

"Uh, yes, if you're going past the library. I'll write you a
note." She had been trying to draw up a coherent list of
things she ought to study, and her wastebasket was full of
crumpled papers. She had reached the stage where igno-
rance was *not* bliss, where she had only a dim idea of how
much she didn't know. So her note simply said, "I want to
study medieval history properly; what do you suggest?"
She gave this and her library card to Kelly, who glanced at
them and said, "Sure, why not? it'll keep you off the
streets," and left in a cloud of giggles and the sound of the
north wind banging the door shut. Big white flakes were

drifting down past Sue's window, and the radio talked of overnight temperatures getting down into the single digits.

At the foot of the Weatherwall it was snowing also, and Amalia spent hours watching the silent flakes fall, like ash after a great fire, and settle onto the steps of the House of the Mists. Sometimes a gentle wind would blow, carrying the snowflakes a few feet past the pillars to lie in thin drifts along the marble floors. And sometimes a great dark storm would blow in, singing its cold song over the roof and around the pillars; but at such times the House would put up some kind of barrier, and the snow would beat against invisible wards and pile up in thick drifts upon the steps. But still the mist that continually welled up in the House drifted out unhindered between the pillars, till the winds caught it up and froze it in an instant into thousands of tiny glittering specks, and whirled it away like a shower of diamonds.

Amalia did not feel the cold; she felt very little except (she thought) the solidity of the floor under her feet and sometimes a breath of wind against her face. Perhaps in time she would go altogether numb. She asked Aumery.

No, he said, *as the years pass you will become more aware of things around you. I have been here two hundred years, nearly, and I see the colors of the sun that change over the Weatherwall, and follow the mists that drift upward against the cliffs; and I hear the wild birds crying, that nest in the crevices outside this valley, and the little trickling drops that fall from the ice on the longest days of summer. Unfortunately, I also feel the cold.*

He was silent, and Amalia cast her Sight outward as far as it could reach, examining the landscape around the House. It was a narrow valley, no more than a mile long from the place where it ran out of a cleft in the rough granite to the cliff's edge that she had climbed. Many trees had once stood in the valley, but they were all dead and most had fallen under the weight of centuries of frost and snow. There was no other side of life, not even a bird or an insect; the birds Aumery spoke of had flown south, maybe, or else they never came into the valley. *Aumery!*

My dear?

Whatever became of Ruk?

I don't know. He has gone out of the sight of any of Imber's creatures. Perhaps he crossed the river and joined the garrison at Hudelsford, or perhaps he's dead. Why do you ask?

I suppose I feel responsible for him, poor wretch. I shall keep an eye out for him; my poor old body has been asleep nearly a day and a night, and it's time I woke it up and took charge.

And assembled an army to lead against Imber. I wish you every strangest kind of luck; you'll need it.

He was silent for a moment, while the sparse flakes swirled in the wind and the mist drifted between the pillars like gauze curtains. *There's one other you should look out for,* he said finally. *He's somewhere in the West, but I'm not sure where; since Ruk went into the West, and my outer envelope has been in Agniran, I've had no news of him. He's been called Amsara sometimes, and Gorbadoc, and Helm. I don't know what his name is now.*

Is he working for the Darkness?

He has seen me, Aumery said after a moment's pause. *He knows what I am. But he has never told the Lords of the West about me; else Ruk would have known it, and Mark of Hellsgarde would have recognized me in your mind. Nor has he fought for Imber. He told me he would, once, but on the day he sided with the Lightlanders instead. No, so far as I can tell he is working only for himself. So long as Imber stands, this man will probably fight him, but if Imber were to fall then I don't know what he would do. So if you see him, be wary.*

How do I know him when I see him?

He's tall and fair-haired, clean-shaven; about forty years old, I think. An ordinary-looking man, you would not notice him if he were standing still. But when he moves, or when he speaks, he makes the air around him cold. He has the air of a commander— but I do not know who, or what, are his followers. I say again, if you see him, be on your guard.

Around two o'clock the phone rang. "Hi, honey," Fred said. "Can I invite Siobhan to dinner tonight? We've got some things to talk about."

"Okay," Sue said, reaching for the Kleenex. "I wasn't— achoo!—planning anything special, but Siobhan won't expect fancy. Will you call her, or shall I?"

"Oh, I will. Thanks. How's your cold?"

"Oh, *it's* just fine. Okay, I'll see you."

It wasn't till after she had finished her tea, and fallen asleep and dreamed of telephoning the local Roto-Rooter to ream out her sinuses and woken up again, that she realized a lot of women would be panicking at this point. In your average real-world marriage, let alone those technicolor couples in the soaps, a husband telling his wife that he and another woman "had some things to talk about" would signal a divorce at the very least. But Sue knew Fred well enough after all these years that no fear rippled over the soggy surface of her mind, only a vague undercurrent that said, "This is some kind of computer business." And that wasn't so dreadful a thought, even though it was probably going to cost them some money.

Feeling at least marginally better for the hot tea and the afternoon in bed, Sue got up around four o'clock to invent dinner. Hamburger out of the fridge, peas out of the freezer, noodles out of the box, and never mind what Marianella might say. (Marianella had one pillow propping up her knees and another squashed down over her eyes against the afternoon sun. Tama had been in to see her twice and she hadn't moved in the last hour and a half.)

Fred came home with an air of suppressed excitement and a fistful of little three-by-five cards, crosshatched with cryptic notes from himself to himself. Siobhan arrived with a pile of paper, manila folders, computer magazines; she stacked them neatly on the coffee table and didn't discuss them during dinner. The kids were being almost unnaturally good; company manners, of course, and then Christmas was coming and they were working on their share of vortex blasters, plastic puppy dogs, and jars of green slime, just add water, batteries not included.

"Okay," Fred said, once the children had been packed away to bed and the adults had taken their second cups of coffee into the living room. "I want to buy us a Christmas present."

"Let me guess," Sue said. "A Christmas present with a keyboard and a video screen. I expected something like that. Are you going to buy the one you've been bringing home?"

"I'd rather not," Fred said. "I'd like something more powerful."

"And more expensive?"

"Not by a whole lot," Siobhan said. "Not an arm and a leg, let's say, just a couple of fingers. What Fred wants to get is this." She pulled a shiny blue folder out of her stack of papers. "This isn't the latest and biggest PS/2, but it's big enough for his purposes."

She flipped through the blue brochure; Sue recognized some, but only some, of the things the little blue computer was supposed to do.

"It's *not* the best you can get," Siobhan said, "but it's widely used in business, and the programs that he's using at work will run on it. And if you're going to learn just one machine, then it's a good idea to do the one that all the businesses are using.

"So he'll start out with the system that comes with the machine, which is what Sav-Mor's using now, and later on you can get UNIX, which is what Sav-Mor *will* be using as soon as it wakes up and smells the coffee. And from there he can go anywhere. Even to the Entworks, if he really wanted to."

"Too long a commute," Fred said, deadpan.

Sue laughed. "Okay, it does everything but change the baby and walk the dog. How much?"

"Oh, if you went to the computer store they'd charge you three grand. Don't faint! And they'd put it all together for you and hold your hand and show you how to use it. But you and Fred don't need their help; I can help you put it together and you can learn to use it on the fly. So you don't need to pay for that up front. Here's last month's *Byte*, it's full of ads, you can mailorder it for half the price."

Sue glanced at Fred. His eyes were eager, anxious. The last time she had seen so much "Oh, please say yes!" on his face was when he had asked her to marry him.

"Well, you won't hear me saying no," Sue said. "Can I get a program to teach me about accounting?"

"Sure, if you want."

"I don't really want, but I thought it might help us to keep track of Shafer. Except by the time I learn anything this project'll probably be over, but there's always a next time."

"No doubt," Siobhan said. "You can get games, too, dungeon-crawling and starships and mazes and . . ."

But Sue started sneezing again, so Fred said good night to Siobhan and got Sue a hot water bottle and poured her into bed.

Amalia came back to herself slowly, as one comes back to one's house after a long absence and reluctantly opens the door on moths, mildew, and mice. Her head ached, her back was stiff, and her eyes were full of sand. She stretched and pulled at cramped muscles, and pumped her lungs full of air. The headache began to recede, and she rubbed her eyes and sat up.

The room was large, and had once been very grand; traces of bright-colored murals still clung to the stone walls. Like many Great Halls, the room was lined with timbers from which curtains could be hung, dividing the sides of the hall into cubicles.

Someone had taken her clothes and boots away and put her into a plain linen shift. An instant of panic flashed over her, and she clutched at her breast. The silver heart still hung round her neck. She opened it a hairsbreadth, and the cold red glow poured out; quickly she shut it again.

There was a blue cloak laid across the end of the bed. She got to her feet, threw the cloak round her, and pushed the curtain aside.

A long table stood in the center of the room, and there were signs that three men had been at work there, three piles of papers, maps and lists and even rough notes sent in from the field on scraps of leather and broken pottery. Mark of Hellsgarde sat at one of the places, looking at a map but not seeing it. Across from him sat a stocky grey-haired man whom Amalia recognized (after a little thought) as Rolf Hammerhand, the master of Light's End. The third place was empty.

"Ah, Lady!" Rolf cried, leaping to his feet. "You're with us again. Welcome to Light's End, though I fear it's not for long. We set off again tomorrow." He bent and kissed her hand. "But don't be alarmed, I have a wagon for your Ladyship."

"Thank you," Amalia said. "I don't expect to need it; I feel quite well." She stretched again. "Or I shall soon. The Duke told you where I've been?" Her hand went to her breast and touched the thin silver shell under the linen, the Heart light and cool as a bubble within.

"Oh, yes." There was respect in his voice. Rolf was used to fighting the Darklanders, but not on their own ground. "And that you've come to Light's End to call for an army. We're doing our best to raise one. There's a great host come in already from the North, plains riders who'd as lief hunt Shadowlings as wolves. They sleep in their saddles as often as not, and they don't fear any darkness."

"Good," Amalia said, attempting to comb out her hair with fingers. All her hairpins were Heaven knew where by the roadside. "Neither do I."

"Maybe you could send your wife to Lady Amalia," Mark of Hellsgarde said. "I suspect she'd like a bath, and a comb, and a new set of hairpins."

That was exactly what Amalia wanted. She had had a sort of a wash at Hellsgarde, but there hadn't been time to heat a big cauldron of water and fill a tub, such as Rolf's wife had done in her own room at the head of the Hall. Amalia slipped out of cloak and shift and stepped into the tub. The Heart—well, probably the water would do it no harm, but she wasn't about to find out the hard way. Carefully she took the chain off and hung it over the edge of the tub. "Mistress Rose," she said, "no one is to touch that. Understand me? No one."

"I shan't touch it, I'm sure," the woman said, "and no one else is coming in here, not if I know it— Agh!" For the Duke of War had walked into the room without any warning, smiling in his distant way and fanning the steam out of his face with his hand.

"Master Rolf just had a good idea," he said. (Amalia settled a little deeper into the soapy water. She was covered up to her modest cleavage in bubbles, and anyway there was nothing about women's bodies that Mark hadn't known before she was born.) "He'd like you to speak to the men tonight, explain to them whatever you think it's good for them to know, make them understand how important this is."

"Heavens! Like the general addressing the troops? I'll speak to them, Mark, but you're the general, not I. Unless you can find a younger man, one who might make a better field commander. Randall of Tower Lost, maybe? I'm told he managed very well, picking up the pieces I left him at Telerath."

"Maybe," Mark said. "For pure skill at leading men, I would have chosen your brother Andri once; but not now, when he's—"

"He's not available," Amalia finished for him. Mark had spent his life in an intimacy of thought wherein there were no secrets except from the enemy; he might have forborne to say "He's on the other side" in front of Mistress Rose, or he might not. "Tell me something." She glanced at the silver heart, hanging from its chain over the tub's rim. "Do the men know about this?"

"Only that it's the Dark Lord's bane, if we can get it to him," Mark said. "About what it is, they know nothing."

"Good. See to it they don't. And I'll give them a rousing chorus this evening. Thank you, Mark." She didn't realize the words were a dismissal until she had spoken them, and Mark bowed and turned away. *What am I now, that I tell the Duke of War to come and go?* The thought chilled her, or perhaps it was the contrast of air and water. She scooped up a double handful of warm water and poured it over her throat.

Mistress Rose was as red as her name, and breathless with her effort not to say what she thought. "Oh, don't be upset," Amalia said. "That's the Duke of War, remember, a very great Seer. He knows what you and I look like even with our clothes on." Rose went two shades darker. "And he doesn't *care*," Amalia said, but she felt she hadn't helped things much.

And it isn't as if he could see *anything*, Sue commented, *as opposed to Seeing whatever it is he Sees. I've seen more skin on the cover of* Playboy—*hell, I've seen more skin on television advertising cream rinse!* She was up to her own breastbone in hot water by now; it was a bleak grey afternoon and a bath sounded like good medicine. The only trouble was that, while she could fill her tub more easily than Mistress Rose could, she could only fill it to a depth of eighteen inches. She scooted down till the water covered her breasts; but this meant sticking her knees out into the air (which fortunately by now was warm). She lay there, the heat comforting about her chest and the steam sweet in her congested lungs, and thought longingly of big wooden tubs, deep enough to cover your whole body. They had them in California—she had seen them on television. Maybe Bingley had a friend who could export one to her? They could keep the marijuana and peacock feathers, if only they'd send her a hot tub. A small one—they must hold a lot of hot water, and fuel wasn't getting any cheaper.

"Ah, thank you," Amalia said as Mistress Rose poured another kettleful of hot water into the tub. She settled in deeper, cross-legged, and let the water lap round her collarbones. It felt good. Once upon a time, she mused, when her friends had chidden her (as friends will) for remaining a virgin—"The pity of it! the waste! you don't know what you are missing!"—she had said that a good hot bath equaled any other pleasure that a healthy body could know. Now she knew more of what she was talking about, and was tempted to take back her words. (Aumery, lean and strong, his skin pale against his dark hair, his touch filling her body like light.) She sat for a long time, till the water began to cool. Then she soaped and rinsed, and scrubbed at her scalp with her fingertips, and rinsed off one last time and climbed out. Mistress Rose brought her a linen towel, frayed at the edges but large and clean, and a wooden comb. She worked the snarls out of her hair, and coiled it high on her head. It made her look two inches taller, and noble and severe. She put on the Heart again, and her red gown, and the blue cloak because her hair was still wet, and went out into the Hall again to deal with the provision of an army.

Kelly stopped by briefly, while Sue was cooking dinner, to drop off Sue's library card and a stack of books and a note from the librarian. "This is mostly survey stuff," the note read. "Life in the Middle Ages, picture books from the National Geographic and so forth, but I've included one straightforward history so you can keep track of who was doing what to whom, and when, and where. And a book of heraldry, and one on costume, and I've renewed all your cookbooks because they were due tomorrow and your friend says you're down with a bug. You might like to take the World History class at the City College; it's a two-year course and the second semester begins with the fall of Rome, 476 AD. When you finish these I'll pick out some more. Take care of your cold."

Around nightfall Marianella got up and called for soap and water and her warm clothing. Tama sent in a maid with them, rather than coming herself—well, and she was busy with the Hall's dinner. The maid was slow-witted, and almost literally dumb with shyness; Marianella knew better than to ask her for news. She knew most of it herself anyway; Amalia had come safely to Light's End and would set out for Meadingham tomorrow.

For her own part, Marianella had abandoned her plans to meet her Ladyship in Meadingham; it would be another week or two before she was fit to travel, and the Duke's party would soon move on to Tevrin for the Solstice. She would go directly to Tevrin, and if Denis preferred to stay in Telerath he might do so, and if Kieran had the gall to show his nose in Tevrin she would look straight through him.

She pulled the bedgown over her head. *Kieran.* Add up his faults till they rose to the skies and toppled over, still there was no man with a softer mouth. *I haven't an inch of my body that's as soft,* she thought, *unless—* Her fingertips brushed across her nipples, and for an instant she could imagine the softness of Kieran's lips. But they contracted under her touch and the chilly air, and shrank into hard forthright dugs: she could have fed twins with them, if she'd had them. *The hell with it.* She rubbed soap into the cloth and began to wash.

Mother! Sue thought, and shook her head as she slid dinner's casserole into the oven. *Nothing I can do to help there, that's for damn sure. Anything I can do for Amalia?*

Do you know anything about making speeches? Amalia asked, softly and from a distance. Most of her attention was on the maps Mark and Rolf had laid before her, and the list of baronies and farmsteads that had sent men and supplies to the mustering of the army, and the rather longer list of those who had promised help that might yet come to them at Meadingham.

Not so I'd notice. You did all right yesterday morning— no, day before last, or whenever that was at Hellsgarde.

You did all right at the PTA meeting. Let us stop patting one another on the back. At Hellsgarde I was talking to my own kind—or so they used to be—and knew how to talk to them. I don't know what to say to ordinary men, common folk without the Sight. But I must, so I shall. It'll come to me.

Night fell, clear and cold with a smooth lavender light in the west, dying into plum and purple and velvet black. Outside the Hall, the men were gathering with torches in their hands, and the garth was as thick with scattered light as the sky overhead. Amalia glanced about, and hugged herself close and shivered. She had the blue cloak over her red wool, and the white furry cloak over that, and was still cold. She would have to look up some more winter clothing tomorrow, or she'd never last till they reached Tevrin.

Someone had built a platform of rough wood, with four steps leading up to it, and they had set Amalia at its top. Lord Mark was behind her, Master Rolf beside her with another torch, held high so that the men could see her. Soon she must speak.

There was a rustling in the ranks, a squirming motion as men stepped aside, and others stepped aside for them, to let someone pass, a man in a horseman's short cloak and hood, pushing his way up to the front. His clothing was dark under the torchlight, and he wore long-heeled riding boots that made his tall body even taller. She could not see much of his face, but he had a short reddish beard, and the men to right and left of him fell back before him as if they respected his authority, or at the very least his temper. His was not the mouth of a kindly man, or of one inclined to let well enough alone. But he came meekly enough to the foot of the steps, and sat on the bottom one so that the men behind him might see over his head. The crowd became quiet. Amalia took a deep breath, and another.

"I have only to say to you what I said to Lord Mark a few days ago, and to Master Rolf this morning," she said. "But they knew already that I have the right to speak, knowing where I have been and what I have been doing. I want you to know that too. I have been to Agniran and back, the citadel of Imber." A murmur went through the listening men. "Yes, I dare to speak his name. I have stood before him, spoken with him; I have seen his face. I no longer fear him. And if you men, by your strength and courage, can bring me to him, then you too no longer need fear him."

"This is all very well," said the man seated at her feet. "It's better than any poet's song, but can we believe it? No offense, madam, but if as you say you've come out of the Shadowlands, can we be sure of whose side you are on?"

Amalia looked down at him, an uncertain shape under the flickering torches. "No offense to you either, sir; I do not know your name."

"Oh, this is Lord Saradoc Ranger, who gathered the men of the highlands to meet us," Master Rolf said. "He was working with us this morning; I'm sorry, I thought your Ladyship had met him."

"Well, milord Saradoc," Amalia said, "you can believe the Duke of War, I hope? He knows all my story, more than I will tell here, and can vouch for the truth of it."

"Very well, very well," Saradoc said, raising his hand as if to wave reproach aside.

"Very well," Amalia repeated. "A month ago my brother, Lord Andri of Fendarath, was taken by two Shadowknights." Another murmur. No one had told these men yet that Shadowknights were abroad again. "I went into the Darklands, searching for him—and I found him too, but he was lost, And I could not save him. But in going through that country, even to Agniran, and coming out again, I learned things for which my brother would gladly have given his life, if he had had the choice. I have the thing that will be the death of Imnber, if we can only bring it to him."

No murmurs now, but cheers, and the men crowded close around the steps.

"The difficulty, of course, is in bringing it to him, since he will not come meekly to us to take death from my hands! That is why I need you, all of you, to make an army that can march along the soft white roads through the Darklands, fight off the Shadowlings and the silverbacks and the cat-riders, tear down the walls of Agniran if need be, and let me come to him. Because if you can do that, then we may yet conquer. And if you can't, then we shall certainly fail and die."

"Well said!" cried Saradoc from his place at her feet. Rising from the step, he seized her hand and kissed it, and climbed to stand beside her. "Lady, forgive me that I doubted you; for now I know you speak truly. You have seen what none has seen before, and found the way to destroy the Dark Lord. With you to lead us, we shall have the victory, and take the curse of the Shadow off our land!"

The men roared. *Now if only I had a great booming voice like that*, Amalia thought, *so to help my rhetoric along!* Saradoc was still holding her hand, so firmly that she could not get it loose without an unseemly tug. He raised his free hand high, to quiet the crowd, and bit by bit they hushed and waited to listen again.

"I have another thing to say," he said. "Since that day two

hundred years ago when Maximus the last King and Aumery his son died on the banks of the Kendal, we have had no leader, but have gone our separate ways under our several Lords and Captains. The Lord of Hellsgarde is our Duke of War, and rightly so, for he is the greatest of our Captains, and now has come out of the Shadow to lead our army. But he is a man of war, not skilled in statecraft."

Amalia, knowing very well how skillfully Mark had dealt with affairs of state without so much as leaving Hellsgarde, was indignant. She turned to catch his eye, but he only raised a finger, as if to say, "Wait."

She turned back to Saradoc. She had missed some of what he was saying, and for a moment it did not make sense. ". . . and make us one kingdom again. She has come out of the Shadow to lead us into the light: Amalia the Queen!"

No cheers now, but gasps and muttering. There had not been a reigning Queen since Atalanta the Red, lost in the mists of legend. Amalia had the sensation of picking her dropped jaw up off the floor.

"We ride to Tevrin for the Solstice," Saradoc went on, "to crown her Queen at Tevrin, that she may reign in Andarath!"

With you at my side, no doubt! Her hand was still held fast; indeed, whether from desire or craft Saradoc had been drawing her steadily nearer him, like a fisherman reeling in his line, so that she could speak almost in his ear. "Quiet them so that I may speak," she whispered, and obediently he raised his hand again and waited till the men fell silent.

Saradoc's hood had fallen back on his shoulders, and the torchlight shone on his fair hair. His pale eyes gazed on her steadily, unwavering. "I know you, Saradoc," she said, "though under a different name. We have a dear friend in common. He too has many names, but I am sure you must remember him. Tall, and very thin, with scars on his hollow cheeks, black hair, great dark sad eyes, and a slow way of speaking, as though it were long since he spoke to men—"

Saradoc had gone pale, and his eyes narrowed. Amalia pulled her hand loose from his grasp and turned toward the men. "This man is a traitor," she said. "Twice traitor, for he would as gladly sell us to the Darklanders as them to us. Take him—"

But Saradoc's arm was round her shoulder, and his other hand held a dagger to her throat. "Move and she dies!"

For an instant there was silence, just long enough for Saradoc to glance about and choose his path of escape. Amalia had just time to think, *This is absurd, I can't die now; I have work to do!* But in the next breath someone started up from underfoot, from nowhere, and pulled down the dagger from Amalia's throat, and the two men tumbled down the stairs in a confusion of legs and arms.

Voices cried, "Seize him!" and "To me!" "Take care!" and "You bastard!" while Master Rolf helped Amalia to her feet and Mark of Hellsgarde shouted orders. Slowly the dust and the confusion settled; of the tangle of men on the steps there remained only a little man in a leather jerkin, holding a bloody cloth to his face.

A sergeant pushed his way through the crowd. "My Lord, I'm sorry. He's got away, with a dozen or so of his men. Their horses were in that grove. They're headed south. We've got men mounted now, and going after them. We should have them within the hour."

"Not bloody likely," another man said, "not with those horses Saradoc's got."

"Keep me informed," Lord Mark said. "Is that man all right?"

"Don't know, sir."

"Get a leech!" someone else said. "He's wounded!"

"No, I'm not," said a muffled voice. "I've a nosebleed, that's all. The bastard had a hard head. Ah, thanks." A soldier had brought a damp rag, and the little man took it and wiped his face. Then he looked up at Amalia. "Good evening, m'Lady. I'd hoped to be here before this, but there was rain on the road. Still, late is better than never."

Amalia sat down suddenly on the top step, and put her hand on Kieran's shoulder, and rested her head on it. "Kieran, get me to bed. Oh, it's all right, Master Rolf, this is my seneschal from Telerath. Get me to bed, Kieran, and then find a bed for yourself. We ride for Meadingham in the morning and I am as weary as the dead."

By the time Sue's cold was on the wane, it was the twentieth of December, and she had to bundle herself into the car and do the Christmas shopping in a rush. She resisted the slime and the blasters, and bought the children clothes and books—and one video game apiece, to go with the computer that they had not been told about yet. She and Fred had already determined—and they would have to harden their hearts and stick to it—that the children could play games only when their homework was done, their rooms were clean, and no grownup needed to use the machine for something resembling work.

Buying the games got her stuck in a long checkout line that wavered just this side of gridlock. This meant she had time to run over her lists, mental and written, of what needed doing next. The written lists were on the backs of envelopes, half-sheets of the kids' school paper, and one old-fashioned IBM punch card that she had picked up from Siobhan. The mental lists were even more chaotic, and seemed to be written on a sheet of rubber that stretched here and shrank there and was continually flapping in a strong wind. Still, she had the general impression that things were in hand. She wasn't going to try to give a Christmas party, not this year, not when she had been lying in bed croaking like a foghorn when she should have been inviting people; but she had promised to bake goodies for a party at the school and another at the church, and— consulting the dancing words on the rubber sheet, she *thought* it would be safe to offer Siobhan a cake or something for the faculty party. With day classes, evening classes, no husband, and two kids, Siobhan didn't have time for things like baking. ("Once upon a time I tried to do it all," she had said. "I was Supermom—house, kids, work, school, the whole nine yards. Something had to give, and what gave was my health. After I got back on my feet I learned to order my priorities. The kids' health, and mine, are on the top of the stack. The house is somewhere around the bottom.")

The shopping mall was full of people and their noise, playing a random bass line to the Christmas carols blaring nonstop over the loudspeakers, and it wasn't until Sue got to the very center, where three corridors intersected in a big open space, that she began to recognize the other sounds she heard. The gentle buzzing sounds of shawms and krummhorns, like dragonflies that had been to the conservatory of music; a rhythmic thump of drums and the thin chime of finger cymbals. She wriggled through the crowds till she could see.

Twenty men and women, most of them college-age or not much older, in a fine mixture of medieval and Renaissance dress. They were dancing a pavane, with slow steps and deep knee bends, and much stately flourishing of the ladies' full skirts and the swords that hung from the gentlemen's sides. Someone had hung a banner from the pillar behind them: three horizontal stripes with wavy edges, blue, white, and green, with a green wreath of leaves of the middle stripe. A sweet-faced woman wearing a tenth-century wimple handed her a sheet of printed paper.

"WELCOME TO THE CURRENT MIDDLE AGES," it said. "We are the Barony of Strange Sea in the Middle Kingdom of the Society for Creative Anachronism. Our purpose is to recreate the Middle Ages, not as they were, but as they should have been. . . ." Sue watched in fascination as they danced, and after the dance held court, and after court demonstrated the art of fighting with broadsword and shield, She watched until her tired arms would no longer be ignored, and when she had to leave she tucked the flyer into her packages.

"Can I see?" Mike asked when she got home, making an unsuccessful raid on her paper bags. "Is it for us? What did you get?"

"Cat's fur to make kitten britches," Sue said, like her mother and her grandmother before her, and stowed the presents in the attic, in the big suitcase with the lock. But when she looked for the Anachronists' flyer, it seemed to have vanished.

It never snowed in Telerath—at least, not within the memory of anyone in the village—but once they had crossed the Medon and followed the east road over the first range of hills, the air got much colder. There were little dirty white drifts on the eastern side of slopes and boulders, and on most evenings fat white flakes fell as thick as stars, and melted before noon.

Marianella was better these days, no longer queasy or feverish, but her body was weak from the long days in bed. Sometimes she rode Rowan in the afternoons, but mostly she rode in the wagon Denis had furnished for her, soft with straw and well-stocked with cloaks and blankets against the cold.

Still, it was pleasant to be out in the world again, to breathe fresh air and see the sunlight every day on a new place. By the end of the week's travel she was riding most of the day, and thinking cheerfully of Midwinter at Tevrin, and the comforts of Rhadath House, and seeing her Ladyship again.

(That Kieran had gone to join the army at Meadingham, that the army was coming to Tevrin in her Ladyship's train, that Kieran might well come with them: that, she would not think about.)

The sun was nearly at the horizon, and a thick mist was forming among the trees that lined the road. Now the sergeant rode forward to take the leads of the draft horses and lead the wagon off the road into a clearing ringed with trees. "This is Fowler's Halt, Master Denis," the sergeant said. "We'll camp here for the night." The sergeant and his men—there were only five of them—tethered their horses behind the wagon and began to set up camp.

"Right," Denis said, helping Marianella down from Rowan's back. "You get in the wagon. One of the men can groom your horse."

"Let me get a blanket over her first," Marianella protested. "It must be nearly freezing, and the sun's not down yet." She took the horse blanket from the corner of the wagon box and covered Rowan with it. Denis crossed the campsite and disappeared among the trees on the other side. Marianella climbed into the wagon and tucked a blanket round her feet. *One more day*, she thought. *Rhadath House. Real beds, hot baths, somebody else's cooking.*

From her place in the wagon she could see the road, muddy during the day but now freezing solid, for forty yards behind them and ten yards ahead. East of Fowler's Halt, just out of sight around the bend, the road hunched its shoulders and began the last and steepest climb into the hills. Midmorning tomorrow would see them over the crest and beginning the long descent into the valley of the Caramath River and down to Tevrin. Across the road the trees closed in, middle-sized oaks and a few conifers. The mist hung between their damp trunks like flimsy curtains. As she watched, shapes appeared on the mist, like breath on glass: men on horseback. Five, ten, a dozen of them. Drawn swords and knives were in their hands.

They spread out slightly as they crossed the road, to cover the whole clearing at once. Could six armed men handle twice as many ruffians at once?

The sun had fallen almost out of sight; it was growing dark, and the leader of the riders pushed back his hood from his head. Marianella had a glimpse of fair hair, a long angular face, a short red beard.

Ohmigod, it's Saradoc, Marianella, that's Saradoc; call Master Denis, quick!

Marianella didn't linger to ask who/what/why. She took a deep breath and tried to think as loudly as she could, *Denis, it's Saradoc. Saradoc and a dozen men. Denis, Denis, Saradoc, Saradoc, come quickly.* She added an irreverent mental picture of Denis interrupting whatever he was doing in midstream and running as if the fiend were after him. Then she looked up at Saradoc. "Good evening, sir," she said. "It looks like a cold night."

Saradoc looked her up and down, lying in her pile of straw in the wagon, and smiled just a little. "Not so cold as you might think," he said, and spurred his horse forward.

But now the sergeant came running from the woods and Master Denis, and the men moved in closer to the wagon. Saradoc raised his sword. But Denis lifted his hands, long and thin as the forefeet of a deer, and suddenly no one could move.

Saradoc's horse stood still in mid-step. Slowly, as if it were stuck in tar, it lowered its raised hoof to the ground. Saradoc's raised sword-arm began to sag. Master Denis folded his hands on his breast. A cool blue light was growing in the air around him, a half-dome of light like the sheen over a moonstone. Within that shell, they could move, and the soldiers moved closer to the wagon and felt the edges of their weapons. Denis took a step sideways, and leaned against the side of the wagon. It was possible they might be there a while.

Stillness and silence. Marianella glanced anxiously at Denis. His face was calm, but she knew that his body's strength was not great and that he must eventually grow tired. Men and horses stood motionless. The sun sank out of sight. The air was growing colder. Nothing could be heard but a bird's cry far off and a faint dripping sound closer to, from snowy branches perhaps that would soon freeze into silence.

No, not dripping branches, but hoofbeats. Four or five horses approaching at a run, and a cry of "Hold on!"

They came galloping round the bend in the road from the east, waving cudgels and clubs and one rusty sword. Five ill-assorted men on ill-favored horses, and their leader—

Master Denis clapped his hands, sharply, and the bubble burst. Saradoc's horses stepped backward, his men blinked and shook their heads, and the five riders were upon them. Outmatched and outnumbered as they were, they attacked the end of the line while the sergeant and his squad moved in to hit them in the middle. Saradoc cried out, and his men massed round him and they withdrew into the forest.

"Let them go," Denis said. They watched them disappear among the trees. Denis and the sergeant stood motionless till the hoofbeats could no longer be heard. "Very good," he said. "We thank you. To whom do we owe the honor of keeping our heads on our shoulders?"

"Oh, I remember you," Marianella said to the leader. "You came to see her Ladyship in Tevrin. You're—"

That's Ruk, Sue told her. *Amalia met him again on the edge of the Twilight. He was going to go off and join the good guys. Evidently he did.*

"You're Ruk," Marianella said with scarcely a pause. "How have you been faring?"

"Well enough, I thank you, mistress," he answered. His men began to dismount. "I went to the garrison at Hudelsford, but they'd have none of me, so I came further west. I fell in with a few of my own sort, and we took to riding up and down this valley, taking out a few Shadowfolk. That bastard—" he pointed over his shoulder where Saradoc had disappeared "—he was doing the same, only he'd take on both things and men. We've fought him a few times. He's bigger and stronger, but us, we have a few advantages." He grinned, showing broken teeth. "We don't fight clean. And the army still won't take us, so we don't belong to anybody."

"You do now," Marianella said. "You belong to Telerath, which belongs to Greywell of Fendarath, and you answer to me. Go help us make camp; we weren't going any further tonight anyway." She pulled the blankets closer about her;

she was shivering from the chill and the excitement. "And for any sake's sake somebody build a fire and make me some tea."

Later, when they had set a watch and the rest of them had rolled up in their blankets, Denis joined Marianella in the wagon. "I've sent a message to Tevrin," he said, "and they'll send men out to run that renegade out of the valley. You were quick off the mark. How'd you come to know Saradoc when you saw him? He was a northern man."

"A little bird told me," Marianella said, and hiccuped, and snuggled down; and Denis held her close till she stopped shivering and fell asleep.

On the last Friday before Christmas, they went as usual to the school play. (Sue had finished costumes for two peasants and a sheep in the nick of time.) The play had gone through a series of changes. Over the last decade the local population had stopped being all white middle-class Protestant. The school, not wishing (very properly) to push the Christian religion on those who didn't subscribe to it, had tapered off on Bible stories in recent years and concentrated on Santa Claus and teddy bears. But the population had continued to diversify, and Christmas had blossomed into a multicultural celebration. The second grade did Santa Claus. The third grade did the Nativity (with the kindergarten and first grade as sheep, which made it unnecessary for them to learn any lines). The fourth grade did Judas Maccabaeus and the Hannukah menorah. The fifth grade did the Indian Festival of Lights, for which they had done an impressive amount of research. But the sixth grade went back to prehistoric times and showed the sun (carried by a child with a bad stutter, as an alternative to having her double a sheep) rising over Stonehenge (two tetherball poles and a lot of muslin and grey paint). Siobhan had written the script and her daughter (Sean's redheaded twin) was playing the old grandmother whose job it was to watch the sun and stars.

> "The north wind doth blow,
> and we shall have snow,
> And what will the robin do then, poor thing?
> he'll sit in the barn,
> and keep himself warm,

And tuck his head under his wing, poor thing.
Summer, goodbye,
Summer, goodbye."

Granddaughter: "It feels like the end of the world. I heard my uncle say, 'The sun is dying.' "

Grandmother: "So we say. We say the sun dies at Midwinter, and is reborn again the next day for the New Year, when it rises over the midwinter stone and starts its journey northwards again."

Granddaughter: "Does that happen every year?"

Grandmother: "I've seen it happen fifty times."

Granddaughter: "Well, what if it *doesn't*?"

Grandmother (exasperated by all the childish questions): "Then it'll be the end of the world!"

They went on to explain a lot of the old Christmas customs. The Yule log and the candles, for example, were symbols of the light they hoped would come back—and sympathetic magic to make it do so. The evergreen tree was a symbol of life, because its leaves never fell, and the holly and the ivy were male and female symbols. (Siobhan's text carefully skirted round this point so as not to offend, not the children, but some of their parents.) Mistletoe was a gift of the gods because it grew without roots, out of the air (or was supposed to). People feasted, and exchanged gifts, and wore their best clothes, on the principle that whatever you did on the first day of the New Year you would go on doing all year long.

Granddaughter: "My grandmother said if the sun doesn't turn it'll be the end of the world."

Boy: "It'll be the end of us, anyway. You know I went up to the hills this summer, with my father, to trade with the hill people. While I was there I saw a glacier pouring down from the mountains—"

Granddaughter: "What's a glacier?"

Boy: "It's like a river of ice, pouring down out of the mountains, covering everything in sight. And at the foot of that glacier, I saw a pile of rocks that it had carried along with it, and left on the ground when it melted back under the summer sun. Just like the piles of rocks we have around here."

Granddaughter: "You mean there used to be glaciers all over *this* country." (looking around) "Where did they go?"

Boy: "I asked my father, and he said, 'They've gone back to get more rocks.'"

The Neolithic people, dressed in their best (bright-colored cloaks and six strings of beads apiece; their mothers must have left the thrift stores bare), gathered together to watch the sun set on Midwinter's Eve. They wept and embraced their friends and family as if they would never see each other again. Then they settled down to wait.

> "This ae night, this ae night,
> Every night and all,
> Fire and fleet and candlelight,
> The gods receive thy soul."

(Siobhan had adapted it from the current Christian version, like a scientist reconstructing Eohippus from the modern horse.)

"This is the night the sun turns," the old grandmother said. "Either our hope comes now, or all hope's end."

There was some kind of disturbance offstage. A foot was thrust out of the curtains behind the "Sunrise stone," and quickly withdrawn. Perhaps the child with the sun had had an attack of shyness? It would be catastrophic for Siobhan's plot if the sun didn't show up. The villagers rose and faced "east," and somebody whispered, "Now."

The sun rose over the painted muslin sunrise stone, and the people cheered. The little girl carrying it was wearing a long dress of red velvet, and had a crown of candles on her head. (Artificial candles with flashlight bulbs, Sue was glad to note.) ("Saint Lucy, by God!" someone whispered behind her.) The Neolithic people joined hands around her and danced, a little hopping dance to the music of a shrill recorder and a small drum.

> "At the dawning of the day,
> Eia,
> When the winter goes away,
> Eia,
> And we see the sun's first ray,
> Eia,

Let us join our hands and say,
Be glad, the sun has risen!
Go away, go away, ice and snow,
let us go, let us go!
Sing, dance as we go, as we go."

Sue found that her eyes were stinging with tears.

They got into Tevrin just before sunset of the next day, and went directly to Rhadath House. Marianella's own clothes were too humble for her new station, and Amalia's too tall for her, so she asked to borrow something from the chatelaine. The gown Mistress Thecla found her was all cinnamon-colored silk, with a close-fitting bodice netted with pearls. Her hair, three-quarters brushed in her haste, went into a net with more pearls, and a cream-colored veil went over it.

I suppose I'll do, she thought smugly, looking herself up and down in Amalia's best mirror. But where in the world was Amalia?

"They're still on the road," Master Denis said. "They'll be here in an hour or so, don't worry, but we must be off if we're to reach our seats through the crowd. You're looking very chipper. Is it the warm bath, or has someone been giving you mulled wine?"

At this point another woman might have gone straight up and turned left, but Marianella had been living with the Sighted all her life, and only smiled. "No, nothing like that. It's just a new dress."

"Oh, is that it. I did wonder." He gave her his arm and they descended the stairs to the door of the Hall, where their horses were waiting.

This will never last, Marianella reminded herself. *He knows, and I know, and we always did know that it couldn't last. But when we part, it will be because he's found one of his own kind, or I've found one of my own kind, or just the world's winds have blown us apart, and not because he never noticed what I was wearing. One doesn't expect a falcon to pull a plow, or a butterfly to cook your breakfast.*

Many torches burned before the door of Castle Tevrin. The air was still and cold, and the stars shone like the torches, bright and without flickering. As Denis had predicted, there was a great crowd, but Michael the Red had arrived just before they did and cleared the way for them, bellowing

"Make room!" in his great bull's voice. Denis found Marianella's seat and put her in it, and disappeared; off to talk with some of his collegues. Marianella was content to sit in a chair with a cushion, whose four legs never moved and whose back never swayed, and watch what went on around her.

The great Hall was the same general shape as the hall at Telerath or any other hold in Demoura, though much larger; and like any other hall it had a row of timber trusses supporting its roof. But here some local carpenter, instead of putting up the standard interlocking triangles, had chosen to indulge himself. He had used perhaps twice as much timber as he'd have needed just to keep the roof up. Large triangles rose from the tie-beam, growing smaller and smaller as they approached the roof, like the branching of fantastic trees. All the wood was centuries old, dark and shiny with age and smoke. Below the beams, the walls were hung with tapestries, some of them rescued from the downfall of Kindarie and Andarath. Directly opposite Marianella hung the famous web of the Field of Gold and the riding of Alban Longsword into the citadel to claim the crown. The sun shone on the golden flowers that studded the grass, and on the spears and armor of Alban's men, but he himself wore no armor, only a cloak as green as the grass and a wreath of flowers on his dark hair. Now Alban was dust, and the weavers were dust, and Andarath was dust and a city walled with beetles' wings, but the web hung here still, bright with a brightness that caught the breath in the throat.

Then she caught a glimpse across the Hall, half-hidden by a lady's tall headdress—a glimpse of a dark head that she would know on the dark side of the moon. She could almost have laughed, if she'd had the breath, because after all these weeks of telling herself she didn't care a bit, at the sight of him her heart turned right over. There was a soured twang like a frayed harp string, all through her body, but again it was only her heart and no one else heard it. Quickly she looked away, and out of the corner of her eye saw a flash of white skin under the dark as Kieran's face turned toward her, and he too looked away.

"I've spoken to the captain of that troop they sent out after Saradoc," master Denis said when he returned to his seat. "They chased him all the way to the Caramath; he has gone into the Shadow. We may see him again in the spring when the war starts, but I hope not. Are you comfortable? Court should begin in a few minutes."

There was a stir in the Hall, the muffled sound of hundreds of people finding their seats, whispering to their neighbors, turning this way and that to see what was coming.

First came two pages dressed in the Heralds' green and gold and carrying armloads of papers. At one end of the Hall a platform stood, set with three great chairs and many smaller ones for the Lord Captains and the Lords of State. (Three great chairs? There had always been two in Marianella's memory, one for the Steward and one for the Duke of War. And the one in the center was one she had never seen before, very large and bright with inlaid pearl and gold, almost a throne.) Along the back of the platform ran a row of tables to hold the necessary paperwork, and the pages went to one of these and began to arrange their books and scrolls and fistfuls of notes.

Now the doors at the other end of the Hall opened, and groups of men and women began to enter: the Steward with his Seneschals in their scarlet robes, the Queen-of-Arms with her Heralds in green and gold, the Seers in sober black. This was their official entrance, but not a formal one, and the people continued to look around and whisper, though in a lower tone. The Lords of State went to the platform and took their seats. The Steward was an old man and frail-looking, but still tall and straight in his gold and scarlet. He sat in the chair to the right of the great throne, and the Queen-of-Arms stood beside him. Aurelia the Red was a woman of fifty, still very fair with her long red braids, and the coronet on her hair was a wreath of laurel leaves, hammered out of the native copper and now green with age. Her staff of office was in her hand, enameled green and traced with vines and leaves of gold, and tipped with a great crystal that caught all the light and threw it back in splinters of brilliance. She bent over the Steward's chair, and they spoke together for a moment. Then she stepped to the edge of the platform, and the torchlight gleamed on the golden leaves in her green gown, and the trumpets sounded. The people rose to their feet.

"My lords, ladies, and gentlemen!" she called out, "the Lords Captains." Her voice was as clear as a trumpet, and she made herself heard all through the hall with little effort.

(They said it was all in the breathing.) "Fulk, Lord Captain of Sallowfell."

Fulk of Sallowfell was a young man, not thirty yet, with his shield arm in a linen sling. Yes, that would be the youngster who had done so well in the battle of the Caramath, and kept the retreat across the river from turning into a rout. He came up to the Queen-of-Arms, bowed to her and to the Seneschal, and took a seat on the end of the platform.

"Eric, Lord Captain of Watermarch." This was another young man; they were taking them in ascending order. The Captains were ranked by seniority. The Heralds kept a list of their names in the order of their creation, and once a year the roll was ceremonially called, from the very earliest down to now, and those Lords Captains who were present answered for the names of those who would never answer again, and would never be forgotten.

Marianella's attention wandered, and her eyelids drooped. Perhaps she should have given the Court a miss, and gone to bed. Her head came to rest against Denis's shoulder, and she forced her eyes open and focused them on a candle, a dozen feet away, whose flame danced and trembled in the wind of those who walked past.

There were candles in the church too, and sleepy children leaning against her side. This Christmas Eve service was a simple one, intended for the whole family: read a Bible passage, sing a hymn—but then they went and held it at eleven o'clock in the evening. A good idea in theory, a struggling whining leaden-eyed confusion in practice. The minister was flipping through his Bible; he must have lost a bookmark. Behind him on the wall hung a satin banner, gold with scarlet lettering that read:

> While all was silent
> at midnight
> O GOD
> Thy Word leapt down
> from Thine
> Eternal Throne

Across the church, another banner read, pale blue and cool green:

Drop down dew
ye heavens
from above
and let the clouds
RAIN
the Just One

But it was not going to rain tonight; it was snowing cats
and dogs.

"Randall, Lord Captain of Tower Lost, Earl of the Sea."
Lord Randall and his party had arrived, then. He strode up
the hall like a man going to the hunt, swift and proud, his
black hair and beard like a lion's mane around his ruddy face,
and he wore his red poppy badge over silver and black. His
boots were stained with riding, but someone had found him a
new cloak that shimmered crimson in the torchlight. He
bowed to the Queen-of-Arms, and then kissed her on the
cheek—she was his cousin—and bowed to the Steward and
took his seat beside him.

"Henrik, Lord Captain of Blackwater, Earl of the Highlands." This was a tall, fair, serious man of forty, one of
Saradoc's blood perhaps, but his noble spirit shone clearly in
his face. His badge was the yellow broom, and his long tunic
and cloak were blue and green and silver like the rain. He had
held the high plains for nearly twenty years against the strange
sendings that came down out of the mountains, things not of
the Darkness maybe, but unchancy and dangerous.

"James, Lord Captain of Ladywood, Earl of the Downs." This
was a small stocky man who looked much younger than he
was, and looked ready to fight bare-handed at an instant's
notice, but he walked like a king. His badge was the wild rose,
and his clothing was all black but for the gold on his belt and
the lining of his long sleeves. He had the Sight and the Voice
and no little measure of luck.

"Paul, Lord Captain of Scarfell, Earl of Tevrin." This was a
smaller man even than the Earl of the Downs, lean and
sprightly, but with broad shoulders and hands like hammers.
His hair and beard were golden, and his eyes sparkled. His
long tunic was sewn in diamond-shapes of blue and white,
and his sleeves were lined with satin red as blood, and in his
hat was tucked the yellow water-flag, badge of his house.

The Earls of the Four Quarters took their seats, and the people (though they were supposed to keep silent till the end) began to cheer. The trumpets sounded, drowning their voices, and the Queen of Arms cried again, "My lords, ladies, and gentlemen! Mark, Lord Captain of Hellsgarde, the Duke of War!"

Lord Mark came through the double doors with his people around him. Yes, his party had plainly arrived a little while ago; they had had time to clean up and dress, and they were as bright as a handful of jewels. Emerald and ruby and topaz and jade, each carrying a lighted candle, for Hellsgarde had no badge that grew in the soil of the earth; and Lord Mark was all in white. (But where was Amalia? Was she too weary to come to Court? Marianella's impulse was to go at once to Rhadath and find her, but the crowd was too great; she could not possibly get through.)

The Seers of Hellsgarde approached the thrones, and the Captains and the Lords of State rose to honor them. Again the people cheered, without waiting for the Heralds to lead them. But again the trumpets rang out to silence them. The Hellsgarde folk took seats on the platform, and Lord Mark sat opposite the Steward, on the left of the empty throne. The Queen-of-Arms stepped forward and raised her staff. The crystal caught the light and bent it into the highest branches of the roof beams. "My lords, ladies, and gentlemen. Amalia Greywell, Lady of Fendarath."

The candles trembled, and there was a great murmur as everyone in the Hall took breath. Most of them had heard at least part of what she had done. Amalia stepped forth into a dead silence, with Adrianna and Genevra beside her. She had put on a loose garment of deep blue, like a wide cloak with full sleeves, but under it the hem of her gown showed like a thin line of blood. Her fair hair was unbound, and streamed down her back like a shower of sunlight. Her face was solemn, nearly expressionless, but even without the Sight Marianella could make a good guess at what she was thinking. Something was going on that she did not know about, and was not about to approve of without taking the cat out of the bag and giving it a good long look.

Slowly the three women crossed the hall; they had not as long a stride as Mark or even Henrik. When they came before the platform, the Queen-of-Arms came down to the bottom step to meet them. "Amalia of Fendarath," she said, "we know of your mission, and the task you have set us; and we accept it willingly, and pledge all our strength to its completion. The scholar, the Seer, and the warrior, all shall follow you in everything; command us, and we obey. For we foresee the truth of what you have said, that what you brought out of the Darkness may lift the Darkness from us."

"I thank you, Lady," Amalia said. "I do not blush to accept all your strength, and your wisdom, and your obedience. For I know that we must risk everything, to the last drops of blood in our veins, sparing nothing. If we do so, we may be victorious; but if we hold back anything we shall never know, as we fall, whether that last trifle withheld might have brought us victory after all."

She had never trained as a Herald, and her voice was low, but so still was the Hall that every word reached its furthest corner.

"We agree," said the Queen-of-Arms. "And we have taken counsel together, and agreed that we need a single leader in this conflict. Even the Duke of War, though he commands the Earls who led the armies on the field, and he himself leads in the air above it; even he cannot rule us all, for this is not his mission, but yours.

"Amalia of Fendarath, the Lords of State have chosen to offer you the throne, long vacant, the Crown and Kingdom of Demoura. Will you accept them?"

Amalia stood as silent as a tree. Now more than ever she needed the skills that had gone with her vanished Sight, for with it she might have known in advance that this was preparing. *Mark!* she thought. *Mark of Hellsgarde, you knew all this was brewing and gave me no warning. Did you think I would run away? Maybe I would. O, let the two of us only live ten minutes after we've won the war, so that I may spend them shaking you till your teeth rattle!* But Mark only looked at her, and smiled. No one ever disappointed Mark of Hellsgarde; he perceived everyone's possibilities to within a hairsbreath, and then called up the impossible out of love.

Oh, it's right but it's wrong, Amalia said. *O Aumery! Shall I wear the crown that belongs to your line, the crown of Alban deep in the fabled past? Should I accept? I don't know how to be a Queen.*

Do, Aumery said. *I'll advise you.*

"I will," she said, and added very low, "May none of us regret this. Tell me what I must do."

Adrianna and Genevra took the blue gown from her shoulders, and left her in the blood-red velvet. They led her before the throne, and had her kneel. The Queen-of-Arms beckoned to a pair of sturdy pages, and they brought forth a wooden casket inlaid with fine threads of silver. From this she took the crown, a thin circlet of silver, ringed with little clusters of pale golden oak leaves. She held it high for a moment, so that everyone might see it, and bent down and placed it on Amalia's head.

It was made for a man, and too large for her, but someone had lined it with twisted silk, and it fitted snugly. *It's light.*

It's small and light, she said. *I thought it would be a wretched heavy thing.*

It is, Aumery said. *You'll find that out for yourself soon enough. I wish I could see you in it.*

Your father's crown. It should have been yours.

A hint of laughter. *I should have made a singularly ill-favored Queen, and there are other difficulties as well. Be content.*

They gave her the Great Seal in its heavy casket, and kindly took it back. They laid the Great Sword across her knees, and put the royal ring into her hands; too large for her finger, it fit her thumb indifferently, and she resolved to find a ribbon to tie it round her neck.

Now she must sit and receive the fealty of the Lords of State and the Lords Captains, kneeling before her and laying their hands on the hilt and blade of the Great Sword. She could not have borne the sight of the Steward, painfully bending his stiff old body to kneel, except that the joy blazed so in the old man's face: it seemed he might go up in flames at any moment, like a wisp of straw.

Then she must confirm all the Lords Captains in their commands, and give awards to two men who had covered themselves in glory on the battlefield—one of them marched in on his own feet to receive his praise and his golden ring, but the other had to be carried in on a litter. Not for all the hard necessities of war would anyone have grudged them their moment in the sun. (Twenty-four other awards, the

Queen-of-Arms whispered in her ear, would be postponed until the next Court.)

Then at last she must speak to people. She told them the same things she had told the men at Meadingham, and she kept it short. "This is the night the sun turns," she finished; "here begins the new year. And since they say the year goes on as it's begun, let us begin with dancing and singing, with feasting and drinking—I understand the folk in the kitchens are quite ready for us and waiting for the word. Gather your children round you and hold them close; you will never have a better time. For whether we live or die, this year is the last year of the war."

Then the Heralds led the acclamation, and the people cheered till they must be hoarse, and then at long last the men came in to set up the tables, and the kitchen wenches brought in the feast. Amalia sank back against the back of her throne with a sigh of relief, and slipped her shoes off under cover of the table. The butler poured wine for the high table, and moved away to supervise the serving down the hall; now she could speak to Mark, close at her left hand. "Mark, what do you all think you are about? This is what Saradoc wanted!"

"A bad man can have a good idea occasionally," Mark said calmly. "I see no reason we should throw away a sword of fine steel, simply because we found it lying on the midden. Ah, here come the plates. Try the salted almonds; the crop was very good this year."

I should rather have had anything of yours than a whole kingdom of your father's, Amalia mused, *but I suppose I must learn to be content with what I have.*

Try to get your outer part to a mirror, Aumery said. *I want you to see yourself, and tell me what you see. When had Demoura ever a fairer Queen?*

Truly, you don't mind?

Truly, only one thing distresses me. If your army, and you, have the victory this summer, then Demoura has a future. And that's a fine thing, except that then you must marry and bear an heir. That bothers me. But you must not let it bother you.

"What're you crying for?" Fred whispered.

"I don't know." The choir sang "Silent Night," and now a very old woman got up from her seat and walked slowly to the nativity scene on the steps opposite the pulpit. The figures were large, most of them a foot high, and they had been brought from Germany early in the century, except for the three camels. Those had been carved in the hospital by a Liberty Hill boy who had lost a leg in North Africa. The little old grandmother took the three-inch-long Baby Jesus from her pocket, put him carefully into the manger, and hobbled back to her seat, and Sue gave up trying either to sing or to see.

Once the feast was over, and the men began to clear the tables to make space for dancing, Marianella at last managed to get through the crowd and reach Amalia's side. "Ah, there you are," said the Queen. "Stay with me, please, and let's hope they choose the Lord of Misrule as quickly as possible. I've got to get to bed before I drop."

"Me too," Marianella said. "But are we going to live in Rhadath House, or here?"

"Here, for the time being. I have to be near the Lords of State, and the Hellsgarde folk and all the Captains are staying here. Those long cold corridors! I'm sorry, it can't be helped."

"Born a King on Bethlehem's plain; Gold I bring to crown him again," Sue sang as she swept up the pine needles on January seventh. Somebody had had a deadly accurate sense of timing—probably the Queen-of-Arms. The twelve days of Christmas had gone by, and still the trumpets rang in her ears; the torches, the gold, the noble lords and ladies still shone before her eyes. Again she regretted that she hadn't realized in time what you could do for the solemnity of the season—not red-nosed reindeer and alcoholic eggnog, but glory and trumpets and the crowning of the Christmas King. Too late for this year, but next year she would give a Christmas party that would knock their socks off.

CHAPTER 12

Closing In

Winter was passing out of Tevrin in a furious rush of wind. Every window in the castle's walls was rattling like a tambourine, and half-a-dozen tiles had fallen from the roof. The Seneschal and his men were in session even now, whether to risk mending them today, or wait till the wind died down.

Aurelia the Red pulled her green cloak closer about her as she climbed the stairs to the Queen's solar, and stopped to close two windows that had blown open in the tower's side, and latch them firmly.

A Guardsman stood at the foot of the stair and another at the top, outside the solar's only door. The rest were no doubt somewhere close at hand; they had taken over the top floor of this whole wing.

Their order was based in old tradition, but Mark of Hellsgarde had established them in the present time of need. One hundred knights, the best in Demoura that were not yet Captains, they were sworn to follow the Queen wherever she led them and to defend them with her lives.

And instead of their own arms, or Tevrin's, they wore on their surcotes a new blazon. *Gules, a heart argent,* Aurelia noted in the old language as she nodded to the Guard at the door. The heart was worked in silver threads and shone against the deep red. Aurelia shifted her staff to her other arm and went in.

The solar atop Tevrin's Lady Tower had been built to catch the sunlight in its big diamond-paned windows. The builder had also had the foresight to include a hearth in the tower's north wall, against days like this when there was no sunlight to speak of, and a pinewood fire was burning in it. Mark of Hellsgarde and Amalia the Queen were seated before the fire, playing a strange game with a set of hares-and-hounds. The board, laid upside down at the Queen's elbow, held empty teacups and half-a-dozen fragments of pottery. The table was spread with the button-sized game counters, red hounds and white hares, and with blue beads and silver buttons and the unstrung corals the Queen had been wearing this morning.

"Good morning, your Grace, my lord Duke."

"Good morning, Madam," Amalia said. She had known Aurelia all her life, but a Herald in her cloak was on duty and would not speak for herself. "My lord of Hellsgarde is trying to teach me the art of strategy, and needs all our prayers. What have you for us this morning?"

"Officer's commissions, your Grace, and the requisitions from the Mountain Quarter. I commend this one especially to your attention; the Duke may have spoken of it. It's the Captain's warrant for Kelvan of Blackwater, the Earl's son of the Mountains. A very promising young man."

"He's that," Mark agreed. "Only twenty, but he's been leading a band of skirmishers deep into the Twilight, three years now."

"And his father praises him with a touching attempt at seemly modesty," Amalia said, reading over the notes attached to the warrant, "and the Lords Captains Henrik and Agilulf praise him without any compunctions at all. I am impressed." She signed the warrant with the pen the Queen-of-Arms held out for her, and set the Great Seal in a puddle of scarlet wax. "Is he taking his own men into battle, or have they given him a more experienced force?"

"He has a hundred of his own men, two hundred of his father's, and some fifty or sixty of Saradoc's—all those Master Donal has been able to look over. They're good fighters and splendid riders, and there's no virtue in leaving them out because they fell under the influence of an opportunist with a voice. Not when Kelvan's got the strongest Voice I've ever heard."

"Even better." Amalia signed the last warrant. "These are for tomorrow's Court?"

"Yes, your Grace. This will be the last formal Court to be held in Tevrin, if we set out on schedule. I thank your Grace. My lord Duke." The Queen-of-Arms gathered up her papers and bowed, and left the solar. Amalia sighed.

"When shall I have a chance to talk to Aurelia as one mortal to another again?"

"When the war is over," Mark said. "Talking of Saradoc, have you heard further of him?"

"Not since last month," Amalia said.

Have you?

He is somewhere in the North, Aumery said, *near the Shadowline, to find grazing for his horses, but as far from your young Kelvan as may be. I don't look to see him again till he joins us for battle.*

In Liberty Hill, too, the winter passed. Sue had spent it in reading and sewing; Amalia had found the time to do some research over her shoulder, and had insisted Sue make herself some suitable clothing. A neat black suit hung in her closet now, with some tweed and flannel skirts and a navy-blue blazer. *I'll never wear them!* she had objected at the time, but now she wore them at least once a week. The computer had taught her a bit about accounting —if not all the subtleties, at least enough of the buzzwords to get by with. Now she was the committee's delegate to visit Robert Shafer, in his office or on the job site. His men had spent February and March putting the repairs into the gym, and all of it was finished except some of the showers, for which parts were still on order. Now with the arrival of warm weather, Shafer had broken ground on the computer wing, and concrete had been poured and walls were beginning to go up, thick with ducting to hold the computer cables.

She had given another dinner in February, for the Carmodys and Randy and Kelly—this time not as serving wretches (Randy's phrase) but as guests. Instead, she had let the children wait on table, in exchange for staying up late and pigging out on lemon fluff in the kitchen. And she had pumped Claire Carmody about people who might be able to donate microcomputers.

"Not us, I'm afraid," Claire had said. "The Entworks writes programs for Cray supercomputers, a little out of your line. Let me ask around the network and see what I can find. There's got to be somebody."

"The old girls' network?"

Claire laughed. "No, the electronic kind. The dealers, not to mention the manufacturers, get tax credits for donations to schools, and if you're thinking they've got about as much milk of human kindness as your friend Shafer, you're right." But she had put the word round, and now the donations were trickling in, with promises of equipment from four companies so far. One had actually delivered five computers, slightly obsolete but still useful, to the school already. Three were under lock and key, and the other two were in the principal's office balancing the secretaries checkbooks and designing posters for school picnics. The committee would have a struggle getting them back again when the new wing was built.

The barberries had begun to perk up as soon as the snow was off the ground, and every plant was an inch higher already. Sue had begun to plant her garden, acting on the strategy she had worked out on graph paper over the winter. She had dug the grasses out of a band a foot wide all round the edge of the lawn, and planted flowers. Violets and cinerarias and shade-loving ferns grew against the front of the house, which would be getting less and less sun all the time as the hedge grew higher. But inside the shelter of the hedges, where the sun would peer over the shoulder of the house, she had pansies and pinks and a line of rosebushes. The roses were old-fashioned ones, not the modern kind with no scent, and came by mail order all the way from California.

Eglantine, damask, musk rose, and the Rosa Gallica that went back to the Roman Empire, the White Rose of York and the Red Rose of Lancaster and the peppermint-striped Tudor Rose that was supposed to combine them both. (The history course she had started at the City College was beginning with the fall of Rome, but there was no rule against reading ahead.)

In the House of the Mists spring never came. The days grew longer, and the sun rose higher each day over the

House and the frozen valley. Sometimes a few drops of water fell from the stone lintels, and spattered on the steps. Sometimes in the depth of a cold, clear night, thin sprays of ice crystals would form along the stony walls and floor. Nothing else grew, and there was no green by day, only by night an emerald star that peered over the rim of the Shadow like a wildcat's eye, every night a little higher.

In the back yard, the grass was springing back, and Sue had a row of lettuces and two rows of bush beans planted. Every Saturday she dug up a few more feet. A length of tall wire fence was on her shopping list, to keep the kids' playground seperate from the vegetables and to give the peas something to climb on.

" 'Every horseman should have a shield, lance, sword, dagger, bow, quiver, and arrows,' " Mark read from the old book of orders.

"Why the bow and arrows?" Amalia commented. "The knights of Maximus's day weren't much good with a bow."

Not on horseback, at any rate, Aubrey agreed. *Some of our people were fine bow-hunters, but only on foot.*

" 'Every man who possesses twelve hides of land must have a mail shirt.' " Mark turned the page. " 'Each soldier should bring rations for three months and clothing for six.' "

"And we were talking about five pounds per man per day, times twenty-eight, times three—oh, surely he wasn't intended to carry all that on his person?"

Of course not, Aumery said, with laughter in his thought. *There was a supply train, a long string of carts carrying stores of flour, wine, and salted meat. Also tools—shovels, carpentry tools, slings to hunt game with—that's what the bows were for.*

"Good morning, Charlie," Sue said, stepping carefully over a pile of ducting. Her shoes were plain black pumps, carefully shined, and her ankles were slender (*still, after three children!* she thought smugly), but her step was firm. Charlie's eyes—he was the foreman for the computer room construction—traveled from her ankle to the even hemline bisecting her knee, to the slim leather envelope that would make do till she got a real briefcase (it held her history notes) to the face, and he smiled. "Good morning, ma'am. Mr. Shafer ain't here today."

"That's all right. I can see him at his office. I wanted to see how you're getting on."

"We're doing fine. The ducting's in, all but the south wall, and we start sheetwalling tomorrow."

"Oh, good." She let Charlie show her around, and tried to visualize desks, students, and computers all in place.

"I'll see you later," she said at last. "I want to check in with the principal's office and see if they got in those diskettes."

"Diskettes? No," the secretary said. "But I'm glad you came in, we've been trying to get hold of you. You weren't at home."

"I was in class, over at City College. What's up?"

"Well, it's Mike. He's got a bad tummy-ache, and the school nurse thought he'd better go home today. Only we couldn't find you. You want to go get him and take him home?"

"Sure I can. What is it, the flu?"

"Sounded more like something he ate. The nurse can tell you."

"Pack horses or mules, twelve pounds of oats, the same of hay," Mark said. "War horses, fifteen of oats and sixteen of hay. We're going to need more wagons to carry it, and that means more mules. There's no forage for them at all?"

"Nothing they can eat, not once we get a day or so beyond the Caramath."

Mike was lying on the nurse's cot, half-curled on his side, the streaks of a few tears on his face. "Hi, Mom," he said. "I feel pretty rotten."

"You look pretty rotten," Sue said. "Why, there's mold growing all over your ears." This was the kind of joke Mike loved, but he managed only a faint smile.

"I threw up twice," he volunteered. "I still feel like it, only there's nothing left to throw."

"He's not so very lively," the nurse agreed. "I think he'd rather be at home."

"Right. C'mon, Mike. Can you walk?"

He could, after a fashion and leaning heavily on Sue's arm. His face was very white, and the freckles stood out like spatters of muddy water.

"Silver Hill Elementary School," the secretary was saying

as they passed her door. "Oh? One moment, please." She covered the mouthpiece with her hand. "Has anybody seen Mrs.— Oh, there you are. Phone call for you."

"Who is it?"

"Christopher Bingley; I think he works for—"

"I'm not here," Sue said. "I left five minutes ago with a sick kid."

"Right," the secretary said, and uncovered the mouthpiece. "Mr. Bingley, she just left a couple of minutes ago. Her little boy's sick and she had to take him home." Sue got Mike into the parking lot under his own steam, but she had to lift him into the car. Putting a carefully neutral look on her face, she started the car and eased it out into the traffic.

"Water," Mark said thoughtfully. "One gallon a day for a man, ten for a horse."

"Don't worry about water, Mark; we'll find it everywhere. The Shadowcover seems to trap it. It never really rains, but the air is always damp. If we happen not to be within walking distance of a pond or a stream, a two-foot well will find water. And it's pure, so far as we're concerned; nothing that could live on us can live under the Shadow."

"Very well." Mark got up and stretched. "I suggest we get some sleep. You have Court tomorrow, and then we set out." He picked up his books and tucked them under his arm.

"Good night." Amalia reached up as he passed, and took his free hand. Neither of them found anything to say, and after a moment Mark nodded and went out.

Mike was able to walk into the house, holding his side and limping. "Does your leg hurt too?"

"No, but it hurts if I straighten it out. Can I watch television?"

"Ungh. You can watch Sesame Street if they're on."

"That's for little kids. Can I watch a movie?"

Sue flipped the dials. The PBS channel was showing a program on ethics for teenagers, and the local channel's noon movie was standard housewives' fare, or sex in the afternoon. She didn't even consider the soap operas. In the end she let him watch an old black-and-white gangster movie, on the grounds that anything that got past the censors forty years ago was old-hat to modern children.

While Mike curled up on the sofa under a blanket, Sue called his doctor. "He doesn't have a fever," she said, "but his stomach hurts and he's been throwing up and he limps."

"Where does it hurt?" the nurse asked.

"Well, in his stomach."

"Above or below the waist?"

"Below."

"Have his bowels moved today?"

"I'll find out." She put down the phone and got Mike's attention long enough to ask.

"He says not. Lots of diarrhea the last couple of days, but nothing today."

"All right, what we'd like you to do is keep an eye on him. If he continues to vomit, if the pain persists, or if he runs a fever, call us back."

"Okay." Sue hung up the phone and stood there for a moment, trying to collect her wits. It was always a disappointment when the doctor didn't produce an instantaneous cure, or at least an explanation, like a rabbit out of a hat. But doctors were only human, after all—she remembered once her own doctor had told her he was like a detective, piecing together bits of clues and tracking down the Most Likely Suspect. She took a deep breath and went into the kitchen. By dinnertime, she might not have an opportunity to cook.

Amalia stood on the cliffs above the Caramath, that fell almost sheer from Tevrin's city gate to the river five hundred feet below. From here, the plain that curved out to the north of the city looked like a peasant's festival gown, a patchwork of every color, smooth and clear in the still morning air. Here and there a spark of light glinted, like glass beads among the embroidery ... but she knew it was sunlight upon steel. The strength of Demoura was drawn up on the plain, four armies under the four Earls, and from here she could see plainly how they were laid out in their quadrants. Mountains to the northwest, plains to the northeast, Sea to the southwest, half-hidden by the cliffs, and Tevrin at her feet, with avenues a furlong wide between. As she watched, a tiny puff of dust moved southward, a messenger on some last-minute errand perhaps, with the rider's helm glittering in its heart.

"It is very beautiful," Amalia said. "Worthy of a song, even if we fall. Maybe the Shadowlings will sing it for us." She turned Pathfinder's head away from the sight and toward the winding road, just broad enough for two wagons to pass each other, that led down the cliff. "Let us go. Please tell the Duke that we are coming."

"I have," Genevra said, her grey palfrey falling into line behind the Queen. "He is expecting us."

As they descended into the plain, the air filled with the sounds of men and horses, the creak of leather and the ring of steel, and with the smells of breakfast cooked and eaten an hour before. The Captains with their men had found places under the Earls, giving each army about five hundred knights and three to five thousand footsoldiers. ("In the old chronicles the army always fought with seven hundred knights," Amalia had said. "That is the number that always appears," Mark had agreed, "which is why we can't trust it. They probably chose it because it scanned.")

They rode north along the dusty avenue, where only a few tufts of spring grass still showed among the hoof-marks. The army of Tevrin to their right, the sea to their left; as they passed, Lord Randall rode forward to salute them. Ryan and Lucas were at his side, tall in their black robes; but Denis had rejoined the seers of Hellsgarde.

Each army had its own wagon trains of provisions, its own cooks and armorers and surgeons. They passed a blacksmith, his shoeing and mending done and his fire douted, tightening the leather straps that bound the cover to his wagon. Everything was in readiness, and something like quiet fell over the men as the Queen's party went by.

In the center of the field, where the avenues met, they found the Duke of War on his great white horse, his scarlet battle cloak bright under the morning sun. There were half-a-dozen wagons to shelter the royal party, which included the Hellsgarde folk, and the hundred knights of the Guard, and two hundred pikemen, and one team of firestarters.

After the Solstice, when Marianella had taken up her place beside Amalia again, Kieran had fallen back a few paces. If he could no longer be at the Queen's side without encountering Marianella, he remained of her party; and when the firestarter teams were parceled out among the armies, he assigned himself and Sala and their companions to the royal party. No one spoke of this openly, except that Genevra noted all these subtle things and quietly reported them to the Queen. She, too, had remained with Amalia all through their stay in Tevrin.

Marianella scrambled out of the wagon as they approached, shaking out her apron and straightening the coif that bound her curly hair away from the dust. "The wagon's prepared, my Lady, if you'd care to rest." She looked over Amalia's shoulder, rather than at her; her face was averted as if too bright a sun shone out of the northeast. Amalia looked that way and saw Kieran and his firestarters, their mounts saddled and their string of pack mules loaded with Teel's firestuff, and she understood. In the last few months she had learned much about how men's bodies betray their thoughts; it was not the same as the Sight, but bade fair to be almost as good. "Thank you, but I think we are setting off almost at once."

And as she spoke, the signal had gone out, and from the four quarters of the field the trumpets blew. Men shouldered their packs and took their spears in hand; knights mounted their horses; from the corner of her eye Amalia saw Kieran leap onto Speedwell's back and take the lead mule by the rein. Men and horses turned their faces to the north.

The Queen and the Duke rode at the head of the army, surrounded by their hundred knights. A young squire on a strong mountain horse rose beside them, bearing the banner of Tevrin on his lance: a tree uprooted. They had hoped to march under the golden banner of Andarath, the sun in his splendor that none had seen for two hundred years, but the old fabric had perished, leaving only a heap of gold wire. Seamstresses had worked to remake it, but they could not finish in time.

Behind the Queen the forces of Demoura spread out in the form of a spearhead, Plains and Tevrin leading in long lines, Mountains and Sea in wider ranks behind. The guard left behind in the city saw them start out, the lance-point of their march glittering with their spears and helms and armor, until the dust rose up and veiled it.

Instead of fording the Caramath at Tevrin, where the river though shallow was very wide, they rode north along the west bank to Hudelsford, so that they could take the road Amalia knew into the Darklands. As they went forward, the Twilight drew ever closer to the riverbank, and presently it drifted across like mist. When they reached Hudelsford, and gave their final orders to the small garrison there, the sky was like silver and all the grass was dead. Craning her neck as they crossed the ford, peering into the north, Amalia thought she saw the place where she had camped that night, and fed the cat Boots with the last of the egg, and seen Ulf take shape out of the darkness. But she could not be sure.

Sue piled sliced tomatoes over shredded lettuce in the salad bowl, covered it with a damp towel, and put it in the refrigerator. She set the bottle of salad dressing on the shelf next to it, where Fred could not possibly miss it. A casserole dish on the shelf beneath was filled with yesterday's ham, vegetables, and rice, with cheese slathered over the top, ready to be heated in the oven. Kathy could set the table, and—

Her ear caught the sound of something unpleasant, and she went into the bathroom. Mike was kneeling on the bath mat, his elbows propped on the rim of the toilet. "I threw up again."

"I thought you were empty."

"Yeah, but I'm a person of infinite resource and sagacity." His face was paler yet, and pinched-looking around the mouth and eyes.

"You poor kid. Let me get you back to the sofa; I'm going to call the doctor again."

"Yes, you'd better bring him in," the nurse said. "Dr. Henderson can see him at two. Don't let him have anything to eat or drink."

"Eat? Are you kidding?" Mike said when this news was relayed to him. "I don't even think I can drink water."

Sue wrote a note to Fred, telling him where they had gone, and stuck it on the television set. She wrote another and stuck it on the refrigerator, telling Fred how to heat up the casserole. (When Mike was being born, she had learned after the fact, Fred had fed the family for five days on cornflakes, hot dogs, and Coke.) Briefly she considered telephoning him before she left home, and decided against it. The Sav-Mor was doing its quarterly inventory, and Fred had enough on his plate. If she made it home before he did, she could take the note down again. She did call the school and left instructions for Kathy and Mark to say in day care until either she or Fred could pick them up. (*And to think there was a time I thought day care was unnecessary because any proper mother would be at home all day!*)

"Okay, Mike. Let's get you into the car." She crammed his shoes onto his feet and grabbed his jacket from the hook by the door as she helped him down the steps.

The examining room had murals on its walls, frolicking kids with complexions of every color, including green and purple. A Grover Monster puppet lay next to the jar of tongue depressors, and a mobile hung from the ceiling, a flock of bright birds with long tails that stirred in every breath of air. The effect was supposed to be cheering.

Dr. Henderson was a small black-haired woman who might have been a year or two older than Sue, no more. She laid Mike down on the paper-covered table and began gently to prod his abdomen. "That hurts," Mike volunteered.

"Uh-huh," the doctor said. "Does it hurt here?"

"Yes."

"Uh-huh." She continued her careful poking and prodding, with running commentary by Mike, for a minute or two. Then she pressed two fingers deep into his right side and quickly drew them back, and Mike howled.

A wind had sprung up at their backs, stirring a wisp of hair at Amalia's temple. The afternoon sun deepened a little, and the silver sky took on a tinge of gold. But before them the Shadow hung like a thick cloud, like a cold front rolling in off the sea, full of the threat of icy rain and howling winds. She pulled her cloak closer about her, and saw Genevra nearby do the same. Then she looked up again.

As if a curtain had parted, or the roiling cloud had taken shape, a face looked down on them. Huge, impossibly high, backed with cloudbanks like massive brutal shoulders, it stared down on them out of eyes that were points of bitter light. Its nose was broad as an ape's, its chin square; its parted toothless mouth lifted at one corner in a cynical smile. Imber.

She bent her head and remembered the figure she had seen in the darkness of Agniran, Imber the dazzling jeweled shape with an embrace made of stars. But this was Imber too. She raised her head again, and it was gone, veiled again in the Shadowcover. She caught Mark's eye, and he nodded, his look grave. She hoped the men had not seen it.

Sue drew in her breath.

"Yeah," Dr. Henderson said. "Reflex tenderness in the lower right quadrant; I'd like to have him seen at the hospital."

"You mean it's appendicitis, don't you?" She felt cold. "That's what I've been thinking."

"Yes, well, I'd like to have them do a few tests and try to rule it out. It still could be just gas, but that's an awfully classic reaction. Why don't you get him dressed, and I'll have the nurse phone ahead."

Mike complained at having his pants fastened over his belly, so she left the zipper at half-mast and covered it with his shirt. When she got him out to the reception area, the nurse was just putting down the phone. "They're expecting you," she said. "You can go right over."

"Before that, can I use your phone? I've got to call my husband."

"Oh, sure." The nurse pushed a button and handed Sue the handset. "Dial 9 to get out."

She had to wait what seemed like an endless time, but was really only two or three minutes, while someone fetched Fred out of the depths of the back room. She explained what had happened and said, "I don't know how long this'll take. So you'd better be prepared to get Kathy and Mark out of day care, not to mention feed them and get them into bed. There's a casserole in the refrigerator, so don't do the Coke-and-cornflakes number again, okay? I'll call after six o'clock, or whenever I know something."

"Would you like me to come home now? We're up to our traditional ass in alligators, but I suppose Stu and Pete could cope."

"I don't know what you could do, except hold my hand. I think they need you more than we do at this point. Just don't forget the casserole, and there's a salad too. I've gotta get Mike over there. 'Bye, love. I'll talk to you when I can."

Once the whole company had crossed the river, they moved

out of the brave spearhead into a defensive formation. The
army of the Plains led now, with the banner at its head, and
the other forces behind them with the Queen's party in the
middle. The supply wagons must perforce go on the road,
their wheels sinking two inches into the soft stoneweed; but
the horse and foot went along the plain on either side. The
Duke had appointed advance riders, rear guards, and scouts to
right and left, and to these Amalia had added Ruk and his
band of irregulars. Some of the captains and constables of the
Tevrin quarter had looked askance, and with recognition, at
these latest additions, remembering them as highway robbers
at worst and mounted nuisances at best. But the Queen had
overruled them all, and now Ruk and his men patrolled along
the front lines of march, beating the bushes and investigating
side-roads for sign of ambush. But there was no resistance, no
sight of any of the Darklanders, and day by day the Queen's
army pressed forward into an empty, silent land.

The waiting room was empty except for themselves.
There was no one in sight except for the secretary who had
taken their names and told them to wait; and an occasional
orderly who passed down the hallways like a ghost, pushing some incomprehensible piece of equipment. When
Sue raised her eyes she saw a bulletin board with a poster
about keeping your child's immunizations current, and a
series of pictures, crayon on scratch paper, documenting
somebody's second grade's field trip. When she lowered
her eyes she saw Mike, his jaw set and his knees drawn
up, reading the same page of a comic book over and over.

Amalia turned her head from side to side, more to relax her
neck muscles than from any hope of seeing something. She
had not realized, last time she crossed these lands, how very
dark the Darkness was. Then, her Sight had shown her the
delicate network of Shadowlife that pulsed through air and
soil and trailed shallow roots in the water. Now all this was
hidden from her eyes, and she could see only the green fruits
of the stonecrop on the road, glowing like tiny jewels until
the hooves and wheels crushed them. Those, and the torches
the armies carried, one to a squadron, and the lamps that
hung above the wagons. Fuel was carefully rationed. They
had lost two horses already, that had stepped in unseen holes
and broken their legs, but no men yet. Three footsoldiers had

fallen into a pit of water that had opened unexpectedly under their feet, but their fellows had fished them out again. And still there was no sign of the Shadowfolk.

"At any rate, we shan't go thirsty on this campaign," she heard the captain of her Guard say to one of his knights. "Not like the Downs, or the Drywall, when we were down to a cup per man per day, and my squire went mad in his saddle."

"No, Captain," the knight said, "but anyone who falls off his horse had better look to it he doesn't drown."

"Mike, the doctor will see you now." There was a nurse standing in the doorway; at least Sue supposed she was a nurse or maybe a lab technician, dressed in baggy shirt and pants and a cap over her hair, all operating-room green. "Mom, you can come too." Between them they got Mike down the hall to another examining room, this one decorated with giant red and pink flowers that never grew on Earth or Demoura, or it is to be hoped not. The doctor—he was a tall, thin dark man who didn't look like Ulf at all—repeated all the tests that Dr. Henderson had done, down to the final agonizing pressure and sudden release in the lower right abdomen. But unlike Dr. Henderson, who talked to her patients as equals whenever possible—*Well, he doesn't* know *Mike,* Sue thought, trying to be fair, but this was no excuse to treat an eight-year-old like a three-year-old. He actually asked the routine question about Mike's bowels by saying, "Mike, have you made poo-poo today?"

Considering how Mike hated being talked down to, he kept his temper rather well. "No," he said, "and I haven't gone to the bathroom either."

The doctor raised one eyebrow, rather like Mr. Spock. "Mmmm," he said. "Let's get some blood tests."

So it was down the corridor with the green-clad nurse again, to a white-tiled laboratory area full of test tubes. The woman in charge—she had a white uniform and a nonstandard red bandanna tied round her curly hair—sat Mike in a chair with an armrest and tied a strip of rubber tubing round his elbow.

"Does it hurt?" Mike ventured.

"It hurts some, not a whole lot," the woman said. "These needles are pretty sharp. You can hold his other hand,

Mom. It probably hurts less than your tummy does right now."

"That's not saying much," Mike said, but he took a deep breath and sat silently while the woman stuck a large-economy-size hypodermic into his arm and drew out what seemed like an enormous amount of blood. *Actually,* Amalia said, cool and silent among the swirling mists, *it's only about an ounce. Don't distress yourself. See how the tip of that icicle catches the last ray of the sun, there! ... a diamond, a topaz, a ruby, a garnet. And now it's gone.* The technician filled several test tubes with blood, dark as garnets, and put them in a tray. "These'll take a few minutes. You can wait out there."

This waiting room was smaller, with only four seats, and no cutesy murals on the walls, only an official announcement on the proper steps for some medical procedure Sue had never heard of. Mike sat on one of the seats, and pulled his feet up into another, and leaned his head against Sue's arm. "I wish they'd hurry up."

"I suppose it takes time," she said, and tried to smooth his hair. "Like baking a cake."

"Well, why don't they use a microwave?" he said irritably, and burrowed his nose into the side of her arm and appeared almost to go to sleep.

Suddenly, Genevra was at her elbow. "They're coming. You'd better get into the wagon."

"No," Amalia said. "I'll fall back among the Guard, but I should stay out here."

"Your Grace, it is not your part to fight in these battles— "

"I know that well. It is my part to be a figurehead, to inspire the men to fight. I can hardly do that hiding in a wagon."

"Oh, Amalia, don't be a fool!" Genevra burst out. "They can't even see you, and they can fight just as well for you sitting under cover as out in the open where something might fall on your head. Do see reason!"

Amalia let herself be persuaded, and crawled into the wagon. Here there was a little light: a single candle burned in a crystal lamp fastened to the wagon's side. "Maybe I'd better put this out," Marianella said. She folded away the needlework that had occupied most of her time since the journey began, and reached for the lamp.

"No, don't," Amalia said quickly. "Remember, it keeps them off, as smoke does flies."

"There's that," Marianella said. She settled back against a cushion stuffed with hay (if the worst came to the worst the horses could eat it) and stared with seeming calmness at the wagon cover overhead. "Lie down, m'Lady. I don't say sleep, but rest your bones at least. We're no use in this war."

"No, I suppose not," Amalia said, and she lay down next to a gap in the canvas and looked, and saw nothing, and listened.

"Nothing on the road, m'Lord," a voice said out of the darkness: Ruk's voice, or one of his harsh-voiced men. "Whatever it is, it's in the air."

"Yes, we've seen it. Go and tell the firestarter fellow, what's his name, Kieran of Telerath. Have him make ready."

There was the tall thin doctor again, standing at the end of the hall, talking to two more of his fellows. There was a slip of paper in his hand, the kind the laboratory put its test results on. *Oh, calm down*, Sue told herself as her stomach turned over. *How many patients have they got in this place? It's nothing to do with you.* But herself wasn't listening.

"Your Grace? Amalia?" Denis's voice spoke suddenly outside the wagon cover, and the lamp caught a quick glimpse of his face under its dark hood. "What's bigger than a silverback?"

"Mmm. Shaped the same, but much bigger, with what look like big scoops for a face, and not very clever? That sounds like a shouf. I wonder if it's the same one I rode into the mountains. I don't think it's a fighter, Denis, but it's an eye, so be sure everything you do is watched."

"Right." Denis closed the wagonflap and rode off, savoring in his memory the scene of the two women curled up among the lumpy hay-filled cushions. The smells of smoke and hay and women, the single candle's light on their faces. They would have posed for an allegory of summer and winter: Amalia, for all her scarlet gown, pale and still and cold; Marianella full of the richness of growing things and a harvest they might never see.

You heard that, Mark?

I did. Withhold the firestarters unless they're truly needed. No sense in giving the Dark One any warning if we can help it.

I'll tell Kieran. He rode on, guiding his horse easily through the gloom, moving toward the taste of Sala's strength and innocent sweetness like a bee homing in on a grove of blossoming trees.

The fortunes of love, Denis mused, *can be worse than the fortunes of war.* Under other circumstances, he and Kieran could have been friends, within the limits of their differences. But as things were, Marianella was between them. *One part injured love, three parts injured pride,* Denis judged, *while I—*

He reined up beside the big granite rock, fluffy with stoneweed, where Kieran's team had halted their animals and stood with lumps of firestuff in their hands. "We heard," Kieran said before Denis could speak. "We're ready."

"Good," Denis said. "But the Duke's word is you're not to shoot, not yet, unless he gives the command or your need is very great. There's something above us that's a spy. We want to keep your lot a secret as long as we may."

"Oh, toads' teeth," Sala sighed, not in rebellion but with disappointment. She scrambled onto her horse's back and from there onto the top of the stone. She stood up, and stretched, and sniffed. "I can't really see them, but I can smell them. Five big ones, and some scores of little ones, and, yes, something very big that smells like a cow. Is that your spy?"

"Yes."

"It's slow and stupid. If it gets close enough, can I shoot at that?"

"Only if you're certain you can kill it. Otherwise leave it alone."

Keeping a part of his attention on those five hovering silverbacks, he rode back to the wagons, seeking a place to lie. He no longer trusted himself infallibly to stay on his horse when his attention was elsewhere, and the middle of a battle was no occasion to fall off.

There's room in the Queen's wagon, Genevra said. *I'm here too.* He guided his horse to the Queen's wagon, tied the reins to the back panel, and climbed inside. He bent his head to Amalia, smiled at Marianella, and lay down beside Genevra. The hay rustled under the carpet beneath his head. Together he and Genevra took wing.

The dark air was tense with the glances of the Seers, rising from every corner of the field like the heat-shimmer over a desert. The silverbacks floated high overhead, patient, barely moving.

Now the rishi began to move in, drifting downwards with a slight rightwards spiral. Denis caught a quick glimpse of Kieran, standing with arms folded, his back against Sala's rock, while she explained what she could see—or smell.

Prepare for attack. Mark of Hellsgarde, floating bodiless in the wind, spoke silent words to Aurelia the Red. Quickly she translated the words into an ancient tongue and back again, before the thin voice could be forgotten and the message lost. Her clear voice rang across the field, and the other Heralds took up the cry and carried it to the farthest outriders. Swords were drawn, spears grasped, and every man looked upward into a dark sky where as yet no enemy could be seen.

Now, Genevra said. Denis watched with critical approval as she rose toward the spiraling rishi, her bright-polished will like a blade toward its heart. She had been a novice when he left Hellsgarde, but now she was a warrior.

A Seer against a rishi was hardly a fair match, since they fought mind to mind and the rishi had none to speak of. One good spark in the right place, and its heart stopped and it fell like a stone to the earth. A grounded Shadowling could still fight, but instead of slicing from above at its opponent's throat, it must now stretch itself to reach above a grown man's hip. Footsoldiers wore the best leg protection they could contrive.

"Mom?"

"Yes, dear."

Mike was sitting up, or trying to, leaning heavily on one elbow. "I wish there was somewhere I could lie down. These chairs are the pits."

"I'll see."

Genevra was putting down her third rishi, or perhaps it was her fourth, when Denis called her away. *We're needed up above. The silverbacks are moving.*

She dispatched the rishi and joined him. The shape of her was a curl of silver, a wave, a wing.

"Is there somewhere my little boy could lie down?" Sue

asked the receptionist. "He's lying across two chairs and it's awfully uncomfortable."

The receptionist looked alarmed, called on for something outside her limited responsibility. But a middle-aged woman in a white uniform—the old-fashioned kind, a dress instead of a jumpsuit—said, "That's Mike with the abdominal pain? Of course he can." She had a British accent and a silver belt buckle. "Put him in Room B, right over there. Who's his doctor?"

"I'm not sure. There's been several."

"Dr. Delfini has his lab report," the receptionist volunteered.

"Fine. I'll tell him." She bustled off, crisp with starch and authority; but she was the first person Sue'd met in this building who used Mike's name without first having to look at his medical records.

The first silverback was nearly in range, and five Seers were already rising to meet it. *Let's not be greedy*, Denis said. *We can wait for the next one.*

That one over there?

Oh yes, he should do nicely. You hit him low, I'll take him high.

Room B was an all-purpose examining room with green walls. There was a sink in one corner, a portable X-ray machine in another (on wheels, and in a plastic slipcover), and a locker full (if the labels on the doors were any clue) of rubber tubing, oxygen masks, and tongue depressors. Sue helped Mike up onto the table and covered him with a light blanket.

The silverback was big, and it was mean, and it ate courage as a man eats crackers. To send only two Lightlanders against it seemed foolhardy. Perhaps the silverback itself thought so. Its moment of overconfidence doomed it. Genevra soared up under its nose, then fell back, fluttering, like a bird with a broken wing—or, say, a bird that feigns a broken wing for purposes of its own. The silverback checked its speed, stooped, bent its massive head to the kill. That was when Denis got it in the nape. They rode its writhing body nearly down to the ground, leaning hard on one flight surface to make sure it didn't hit anybody.

"It hurts," Mike said.

"I bet it does. Poor kid. Anything I can do?"

"When's the doctor coming back?"

"As soon as he can, I imagine."

"What's he *doing*?"

"Mike, remember I told you a doctor's like a detective. He finds the footprint so he goes looking for people with size-nine feet, and then he finds the gnawed chicken leg so he knows that rules out Colonel Sheldrake who's a vegetarian, and then he finds the single mink hair in the ransom note and that tells him it's the aging movie star who's holding George Lucas hostage until he casts her as Lady Vader. . . ." Mike giggled feebly.

"So the doctor's doing the same sort of thing with your blood tests."

"If he finds a mink hair in my blood I want a different doctor." Mike shifted position on the table, and sniffed. "It hurts."

The third silverback was down. The fourth was falling. The Shadowlings were down, most of them, spitted on Demoura's spears. The last silverback wheeled high overhead, disdaining to close with those who challenged it. It circled again, as if it searched for a target worthy of it. Then suddenly it stooped—

"It hurts," Mike said again.

"I know, dear. There's not a whole lot I can do about it."

"Is the doctor coming?"

"I'll take a look." She went to the door and looked out. The corridor was empty. Nothing could be seen of the receptionist except her sneakered feet, just visible past the doorframe. "No sign of him, Mike, sorry." Mike sniffed again. "Would you like to blow your nose?"

"No."

The silverback stooped, and fell past its enemies as though they were not there. It banked and turned; it spread itself out and turned the speed of its fall into the speed of attack; it was headed directly toward the Queen's wagon. *There, quick!* Denis called to Genevra, but they were too far away. And somewhere in a deep eddy of his mind the thought came, *But our bodies are there, we could die in this.* That was important for some reason, he thought, but couldn't quite remember why.

"Can I have some water? My mouth's so dry."

"You're not supposed to. Why don't you rinse your

mouth and then spit. They must have a basin around here." She found one, the traditional kidney-bean shape in pale blue plastic, and held it while he spat. "Maybe they'll let you have some cracked ice later. That's what they gave me when I was in here having you guys."

There was a light in the darkness, a flare of real light that could be seen with the eyes. Arrows, slingloads of firestuff, Sala's narrow face flickering in a light of her own making as she set them off. The silverback flinched, pulled up just a little, pained by the light; and then the missiles hit it. It screamed like a whole choir of angry sopranos at once, and caught fire and fell to the ground ablaze. It missed the wagon and hit the road, and men busied themselves in putting out the stoneweed before the fire could spread.

"It hurts."

And suddenly it was all over. Nothing remained aloft but the shouf, which hovered for another few minutes and then turned and made off into the east. Denis descended into his body again and looked round. His arm was under Genevra's head, and as he watched her eyes opened. *That was fun. Let's do it again.*

"Well done, Kieran," said Mark of Hellsgarde as he rode past, seeing that the column reshaped itself properly.

"Thanks, m'Lord," Kieran said. "By your leave, m'Lord Duke, we held off as long as we could.

"And by your leave, m'Lord Duke," he muttered once the Duke was past, "maybe we won't hold off so long next time. We nearly lost them."

"Mom?"

"Yes, dear?"

"What happens if I die?"

Sue took a breath. "Then you go to Heaven. But I don't think that's very likely."

"Do I have an appendix?"

"Everybody has an appendix, and maybe yours is what's bothering you. But even if it is, the doctors can handle it. It's a simple operation and they've done it lots of times." *I suppose.*

"Even on little kids?"

"Especially on little kids. So don't worry."

"But you're worrying, Mom. You've chewed all your lipstick off."

Sue could think of nothing to say. After a moment Mike turned over, and said "Ow!" and turned back.

Not much of an attack, Donal remarked. The council of Hellsgarde, drawn from its various wagons, was in session upon the lower air. *Nothing you'd bother to put in the histories.*

There was an agreement. *I am thinking in particular,* Mark said, *that we saw no Shadowknights, and the Queen said he has two, or in a pinch three.*

A feint, to draw our attention? If so, he failed in that.

No, for there was no second force attacking once the first had engaged us. I think he meant to test our strength, and tempt us, maybe, to underestimate him. Nonetheless, we must be wary. Scan from horizon to horizon. We have now to cross the causeway Amalia told us of, that runs for miles between those low wet fields. We shall all have to take the road, horse, foot, and wagon, and be strung out for miles till we reach the high ground again. If I were any good as a commander, and I saw an invading army along such a road, that is when I should attack. So keep watch.

"Yeah, the profile on the bloods is absolutely classic—" The door swung open, and a short plump red-haired man in surgical greens puffed in like a very small, very energetic locomotive (a small switching engine, perhaps). "Hi. Hi. I'm Dr. Thorvald. Dr. Delfini asked me to take a look at Mike. Now, let's see here." He turned Mike gently onto his back and ran his fingers over the child's abdomen. His face became very thoughtful. "Mm-hmm. I tell you what, Mike, it looks as if, for once in a way, the signs aren't fooling us. I think we need to take your appendix out. You know what that means?"

"Well," Mike said, "first you put a gas mask over my face, and—"

"Naw, naw," the doctor said. "That's old-fashioned. You've been watching old movies on television, that's what. No, we give you a shot in the arm. We give you one right now, or in a minute or two anyway. You think you can handle that?"

"Yeah," Mike said.

"So this shot makes you very sleepy. Then we put you on the cart and wheel you into the operating room, and start an I.V. in case you miss dinner. Then we give you another shot, which by this time you probably won't feel it anyway, and that sends you straight out into left field and by the time you get back it's all over. Then in a couple days you go home, and then you have to take it easy till your stitches heal. Okay?"

'You're the doctor," Mike said. "Can we do it now?"

The doctor raised both eyebrows. "If it's okay with you, Mike, it's fine with me." He glanced at Sue. "This kid must watch M*A*S*H. *He* isn't afraid of hospitals."

"He isn't—" Suddenly Sue couldn't speak. She swallowed hard. "He isn't even afraid of the dentist. I think you can go ahead."

"Super." Dr. Thorvald took a tube of liquid from one locker, a needle from another, and injected Mike's arm. "Did that hurt? Oh, not much. Well, that's the most it's going to hurt from now on. You wait and see. I'll go get the gurney." He hurried out.

The farm-paddies stretched out to the horizon on either side. There was room for four soldiers side by side, or two horsemen, or one wagon. The line was very long. "There's *something* overhead," Denis told Amalia, "but it doesn't seem to be doing anything. Just hanging about watching."

"Perhaps it's the shouf again?"

Denis shook his head. "Too many brains for a shouf. Could be the Shadowknights. And here we are, four men wide and a thousand long, so why don't they attack?"

"But they are," Genevra said, unexpectedly. She sat up and tucked her feet under her. "Somebody up there—" she jerked her thumb toward the wagoncover "—is sitting up there telling our men they're not going to make it. Can't you hear him? Can't you feel them? There's somebody up there with a Voice."

Denis's eyes met Amalia's. "Andri," he said softly.

"Can it be? He's got the Voice, but never this much of a range."

"Well, he's studied under a master this past year, poor fellow," Denis said, "and now we've got to deal with him." *Mark!*

I noticed, Mark said. *We have Kelvan of Blackwater starting up a counter-song; that ought to help.*

"Let me out there," said Amalia once this was translated. "Get me my horse, and a couple of squires with torches."

She rode to the head of the line, where the banner-bearer and the Duke led out onto the emerald-lit stoneweed. Mark remained where he was, but he sent Kelvan of Blackwater back along the line with Amalia.

Denis was fond of music, when he had the time for it, and he listened with interest to the polyphony being sung before his mind's ear.

Despair, it sang from the sky. *Your spears are broken, your lances shattered, your bones will lie in strange soil and never even feed the flowers. Turn back if you can. Run away and hide. Lie down and die.*

"You okay, Mike?"

"Mmmm," he said. "Not so bad. Now I know why people get addicted. Are we going now?"

"Not yet. Just relax."

"Couldn't relax—nng. Couldn't *not* relax if I tried."

But Kelvan sang, *Courage!* and his Voice was steel under velvet, rich and dark and strong. (But the man was a high tenor when he opened his mouth!) *They fear us, they cannot withstand us. We are the army of Light riding to conquer Darkness. Golden are our trumpets, bright our torches, sharp our sword-blades; we go to plant our tree again in Andarath.* And the men marched on.

"Okay," the doctor said. "Let's get you onto the cart, Mike, and we'll get going. Give your Mom a hug. If you'll stop by the receptionist, Mom, she's got one more paper for you to sign. It's a drag, I know. After we fix up the patient, we have to give his Mom therapy for writer's cramp."

We are coming to the end of the causeway, Mark told Denis. *The plain widens here, and they are all over it, drawn up in good order, waiting for us. I don't think they intend to let us off the causeway. But I have an idea. Send all the firestarters forward. And when we've all come off the causeway, then draw a wagon across the end of it, and set it afire. They'll not sneak up on us; nor can we think of retreat. Oh, yes, and get Her Grace back into that wagon.*

"Okay, you need to sign this release," the receptionist said.

The firestarters came forward, their bows strung, bags of firestuff slung across their shoulders, to where the Duke stood at the head of the line. Before him, the shining green/white road sloped down about twenty feet to meet the plain; and scarcely another twenty feet beyond there stood the first ranks of the Shadowlings, mounted on cats, their sharp little swords in their hands.

"Okay, thanks. Dr. Thorvald is scrubbing now; they'll be going into surgery in a few minutes. Would you like some coffee or something? You look pretty beat."

"I better call my husband first."

"Loose," cried the Duke of War, and pointed. The bowmen and slingers obeyed, all their missiles converging within a few feet of each other. Sala and her brothers linked hands and set light to everything they could reach. And the stoneweed of the road went up in flames.

Sue called Fred and brought him up to date. "Do you want me to come get you?"

"No, I think I'd stay till he gets out. I'm not worried, Fred, really," she lied. "You can tell when somebody knows his job. You just sit on Mark and Kathy and don't let them get eaten by bears. You take care too. 'Bye, Fred. I love you too."

The burning road sent a thin line of chaos right through the strength of the Darklanders. Many were killed outright, and the rest driven back, so that the Shadowknights (two Shadowknights, now plainly to be discerned on their dragons above the battlefield) took more than two hours to draw them up again.

"Now why don't you go get that coffee," the receptionist said. "The cafeteria's down on the first floor, you get out of the elevator and turn right."

"Yeah, I guess," Sue said. *How're you guys doing?*

No one answered. The last of the men were coming down off the causeway now, and moving into battle order, and the Duke's servants drew the wagon across the road and fired it. It made a pitifully little light at their backs. The road had all burnt out.

Good luck.

High above them, two sparks of light glinted out of the Shadowcover. The eyes of Imber, looking down at them with contempt and delight. The ranks of the Shadow had taken form again. The first of the knights started forward.

And nothing. It was as though someone had pushed the

PAUSE button: men and Shadowfolk standing still, the very torches unmoving. Sue went downstairs and got her coffee.

The cafeteria was nearly deserted—it was the middle of the evening shift, not time for coffee breaks, and the other visitors had gone home. Remembering that she hadn't had dinner, she bought a sandwich and ate three bites of it.

She closed her eyes, hoping to escape into Demoura . . . but her mind would not take wing.

Slowly they took shape around her: Amalia, grave in her martial scarlet, and Aumery in somber black; Marianella, drying her eyes on the corner of her apron, and Kieran in his leather jerkin and the sea gull's feather tucked behind one ear. *Don't be afraid,* they said. *We're here.*

I know.

Give me your hand. She let her hand rest on her knee, and Kieran's hand curled round it.

I wish some of you could be at my house, to cope with the kids.

A woman dressed in surgical green padded down the aisle in soft plastic slippers. She didn't look at them.

Eat, Amalia said. There was a south wind flowing up into the Weatherwall from the plains, and blowing the mists away from the steps of the House. From where she stood, she could see six stars. *Eat,* she repeated. *It's fuel for the body.* From a long distance away, Sue picked up the sandwich and bit into it.

CHAPTER 13

Single Combat

Nine o'clock. Sue got up and went for another cup of coffee, not because she wanted it but because it was something to do. She had spent the last few hours, her friends silent around her and almost transparent, watching her thoughts chase each other round her brain like frantic squirrels—squirrels, she clarified, that were high on amphetamine, had one sprained ankle apiece, and thought they were on their way to Portland to address the Rotary Club.

She looked at her watch again. Nine-seventeen. Surely they ought to have been done with Mike by now. It hadn't taken this long to *have* him. Her face was hot and her feet were cold, and her eyes kept going out of focus. *Something's gone wrong, or is going wrong, and they haven't come out to tell me yet. Or else they're waiting for me up at the receptionist's, rather than page me and give me a heart attack or something.*

She began to get up, then stopped herself and sat down again. She had been up to the reception desk every few minutes, it seemed, for hours; they must be sick of the sight of her.

You really haven't been here that long, Amalia said. *I know it seems longer but it's just your mind.*

Sue hunched her shoulders and turned her head this way and that, trying to get the muscles to relax. *It's a*

282

routine procedure anyway, isn't it? They do it every day. It's like changing a fuse. Tell me I'm right.

I believe so. Your doctor didn't seem concerned about the outcome; please don't be troubled.

I'm not troubled. That was the trouble, she realized suddenly. She was not worrying, only remarking within her mind that the matter was serious and one really ought to worry. *It's not really bothering me. Even if Mike dies—* She put her hands over her face. *Even if he dies, I'll manage all right. And now will you listen to me? My child is up there being—And I sit here reassuring myself that it's all right, I can cope, it won't upset my equilibrium! God forgive me. Lord have mercy on us. God, will you please take a sharp stick and poke me till I come to my senses. Amalia, I am like you, my soul is frozen in ice.*

That doesn't follow, Amalia said. *I still know fear and grief, love, yes, and exasperation, none the less for standing here. I think you are numb with shock. You'll come out of it presently.*

I'd better, hadn't I? And because she could no longer sit still in one place, she thrust herself out of her chair and walked to the end of the room and back, her hands clenched behind her back.

A man stepped into the room, and it was Chris Bingley. Sue stood and gaped. Imber in his blazing cloak, his starry body-stocking, would have been less incongruous.

"Well, hello," she said after a moment.

"Hi," Chris said. "How's your little boy?"

"He's still in surgery. I suppose he's okay; the doctor acted pretty confident about it all."

"Where's Fred?"

"Home sitting with the other kids."

"Why isn't he here?"

"Because he's home sitting with the other kids," she repeated, raising her voice maybe just a little.

"How long have you been here?"

"Mid-afternoon. Mike took sick about lunchtime."

"I know. I just missed catching you at the school. Then I wasted a lot of time calling doctors' offices. None of them would say whether you were their patients or not."

"Well, of course not. Would you want your doctor telling strangers about you?"

"Then when I called your house, you were already gone," Chris went on unheeding, "and then I called here and got the same runaround. And where was Fred all this time?"

"He was at work, of course. Till just before six, when he had to get the kids out of day care. Where did you suppose he'd be? They're doing inventory, remember?"

"Oh, sure. The devoted employee, no personal loyalties can stand in his way, no sacrifice is too great. Who's he think he's trying to impress?"

"Not you, obviously." Sue looked with disgust into the inch-and-a-half of cold coffee in the bottom of her cup, and picked it up with two fingers to throw it into the trash.

"So then I had to go to a meeting," Chris was saying, "and then a business dinner. As soon as I got out I started hunting again. I could've called your house, I suppose, but I didn't want to, I wasn't sure I could keep my temper."

"Chris, I'm very tired, it's been a rough day and it's not over yet. Do you suppose you could come to the point?"

He stopped in mid-gesture and glared at her. "I wanted to find you. I want to be with you, give you some support maybe, since it's for damn sure you aren't getting any out of Fred."

"I do not need any support," Sue said. "I am doing just fine. Kathy and Mark, on the other hand, are probably worried sick. I don't envy Fred the job of getting them through the evening and into bed."

"It beats sitting here in an empty cafeteria drinking crummy hospital coffee."

"Actually, the coffee's pretty good; or it was while I could still taste it."

Chris sat down beside her and took her hand. "I'm here, Sue," he said.

"I know you are. Don't you think I have enough problems already?"

He dropped her hand and without another word, got up and walked away. *Oh shit*, she thought. *I think I just blew it. We just took the wrong exit from life in the fast lane.*

Good riddance, Kieran said, and she turned to clasp his hand.

"You shut up, shorty!" Bingley shouted, and vanished around the corner, leaving Sue agape.

Did he really say that? Can he see Kieran? Or did I only imagine I heard him? How tired do you have to get before you start hallucinating? She turned back to Kieran, who shrugged.

Does it matter? He's got no manners and no style, the sort that gives us peasants a bad name.

She looked at her watch. Nine-thirty-five. Time to go bug the receptionist again. She slung her purse over her shoulder and went back to the elevator.

The receptionist looked up and smiled. "Oh, hi," she said. "I was just going to have you paged. They've just come out. Mike's in the recovery room."

"Everything okay?"

"Everything looks good. Right through that door."

Mike looked very small in the big bed, his skin almost as pale as the sheets, his eyelashes long and dark against his cheekbones. But his breathing was regular, and any resemblance to a deathbed scene was spoiled by the look of the man sitting beside him. His white uniform was rumpled, and he was sitting on the bottom third of his spine, long legs stretched out in front of him, reading a comic book full of Japanese monster robots. Every thirty seconds or so he'd take a glance at Mike.

"Oh, hi," he said. "Are you Mike's mother? Have a chair. He's fine, he had a really boring operation, it was so simple, and now we just have to watch him till he wakes up and then he can go back to sleep." He yawned. There was a nameplate on his shirt, 'Arvid Janssen, R.N.' "And then so can we. It's the rules."

It was another twenty-nine minutes by Sue's overworked watch before Mike wrinkled his nose and opened his eyes. "Hi, Mom," he said. "What happened?"

"Don't you remember? You had your appendix out."

"Far out! Can I keep it?"

"Well, uh—"

She glanced at the nurse, who had folded his comic book and gotten up. "In a jar, do you mean? I'll see what I can do. It probably went down to Pathology; I'll see if I can rescue it before they throw it out." He winked at Sue.

"I knew a guy once who collected gallstones. They were supposed to be all his own, but we think he cheated. Okay, Mike, give your Mom a hug and then you can go back to sleep. I'll take you to your room. No, you don't have to get up; you're on wheels."

Sue kissed Mike, smelling disinfectant and little boy incongruously mingled. "I'll see you in the morning," she said. "Goodnight—" But he was already asleep again. "Goodnight," she said to the nurse. "When are visitor's hours tomorrow?"

"Okay, for parents it's twenty-four hours a day, except during doctors' rounds," he said. "Why don't you go get some sleep, and come by after breakfast. You look pretty tired. G'night." He wheeled Mike's bed away, the wheels going whisper-click-whisper-click down the echoing corridor.

"Fine," Sue said. But she didn't feel sleepy; she was too keyed up. There was something still that demanded her attention. Not a class assignment, nothing about the PTA. It nagged at her. Something she had to do. She said goodnight to the receptionist, got down to the parking lot, was putting her key into the ignition before it struck her.

Amalia took one long look at the eyes of Imber overhead, and pulled her head back inside the wagon. *These may be my last hours,* she thought. *I must remember everything.* She felt the wood of the wagon box under her fingertips, rough and ridged, each line of grain a thin little streak of smoothness. A patch the size of a fingertip, soft, smooth under her touch like powder. She shifted her body so that the lamp's light could fall on it. A few early threads of spiderlime, breaking ground, colonizing the wood to break it down to Shadowdust. She scraped it away with her fingernail, but doubtless there were more. Outside she heard the clash of metal, armor against armor, stirrup against greaved ankle, swords rattling out of their sheaths, and the voice of a sergeant, just audible over the distance: "Come on, you sons of bitches; you want to live for ever?"

Sue's car was crawling down Market Street behind the City Hall, the closest thing to urban decay Liberty Hill had come up with so far, with its third-rate movie theaters and porno shops. There was scarcely another car in sight, thank Heaven; she didn't *think* she had just gone through that flashing red light, but she couldn't be sure; she hadn't been watching. Better to get out of the center of town before she ran into something, or something into her. She signaled and turned right. It was the last conscious act she made for some time.

"Now, make ready," Michael the Red told Kieran as he rode by. "There's no chance left of surprising them, so hit them as early as you can. Master Denis says there's a whole battalion of them coming in, as thick as geese in autumn. Aim for the big clusters if you can, but almost anywhere you shoot you should hit something."

"We'll be ready," Kieran said. His fingers were on his bowstring, the new one he had carried wax-sealed in a jar against this hour.

"There is a great host," Denis said, "several hundreds at least, on cats, coming slowly toward us."

"I have seen them," Mark said. "They outnumber us, I believe, by a few. Let us not give them the advantage." He turned to Aurelia the Red, who had ridden this far with him knee to knee. "Madam, sound the attack," he said. "And then fall back, if you will, and get you to the wagons." He smiled. "Aurelia, if we don't meet again in this world, farewell, and remember me. You always were my favorite cousin. Take care." He leaned down and kissed her, and then spurred his horse forward to ride beside the banner-bearer. Aurelia reined in, and let the files of horsemen pass her till her trumpeter came level with her. "Sound 'Knights to the attack,' with repeats to the four quarters. Now."

As she rode back toward the wagons the trumpets took up the call, answering one another in all directions. The knights moved close together, knee to knee, their lances faint gleams in the torchlight. They urged their horses across the plain, heedless now of the dark, and galloped toward the whispering Shadowlings.

They hit the Shadow line like the blow of a mace, a blow that would have shattered an army of men. Unfortunately, the Shadowlings were not intelligent enough to see the implications of the blow and be demoralized. The Lightlander cavalry broke their line into four pieces, but each piece fought on as if they had split up by design. The Shadowlings were courageous, not by choice, but because they knew of no other way; and each one, separated from all his fellows, would still fight on till he was hacked to peices. The knights had their hands full. Behind the front ranks, the pikemen lowered their pikes, like a forest of long reeds, against a possible counter-charge. Kieran nocked an arrow to his bow and moved closer to Sala. Her eyes were half-closed, looking into the blank sky.

Fortunately, the Shadowcats were smarter than their riders, and a sword-cut that took the legs out from under one would persuade a dozen of its fellows that they might have better luck elsewhere. The front edge of the Shadowline began to soften.

There was a high thin whistling in the air, like wind through harpstrings; the men of Demoura could only just barely hear it, but it served the Shadowlings as a trumpet call. A fresh wave of Shadowcats were advancing to fill in the line. The knights closed up their ranks a little tighter.

But now Mark brought in his second mass of cavalry, from where they had been waiting behind a line of pikemen on his right. Swords and lances at the ready, they hit the enemy's flank, and the nearest Shadowlings turned to meet them.

But only the nearest. Those Shadowlings who were not yet themselves under attack would continue to obey their orders, to press forward and shore up their forward line, without seeing or caring that their next neighbors were being cut up like chickens for the pot.

For perhaps fifteen minutes, no one could have told which way the battle was moving. There was death being dealt on both sides. But again the thin whistle sounded, and now the Lord of Darkness attacked from the air. Silverbacks and pearlbacks and rishi came spiraling down, and some nasty little things that even the Hellsgarders had not seen before. These were blade-shapes about the size of a man's hand, sharp as spearheads, that flew about of themselves. They seemed always to attack an enemy at his highest point, and their strength was not enough to pierce the knights' helms. Some of the riderless horses were killed, though, pierced at ear or eye or nose, and more than one knight found sudden blinding death when a flyer got in at the eyeslits.

Now the firestarter teams came into their own. A single firebolt, well-aimed, could scald half-a-dozen Shadowlings and their rishi, crippling their attack and sending them plunging into the ground, or soften up a silverback for the attention of the Hellsgarders, or take out a whole flock of flying spearheads like moths around a bonfire. Only over the cavalry were the Shadowfolk making headway. The firestarters tried sending a few shots low over the knights' heads, but it was ticklish to aim correctly and the firebolts had no calming influence on the horses.

"We ought to be out there," Sala said. "Look how many dead horses are lying on the field. Couldn't we creep from one to the next?"

"We shall probably be killed," Kieran said. "Shall we try it?"

"Better killed than beaten," Sala said. She slid down from her rock and beckoned to her team. "Come on, you sons of bitches," she said. "I forget the rest."

They made their way across the dark plain, invisible except when someone else's firebolt went off. Sometimes they felt their way with their toetips; sometimes they had to creep on hands and knees.

They paused to take breath behind a fallen horse. Its rider had tried to leap clear, and failed; he lay crumpled, his legs pinned under the animal's bulk. His helm had been knocked from his head, its chinstrap broken, and it lay on the ground beside him.

Kieran lay flat on the ground beside the fallen knight, his head pillowed on his arms, and inhaled the faint beehive fragrance of the groundcover. *Another hundred yards*, he thought. *Two hundred would be even better. Then we'll be in the thick of it.* His face itched with sweat, and he rubbed it against his sleeve. *No doubt we'll never make it back. It doesn't matter.*

"You," a voice said. Kieran raised his head. The fallen knight had opened his eyes and was looking at him. "You're the firestarter, aren't you? Kieran of Telerath."

"Yes, my Lord."

"You're going out there? Good man. Better give the girl my helm."

"Thank you," Kieran said, but the knight had closed his eyes. Kieran fitted the helm onto Sala's head, and they crept on.

Further back behind the lines, Amalia sat in her wagon and

brooded. Denis and Genevra lay in the wagon-bed, unheeding of what was around them, their minds far away where the battle raged. Genevra had turned onto her side, curled up in the crook of Denis's arm, and his head was turned toward her. Amalia and Marianella exchanged glances, and faint smiles.

"This is all very well," Amalia said, "but—."

"My Lady, if you can think of anything useful you can do, you have my leave to do it," Marianella said. "*I* can't think of anything."

Another pause, in the shelter of the mound where two horses and a Shadowcat had died on one another's bodies. The starless air was full of the whispering speech of the Shadowlings, and somewhere within earshot a man's voice was weeping, quietly, as if he had been doing it for a long time. Something shrieked overhead, thinly, like a bat.

Already Kieran was feeling tired, desperately weary, and they had not yet reached the front lines. Tears stung his eyes, and he laid his head down on something soft— the webbed furry paw of the shadowcat—and blinked the dampness away.

A voice cried out overhead, a human voice, but in some strange language having vowels fit for an owl and consonants designed for a snake.

Kieran looked up. For an instant he saw it, outlined by the last light of a fireburst: a man in a flowing cloak, flying astride a hideous dragon shape, all bat wings and snaky neck and tail. The dragon flinched as the light struck it, and buried its head in its shoulder; but the man struck it with something—a riding crop?—and made it fly onward. He cried out again, cursing it perhaps; even through the horrible inhuman language Kieran could hear the shrill note of fear in his voice. The beast answered in a low roar that rumbled back across the field like distant thunder.

One of the Shadowknights, Kieran thought. One of two, the Queen had said. Except sometimes she said there were three, and when her Lords of State asked her about it she changed the subject. But the Duke of War seemed to know about it. Two, or maybe three, human renegades that had gone over to the Darkness, and one of them the Queen's brother, poor Lord Andri that had the Voice. That was where this weariness, this feeling of despair, was coming from. Well, Lord Andri wouldn't have the better of Kieran, the Queen's seneschal of Telerath, not just yet. "Come on," he said. "We're moving on. It's not far now."

And all this time there was no light but the firebolts from the other teams that exploded overhead, for the torches had all gone out. Some thoughtful Seer had taken the trouble to notify one of the other teams, and they were casting their bolts low overhead, to cover Kieran's advance. In the past hour Kieran had given up most of his interest in the future, but he hoped he might live long enough to thank them.

The Duke of War sat up a little straighter in his saddle, and opened his eyes. "He's gone back," he said to the captain of his guard.

"Who, my Lord?"

"Oh, sorry. The Shadowknight that was hanging over the lines, singing at us. His mount got a touch of light and turned back. A pity we couldn't have downed him. Where's Captain Kelvan?"

"Got a dart in his shoulder, my Lord. They've put him in a wagon and the leeches are seeing to him. We shan't see him on the field again today, but he ought to be able to sing again in a while."

"Good. I hope so." Mark closed his eyes and ascended again. *Denis*, he called. *Kelvan's down. Do you suppose the two of you could take out that Shadowknight?*

Nobody's ever done it, but we could give it a try I suppose. Thank you for your confidence, Mark, I hope it isn't misplaced. Look there, by the way. Something big's coming up.

Mark looked into the east, where the Darkness was deepest. Yes, something was moving there, a massive attack on a weak point in their line. Twin spearheads, on the ground and in the air, led from above by the Shadowknight. Already the cavalry were turning that way to defend the line, and the pike squares had shifted their pikes to reinforce it, and overhead six or eight Hellsgarders were stooping like eagles toward the Shadowknight.

"Well," Kieran said. "How do you like that? We get here to fight and they go off somewhere else." The spearhead of the Darklander army had passed them by at no more than twenty yards' distance, and the last of the air attack was still whistling overhead. "Discourteous, I call it. Let's meet bad manners with bad manners and stab them in the back."

He raised his bow and loosed the bolt. His companions did the same. Sala thumbed her nose at the Shadowlings' backs, and set all the missiles afire in one breath-holding burst of effort. There was a satisfying burst of light across the dark sky, and a dozen rishi fell whistling and shrieking from the sky. "Right," Sala said, panting for breath. "Let's do that again."

The Darklander spearhead was blunted, its advance slowed down to a crawl; the Shadowknight had wheeled away and fallen back. "Good," Mark said, smiling at the shaken banner-bearer. "If that's the best he can do—what's that?"

Shouts were going up on their left, and the sounds of clashing metal and the purr of running paws and the whistle of wings. Mark gulped for breath and went aloft again.

The first attack had been a feint, to draw away their defenses, and now the weakened line was buckling, giving way at the point of penetration. The Shadowlings were pouring in. Overhead, a great mass of rishi as thick as a swarm of bees followed the advance of all three Shadowknights. Curiously, the dragonriders were in the form of an inverted triangle: instead of one leading two, the other way around, like a king preceded by two swordthanes. Mark swooped down. He wanted a look at that Shadowknight.

The Hellsgarders were wheeling to the defense, knocking the nearest rishi out of the air, and the five firestarter teams within range were peppering them with light. But there were so many of them.

On the ground, the Shadowcats formed the cutting edge for a massive wedge of Shadowlings afoot, small but deadly. As they surged through the Demouran lines, the men swung round to attack them on the flanks, and this did some damage but not enough. There was not so much that footsoldiers could do to charging cavalry, not unless it were charging at them to be impaled on the pikes. Mark's banner-bearer, leading by the bridle the horse of his absentminded lord, realized with a prickling of his scalp that the Shadowlings were headed directly for the royal wagons, as if they had known from the start where they were. "My Lord!" he cried, and touched Mark's sleeve in defiance of orders.

"I know, I know," Mark muttered, and pulled his hood over his face.

In the air, the Shadowknights were riding three abreast, circling this way and that, spurning the attack of the Hellsgarde circles. Such power was in the two flanking dragonriders that not even Mark could come at the one in the middle. He was close enough to get an impression of the man, though, just as an ordinary man afoot can get an idea of another's state of mind from the way he walks. It was very strange. There was the flavor of long age and suffering, a barren life under the Shadow and the heavy hand of the Lord of Darkness. But with it, there was something of a young man and light-hearted, walking in springtime, pushing aside a too-playful dog, walking across blossoming fields to the cottage where his girl was waiting for him. Slowly, as if they had plenty of time and could linger to enjoy their journey, the Shadowknights were making for the Queen's wagon.

Will they, hell! Denis said. *Come on, girl.* Genevra was beside him, and at his word she moved up and meshed with him so smoothly that they seemed almost one creature, as if two eagles in flight could have woven their wingtips together, feather by feather, and flown on.

It was like having his second eye restored, Denis thought, and seeing in depth after long half-blindness. Together with two viewpoints and one judgment, they looked over the two flanking Shadowknights. The one in the center was for Mark, he had said it; and the fellow on the left was a canny flyer, no sign of an opening there. The man on the right, now ... yes, watch there, as he turned. Wasn't there a bit of a jog in that smooth curve?

He turns too close, Genevra/Denis told Denis/Genevra. *He crowds his lord too close on the right, and turning left, comes within his wing-beat and must turn away again. See, when they turn right there's no difficulty. But if we/I can be on hand when they turn left again ...*

Faintly echoing the excitement of their spirits, their bodies were locked tight in each other's arms. Genevra's head rested on Denis's shoulder, and his lips murmured into her ear. Amalia, lying close behind Genevra, strained to overhear the syllables, while Marianella put down her needle and folded her hands in her lap to keep them from twitching.

Amalia's face had gone very white. "Oh, Heaven," she said at last, and got up. She shook the wisps of straw out of her skirts, careless of how they scattered over her unheeding companions, and climbed out of the wagon.

Here, away from the front lines, torches still burned, and overhead fireburst lit up the air. She could hear the clash of battle, now, ahead and a little to her left, as the spearhead of the Darkness came nearer. Overhead the windless air whistled with the beating of wings. Somewhere up above there were the Shadowknights, come to take her. *Oh, love. Aumery.* The Shadowlings were very close now.

Then a horn sounded, somewhere off to the north, badly blown and not musical, an uncalculated challenge. Shouts, and hoofbeats, and a fireburst overhead revealed a band of horsemen, at least two hundred of them, charging into the Darklander spearhead and braking it off at the tip. They were an ill-assorted crew, riding under no banner, and their black-helmed captain fought like ten men and seemed to have eyes in the back of his head and another at his swordtip.

Within minutes it was over. There was some backslapping reunions among the Queen's men and the newcomers, and a few loud-voiced recriminations, too. The captain leapt from his horse and strode toward the Queen, tossing his dark helm aside.

It was Saradoc, come out of the Darkness to their aid, his coat turned yet another time, walking like a conqueror. His eyes were fixed on Amalia, and a little smile was taking shape in the corners of his mouth, framed by the reddish beard.

Then, almost at his feet, a fallen Shadowling raised its arm out of the tangled shroud of its rishi, and hurled a dart. It struck him in the side, between the leathern lacings of his breastplate, a handsbreath below the heart.

Saradoc took another pace, and stopped. With two fingers he plucked the dart out, glancing at it disdainfully, and flung it away with a flip of his wrist. He came on, a little slower now, to the wagon where Amalia still stood.

He was breathing through his mouth, carefully and almost silently, as if it hurt. He gripped the wagon-box with one hand and put the other round the back of Amalia's head, and covered her unresisting mouth with a hungry kiss. When he had to draw breath, he let her go.

"Mmm," he said. "Your Grace," he said, faintly mocking. "If I had ten more minutes I'd show you what a man's made of. But time presses." He closed his eyes and leaned against the wagon. One of Amalia's Guardsmen, passing by, caught him as he slumped and gently lowered him to the ground. He opened his eyes again and caught Amalia's eye. He smiled once more, and kissed his hand to her, and died.

Now. Denis/Genevra had been waiting, hovering as lightly as a breath above the conflict in the air, while the Shadowknights wheeled in slow infuriating circles always to the right. But now something was happening below that had attracted their attention; the central Shadowknight had turned sharply downward, banking to the left, and his companions followed him. And once more the right-hand dragon moved in a little too close, and had to turn away again. Denis/Genevra slipped down along the thin shifting layers of air, and caught him as he turned.

The Shadowknight raised his hands to his face. The dragon at first did not notice anything had happened, and went on spiraling to the right. The Shadowknight, recovering, put one hand on the bony knob at the base of its neck, to bring it back into control. In his other hand he raised the black whip that was his direst weapon, deadly against spirit and flesh alike. But wherever he struck, Denis/Genevra were somehow not there. Their trailing wingtips drifted past his face, confused his senses, teased the shrieking dragon to strike this way and that. He raised his whip high, brought it round in a great circle that might have taken anything within range. But all he caught was his own dragon's wingtip, for Genevra/Denis swooped in under his arm and engulfed him, blinded and deafened him, Denis shrieking cacophony in his ears and Genevra a taste of springtime upon his lips, till they pulled free and vanished a split second before he crashed into the earth.

What'd you want to go and kiss him for?

I thought it might be useful. Wasn't it?

You'd better leave Hellsgarde, my girl. You're picking up bad habits.

"I don't believe it, they got him!" the banner-bearer cried.

"Yes," Mark said. "Well done, Denis. And the other two are moving off again."

On the ground and in the air there was still confusion, but

the men of Demoura had formed rough quick alliance with those of Saradoc's who had survived the charge, and were going about mopping up. Any Shadowcreatures that could fall back were doing so, leaving an open space of about a quarter mile. A truce seemed to be in force.

Torches were being relit, and for the first time Amalia had a good idea of where she was. The ground on which they stood was covered with burnt stoneweed, but only a hundred yards away the line of burning ended, and the road shone white again. In all this turmoil, over several hours of battle, neither side had gained or lost ground.

"Damn," said a voice behind her: Ryan, slumping on his horse and scratching his head. "Pardon me, Your Grace. I can't quite follow what the fellow's saying."

"What fellow?"

"The Shadowknight, the other one. He's acting as herald for his master, calling for—parley? No, not exactly. He's calling for— "

"Trial by single combat," said Mark of Hellsgarde, riding up to them. "He calls on your Grace to face him. I will fight for you, if you wish."

Amalia turned. Far across the gap, where the shadowcreatures stood in a long line and the white stoneweed shone faintly green, a tall dark figure stood waiting. "No, thank you, my Lord Duke," she said, touching the faint spot of warmth where the Heart lay against her breast. "This is no one's hour but mine."

Without anyone's giving an order she could hear, the hundred picked knights of her Guard fell in behind her as she walked across the burnt stoneweed. Behind them came the pikemen, led by the torchbearers and followed by everyone who could walk. By the time she reached the boundary of black and white upon the ground, the sky behind her was milky with the torchlight, and the Shadowlings were falling back. The dark figure raised his right hand. The torchbearers stopped. The two of them were alone in a wide circle, surrounded by their armies.

Amalia went forward, the silver medallion brilliant upon her scarlet gown. As the dark shape approached her it blossomed forth into that cluster of lights in man's shape whose familarity and deadly beauty made her heart turn over. Her men behind her were murmuring with awe. Thirty yards, twenty yards, and she saw the shining body beneath the shining cloak, the long-fingered hands (emeralds and sapphires in the nails) that had kindled fire in her body and resolution in her heart. Stars lay on his shoulders like drifts of snow. The points of his crown were the bitter green of winter. Still she could not see his face.

At ten paces' distance he stopped, and his hand went to his breast. A faint ruby shape went to his lips, and hung there, and fell away. And the lights of Imber flew away like silver moths, and Aumery stood there again in his black cloak. She could make out his face in the torchlight, just, and he was smiling.

"My heart's love," he said. "I see you again; it's more than I had hoped for."

Break the Heart, he said. *Kill me, if you can. Do it at once.*

"Aumery," she said. "I daren't touch you, I should lose all my resolve."

"Touch me anyway," he said. "Kiss me, and give me farewell. Death is very close now."

Do it! Break the Heart! You waste time.

I'll spend my time as I choose. None can choose for me now.

She reached up and took his face between her hands, and guided him down to her kiss. The beard along his jaw was soft and sleek under her fingers. There were tears upon his face, and his mouth tasted of blood.

She stepped back and opened the medallion. The Heart fell lightly into her hand, and she held it, faintly warm, between her fingers. Aumery said, "Dear love, farewell."

Break it! Break it!

Amalia watched the lights begin to return, like evening bees to their hive. The crown blazed, the cloak swirled like the fringe of the Galaxy, the shining arms stretched wide as if to embrace her. And Amalia smiled, and dropped the Heart. It fell between her feet, and did not break.

The Dark Lord stepped closer. Beneath his crown his face was taking shape: the fiery eyes, the squat ape's nose. The ugly mouth smiled, and he held out his hand, palm up.

Amalia held out her closed hand, and opened it, and there was nothing on the palm. She held out her other hand, and opened it, and it was empty. And she took one step to the side, and brought her boot-heel down upon the Heart. It splintered like glass; it burst like a soap-bubble. Imber fell back.

His lights began to leave their positions, moving back and forth in erratic little circles, glowing yellow amber now instead of white. In seconds they had lost all man's shape and were moving in a spiral, like a dust devil, shining ever deeper red like fires that are going out. They spun apart, shot past Amalia's face like sparks, and winked out one by one. The dark body they had shielded fell heavily to the ground. Amalia fell to her knees beside it and laid the head on her lap. Her men behind her were cheering. She spat out a tendril of hair that had drifted into her mouth, and tasted the salt of her own tears.

A shaft of light fell over Aumery's face, illuminating his shadowed eyelids, his bloodless lips, the grimy streaks of sweat and tears over his pale skin. Amalia looked up, startled. There was a break in the Shadowcover overhead, and the sunlight was pouring in. As she watched, another break opened up, and another. Imber's clouds would not survive him long.

The Shadowlings turned to flee, but there was nowhere they could go. The deadly light was pouring down upon them, and they fell and began to crumble where they lay. A silverback hit the ground fifty yards from Amalia, with a thump that she could feel as well as hear. She arranged Aumery's head more comfortably on her lap, as though he could feel it, and wiped away the grimy streaks from his face.

Like a leaf falling, a tattered rishi came spiraling down, to land almost at Amalia's feet. Its rider spilled out and rolled over the ground, coming to rest at her side. It was still alive, and it turned from side to side, clutching at its head. Its mouth gaped open like a young bird's beak, gasping as if for breath, for something it needed in the air that was no longer there. It shuddered, and flung its hands wide, and lay still.

I did not will this, Amalia thought. *If only we could have lived together somehow.* But she could not think of any way that could have been.

Now the men of Demoura were coming out on foot to meet her, weeping and cheering, and Mark of Hellsgarde at their head with compassion on his face. And who was that, and what was that she was carrying?

Marianella, her face alight, came half-running out of the

midst of the crowd, the banner-bearer close behind her. She was teasing him, keeping something out of his grasp, carrying it to Amalia. As she came close, she shook the thing out: a banner, bright in the sun, the golden sunburst of Andarath on a field of deep blue. "Good heavens," Amalia said mildly. "Where did you get that? I thought it had all perished."

"I've been working on it," Marianella said. "What did you think I was sewing on all those hours in the wagon? Tiny garments?"

"I didn't inquire," Amalia said. "Give it to the poor man and let him do his job."

"Oh, here." Marianella made a face, but she gave the sun of Andarath into the hands of the banner-bearer, and hugged him into the bargain. "My Lady, aren't you pleased?"

"Of course," Amalia said. "I think you were very clever."

The destruction of the Shadowcover, which had started directly over their heads, had reached the horizon by now. Somewhere in the distance there was a boneshaking thud as a shouf fell out of the sky. It was a bright spring day, full of thin clear cold sunlight, and getting on to late afternoon.

Marianella fell to her knees beside Amalia. Her eyes were on Aumery. "Who's that?"

"Someone I used to know." She brushed a wisp of his dark hair back from his face, and picked a bit of stoneweed out of his beard.

Far away, where the House of the Mists stood under the shelter of the Weatherwall, there was a strange sound. It had been a sunny day, and drops of water had been falling from the ice all afternoon. Now the sounds of the drops were louder, and closer together, and what was that? It sounded like a fountain—Amalia did not realize that she could turn her head to look, until she had done it. Wherever she looked, the ice was melting. She could move her hands, her arms; she raised her hands to her face and perceived that though her spirit would have been hidden from the outward eye, her Sight could see her hands plainly. Her feet broke free of their invisible shackles of ice, and she turned away. She walked down the length of the House, with the open pillars on her left and an inner chamber (strange paintings dim upon its walls) on her right, following the sound of the fountain.

The place had been a garden once; she could see the trunks of trees, and banks that still held the remains of flowers that had grown there, blue and white. They had been preserved in the ice that had come upon them so suddenly; now the ice was melting. Drop after drop ran along the withered vines and fell into the pool that was forming. As she watched, the pool overflowed and began to run along the channel that had been dry. A puff of air went past her face, heavy with cool mist; it condensed upon the rock face at the other side of the clearing and began to flow downward, drop by crystal drop, to join the flowing spring. The source of the Kendal was coming alive as she watched. Winter had gone, Imber had left the earth, and it was spring.

Amalia looked up again. Before her stood her brother Andri, disarmed and guarded by two armed men. "Well done, Amalia," he said. "Once again you've pulled my chestnuts out of the fire, and I thank you."

"What are sisters for?" she said. "I'm glad to see you alive, I was afraid—"

"No," Andri said heavily, and sat down beside her. "No, that was Guiard. Two Hellsgarders thought of something new, I'm still not sure what it was, and blinded him and brought him down. Broke his neck."

"Poor Guiard," Amalia said. "From beginning to end, he never had any luck."

"And then there's this man," Andri said, indicating Aumery whose head still rested on Amalia's lap. "I know his story. May Heaven give him rest; he has paid for one days' pride and folly with two hundred years of wretchedness. And he was a good commander, and gentle toward us; it would have been my delight to serve under him, if we had both been on the other side."

Behind her, something stirred, more powerful than sunlight, more generous than the mist. She turned, and Aumery took her into his arms. All the clarity of his spirit, long subdued like banked fires, blazed up like a beacon. Now she saw the image of his body, illuminated as from within; now only the bright shape of his soul released from bondage. It was too much to comprehend, there would be time to sort it out. And his head stirred on her lap, and his eyes opened.

For minutes for hours they sat there they stood there while shouting men surged round them while the spring dropped crystal drops into the Kendal with the sound of music. At last they looked around. Andri was kneeling on the ground, his face hidden by his hands. Marianella was seated beside him, her legs crossed tailor-fashion, her face a careful portrait of long-suffering patience that has been tried almost too far.

"Your Grace, I'm sure I've no wish to pry," she said. "It's just that you've always told me everything before, and am I to know who this is?"

"Of course," Amalia said. "This is Aumery, the King's son, freed from prison now, and ready to take his rightful place among men."

"What will the Council say?"

"The Council will listen to me, I hope, and even if they did not: the man the Queen weds, is he not King?" She and Aumery smiled. Marianella threw up her hands, and got up and walked away.

Sue opened her eyes. She was, she was pleased to discover, neither in a police station nor back in the hospital as a patient this time. She was sitting in the last pew of a church, a Catholic church she supposed, full of gilt and glitter and brightly painted statutes. A golden canopy, impossibly ornate and standing on four pillars twisted like crullers, stood over the altar. A small forest of candle flames burned before a statue of the Virgin Mary. Bright banners hung on the wall, and the smell of incense hung faint and sweet in the air. It was a festive place, and suited her present mood.

"Excuse me," a voice said. It was a young priest, she supposed; at least, he was wearing a black T-shirt with a white clerical collar. Beneath that he was wearing scruffy blue jeans, and his tennis shoes were in a state that meant either he preferred comfort to style, or he took his vows of poverty seriously. "We're about to close up the church for the night," he said now. "If you'd like to talk, we could go into the rectory. Would you like some coffee?"

"Oh, no thanks, uh, Father," she said. "Everything's fine now." She looked about her, found that her purse had stayed with her throughout her wanderings, and picked it up. "I'm going home. Good night."

The young priest walked her to the door. "Good night," he said. Behind her she heard the heavy lock snick shut. Her car was parked in front of the church, in a no-parking zone, but it hadn't collected any tickets. But it was nearly midnight. She'd better get home.

Marianella pushed through the crowd, not caring whom she jostled. Her only thought was to reach the wagon and hide. She was happy for the Queen, she wouldn't deny it, but just now the reversal in their fortunes since last fall was very hard to bear.

A figure barred her way. She sniffed, and blinked hard, and stared. Kieran stood before her. "I have a frightful temper sometimes," he said. "But I'm neat and tidy and I always pick up my clothes."

She looked at him for a long moment. With all the good will in the world, you couldn't call that much of an apology. But there was pleading in his eyes. "Then I think I'll keep you," she said at last. "Just as well. Come on to the wagon, we've got to talk."

Ah, *that* was where she was; across the street from the church was the Record Barn. It wasn't quite midnight yet; Randy might still be working the late shift. She crossed the street and went in. The man clerking for the rock-and-roll section was almost asleep; he barely stirred his head on his supporting hand as she went by. On the other side of the corridor she stopped short, as if she had been struck by lightning. What sounds were these? Gongs, little bells, deep drums, striking in a complicated rhythm, deep blue-green notes out of the depth of a rain forest, and the thin reedy tone of a little flute! The music of Agniran, lost to Demoura with Imber and all his works, had reappeared, unhoped for, on Randy's CD player.

The room was littered with papers and beer cans, the residue of some kind of party. Randy was picking the pieces up and dropping them into the garbage, not very rapidly. "Oh, hi, Sue," he said. "Gosh, you missed the party altogether. I tried calling you, but you weren't home."

"Randy, what is this?" She gestured into the air, the deep blue notes almost palpable to the touch, cool and smooth as the gongs that made them.

"Javanese gamelan music. Like it? I put it on to get me

through the cleaning up. The party's over, I'm afraid. Even Kelly's gone home."

"I wasn't really in a postion to party," Sue said. "I've been seeing Mike through an appendectomy. Yes, he's fine now. I was just about to go home to bed. What was the party about?"

"I got my scholarship," Randy said, tucking his thumbs behind imaginary suspenders and waggling his fingers. I'm going back to school and get my Phud."

"Your what? Oh. Oh, Ph.D. That's great, Randy. Does Kelly know? Oh, yeah, you said she was here."

"Yeah, that's the other thing," Randy said. "We're engaged."

"Oh, that is nice," Sue said, and meant it. "You couldn't do better, either of you."

"I didn't tell the guys. They're not into engagements, they just live together. Sometimes by fives and threes. But we decided to take a leaf from your book and be old-fashioned."

"Well, I couldn't be more pleased. But my God, Randy, it's midnight. I've *got* to get home. I'll talk to you later. Gamelan music, you called it? I'll be back later, with money." She kissed him on the cheek and went out to her car.

"Let me get this straight," Kieran said. "You're with *what* and you think we should be *what?*"

"You heard me," she said. "And if you give me any of your sauce I'll go to the Queen."

"Dear heart, I wouldn't dream of it. But what about Master Denis?"

"Oh, Master Denis is going to marry Mistress Genevra. She knows it, I know it, everybody knows it but him. I give them two months."

Sue crept into bed as quietly as she could, but Fred woke up anyway. "Hi," he said. "Mike okay?"

"He's fine," she said. "They're going to give him his appendix in a bottle. One more thing to dust."

"You'll cope," he said. "Oh, yeah, Bingley called. he said to keep it under my hat till Monday, because he has to write a letter to Detroit. You are looking at the next manager of the Green Valley Sav-Mor, or you would be if it wasn't dark."

"Yeah, it figures," Sue said. "Good for you. Good for us. Move over a little, will you?" She curled up in the crook of Fred's arm, as familiar to her as the palm of her own hand. Marianella drifted towards sleep, Kieran's head pillowed in its old place on her arm. Sweaty, exhausted, reeking of burnt firestuff and unspeakably dear, he shifted a little in her arms and began to snore softly. She smiled. Deep down, so softly that she could not be sure she did not imagine it, her child stirred. *Weddings,* she thought. *We shall have to contrive something, quick. It doesn't matter so much about me, but I'd never have thought her Ladyship would throw her bonnet over the windmill!* . . .

For Amalia had refused to let custom or propriety separate her from Aumery, and they lay together now in a pavilion pitched a few yards from the wagon. Aurelia had been shocked, but then public seemliness was part of her job. Mark had only laughed.

Amalia had fallen asleep at once, but Aumery lay long awake, his head resting on his hand, looking over every feature of Amalia's face. For a late moon had risen, and the stars shone, and darkness would never be completely dark again.

Sleepless in a cleft of the mountain, Amalia and Aumery stood and watched the stars. Slowly they turned overhead, around the green Pole Star that hung a handsbreadth above the Weatherwall. To the Sight they were cold, but alive, and each sang like an angel in its own range, from the piercing sweetness of the great blue-white to the deep soft murmurs of the dim old red dwarfs. The air was clear and cold. Already the south winds were bringing them seeds to plant their garden.

CHAPTER 14

Ceremonies

"I suppose she counts to ten," the woman said. "Whatever crops up, she just takes a deep breath, and smiles, and then she copes with it. Either she can count to ten faster than anyone else I know, or else she's a witch."

Sue smiled. The women had met in the hall—one on her way to the bathroom, the other on the way back—and presumably didn't know Sue could hear them from the kitchen. *In other words, I keep my cool. Thank you, ladies. Not so hard to keep my head on my shoulders, living among these things for the refreshment of my spirit.*

Amalia stood upon the steps of the House of the Mists, looking over the garden that was taking shape between the rock faces. The mist that blew across the valley formed droplets on the stone that ran down into the stream, and beneath them crisp strands of moss were growing. The dead tree-trunks were crumbling into mould, and they were green. Windblown seeds had sprouted, and maybe even some that had been frozen were still alive. Already three blue flowers had opened among the green moss. Cool; green; moist; crystal; the gentle veil of mist blowing across the water.

She poured boiling water over the tea leaves and over the coffee in the glass filter. (She had been willing to accept that some people just aren't into tea-drinking, not even in mid-afternoon.) Plates of cookies, plates of pound cake; and to take pity on everyone's diet, she had added plates of raw vegetables with cheese and vegetable dips.

She shook out a fresh paper bag to line the garbage can, ready to receive cheese wrappers and a cracker box. A sheet of paper fluttered out of it and grounded itself under the toe of her shoe: "WELCOME TO THE CURRENT MIDDLE AGES." So that was where it'd gotten to. . . .

Of the walls and towers of Andarath that had fallen two hundred years ago, nothing remained: spiderlime and stoneweed had broken down timber and stone to dust. Of the strange tubes and mounds, shiny as beetles' wings, that had formed the city of Agniran, nothing remained: the sunlight had destroyed everything, and the first men to arrive there had found only dust and ashes, and a few green weeds beginning to sprout.

All the land was like that: the soil was dead, but fertile, and it was no trouble getting seeds to grow. Getting them to thrive was another matter, since all the tiny life of the soil was gone. Every midden and pigsty in the west was being mined for its muck, its earthworms, and its small invisible living things.

On the plain by the river, the ground was spiderwebbed with pegs and string. The city was to be rebuilt, as close as might be to what it had been; the builders were going by the King's memory and the deposits of nails that had been left, preserved by growths of ironcrop that now were gone. Most of the nails were still reusable. And where the King's house would one day stand, a cluster of pavilions spread white canvas against the sun big enough to shelter hundreds of people.

"My goodness, how nice," said Meade Bingley, looking at the cookies as if they were chocolate-covered ants. "You don't worry about calories, do you?"

Cool; green; crystal. "I like to provide a choice," Sue said. "There're carrot sticks here, and mushrooms and zucchini; this dip is blue cheese, and the green one's avocado."

(She hadn't quite figured out where Meade Bingley was coming from. Chris had brought his wife down for the week, and she had been skating over the thin ice of everyone's feelings ever since she arrived. She was intelligent, and well-educated. She was impeccably made up and beautifully dressed, and her family had money—you couldn't talk to her for ninety seconds without managing to be told about that. Maybe she was part of the reason her husband behaved like such a turkey.

"And you do this every Wednesday?" she was saying. "Just for tea and gossip?"

Wind stirring the frail moss, crystal drops trickling over the stone. "Well, that too," Sue said. "We started out as a subcomittee for the PTA, to get the school some computers. Now we're looking for a new direction to take. We've discussed raising funds for a science lab, and there's been some talk of sponsoring a branch of the Young Astronauts. Our children's future is in space, after all."

"You're sure about that?" Meade said. "Mine seem determined to be punk rock stars."

There was a pool at the valley's edge, its surface as still as glass, and here the waters gathered before pouring over the cliff, smooth and even from rock face to rock face. The climb that Amalia had made with such fear, and gone down again with such difficulty, was a solid sheet of water now, with slippery strands of moss beneath. No one would climb that face again, if not a hero unequalled in living memory.

"Well, when my kids were born, I hung mobiles over their heads," Sue said, "so that as soon as they felt like it, they could start learning that there are different colors in the world. Now I'm dangling the planets and stars in front of their noses. It seems to be working okay. And at the moment, what we have to do—" she tapped the rim of her cup with her teaspoon, and the chatter started to die down. "What we have to do today is to think about the rededication ceremony for the gym, and the opening for the computer room. Ideas?"

Late spring had turned as warm as early summer, and men had stretched a canvas sunshade over the place that would be the Queen's garden. A few small trees had been brought in, in tubs, and a dozen rosebushes, and here the Queen sat with the ladies, waiting for Court to begin.

"But where's the little Marianella?" said Elisa of Rockridge. "Nothing wrong with her, I hope? Such a dear little thing, and so helpful when the seamstress went down with fever the week before my wedding."

Amalia smiled. Ketil of Rockridge had married Elisa for her beauty, and she still had that, but she had never had much sense.

"She's still here," she said, "but resting till court begins. She's in her seventh month now, you know, and she grows weary. She and her husband are leaving Court tomorrow."

"Oh, dear," Elisa said. "Why, whatever for? I'm sure I've heard nothing against them—at least nothing to send them away. There was that celebration bonfire, of course, where some of the firestarters got a little out of hand, and that one tall girl—oh dear. Do you suppose—"

"Elisa." The Queen held up one finger. Drops of water, soft upon the moss, and three blue flowers. "It's all been provided for; wait and see. And they're going into the west so their baby can be born at home."

"Oh. Oh, I see," said Elisa, who plainly didn't. She made a curtsey and turned away, and as she did she cast a sharp glance at Amalia's own waist. But the gown of grass-green velvet was loose about her body, and the Queen kept her own counsel.

A royal heir, Aumery said as they stood intertwined at the water's edge. *I never thought life would flower from my undead flesh, but through you the line of Alban will blossom again to enrich the land. Look, there is a waterfly.* They watched it, frail legs and gauzy wings, skimming across the water's surface. *What can it find to eat here?*

I don't believe it eats at all, Amalia said. *It can lay its eggs in the water, though, and its grubs will feed off the moss.*

"I have one idea," said Myra Stone. "When the gym was originally dedicated, back in 1950 which none of you kids remember, the address was given by the pastor of Trinity Methodist, the Reverend Henry Davis. He's in a nursing home now, out near Petervale. I haven't seen him yet, so I don't know what shape he's in."

"See him, would you please?" Sue said. "If he's able to speak coherently, he can give the invocation. If he can't speak, but he is able to attend, he can be an honored guest."

"And if he can't come at all?"

"Then we can visit him with some photographs and some cookies. Find out about it, will you, Myra? Thanks."

Now the trumpets sounded, and the King came into the garden followed by many nobles. He had laid aside the black cloak of the days of his misery, and he wore a scarlet robe, its full sleeves deeply embroidered with gold. The squire who followed him, arms full of his blue velvet mantle, was hard put to it to keep up with the King's long strides.

He wore the Crown of Alban now, which fitted him better than it had Amalia; under it his eyes were alight with wisdom, and strength, and joy. He went to the Queen and took her hand, and bent his knee to kiss it. He never let the Court forget that she had sat on the throne before him, and he delighted to honor her.

Then he raised her to her feet, and led her toward the great pavilion that did duty as hall. The breathless squires had just time to throw the blue mantles over their shoulders before they went in.

When the King and Queen were seated, on twin thrones carven from the halves of a sundered oak, Aurelia the Queen-of-Arms stepped forth with the list of honors, but the King waved her back and rose to speak.

"It was with joy," he said, "—or so she insists—that Our Queen gave up the Crown of Alban for Our crowning. Happy was Demoura on the night that so great a lady came out of Darkness to bring light to the world. Now We wear the battle-crown, symbol of strength and the power of the land. But let no man forget that it was she whose valor brought us the victory, and life out of death." He beckoned forth a pursuivant with a casket of polished wood. "—And since the Queen's crown of old was lost when this city fell—" He lifted from the casket a circlet of gold, twined with flowers and leaves of blue and green enamel. Pearls clustered like berries among the leaves, and crystal drops rested on the petals like dew.

Only a shadow of the beauty of this place, Aumery said, *and a shadow's shadow of your beauty. But the flowers will look well above your eyes.*

Amalia would have knelt, but he stayed her, and set the crown on her head as he looked into her eyes. Then he kissed her before all the people, and a murmur of delight went round the pavilion before it was drowned by cheers.

"I wish this day were over," she whispered, under cover of the noise.

"Patience," he said. *My spirit will never leave your spirit's side.* "After court, and when the feast is over, we will walk under the stars alone, and lie down together without any hindrance."

Then he called Aurelia forth with the list of honors, and the scroll was as long as her arm, for all the nobles must receive again of the King the lands their ancestors had lost to the Shadow, and do homage. And first of all she called forth Andri Greywell of Fendarath.

"Andri," said the King, "We call you first, in token that all your past actions are pardoned. For if the people have forgiven Us the deeds We did under the Darkness, how much more must We forgive you?" And he gave the charters into his hands, and said, "Receive again the honors of Greywell, and Fendarath, and Hill House upon the Scarfell, and Rhadath House in the city of Tevrin, their castles and lands. But one thing We withhold: the fief of Telerath, its lands and its sea-keep. Forego them, of your courtesy; We have another use for them."

"Your Grace," said Andri, "I could give up all my lands, and my very life, and still count myself rich in your gift. I have not forgotten your kindness to me, when we were both under the Shadow. Receive the honor of Telerath, and may it bloom beneath your hands." Then he swore fealty to Crown and King, and withdrew.

"Kieran of Telerath," Aurelia said now. There was a stir in the pavilion, and some craning of necks. Those standing near him saw Kieran raise a quizzical eyebrow, but he said nothing as he helped his wife to rise from the chair the Queen had set for her.

Marianella had lost weight from her face, and gained it in her body, and a blind mole with one eye covered could see that her feet hurt. But her face was radiant, and she walked cheerfully up the pavilion's length on Kieran's arm. From the looks that passed between them, it was plain that she had known beforehand what was to do, and that he had not.

Kieran knelt before the King, but the Queen called Marianella to sit beside her.

"Kieran, son of Brennan," said the King, "your valor deserves reward. More, your audacity deserves recognition; and since you decline to be a Captain, We can only make you a Baron. Receive the honor of Telerath, its lands and castles, between the Medon and the Moors. And as you have asked, We give you leave to return there, so that your son may be born on his own lands." And he set a golden circlet on Kieran's head, and embraced him.

"How d'you know it's a son?" Kieran murmured, too low for the crowd to hear.

"I asked Mistress Adrianna," Aumery said in the same tone. "She's never been wrong yet."

Amalia kissed Marianella, and Kieran, and Kieran kissed her back right soundly. "I should've done this before, back along the Medufar," he said. "Think what I've missed." But the Queen only laughed, and let him go.

"You'll miss her," said the King to the Queen, under cover of the applause.

"Yes, I shall," she said, "but not so very much. My life is so full."

("And besides," Kieran said to his wife as they went back to their places, "I've got to find husbands for the daughters of Helg. Now the war's over, they're getting restless, and I don't want them bearing little firestarters to person or persons unknown.")

There were many more honors and lands to be given out, and other men to be ennobled. In many cases the ancient family of a place had all died out, and the land was to be given to someone else to be reclaimed, reforested and brought under cultivation. The Queen had worked out the list with the aid of the Seneschals, and it was she who gave out the charters to these lands.

What a long day, Amalia said. *The sun is still high overhead, and our mortal backsides will grow very tired, I fear, before it sets.* The waterfly had been joined by two others, and they spun in a tiny dance over the surface of the water.

Meade had retreated into a sullen silence. *Poor thing,* Sue thought. *No one has time to envy her, and so she's miserable. Maybe she thinks Chris married her for her money. (Maybe he did.) I'll have her over tomorrow if I can, when we can be private. Maybe she'd like to talk.*

They drifted along the edge of the water, back to the House of the Mists. Even under the full sun, wisps of vapor were still pouring out of its inner chamber; they sparkled and shone in the bright air, and on the rocks and mosses and the fallen tree trunks.

My outer part looks forward to her first child, she thought, *and I to my first tree that shall take root here.*

They went up the steps to the House, to the subtle images on the inner walls whose study brought wisdom. Some day, she knew, their mortal bodies would age and die; some day they would step within the veils of mist into the inner chamber, resting place of heroes. It was a gate, to what as yet she only dimly guessed. Even under the greatest power in the world, the soul is not bound to the world forever.

And the doorbell rang, and the nearest person on her feet went to answer it. "Hello, my name's Bingley, I've got a wife here, I think," the deep voice said. "I know I've got some friends here; hello, Sue, Siobhan. Hi, Meade. You ready to go?"

"No, I'm not," said Meade in her thin voice. "I'm enjoying myself."

Well, I'll be. "Have some coffee, Chris," Sue said. "And we haven't any fruitcake, but try these cookies; they're Swedish, and the name means 'Dreams.'"

"Neil Hillranger." This man led a cadet branch of an old family, rich in portable wealth and renowned in war, but with no lands. The Queen had chosen this grant carefully. "Neil, in latter days your people ranged the highlands of Sallowfell and Scarfell and the foothills of the Weatherwall. We have chosen for you the hills of Amberlime in the highlands of Markrath, and the valley of the Lime that flows into the Rath. Care for them well. You'll find that the dead fibers of stoneweed will hold most of your soil through this winter, but in spring you must be ready to replant. Time was when the forests of Amberlime were the fairest in the world. Make them so again."

"Yes, your garden is looking great," Chris said. He had found a low hassock beside Sue's chair, and looked up at her thoughtfully as he sipped his coffee. (If the man wanted to look like a suppliant at her feet, well. . . .) "Already, I can tell your house from the others as I come down the street, and your roses are real heartbreakers."

It appeared she had been talking about the garden. Well, and so she had, the inner garden, Demoura within Earth held as close as a nut in its shell. Everything she saw was pregnant with its deeper counterpart, its secret meaning. Earth had become an eggshell crust on the surface of Demoura, needing only a touch to break through, and translucent to a splendid light.

"May you have steadfastness and courage in the labors ahead of you, and may your heirs say in your praise: "These things that were dead, our father restored to life.""

"Thank you," Chris said, very low. "I wish—but we can't have what we wish for, can we."

"Oh yes we can, if we wish for the right things."

Chris did not answer, but sat quietly, looking at her. Meade broke into the silence. "Well, Sue, now you've got the PTA well in hand, what's next? A seat in Congress?"

"My husband keeps saying that. He's kidding—I *think*. No, I'll stick with the PTA while my kids are in school. One circus at a time. After that, we'll see. Maybe I'll write a book, or take a degree. There are always possibilities."

Outside her window the white rose of York danced in the sun, the white walls of the pavilion rippled, the hedge grew lustily, secretly preparing a secret place. Beyond that, a wide world, a planet full of circuses, a stepping-stone to the stars. Kieran rocked back on his heels and stretched unobtrusively, unconscious of Elisa's covetous eyes. Proud as a stag on the mountains, crisp and fresh as a drake on the green, his eyes blue as the sea, his mouth the flower of forgetfulness in the deep wood. Chris was still looking at her. She smiled diplomatically, and caught Siobhan's eye; time to call this chattering mob to order and put together some solid plans. Trumpets sounded, and the King rose to lay honors on the shoulders of Kelvan of Blackwater. Glory in his face beneath the ancient crown, a kingdom reclaimed ready to blossom under his hands.

Far back in his eyes, and in the eyes of the Queen, the great Seers could faintly sense the flavor of green, the color of moisture, the scent of water: the House of the Mists, the pool of the Kendal, pure source of healing: shining Aumery, the rose at the heart of the world.

Paksenarrion, a simple sheepfarmer's daughter, yearns for a life of adventure and glory, such as the heroes in songs and story. At age seventeen she runs away from home to join a mercenary company, and begins her epic life . . .

ELIZABETH MOON

THE DEED OF PAKSENARRION

"This is the first work of high heroic fantasy I've seen, that has taken the work of Tolkien, assimilated it totally and deeply and absolutely, and produced something altogether new and yet incontestably based on the master. . . . This is the real thing. Worldbuilding in the grand tradition, background thought out to the last detail, by someone who knows absolutely whereof she speaks. . . . Her military knowledge is impressive, her picture of life in a mercenary company most convincing."—**Judith Tarr**

About the author: Elizabeth Moon joined the U.S. Marine Corps in 1968 and completed both Officers Candidate School and Basic School, reaching the rank of 1st Lieutenant during active duty. Her background in military training and discipline imbue The Deed of Paksenarrion with a gritty realism that is all too rare in most current fantasy.

"I thoroughly enjoyed *Deed of Paksenarrion*. A most engrossing, highly readable work."
—**Anne McCaffrey**

"For once the promises are borne out. *Sheepfarmer's Daughter* is an advance in realism. . . . I can only say that I eagerly await whatever Elizabeth Moon chooses to write next."
—Taras Wolansky, *Lan's Lantern*

*　　　*　　　*　　　*　　　*

Volume One: Sheepfarmer's Daughter—Paks is trained as a mercenary, blooded, and introduced to the life of a soldier . . . and to the followers of Gird, the soldier's god.

Volume Two: Divided Allegiance—Paks leaves the Duke's company to follow the path of Gird alone—and on her lonely quests encounters the other sentient races of her world.

Volume Three: Oath of Gold—Paks the warrior must learn to live with Paks the human. She undertakes a holy quest for a lost eleven prince that brings the gods' wrath down on her and tests her very limits.

*　　　*　　　*　　　*　　　*

These books are available at your local bookstore, or you can fill out the coupon and return it to Baen Books, at the address below.